Grave Endings

GRAVE ENDINGS
A Novel of Suspense

ROCHELLE KRICH

BALLANTINE BOOKS
NEW YORK

A Ballantine Book
Published by The Random House Publishing Group

Copyright © 2004 by Rochelle Majer Krich

All rights reserved under International and Pan-American Copyright Conventions. Published in the United States by Ballantine Books, an imprint of The Random House Publishing Group, a division of Random House, Inc., New York, and simultaneously in Canada by Random House of Canada Limited, Toronto.

Ballantine and colophon are registered trademarks of Random House, Inc.

www.ballantinebooks.com

Library of Congress Cataloging-in-Publication Data is available from the publisher upon request.

ISBN 0-345-46810-4

Manufactured in the United States of America

9 8 7 6 5 4 3 2 1

First Edition

Book design by Susan Turner

For Sara Ann Freed

My editor, my friend.
I am privileged to count myself among the many who benefited from
her wisdom and kindness.

ACKNOWLEDGMENTS

I am grateful to those who were generous with their time and information for this work of fiction: Renne Dvorak Bainvoll, Ph.D., clinical psychology; Detective Paul Bishop; Detective Jeff Brumagin, West L.A.; Detective III Terry Pearson, Officer-in-Charge, West Traffic Division, Detective Section. Many thanks to D. P. Lyle, author of *Murder and Mayhem* and *Forensics for Dummies,* and to Assistant District Attorney Mary Hanlon Stone, for their invaluable advice.

Special thanks to my wonderful champions: my Ballantine editor, Joe Blades; my agent, Sandra Dijkstra, and her staff, with special appreciation to Elisabeth James and Babette Spaar; Eileen Hutton and everyone at Brilliance Audio; Marie Coolman, Gilly Hailparn, Kim Hovey, Heather Smith, and Margaret Winter; and Carol Fass, Carolyn Hessel of the Jewish Book Council, and Daisy Maryles for their friendship, guidance, and support.

To my friends and family: Thank you for tolerating my obsessiveness and my deadline-inspired absence from your lives. And to my daughter, Sabina, and my husband, Hershie: Thank you for providing me with a last-inning save.

Rochelle Krich

A Note on Pronunciation

Yiddish has certain consonant sounds that have no English equiva-
lents—in particular the guttural *ch* (achieved by clearing one's
throat) that sounds like the *ch* in *Bach* or in the German *ach*.

Some Yiddish historians and linguists, including the Yiddish
Scientific Institute (YIVO—Yidisher Visenshaftikhe Institut), spell
this sound with a *kh* (*Khanukah, khalla*). Others use *ch* (*Chanukah,
challa*). I've chosen to use *ch*.

To help the reader unfamiliar with Yiddish, I've also doubled
some consonants (*chapp, gitte*).

Zh is pronounced like the *s* in *treasure.*
Tsh is pronounced like the *ch* in *lurch.*
Dzh is pronounced like the *g* in *passage.*

Here are the YIVO guidelines for vowel pronunciation, which
I've followed in most cases, except for those where regional pro-
nunciations vary (*kliegeh* instead of *klugeh, gitte* instead of *gutte*):

a as in *father* or *bother* (*a dank*—thanks)
ay as in *try* (*shrayt*—yells)
e as in *bed*, pronounced even when it's the final letter in the
word (*naye*—new)
ey as in *hay* (*beheyme*—animal)
i as in *hid,* or in *me* (*Yid*—Jew)
o as between *aw* in *pawn* and *u* in *lunch* (*hot*—has)
oy as in *joy* (*loyfen*—to run)
u as in *rule* (*hunt*—dog)

With a little practice, you'll sound just like Molly's Bubbie G.

—Rochelle Krich (ch as in *birch,* but that's another story)

GRAVE ENDINGS

CHAPTER ONE

THERE IS A CENTURIES-OLD TRADITION, GLEANED FROM the arcane pages of the Kabbalah and supported by stories too numerous to dismiss as myth, about a red thread whose mystical power wards off the evil eye lurking behind envy and arrests its malignant reach. Women yearning to conceive hope the thread will work where nature and science have failed. Pregnant women wear it to ensure a safe delivery and a sound child. Those who are ill or face adversity wear it to reclaim their health or find better fortune, and those who are fortunate wear it to hold on to their blessings.

I've seen the thread circling a person's neck or entwined around the band of a watch. I've seen it looped through the slats of a newborn's crib or peeking out from the doughy folds of a tiny ankle. Mostly I've seen it worn as a bracelet, usually on the left wrist, tightly knotted and left in place until the fibers are frayed by water and soap and body oils, and time.

The thread looks thin and ordinary. What makes it special, and potent, if you believe the stories, as I do, is the larger skein from which it has been snipped, a length of red wound seven times around the tomb in what is now the center of Bethlehem and that, centuries ago, was the desolate spot where Jacob buried his true love, Rachel.

Rachel, who died while giving life to her second son.

Rachel, who cries for all her children, those who emerged from her womb and those of future generations, and intercedes on their behalf.

Ten years ago, when I was nineteen and about to return home after a year's study in an all-girl Orthodox Jewish seminary in the hills of Jerusalem, I took a cab to Rachel's Tomb on a June day so hot that the air baked my face and dried the perspiration before I could lick it off my lips. Ten years ago Bethlehem was free of sniper attacks and consequently safer to visit, though even then my parents had warned me to be careful. Ten years ago the tomb wasn't surrounded, as I hear it is now, by tall walls and guard towers that offer protection to the many who, despite the danger, travel in bulletproof Eged buses to pray at the side of Rachel's resting place.

There were throngs of people when I arrived that day. Bare-headed men in slacks or shorts; men wearing yarmulkes, some of them with beards. Some of the women, their hair covered with wigs or scarves or berets, wore modest clothing and stockings that defied the heat. Others defied strict rules of modesty with short sleeves and with skirts that revealed tanned bare legs and brightly polished toenails. More than a few of the women were big with child, their hands resting on swollen bellies that strained against the cotton of their blouses.

After dropping coins into the cupped palms of several hunched elderly turbaned women who formed a queue near the entrance to the white stone building, I passed through the anteroom into the cool interior of the domed edifice and, with more than a little awe and reverence, I approached the black-velvet-draped sepulcher. My eyes quickly adjusted from the sun's glare to the soft dim light of the chandeliers, and my low voice joined the hum of the other supplicants. Then, with the help of a middle-aged woman who held on to the end of a spool of red thread I'd purchased a few days before, I walked around the sepulchre, reciting a special psalm as I pressed the thread against the velvet while the woman, smiling and nodding approval, counted each circuit aloud until I had completed the seven.

Outside, I snipped a length of my red thread and asked someone to tie it around my wrist. Days later, back home in Los Angeles, I gave lengths of the thread to friends and family. My father, my mother, my three sisters and three brothers, my grandmother and grandfather, aunts, uncles, cousins. My grandfather, Zeidie Irving, wore the thread around his thin wrist, but it didn't avert the heart attack that took his life a few months later.

And it didn't protect my best friend, Aggie Lasher, from the person who killed her almost six years ago.

"Is that the one?" Detective Andrew Connors asked now, pointing to the rectangular silver locket he'd taken out of a brown evidence bag and set on the table in front of me.

He was watching me, and I was staring at the locket. Its face was embossed with the image of Rachel's Tomb, just like the face of the locket I'd bought in a Pico Boulevard store that sells Judaica. There are thousands of similar lockets, I told myself, sold in hundreds of similar stores all over the country and abroad.

"Molly?" Connors prompted.

"Can I turn it over?" I wanted to pick it up, dreaded touching it. I'd arrived at my apartment only minutes before Connors, and the heater had just begun to battle the chill of the February day, but my lips were as parched as they had been that summer day ten years ago.

"Go ahead." He nodded. "It's been printed."

Still, I didn't rush. For nearly six long years I'd hounded the Wilshire Division detectives, phoning the station every few months, sometimes more often, asking whether any leads about Aggie's murder had surfaced, knowing I was making a nuisance of myself but not giving a damn. For nearly six years there had been nothing.

Then around eight-thirty this Thursday morning Connors had phoned. Something he wanted to show me, he'd said. Could I come to the Hollywood station?

"Can it wait till tomorrow, Andy?" I'd asked. "I have a wedding gown fitting in half an hour, then tons of errands, and a six o'clock tasting at the caterer's. In that order, or they'd have to let out a few seams." I was prepared for a wisecrack—Connors and I do lots of friendly verbal jousting—but it didn't come.

"How about between the fitting and one, Molly? I can come to your place if that makes things easier. Unless your errands are with your rabbi?"

"I wish." My rabbi, formerly the high school heartthrob who dumped me, is my fiancé, a fact that my family and many of my friends find humorous, and I do, too, at times. "Zack has meetings all day at the shul. This is a switch, *you* calling *me.*"

I write books about true crimes under my pen name, Morgan Blake. I'm also a freelance journalist and I collect data from detectives in police stations all over the city for my weekly *Crime Sheet* column that appears in the local tabloids. That's how I met Connors.

"How's eleven?" he asked.

"Eleven is fine." His solemnity was making me uneasy. "What's this about? Did I step on any departmental toes?" Not everyone in the LAPD appreciates my inquisitiveness and persistence.

"Tell you when I see you," Connors said, and hung up before I could press.

He showed up early. I was still in my powder blue wool suit but had kicked off my four-inch BCBG stiletto heels, so the gap between my five feet five and his lanky six-two seemed greater. I was about to make a quip, but the somber look in his hazel eyes stopped me. That and the absence of his usual slouch, and the brown paper bag in his hand.

"What's up?" My heart did a little flip, even though I'd talked to my mom minutes ago and knew my family was fine. I wasn't thinking Aggie. Connors is with Hollywood Division, and Aggie's case belonged to Wilshire.

"Can we sit down, Molly?" he asked.

I scowled at him. "You're making me nervous. Just tell me why you're here." I pointed to the bag. "What's in that? Leftovers?"

He hesitated. "Something that may have belonged to your friend."

He spoke gently, but the words rocked me as though I'd been slammed against a wall. My legs were wobbly, my chest was hollow. I felt his hand steadying my elbow, and a minute later we were sitting across from each other at the breakfast room table, the space between us occupied by twin towers of the wedding gifts that had arrived yesterday, still wrapped in bright-colored floral papers and ribbons that looked obscenely cheerful.

Connors pushed aside a stack of boxes, slipped the locket out of the bag, and placed it in front of me.

"Where did you find this?" I'd described the locket to Connors years ago. I'd described it to the Wilshire detectives, too. I never thought I'd see it again.

"On a guy named Roland Creeley. Does the name ring a bell?"

I shook my head. My heart pounding, I picked up the locket and read the inscription on the back:

לאגי

חברתי הטובה

"That's Hebrew, right?" Connors said. "What does it say?"

"For Aggie. My Best Friend."

Saying the words filled my eyes with tears. I unsnapped the tiny latch. There was the coiled red thread I'd tucked inside the locket I'd given Aggie a year before she died, the locket that she wore daily but that was missing when the police found her body in a Dumpster.

"So it's hers?" Connors asked.

"Yes." I clicked the locket shut. "But you knew that," I said with a prickling of resentment.

"We had to make sure. I know this is tough for you, Molly. I'm sorry."

In my mind I was sitting cross-legged on the daybed in Aggie's bedroom, watching her pry the locket open with her long, slim fingers, taking pleasure in the delight that warmed her dark brown eyes and the smile that widened as she pulled her curly black hair to one side and fastened the silver chain around her neck. *Oh, Molly, this is perfect.*

At some point I realized Connors was talking. I wiped my eyes and looked at him. "Sorry. What did you say?"

"I need it back, Molly."

He sounded awkward and apologetic, which is rare for him, and now I felt awkward, too, as though I'd been caught taking something to which I had no right. My face flushed, I dropped the locket into his outstretched hand and watched it disappear into the brown bag.

"It's evidence, Molly. When we close the case . . . Maybe her parents won't mind. . . ." His voice trailed off.

"You think this guy Raymond killed her?" I asked after an uncomfortable silence broken only by the clanking of the heater.

"Roland—aka Randy. He has a long sheet." Connors relaxed against the chair back and stretched out his long, jeans-clad legs. He was on easier turf now. "Apparently he's been stealing to support a drug addiction since he was a teenager. A busy guy, Randy."

"So Aggie died for a thirty-dollar locket and the contents of her wallet," I said, the words leaving a bitter taste in my mouth.

It's what the police had speculated. I'd had almost six years to come to terms with the fact, but the outrageousness and banality— that Aggie's life, full of promise, had been snuffed out so a drug addict could shoot up—shook me as though I'd just learned of her death.

"Did you tell her parents yet?" I asked.

"I'm going there right after I leave you. I wanted confirmation on the locket. When was the last time you saw her wearing it, Molly?"

"What's the difference?"

"We need to establish a time frame."

I curled my lips. "I told you *before,* but I guess you weren't paying attention."

"Tell me again," Connors said, countering my surliness with annoying patience.

I was being unfair, making him the butt of the anger I felt toward Creeley and the Wilshire detectives who hadn't found Aggie's killer all these years. At the moment, I didn't care. I wanted to punch someone.

"A week or so before she was killed. I gave her the locket seven years ago. She'd just started working at Rachel's Tent, and I thought it was the perfect gift. Rachel's Tomb, Rachel's Tent? Aggie thought so, too. She wore it every day." I was back in her bedroom. I blinked away the image and the tears that stung my eyes.

"What's Rachel's Tent? I know you told me, but remind me."

"Why are *you* here, not Wilshire?" The fact had just registered. "Or did they send you to do their dirty work?"

"Because *we* found Creeley and the locket. About Rachel's Tent?"

"It's a women's social services agency." I uncurled my fingers, which had formed fists. "Wilshire knows all this. It's in Aggie's file. Maybe you should read it."

"Believe it or not, the thought occurred to me."

"If you can find it, that is. I wouldn't be surprised to learn that they misplaced it."

Connors sighed.

"I'm sorry," I said after another uncomfortable silence. "This isn't your fault. It's just . . ." I bit my lips. "Thanks for not telling me when you phoned before."

He reached over and covered my hand with his. "This must hurt like hell, Molly. But at least now you know."

There was something to that. "And I'm glad it was you, not Wilshire, Andy."

"So is Wilshire." He flashed me a wry smile. "Want me to stick around awhile? You can show me the loot you got." He nodded at the stacks of gifts.

I shook my head. "But I appreciate your asking."

He repeated the offer when I walked him to the door. "You're sure?" he asked, raising the collar of his cowhide jacket.

"I'm sure." I needed to be alone. "Can I see him, Andy?"

"Molly—"

"I won't make a scene. I want to tell him what she was like, Andy. I want him to *know*." My fists were clenched again. Hate for Roland "Randy" Creeley twisted in my stomach.

Connors put a hand on my shoulder. "Creeley was dead when we found him, Molly. He overdosed last night."

"Gee, how sad."

"Yeah."

My grandmother, Bubbie G, says that anger is like a thorn in the heart. I felt a surge of satisfaction that disappeared by the time I shut the door. With Creeley dead, I'd never achieve the closure I'd been seeking all these years.

The thorn was still there.

I imagined Aggie's parents would feel the same when Connors told them.

CHAPTER TWO

Monday, February 16. 9:12 A.M. Intersection of De Longpre
Avenue and Ivar Avenue. Angry that a man spit on her vehicle,
a woman chased the man on foot on the parkway and tried to hit
him with a set of jumper cables. The suspect, turned victim, told
police he turned his head to avoid being struck by the cables. The
woman attacker was described as a 35-year-old, standing five
feet four inches and weighing 135 pounds. (Hollywood)

VINCE PORTER NARROWED HIS BLUE EYES FOR EFFECT AND
scowled at me across a desk cluttered with stacks of blue binders
and folders and six bottles of water lined up like bowling pins.

"What do you mean, why did Creeley have the locket?" he
demanded. "Because he took it when he killed your friend, that's

why. Probably wanted to make it harder for us to identify the body."

Porter is in his mid-thirties, six feet plus with the kind of muscular physique that says he works out daily, and not just to meet the LAPD fitness requirements. Add the baby blues and wavy blond hair and substitute a Speedo for the tapered olive green shirt and beige slacks that showed off his flat abs and tight butt, and he could step into an episode of *Baywatch*. He knows it, too, which is why, Zack aside, if it were just Porter and Connors, I'd pick Connors with his receding hairline and bald spot any day.

Porter is one of the Wilshire Division detectives I've been nagging about Aggie's murder. As you can imagine, that hasn't endeared me to him, but our relationship warmed up to tepid several months ago when I proved helpful in an investigation that he and Enrico Hernandez were running. I would have preferred talking to Hernandez, who has more class and less attitude, but he was on vacation. And tepid is better than frigid, which is how I'd characterize my relationship with Wayne Berman, who handled Aggie's murder and has since retired and who never returned any of my calls even before he did.

"But why didn't Creeley *sell* the locket?" I'd been brooding about the locket and Creeley all weekend. "Or pawn it? He could have used the cash to feed his drug habit."

Porter kneaded his forehead in exaggerated concentration. "Connors says the locket's inscribed to your friend, right? I'm going out on a limb here, but could it be that he didn't want to get nailed for the murder?"

I ignored his sarcasm. "Then why didn't he dump it? Why would he be interested in a locket with an image of Rachel's Tomb?"

"You must have been a joy in school with all those *whys*." Porter's expression was dour. "Maybe he thought it was his lucky

charm. You're the one who said the red thread's supposed to protect people."

"That's a mystical *Jewish* belief," I reminded him. "Was Creeley Jewish?"

"No."

"Then it wouldn't mean anything to him."

Porter's answer was a shrug.

"By the way, where did they find Creeley?" I asked. "Connors
didn't say."

"What's the difference?"

"Just curious." I wasn't about to tell Porter about the alternat-
ing images that had been running in my head since Connors's visit.
Creeley lying in the gutter of a narrow, litter-strewn alley, jerking in the final throes of a drug-induced death. Creeley writhing
in his roach-infested apartment. I wasn't sure which one I liked
better.

"He was on his bedroom floor," Porter said. "Does that do
it for you? Can I go back to playing detective and earn my
salary?"

Obviously, any points I'd earned months ago with Porter had
expired. "What was Creeley like?"

"Dead." Not a hint of a smile.

"Connors told me he was a career criminal."

"Right."

"Can I see his jacket?"

"Connors's?"

I had to admit Porter did deadpan well. I dug my nails into
my palms. "Creeley's."

"No."

"Why not?"

"Why do you want to see it, anyway?"

We'd graduated from monosyllables to sentences. I supposed
that was progress, but Porter's crankiness was beginning to grate.

"I'd like to know something about the man who killed Aggie. Is that so hard to understand?"

Porter sighed. "No, it isn't. You wait all these years for us to find the guy who killed your best friend, and then he shows up dead. I'm sorry. I really am."

His unexpected compassion made my eyes well. I decided I preferred his sarcasm. "I want to know why he did it. Why Aggie."

"Sometimes there is no big answer. Creeley was a bad guy when he was alive, now he's a *dead* bad guy. That won't bring your friend back, but at least the streets of L.A. are safer. Who knows how many other people he's killed, or would have killed?"

I'd been focused on Aggie and hadn't considered that possibility. "He's a suspect in other murders?"

"Not what I said."

I leaned forward. "C'mon, Detective Porter. Why can't I see his jacket? He's dead."

"For one thing, my showing it to you would be a misdemeanor. And like I said, there's nothing in it that will give you the answers you're looking for."

"Maybe it'll give me some closure."

"Closure isn't all that it's cracked up to be. It's just a fancy word shrinks use, and ex-girlfriends who like to talk a thing to death."

I wasn't in the mood for Psychology 101 à la Porter, who probably has a host of exes and is no Dr. Phil. I wished Hernandez were here. Picking up my purse, I stood. "Thanks for your time. If you change your mind—"

"So what exactly do you want to know about Creeley?"

The change of heart surprised me. Either Porter was taking pity on me, or he figured I'd be back to nag him. Probably the latter. I sat down again. "Anything you can tell me. What he looked like, his background."

Porter opened a manila folder that he removed from the bottom of a stack and held it up so that I couldn't take a peek. "White male, five-eleven, one hundred eighty-two pounds. Brown eyes, blond hair—with a little help from Miss Clairol, is my guess." He flipped a page. "High school education. No steady job except for a few years, unless you count his street activity."

"Was he working around the time Aggie was murdered?"

"Yeah."

"Doing what?" I prodded when Porter didn't say.

"Nothing that would get him into *Forbes.* He wasn't making his mark on society, Blume. He was making *society* his mark."

I smiled to show I appreciated the witticism. "Can I see his mug shot?"

Porter shook his head. "He was good-looking, if that's what you want to know. *Too* good-looking, according to his daddy. That was Randy's downfall—that plus his dream of becoming the next Brad Pitt."

"That's in the rap sheet?"

"That's what Roland Creeley senior said when we told him the good news."

"What about the mother?"

Porter raised his hand and waved good-bye. "Walked out when Randy was nine. Left hubby to take care of Randy and his sister. The sister wasn't even two when Mom skipped. Different lyrics, same old sad refrain. 'My momma done left meee.' "

Porter has probably earned the right to be cynical, but I felt a flicker of unwelcome sympathy for the boy whose mother had abandoned him and his family. That's the danger in finding out a person's history.

"Young Randy started early," Porter said. "Petty theft when he was thirteen. He got probation for that. He was in and out of the system for years. Vandalism, truancy, DUI. Not an impressive report card. Then our hero graduated to felonies."

"He was convicted?"

"Twice. He did a home robbery at sixteen and spent a year in a juvenile facility."

"And the second time?"

Porter glanced at the sheet. "Eleven years ago. He did four years at Chino—double what he would've served if he didn't have that first strike."

So Randy had been released seven years ago, less than a year before Aggie was killed. "Nothing since then?"

"That we know of—until he murdered your friend." Porter shut the folder. "He probably improved his skills. He had to, if he didn't want to spend the rest of his life as a guest of the state."

I nodded. California's three-strikes law mandates twenty-five years to life in prison for a third felony conviction. "What was the first strike?"

"A street mugging."

"Just like with Aggie," I said, and was treated to another one of Porter's shrugs. "Did he use a knife?"

He'd used a knife on Aggie. The weapon was never found, but my imagination, which has forced details on me that detectives had withheld and that I hadn't really wanted to know (how many times she was stabbed, the location and nature of the wounds, the ultimate cause of death), shows me a long, slender blade and a wood handle, both darkened with her blood.

"He was unarmed," Porter said. "Otherwise, the judge probably would've tacked on another five years."

In my dreams, which have resumed in frequency and intensity since Connors's visit, I see Aggie as she looked on that warm July night almost six years ago. I see her wistful smile, the urgency in her deep brown eyes, *Come with me, Molly,* a few rebellious dark curls that escaped her crocheted navy scrunchy, the silver locket gleaming against the navy of her three-quarter-sleeved cotton sweater. I hear her purposeful tread as she hurries from her car in the darkening night toward a synagogue hall she will never reach where hundreds of women have joined to recite psalms for a young mother stricken with cancer.

In my dreams a man follows her. He is a hulking figure, his face masked in shadows, and there is menace in the stealth of his gait, in the set of his granitelike shoulders. I scream Aggie's name, to warn her, but the sound dies in my throat, and I watch, helpless, bound by shackles of sleep, as he accosts her and drags her into an alley. I see the glint of steel as the blade slices the air, again and again, but even in my dream my subconscious takes pity on me and I see nothing else.

Porter glanced at his watch. "Is that it? Are we done playing twenty questions?"

"I guess."

I would never be done. I now had a name for that shadowy figure, but still no face. I had questions whose answers had died with Creeley:

Did Aggie hurry when she heard his footsteps, or was she suddenly aware of him looming above her? Did she sense peril, or did he put her off guard by asking for the time or spare change before he attacked? Did he clamp his hand on her mouth to stifle the screams I hear in my head?

"You okay?" Porter asked. "You look a little green." He sounded uncomfortable, probably trying to figure out what to do if I fainted—or worse, started crying.

"I'm fine," I said, though my upper lip was beaded with sweat. My legs felt shaky when I stood.

"I know this is rough, Blume, but at least you can put it behind you."

I could hear in his voice that he was impatient for me to be gone—away from his desk, from the station, out of his life. I also heard, again, what sounded like genuine solicitude, which brought me this close to crying, something I refused to do in front of Porter.

I bit the inside of my lip until the quivering stopped. "By the way, how old was Randy when he died?"

"Thirty."

Zack's age, and in two months, mine. And Aggie's, if Creeley hadn't killed her. I didn't want to, but I couldn't help thinking about Randy Creeley and the road not taken.

CHAPTER THREE

I WAS TEMPTED TO GO HOME AND HAVE A GOOD CRY, BUT I normally collect data for my *Crime Sheet* column on Mondays and Tuesdays, and keeping busy would be therapeutic. After copying material from the Wilshire board, I did my rounds at several other police stations, then picked up Zack from his shul office at a little after two and drove to my brother Judah's Judaica store in a nearby Beverly Boulevard strip mall to select Zack's *kittel*. It's a ceremonial white cotton robe that, like the white of the bride's gown, symbolizes purity. A married male wears a *kittel* on Yom Kippur and at the Pesach (Passover) seder and is buried in it (after a long, happy life, one hopes). Zack would wear his for the first time on our wedding day, a private Yom Kippur that would erase all our sins.

"Another plus for matrimony," I'd commented last Monday night to my three sisters at our weekly mah jongg game, earning smiles from Edie and Mindy and a frown from Liora, who was subbing for my sister-in-law, Gitty. Liora is twenty, the youngest of us Blume women. Since her return last June from a year's study at a girls' seminary in Israel much like the one I attended, she's also become the most earnest and pious.

"Don't joke," she'd warned.

The truth is, I was only half joking. I can't speak for Zack, but I'd amassed a fair number of transgressions over the past few years (many of them in the thou-shalt-not-gossip category) and I welcomed a clean slate.

Judah wasn't in—he teaches two classes at one of the local Jewish high schools—but he had set aside a selection of *kittels* for Zack, who tried them all on before choosing one with vertical pleats and embroidery at the collar. Sarah, the middle-aged saleswoman Judah had recently hired, was doting on Zack and enjoying the fashion show. So were two other women, one of them a young blonde, who were pretending not to stare. My rabbi, in case I haven't mentioned it, is a hunk. Six feet tall, black hair, a smile that makes my knees weak, gray-blue eyes that see into my soul. I had a fluttery feeling watching him, picturing him standing next to me under the chuppa. Only sixteen more days . . .

"My mom wants to know if you've decided on candlesticks," Zack said after I had paid for the *kittel*.

According to a tradition that Judah says goes all the way back to Adam and Eve, the bride's family provides the *kittel* and the *tallit* (prayer shawl). The groom's family presents the bride with Shabbat candlesticks.

"Not yet. I haven't had a chance to really look."

I'd planned to look on Sunday, but Connors's revelation had dampened my mood. And if you want to know the truth, I hadn't figured out what to do with the pair my ex in-laws had given me four years ago and that I've been using every Friday, even after Ron moved out. Returning them would be hurtful and rude, but I didn't want to bring them into my new life with Zack. I was considering donating them to an organization that helps needy brides.

The lingering filaments of divorce, I thought as Sarah placed pair after pair of sterling silver candlesticks on the counter in front of me. I looked at more than twenty until I finally found a set I loved with simple, clean square lines, as different as possible from the ornate, filigreed towers sitting in my china closet.

From the Judaica store we drove to a dairy restaurant in another strip mall just a block away. Yes, it's embarrassing, and right out of *L.A. Story,* if you remember the Steve Martin film that skewered us Angelinos, but I wasn't about to leave my Acura in the lot across the street and risk having it towed by the owner of one of the other stores.

We ate our late lunch at an outdoor table. It was a perfect February day—crisp and sunny, with the temperature in the mid-sixties and a mild breeze that pinked my cheeks and justified my large cup of steaming hot chocolate. Not that anything chocolate needs justification, in my opinion.

Most of the other tables were filled—no surprise, since the place is popular with the Orthodox community, especially for those of us who live or work in the Miracle Mile area. The draw is not the ambience: The mall consists of an L-shaped arrangement of ordinary stores that face an always crowded parking lot. You may get an occasional whiff of tantalizing aromas—tomato, cheese, and sausage from the (nonkosher) pizza shop at the far left; fresh bread and pastries from the corner bakery; sautéed onions and grilled steak from the kosher meat restaurant behind you. But the predominant perfume is car exhaust, and the only music you'll hear is the blaring of horns and the rumble of engines accompanied by the angry shouts of people vying for a parking spot. Still, the food is tasty, if not haute cuisine, and it's kosher. And chances are you'll see someone you know, which is part of the fun.

It was a major part of the fun for Aggie and me. Whenever we would come here, which was often, we'd have a contest to see who could identify more people and invent the most outrageous stories about those we didn't know. (The loser paid the tip.) I found myself scanning the people at the other tables. Five I knew by name. Three more looked familiar, but Aggie wouldn't have given me points for those.

I felt a familiar lump in my chest and waited until I was in control before I turned back to Zack.

"Thinking about Aggie?" he said.

My eyes were like leaky faucets. "Everything reminds me of her. I don't mean to be a downer, Zack."

"You're going through the trauma of her death again, Molly. I'd be worried if you *weren't* grieving." Leaning across the table, he blotted my eyes with a tissue, a gesture that, given the Orthodox rules, was as close to a caress as he could offer. "I wish I could make things easier for you."

Last night in my apartment he'd listened to me talk about Aggie for hours. I would have loved to lean against his shoulder, to take comfort in his arms. Solace, not sex. Sometimes the rules are hard to follow.

I took the tissue and blew my nose. "I spent half an hour with Porter and learned almost nothing. I still don't know what Creeley looked like. It probably doesn't make sense, but I need to know."

Zack wrapped his hands around his coffee cup. "When my friend was murdered on the Jerusalem bus, I checked the papers every day to see the face of the suicide bomber who did it. I wanted to focus my anger on the person responsible for the horror."

Zack had almost been on that bus. From his somber voice and the distant look in his eyes I knew he was pondering the what-if, reliving the tragedy that had turned his life around and set him on the path to becoming a rabbi.

"Did you ever see the bomber's face?" I asked.

Zack nodded. "He was average-looking, not someone you would've picked out from a crowd and said, 'That guy's going to blow himself up.' He was twenty-three, my age at the time."

Another road not taken. "Did seeing it help?"

"A little. Not enough." He took a sip of coffee. "Doesn't the detective have a mug shot of Creeley?"

"Porter wouldn't let me see it, or Creeley's rap sheet. He *did* toss me a few crumbs." I repeated what the detective had told me. "I understand why Creely was afraid to sell the locket. But he's not Jewish. Don't you think it's odd that he held on to it?"

"It's odd," Zack agreed. "Unless he studied Kabbalah and learned about the significance of the red thread."

"Oh, please." I picked at my tuna salad.

"A lot of people are studying Kabbalah, Molly. Jews and non-Jews. It's been getting a lot of press because of celebrities like Madonna and Guy Ritchie."

"And Roseanne and Sandra Bernhard and Demi Moore. I read *People*. But Creeley was a petty thief and drug addict. How would he end up at a Kabbalah center?"

"Maybe he was looking for spirituality, for something other than drugs to fill a void. What did Porter say?"

"He didn't. He shrugged. He shrugs a lot. I think he enjoys showing off his pecs." I exaggerated the detective's shoulder movement, and we both laughed, something I hadn't done in days, so it felt especially good.

I worked on my tuna, which I alternated with sips of hot chocolate, and reviewed my conversation with Porter. I was still thinking about it when Zack finished his sandwich and took a sheet of paper from his jacket pocket.

"I'm leaning toward 'Adon Olam' for me," he said.

My mind was still on Porter. " 'Adon Olam'?"

"For the procession? We were going to decide on the songs today, remember? We have to tell the band no later than Wednesday."

I remembered. " 'Adon Olam' is great. I love it."

"If you're not up to deciding now, I can come to your place tonight, after mah jongg. Or we can do it tomorrow."

"No, let's get it over with."

He raised a brow. " 'Let's get it over with'?"

I blushed. "I meant we should decide so we can tell Neil." The bandleader. "I care about the music, Zack. I was thinking about Creeley. I really *do* love 'Adon Olam.' "

"Why don't we hum a few bars," he said, but a smile played around his lips. "So what's bothering you?"

"For one thing, Creeley had a job around the time Aggie was killed. So why did he mug her?"

"Last I heard, drug habits are expensive, Molly. It's not as if he was a CEO making big money."

"But Creeley was never violent before. He was unarmed the first time he mugged someone. Why didn't he grab Aggie's wallet and run? She would have given him whatever he wanted. She didn't care about material things."

"People don't always react rationally when they're frightened." He gazed at me with interest. "Are you saying Creeley *didn't* kill Aggie?"

"Maybe." The possibility had blossomed in my head sometime after I left Porter's office.

"Then how did he end up with her locket?"

"He could have been looking in the Dumpster where the

killer put her body and found the locket. Or someone could have planted it on him."

"Molly—"

"Something's off. It's not just Creeley. It was Porter's attitude when I asked basic questions he shouldn't have minded answering. He was defensive. I think he's sitting on something, Zack. I owe it to Aggie to find out what happened. I don't want to let her down again."

"Aggie's murder isn't your fault, Molly," Zack said, but I was rummaging in my purse for my cell phone. He took out a pen and scribbled something on his list. I couldn't tell if he was annoyed.

Porter was, when he came on the line. "What now?" he said, his tone a close imitation of a seal's bark.

"Just a few more questions, Detective?" I said with enough sugar to reverse insulin shock. "Aggie wasn't the kind of person to put up a fight. So why would Creeley kill her for her wallet and locket if he never killed before?"

"Like I *said,* we don't know that he didn't kill before. Just that he wasn't caught."

"But you told me he was unarmed when he committed the last burglary. And he had a job. And he stayed out of trouble for the past seven years. That says something."

"It says I shouldn't have told you a damn thing, Blume. Believe me, it won't happen again."

"Seriously, Detective. Doesn't all this *bother* you?"

"*You* bother me." Porter's voice was rising. I held the cell phone an inch away from my assaulted ear. "I told you Creeley had two strikes. If Aggie Lasher ID'd him, he could've been sentenced to life. He couldn't take the risk."

Porter had a point, but I wasn't convinced. "Still, the violence doesn't fit his profile."

"When did you graduate from Quantico, Blume? It's over. Case closed."

"What if Creeley was framed, Detective Porter? What if Aggie was deliberately targeted by someone else?"

"What if cows were ducks? You want to know what I think, Blume?"

"I'm sure you're dying to tell me."

"You *want* it to be someone else, something bigger," he said, not unkindly. "If you'd been with her that night, maybe Creeley would've mugged someone else. But if she was specifically targeted—well, even if you'd been with her, she would've been killed some other night. So you're off the hook."

My face burned with anger. I wanted to yell at Porter and tell him he was wrong. But I didn't, because on some level, he wasn't.

"Connors tells me you're getting married in two weeks," Porter said. "Why don't you leave the police business to us and concentrate on your fiancé. I ought to send him a condolence card. The poor guy probably has no clue what he's getting into."

"You don't care if Creeley *didn't* kill Aggie, do you?" I said before my mind could put the brakes on my mouth. "You want to close a cold case and up your solve ratio."

Porter hung up. The sound reverberated in my ear.

I flipped my phone shut and dropped it into my purse. "Well, *that* was productive." I managed a tight smile.

Zack was frowning. "Do you really believe that the police are just interested in closing the case?"

"Not really. Although Andy Connors is always telling me that the big brass are upset with the number of unsolved cases." I tapped my fork against my plate. "Porter annoyed me. I wanted to annoy him back."

"What did he say?"

"He felt sorry for you 'cause you're getting stuck with me." I made a face. "He said I should leave the police business to him and focus on you."

"I like the last part." Zack smiled. "The focusing on me."

"You think I'm obsessing, don't you?" I tend to be like a dog with a bone. It's a flaw or a virtue, depending on whom you talk to, or if you're the bone.

"That was a joke, Molly."

"But *do* you?"

The furrow between his brows told me he was choosing his words. "When you care about something or someone, you get intensely involved," he said. "It's one of the qualities I love about you."

I braced myself. "But . . . ?"

"What if there's nothing to find out? You've been living with this for almost six years, so it's hard to let go. But at some point you'll have to, or this will eat at you forever."

I thought about one of Bubbie G's Yiddish sayings. *Az me laigt arein kadoches, nemt men arois a krenk.* If you invest in a fever, you'll realize a disease.

Was I investing in a fever, or was the disease already there?

CHAPTER FOUR

Tuesday, February 17. 11:40 A.M. Corner of Vermont Avenue and Sunset Boulevard. A robber approached a man from behind and put a knife to his stomach. He demanded the victim's money and backpack. A second robber pushed the victim to the ground and the two fled with the victim's wallet and $585. (Northeast)

I HAD A SLUGGISH START TO MY DAY THAT A HALF HOUR on the treadmill and two cups of coffee didn't help. After mah jongg at Edie's last night, Zack and I had stayed up past three finalizing the wedding music and cataloging the gifts that had usurped most of the space in my small apartment and would do so for several weeks until we closed on the house we had bought.

I felt awkward about the gifts, especially those from people who had gifted Ron and me four years ago and might be wondering if this marriage would "take." (Ron and I had lasted fourteen months.) I felt awkward about the wedding, too, which my parents have insisted on paying for, despite my repeated offers to use money from my divorce settlement. I would have preferred an intimate affair, but I couldn't blame Zack's parents for wanting to share the nuptials of their only child with all their family and friends. And of course Zack had to invite the entire congregation, including the Hoffmans (Ron's parents), and Ron, who had been close with Zack in high school and sits on the synagogue board. The Hoffmans, not surprisingly, had written that they'd be out of town. Ron hadn't responded. I couldn't imagine that he'd want to watch his ex-wife standing under the chuppa with another man. My guess was that he wouldn't come but was enjoying dragging out my discomfort.

With a third cup of Taster's Choice French Vanilla steaming my face and my new flat-panel computer screen, I began entering *Crime Sheet* data. I inherited the column four years ago from Amy Brod, a friend from a UCLA journalism extension course who suggested me as her replacement when she moved to the L.A. *Times.* Amy had warned that the data entering was mind-numbingly tedious, but two years of writing newsletters and brochures for corporations and fund-raising organizations had inured me to "boring," and I'd had only modest success placing feature articles in magazines and local papers, including the *Times.* A weekly byline, I'd hoped, would give me exposure and credibility and a toe in the larger media door, along with access to detectives who could help me research the true-crime book I'd begun writing. Like my grandmother, I've always been fascinated and repelled by crime and criminals, real and fictional. Aggie's murder had intensified my need for answers—not just the *who,* but the *why.*

Amy was right about the data entering, particularly since my editor, George, discourages ironic commentary. But overall, the job is great. It's been a window on the complex, layered identity of the city I love and from which Orthodox Judaism has insulated me most of life. If you're Orthodox, you tend to live in close-knit communities that provide the necessities: Orthodox private schools; kosher markets, butchers, and bakeries; a ritual bath; synagogues within walking distance. Until I strayed from Orthodox observance in my early twenties, most of my friends—many of whom I'd known since elementary school—were Orthodox, too.

I also enjoy the camaraderie with many of the detectives I've come to know, and I still feel a thrill of anticipation when I step into a police station. The crimes I report are mostly repetitive and often mundane, but there are invariably entries that pique my interest. A few have taken me in unexpected directions in the quest for truth, and one, on a dark journey that almost cost me my life and still has me shaking when I allow myself to think about it.

Today, though, my mind was on Creeley. The only crime that mattered to me was Aggie's murder; the only truth, Creeley's involvement. After an hour during which I found myself rereading the same crime data three or four times and making more typos than sense, I phoned Connors. He wasn't in. I had no intention of contacting Porter, who probably wouldn't take my call anyway. So I went online.

My mailbox was cluttered with the usual variety of enticing offers: Russian mail-order brides; Viagra and other prescription drugs that you can get cheaper anywhere in the world than in this country (which, as you probably know, spends all the research and development dollars for said pharmaceuticals); fast-track college diplomas; enhancements for male genitalia ("Ladies, your man needs this bad!"); septic tank repair; "Bikini Zone" No Diets; tips to help stop annoying pop-ups; search engine secrets; LOWEST

MORTGAGES IN 35 YEARS!; new technology that will enable you to find anyone (with the exception of the person sending you this offer); frightening, sordid, and pathetic invitations to engage in teen sex.

When I'm particularly offended, or when I have writer's block or am procrastinating, I report spam to my Internet service provider (ISP), which promises to block future posts from the offenders. But the ingenious, friendly folks who send spam seem to have all the time in the world along with an endless supply of e-mail addresses, and I'm pretty certain that my missives to my ISP end up in a virtual circular file. So most of the time, I press DELETE.

That's what I did now. Then I logged on to Google, a search engine that more than makes up for the spam, and typed, "Roland Creeley in Los Angeles, California." *Creeley* is an unusual name— a plus for me—and there were only two hits: One was on Goldwyn Terrace, the second on Cherokee. A visit to MapQuest showed that Goldwyn Terrace was in Culver City. The Cherokee address was just north of Hollywood Boulevard.

I assumed that Culver City Creeley was Roland senior, and since Hollywood Division was handling Randy's death, Chero-kee Creeley was probably Roland junior. I wrote down both ad-dresses and the phone numbers Google thoughtfully provided, then placed a call to Cherokee Creeley.

I did it to try to verify that I had the right man. I did it be-cause he might have left an answering machine message and I needed to hear his voice. I drummed my fingers on my desk and sat up straighter when a machine picked up after four rings and what seemed like an interminable wait.

". . . Randy Creeley. Leave a message and I'll call you back. If you need to reach me right away, call me on my cell phone. . . . Peace and love."

My heart pounded as I listened to the pleasant timbre of a

voice that belonged to a man now dead—a man who had wished his callers peace and love, though that didn't prove anything, certainly not according to the police, who insisted that Creeley had killed my best friend and who could be right. I pressed REDIAL, listened to the message again, and copied down Creeley's cell number.

I had sheets of police reports with *Crime Sheet* data to enter. I had wedding favors to wrap, gifts to *un*wrap and record, a four o'clock appointment with the florist. Zack's words echoed in my head, and I could hear Connors's warning:

Leave it alone, Molly.

But as Smokey Robinson will tell you, nothing could keep me away from my guy.

CHAPTER FIVE

LIKE SUNSET BOULEVARD TWO BLOCKS TO ITS SOUTH, Hollywood Boulevard is more a state of mind than a locale and has more personalities than Sybil. East of Vine it's Anytown, USA, a wide street lined with industrial shops, groceries, and other stores that serve the needs of the area's polyglot residents. At Gower there's a car dealership where I get my Acura serviced and from whose lot you can see the famous HOLLYWOOD sign (originally, HOLLYWOODLAND). And between La Brea and Highland is the Hollywood you've probably read about or may have visited, a giant marquee that has been flashing hope and promises of fame to thousands of would-be actors—among them, apparently, Randy Creeley—and that invites us all to watch the show, to believe in the magic.

In recent years the magic had all but disappeared. Like an aging star desperate for roles in B movies she would have shunned in her prime, Hollywood slipped into disrepair. The street that once was the scene of glamorous, red-carpeted premieres attended by paparazzi and crowds of exquisitely dressed celebrities and their fans was pocked with dozens of peep shows, tattoo parlors, and tawdry souvenir shops selling sleazy, overpriced products. Standing in for the celebrities and fans were prostitutes and their johns, the homeless, runaways, drug dealers, users. When the local citizens would complain, the LAPD would periodically chase the street people away, but without conviction, the way you halfheartedly swat at flies buzzing around your barbecued ribs and corn. You know the flies will be back the minute you stop waving your hand, and they know that you know that after a while you'll get tired of waving.

Lately Hollywood has undergone a face-lift. The boulevard will never be synonymous with *subtle* (there's the new Erotic Museum, and Heidi Fleiss is opening Hollywood Madam), but the sordid souvenir shops are being replaced, slowly, with trendy eateries, boutiques, and nightclubs. And though the prostitutes and drug dealers do trickle back, along with the homeless, and it's not a neighborhood you want to visit at night, and definitely not alone, the area has improved.

The glitz is back. Turning right from La Brea onto the wide boulevard, I was greeted by the vertical "Hollywood" spire that topped a silver gazebo with life-size silver statues of four multicultural, evening-gowned stars: Mae West, Dolores Del Rio, Dorothy Dandridge, and Anna May Wong. Several blocks farther east I passed the $600 million–plus Hollywood & Highland project (new investors recently bought it at a fire sale for $200 million), a two-block structure with a Cecil B. DeMille–grand marble arch that invites you inside to an open-air entertainment complex with shops, restaurants, and the Kodak Theater. It's the new home of the Academy Awards ceremony and is across the street from Oscar's original residence, the refurbished Roosevelt Hotel.

The grand old theaters, all within a block or so, have been restored, too. The Egyptian, with its Egyptian-style columns, hieroglyphics, and a twelve-foot dog-headed guard god. The El Capitan, where you can still hear a live organist and pretend you're watching a live stage production with Clark Gable or Buster Keaton. Grauman's Chinese Theatre, across the street from the Egyptian, stands out with the huge dragon draped across its pagodalike architecture. You've probably heard about its forecourt, where autographs of over 170 celebrities, along with impressions of their feet and hands, have been preserved in the concrete.

I love movies and movie stars. So does most of my family, including Bubbie G, who used to enjoy watching the classics on cable before macular degeneration stole most of the central vision from her once bright blue eyes. When we were kids we'd visit Grauman's and try to fit our hands and shoes into the prints made by celebrities we adored, like Judy Garland, Jean Harlow (my mom's favorite), Bette Davis, and Meryl Streep (mine). My ex-husband, Ron, claims he's a perfect match for John Wayne and Cary Grant (not), and when my youngest brother, Joey, was in his *Star Wars* phase, my dad teased him and told him he saw a striking similarity between Joey's hands and R2D2's treads.

I wondered whose footprints Randy Creeley had tried to step into. Brad Pitt's, according to Creeley senior, although that was probably Porter's embellishment.

Only a few empty spaces remain in Grauman's forecourt, by the way, but there's still room for your bronze star to be embedded in the sidewalk along with the other stars on either side of Hollywood between La Brea and Vine. Bob Hope has four stars—one each for radio, stage, TV, and the movies. Gene Autry has a fifth, for music.

There would be no bronze star for Roland Creeley on Hollywood, and there was no star on the sidewalk in front of the two-story blue stucco apartment building where he had lived and died. A wall under repair looked as though it had been electrocuted by lightning bolts of gray plaster, the white paint on one window's trim was flaking, and another window was shuttered with cardboard. I found a parking spot in front and was careful to turn the wheels toward the curb. Cherokee climbs steeply from Hollywood to Yucca, and I didn't relish having my Acura roll down the street.

The building manager, Gloria Lamont, was wary even after studying the business card I'd pressed against the privacy window of her door, and she wasn't keen on talking to me about Creeley.

"I got nothin' to say," she insisted. "All's I know is, he's dead." She didn't sound all that sorry.

I put her in her mid-to-late fifties, judging from the salt and pepper in her cornrows and the fine lines around brown eyes several shades darker than the coffee of her skin. She was around my height, five-five, with a generous figure that she showed to advantage in black spandex leggings and a black sweater with a peacock design that gave a welcome jolt of color to the drab hallway.

She was standing in the doorway to her ground-floor apartment at the front of the building. Behind her Marvin Gaye was offering "Sexual Healing," presumably not to the young voices whose squeals I heard ("I mind my daughter's two young 'uns after school till she comes home," Gloria told me with weary pride). The smell of fried onions and garlic and tomatoes made me wish I'd had more for lunch than a Power Bar and glass of milk.

"The police said Randy overdosed on drugs," I told her.

Gloria folded her hands under her ample bosom and fixed me with a warning frown that would have stopped a battalion. "I don't know nothin' about drugs."

I'd obviously touched on a sore subject. I wondered if the

manager's statement was for my benefit or for the benefit of ears that might be listening. I'd heard the clack of a door being opened farther back along the hall. Gloria had heard it, too. She'd turned her head and was frowning in the direction of the sound.

"But did you suspect that Randy was an addict?" I asked.

"I get paid to take care of the building and collect rent, *not to stick my nose into other folk's business, like some sorry people who don't have nothin' better to do,*" she finished, her raised volume aimed at the door behind me.

The door closed with a *thunk*. Gloria returned her attention to me. "Randy was into drugs again, he got what he deserved. I don't need his garbage comin' down on me. I don't need the police on my back."

Her voice was quieter but shook with anger—at Creeley or the police, maybe both. The look in her eyes—a combination of fear and defiance—said she suspected that something illegal might be going on behind the doors of the apartments in the building she was managing, that there was nothing she could do about it.

My knowledge of drugs is limited to what I learn from the news and movies and TV, and to the occasional sad stories of Orthodox Jewish teenagers caught in their snare. I felt a wave of sympathy for Gloria and was counting my blessings when I heard a screech from inside the apartment, followed by a whoop of laughter.

Gloria whipped her head around, sending her cornrows flying with the clicking of castanets. "Jerome Warren, keep your hands off your sister or I'll give you what for!"

The noises stopped. Gloria faced me again.

"I can imagine this hasn't been easy for you," I said. "Especially with having to take care of your grandchildren. How old are they?"

"Jerome's goin' on seven. Jasmine just turned five." Her tone was stingy, as if I were a social worker and she wasn't sure what I planned to do with the information.

I smiled. "I have nieces and nephews about the same age. They can be a handful."

"They good kids, doin' real well in school," she said in that same guarded voice that wasn't buying my pitch at camaraderie. "You said you're a reporter. Who do you write for? The *Times*?"

"Sometimes. I freelance for different papers."

She nodded. "My husband Earl, rest his soul, liked to write. Poetry, mostly. He never had anything published, though. So you're fixin' to write about Randy, huh? I can't see why any-body'd care. He wasn't nobody special."

"Do you know where he worked?"

"No one place. He had a job, was makin' good money from what I could tell, but he lost it 'bout eight, nine months ago when he took sick."

Something Roland Creeley senior hadn't told Porter. Or maybe Porter hadn't shared it with me. "What happened?"

"He got hold of some bad stuff and almost died. I don't know where he got it," Gloria added. "Not my business. After that he told me he wasn't gonna have nothin' more to do with drugs. He had me believin' it, too."

Gloria's shrug said she didn't much care, but I sensed she was angry and disappointed with Creeley's relapse and her misplaced faith.

"How did he pay his rent after he lost his job?"

"He worked some of it off, did jobs around the neighborhood. Fixed doors and screens, small paint jobs, things like that?" She was friendlier now. The arms had come down, like the wooden bars at a railroad crossing when the coast is clear. "He was supposed to paint that outside wall what has cracks, and he was gonna take care of that front window, but then he up and died," she added with a hint of her former resentment.

So Randy was a handyman, when he wasn't mugging people to support his habit. "I understand that he wanted to be an actor. I heard he was very handsome."

"Well, he wasn't no Denzel. But yeah, Randy wasn't hard on the eyes." The woman allowed herself a chuckle. "He talked all the time about makin' it big in the movies. He was a smooth talker, I give him that. He could make you believe night was day and day was night. He'd borrow ten dollars and tell you he gave you back twenty and you owed him ten." Gloria's voice held equal parts of exasperation and admiration.

"He sounds like my ex-husband." Ron had smooth-talked his way through an affair and for a while had me doubting the truth, even after I confronted him with proof of his infidelity.

"Is that right?" Gloria clucked. "Well, I have to say the fear of dyin' shook Randy up some, 'cause he straightened up his ways. He started goin' to church regular. He paid his rent on time, prob'ly 'cause he wasn't spendin' most of his money on drugs. A few months back he gave me two hundred ten dollars. I said, 'Randy, what's this about?' An' he says, 'Mrs. Lamont, this here is money I been owin' you a long time, and there's more comin' but I don't have it just yet.' An' even before that he'd bring candy for my grandkids, and once in a while, some toys he knew they wanted. He was nice like that." For the first time she sounded sad that Creeley had died.

I wondered if Randy had paid for the toys or helped himself to them. Maybe he'd been playing Robin Hood. "Did he ever get into fights with the other tenants?"

"If he did, I didn't hear about it. I know he did time, but I didn't hold that against him. People change, you know? 'Course, I'm not sayin' I didn't keep my eye on him at first," she admitted.

"But he was always friendly, never gave me a lick of trouble. Until last week, that is. He more'n made up for it then."

A sharp cry from her apartment drew her attention. Gloria turned and listened. "TV," she told me when she was facing me again.

"Who called the police, by the way?" I'd forgotten to ask Connors or Porter.

"I did, one o'clock in the morning. His girlfriend Doreen woke me and made me open his door. She knowed something was wrong 'cause Randy was supposed to meet her and he didn't show, didn't phone? She screamed loud enough to wake the dead when she saw him lyin' there on the floor. He wasn't good-lookin' then, unh-unh." The manager pulled her lips into a grim line.

I took out a notepad. "Do you have a phone number where I can reach Doreen?"

Gloria shook her head. "I don't know her last name, neither. The day after Randy died, she came by to get some clothes she maybe left in his place, but the police had that yellow tape up? I told her, 'Gimme your number, I'll call you when they done,' but I must've took down the number wrong 'cause when I phoned two days later after the police took down the tape, the lady who answered didn't know Doreen. I expect she'll be by."

I handed her a business card. "When Doreen *does* come, would you give her this?"

"I guess I can do that."

"Would it be okay for me to see Randy's apartment, Mrs. Lamont? You said the police were done, right?" I added when she frowned, "I promise I won't take anything." I heard the anxiousness in my voice.

Gloria heard it, too. She was looking at me shrewdly, those brown eyes narrowed. "What do you need to see his apartment for, anyway?"

"Sometimes you can understand a person better from seeing where he lived." Which is true.

"So this is for your story, huh?" She crossed her arms again. "That's a load of you-know-what. What's going on?"

I debated, but not for long. "My best friend was killed six years ago. Now the police are saying Randy did it. I need to know if it's true."

I had startled her, but the shock turned to anger. She glowered at me. "Why didn't you tell me that in the first place?"

"I didn't know if you'd talk to me."

"Uh-huh." She studied me for a moment. "So that part about writin' a story on Randy, that's all lies. Not much difference between you and him, is there?"

Well, of course I felt myself blushing. "I may end up writing something about him. Right now I'm trying to find out what I can."

"Uh-huh." She cocked her head. "How do I know you're not givin' me another *story*?"

I took out my wallet and showed Gloria a photo Mrs. Lasher had taken of Aggie and me in the Lashers' backyard against a background of hot pink bougainvillea on a June day a month before she died. "That's my friend," I told the manager. "Her name is Aggie. She was killed on July 23, almost six years ago. She was twenty-three."

"An' the cops're sayin' Randy did it?" Gloria looked at the photo, then at me. Then back at the photo. "But you don't think so?"

"He could have. But you said he never fought and never gave you any trouble. And he never killed anyone before, as far as the police know."

"I seen people do things when they drunk or on drugs they wouldn't do otherwise. Just 'cause a man brings candy to a child don't mean he can't turn ugly."

She pinched her lips, and her eyes had a pained, faraway look. I wondered if she was reliving a memory.

"Ten minutes," she told me.

"You can watch me the whole time, Mrs. Lamont."

She dismissed my smile with a snort. "You got *that* right."

CHAPTER SIX

AFTER GIVING STRICT INSTRUCTIONS TO JEROME NOT TO open the door to anyone ("Not even the chief of *police!*") and promising she'd be back in ten minutes, Gloria took a ring of keys, locked her door, and led me through a narrow, musty hall-way to a second-floor apartment at the back of the building.

"Randy's daddy was supposed to empty the apartment yester-day so's I can rent it, but he didn't show," she said with annoyance as she unlocked the door and pushed it open. She flipped up a light switch. "Well, here it is."

Stale air laced with an unpleasant odor I couldn't identify greeted me like a ghost. I followed Gloria into a generous-size L-shaped living-dining room. The "living" part said bachelor's pad: cushy red leather sofa, black area rug with a red-and-white swirling pattern, one-piece Lucite coffee table with curved ends. The sofa faced black speaker boxes the size of refrigerators that were hooked up to a sound system housed inside a black lacquer cabinet crammed with CDs, and the DVDs Randy would have viewed on the sixty-inch projection TV positioned between the speakers. Next to the sofa was a black lacquer desk whose working surface was taken up by magazines and a combination phone–answering machine and multipurpose fax machine.

"He got all that about five, six years ago," Gloria said when I asked her about the TV, which ran over three grand four years ago when my ex, Ron, had lusted for one. "That and his Porsche." She pronounced it "porch." "Like I said, he made good money 'fore he took sick, but I think a lot of it went up his nose."

She didn't know what kind of work Randy had done and didn't have the time right now—or the inclination, I thought—to look through her files to see where he'd worked. "Ask his daddy," she said.

There was a black mug on the coffee table, which was piled with stacks of newspapers and magazines. *Variety,* the *Hollywood Reporter,* a church newsletter. More of the same on the desk. With Gloria breathing down my neck, I opened the drawers. Pens, paper clips, pencils. A rubber-banded stack of bills looked tempting, but Gloria said she didn't feel right letting me look at those, a man was entitled to his privacy, and I didn't even ask if I could STAR-69 the phone to find out to whom Randy had made his last phone call.

In the dining area, next to a kitchen not much bigger than my teeny galley, were a white bistro table and two white chairs with black vinyl seats, one of which was torn. A dinner plate on the beige-tiled kitchen counter bore the congealed remains of what looked like lasagna. Next to the plate were four empty

Heineken cans, a half-empty bottle of Jack Daniel's, and the glass, with a cloudy amber coating on the bottom, that he'd used in emptying it.

An eclectic mix of unframed movie posters brightened the ivory walls throughout the L. *The Sting. The Truman Show. Terminator 3. The Matrix. Braveheart. Lord of the Rings. North by Northwest. Legends of the Fall.* In the center of the living room a green plastic bucket sat on the worn beige carpet, directly beneath a large, nasty-looking brown blister on the ceiling.

"Randy was goin' to take care of the leak, too," Gloria said. I sensed she was sorry about his death and not just about the repairs he hadn't completed.

The bathroom off the living room was tiny. I didn't find anything of interest in the medicine cabinet, just the essentials. Creeley's bedroom, around ten by ten with a window not much larger than my eighteen-inch flat screen computer panel, barely accommodated the king-size platform bed and black lacquer nightstand. On the wall at the head of the bed, which was a tangle of brown sheets and a black comforter, Randy had hung a cross. From the rectangle of paint around it, lighter and fresher than the paint in the rest of the room, I could see that the cross was a recent addition.

The odor was stronger here, and I had no difficulty identifying it as vomit. Neither did Gloria.

She crinkled her nose. "I sprayed yesterday, but I'll have to get the carpet cleaned to get rid of the smell. That's where I found him," she said with somber theatricality, pointing to a darkened area of matted carpet between the bed and the opposite wall.

I followed her finger with my eyes and pictured Creeley jerking on the floor, dying. Somehow it didn't give me the satisfaction I'd anticipated. I glanced at the walls, covered with more movie posters and a framed black-and-white headshot of a handsome young man whom Gloria identified as Randy Creeley.

"I tol' you he was good-lookin'," she said. "Sexy, too."

He was. Artfully tussled longish blond hair with darker roots; large, expressive dark eyes; a chiseled nose; a strong, square chin. He didn't look like a killer, but neither had Ted Bundy or the man who had tried to choke me seven months ago.

I studied the photo a while longer, but if there were hidden clues to Randy's identity, they eluded me.

I looked through his closet. Randy's wardrobe had been mostly casual: a dozen pairs of jeans, a lineup of athletic shoes, flip-flops, and two pairs of dress shoes. A couple of Hawaiian print shirts looked especially gaudy next to the dress shirts, dark twill slacks, and black loafers that I assumed he wore to auditions. I flipped among the slacks and shirts but didn't find any clothing that would have belonged to the girlfriend. Unless Doreen had a key to Randy's apartment and had removed her things?

"She didn't have a key," Gloria said when I asked. "If she did, she wouldn't of needed me to open his door, would she? I guess she didn't leave stuff after all."

I returned to the books stacked on the nightstand. The top one was a thick text. *Alcoholics Anonymous.*

"Can I look at these?" I pointed to the stack.

"I guess so, seein' as how the police are done."

I picked up the book. It was well worn, I saw as I paged through it, with many passages highlighted in yellow. Serving as a bookmark in the middle of chapter nine were two color photos. One was of Randy with his arm around a pretty, petite, light-brown-haired, ponytailed young woman in jeans and a T-shirt. The girlfriend?

"No, that's Randy's kid sister, Trina," Gloria said when I showed her the photo. "She came by 'bout once a week, more when he took sick. Randy's momma died when he was just a kid."

Dead to Randy, and to his family? It was probably less painful to say his mother had died than to deal with the complex emotions of being abandoned.

The other photo showed Randy as a stunning child (five or six?), cheek to cheek with a beautiful woman I assumed was his mother. There was something artificial about the pose and the smiles and the woman's long golden hair that seemed to blend in with her son's. Someone—Randy? his father?—had ripped the photo and Scotch-taped the parts together unevenly, creating a faint, jagged line that scarred her face.

I replaced the photos and shut the book. "Do you know where I can reach Trina, Mrs. Lamont?"

"She lives a couple of blocks from here. I don't know the address. I have her phone number, though. After Randy took sick, she gave it to me, just in case. Work *and* home numbers. I called her after the police and she came right over. She took it bad, poor thing." The manager clucked.

I have three brothers and three sisters and can't imagine how I would deal with losing one of them. The thought made me shudder.

I checked the rest of Randy's reading material. A well-worn Bible, other books on addiction and self-help.

"It looks like Randy was serious about trying to quit drugs," I said as we were leaving the apartment.

"Well, like I said, he was shook up bad when he almost died. He told me he was never gonna do that stuff again, and Trina, she watched him like a hawk. But once you hooked, it's hard to get free, you know?" She locked the door. "My daughter's husband swore ten times he was done with all that, and I believe he meant it, every time. Shirrel left him 'bout five months ago, and I hope she doesn't go back."

CHAPTER SEVEN

CONNORS WAS IN A HORIZONTAL POSITION WHEN I EN-
tered the Hollywood Division detectives' room at one-thirty, his
scuffed tan boots propped on his desk, his ankles crossed. He was
engrossed in a phone conversation, and acknowledged me with a
nod, minus his usual smile. Not a good sign.

I took off my peacoat, pulled up a chair, and inhaled the
smell of coffee from the mug on his desk while I waited.

"The answer is no," Connors said in his flat Boston accent
when he put down the receiver.

"No, what?"

"No to whatever you're selling."

"You're sure? I have Girl Scout Cookies, wrapping paper,
Amway products, magazine subscriptions—"

"Cut it out." He swung his long legs down from the table and sat up straight.

"I take it Porter told you about our conversation."

"He's ready to lock you up." Connors scowled at me. "Why would you piss him off like that, Molly?"

"Because he was being stubborn, and he's a jerk." I hesitated, a little nervous to test the water. "And maybe he *is* too eager to close Aggie's case."

"Porter wouldn't do that." There was a warning in Connors's voice and in his hazel eyes.

"Then why wouldn't he consider the possibility that Creeley didn't kill Aggie?"

"Because logic and the evidence say Creeley did it."

"By *evidence* you mean the locket. Creeley could have gotten it from someone else, Andy. Or he could have found Aggie's body in the Dumpster and taken the locket."

"The locket's only part of it."

That was a surprise. "What else do you have?"

Connors shook his head. I could see from his expression that he regretted what he'd said.

"Come on, Andy. I won't let on that you told me."

"Like Porter wouldn't figure it out?" He drained his coffee mug and set it on a stack of papers.

I wondered what other evidence there could be, and why Connors wouldn't share it with me, why Porter had been so evasive. "I spoke to the manager of the apartment building where Randy lived."

Connors *tsk*ed. "*Only* the manager? You're usually so thorough."

"I left my card with the other tenants." Including the person who had been listening in on my conversation with Gloria. I'd rung his (her?) bell, knocked a few times. My eavesdropper had either left the building or turned shy. "The manager said Creeley reformed when he almost died eight or nine months ago after a drug episode gone bad. He swore to her that he stopped using."

"Creeley wouldn't be the first to start using again, Molly. Rehab clinics are full of repeaters."

"But he started going to church, Andy. He repaid money he'd borrowed. You were in his apartment, right? So you saw the books on his nightstand. *Alcoholics Anonymous,* other books dealing with addiction and self-help."

"I have *Atkins* on my nightstand and still eat too many carbs."

"Show-off." Connors is in his mid-thirties but has the metabolism of an eighteen-year-old and a stomach as flat as a marble countertop. I sucked in my own. "The manager told me Randy's girlfriend, Doreen, came by the day after he died to pick up some clothes she'd left at his place. There was crime-scene tape on the door, and she said she'd come back." I paused.

"Is there a point here?"

"Doreen hasn't come back, and I didn't see any women's clothes in Randy's closet. The manager let me in," I added in response to Connors's questioning look.

"Maybe Doreen came back and let herself in." Connors picked up a pencil and rolled it between his palms.

"Apparently she didn't have a key. And if she *had* a key, why did she need the manager's help to get into Creeley's apartment?" No reaction from Connors. "There's not one feminine toiletry item in his medicine cabinet. Either Doreen never stayed overnight, or she cleaned out all her things. And when the manager, Mrs. Lamont, tried phoning her to tell her the police were done and she could come by, the person who answered said she didn't *know* Doreen." I ended with a flourish that was wasted on Connors, judging from his deadpan expression.

"So Mrs. Lamont copied down the wrong number," he said. "People do that all the time."

"Maybe. But what if Doreen intentionally gave her the wrong number?" And why wasn't Connors wondering the same thing?

"And she would do that because . . . ?"

"Because she was involved with Randy's death," I said, barely restraining my impatience. "Suppose she had a key but didn't want to be the one to find the body. Suppose she had to get into the apartment the next day to make sure she didn't leave any incriminating evidence."

"Suppose Saddam Hussein had weapons of mass destruction." Connors put down the pencil. "Maybe Doreen *did* have a key. She found Creeley dead, but didn't want to be involved. So she left and then went back and had the manager open the apartment. And she gave her a wrong phone number."

I had to admit that made sense. "Did they do the autopsy?"

"On Friday. Creeley overdosed, like I told you."

"I didn't see any drug paraphernalia."

"It was there. We took it. We just didn't think to give you an inventory," he added. "Plus Creeley went to town on the booze. If you checked out his apartment, you must've seen the empties."

"That doesn't mean he drank the stuff. Someone could have emptied the beer cans and half the whiskey."

"Someone *could* have, but Creeley had enough alcohol in him to open a bar. A guy goes off the wagon, he usually does it in a big way."

"I wouldn't know. Did they find fresh needle tracks?"

"You're watching too much *CSI*. Yeah, they did. Do yourself a favor and let it go, Molly. Creeley killed Aggie. He overdosed. It's over."

"He never killed anyone before, Andy."

"He never got caught."

"If you say so." I was playing a broken record and getting nowhere. I stood and returned the chair to the adjacent desk. "By the way, when's the funeral?"

"Ten o'clock Thursday morning."

"Where?"

Connors named a cemetery in Downey. "What're you planning to do, open the casket and make Creeley tell you what happened?"

"I'd get more information from him than I've gotten from you guys."

"Don't mess with the investigation, Molly."

"What investigation?" I slipped on my jacket and slung my purse strap over my shoulder. "Creeley overdosed. He killed Aggie. Like you guys keep saying, the case is closed."

"It *is* closed. There's stuff you don't know, Molly."

"Because you won't tell me. This whole thing with Creeley doesn't feel right."

"It doesn't *feel* right?"

"Why didn't Creeley leave Aggie where he killed her? Why did he take her body to a Dumpster behind a restaurant several miles away?" That had been puzzling me all along.

"What did Wilshire tell you?" There was a note of caution in Connors's voice.

"That Creeley wanted to delay discovery of the body. That moving a body can make it harder to pin down the time of death, and that helps the killer establish an alibi."

Connors nodded. "So there's your answer."

"What's going on, Andy? Why are you so uncomfortable?"

"You're asking questions about a six-year-old case that isn't mine and never *was* mine, Molly. If you want answers, go to Porter."

"Yeah, right." I sniffed.

Connors sighed. "Why do you have to make this so hard?"

"Because she was my *best friend*!" Heads turned our way. I lowered my voice. "What if Doreen killed Randy, or knows who did? Maybe she planted the locket so you guys would think he killed Aggie. And if Creeley was killed, maybe Aggie was a specific target, not a random victim. Have you even considered that? Of course not. You guys are *so* eager to wrap this up."

Connors had risen from his chair and was inches away from me. "Do you have any reason to believe that Aggie was mixed up in something that would put her in danger?" he asked with an intensity that made me flinch.

"No. Of course not."

"Was she worried about anything? Was she scared of anyone?"

"I answered all these—"

"*Was* she?"

This was a Connors I'd never seen. There have been times, when I've pressed too much, that he's told me to back off, but now he was angry. I had a glimpse of how intimidating and effective an interrogator he could be.

"Aggie wasn't scared," I said. "She was happy. She loved her family, her life, her job. She loved helping people. If she was concerned, it was about her clients at Rachel's Tent. She took her work seriously."

"Exactly." Connors practically spit the word. In a calmer voice, he added, "So why the hell would someone kill her? And why frame Randy Creeley for it?"

CHAPTER EIGHT

TRINA CREELEY, I LEARNED WHEN I PUNCHED THE PHONE number Gloria Lamont had given me, worked at Frederick's of Hollywood—on Hollywood Boulevard, hence the name, and as it turned out, only blocks from Creeley's apartment. Had I known, I would've walked to the store after talking to Gloria instead of wasting my time with Connors. I was muttering to myself on the drive back, and my mood wasn't enhanced after I circled Frederick's three times without finding a parking spot. I ended up leaving my Acura three-fourths of the way up Cherokee, almost where I'd parked it before. I had new sympathy for Sisyphus.

I'd heard of Frederick's and the sexy lingerie it sells, and you may have seen versions in a mall near you, but this pink-awninged gray building, formerly a garish purple, is the original flagship store. Even if I hadn't been engaged to a rabbi, I would have felt self-conscious entering an establishment where you can buy musical panties that play "Happy Birthday." Of course, if one of Zack's congregants saw me exiting the Art Deco tower, I could have used a variation of the I-only-buy-*Playboy*-to-read-the-articles excuse and say I'd been visiting the Lingerie Museum inside.

The stars on the sidewalk in front of the entrance—Jack Palance and Fleetwood Mac—were echoed in the star-studded motif of the gray carpet inside the store. The walls were purple, the clientele mostly adult, although two women were pushing strollers, and a pregnant customer had a young child in tow.

To be honest, I was disappointed. I'd expected "outrageous," but aside from a display case offering specialty items (Body Icing, Whipped Body Cream, a Honeymoon Kit, Edible Panties, Passion Powder) and a rack of costume lingerie (French maid, Cleopatra, a nurse, a sailor), most of the merchandise—nighties, teddies, and other items that echoed the theme "Less is more"—didn't look all that different from what you'd see on a Hollywood celebrity at the MTV Awards, or at Victoria's Secret, whose latest Christmas catalog offered panties with holiday jingles. Gives a new meaning to "naughty and nice."

The sales staff, all women, were dressed in black. I looked around but didn't see anyone I thought was Trina. When I asked for her, a licorice-thin, willowy six-foot-tall brunette who introduced herself as Jonnie pointed to a woman several feet away holding up a rhinestone-studded bra for a male customer's approval.

I wouldn't have recognized Randy's kid sister. According to Porter, she was seven years younger than Randy, which made her twenty-three, but she looked older. Makeup had added the years and a measure of sophistication, and she'd exchanged her brown ponytail for a strawberry blond shag that overpowered her thin face. Fitted black slacks and a long-sleeved black Lycra scoop-neck top showed off a flat tummy and generous curves and an inch of what I supposed was a black lace Frederick's of Hollywood bra.

"She's going to be a while," Jonnie said. "I can help you, if you like."

"That's okay. I'll wait."

Glancing in Trina's direction every twenty seconds or so, I flipped through racks and was checking out the French maid costume when my cell phone rang. It was Zack.

"How about grabbing lunch?" he said. "I'm working on the expense report for the board and my eyes are glazing."

"It's two-thirty. Kind of late for that," I told him, though my stomach said otherwise. Since leaving Gloria Lamont, I'd been snacking on Hershey's Kisses and I craved something substantial.

"A cup of coffee, then. Water. Anything." He lowered his voice. "I miss you."

Even over the phone, he made me all tingly. "I miss you, too. But I'm kind of tied up right now."

"Literally or figuratively? With any other woman, I wouldn't ask."

"Ha, ha."

"So where are you? Looking at carpet samples? I could join you."

"Frederick's of Hollywood."

"Maybe not." Zack laughed. "Frederick's, huh? Somehow I pictured you in Christian Dior or Vera Wang."

"They have some nice things here. And costumes." I described a few. "Maybe I should get one for the shul's Purim party."

"You'd definitely make a statement. So what *are* you doing there?"

I hesitated, then told him. "And before you say anything, I'm not getting my hopes up that the sister will have any answers for me."

"You already have, or you wouldn't be there."

"Don't be so damn smart." I fingered a black teddy. "As long as I'm here, I may try on a few things, get something special for our honeymoon. Shmuley Boteach would approve." The author of *Kosher Sex*.

"That's because he doesn't have a report to finish. If it's full of mistakes, I'll blame you. *How* many days till the wedding?"

"Fifteen." I pictured him at his desk, shirtsleeves rolled up, tie loosened, top button undone, black suede yarmulke off center the way it always is.

"Too long," he said.

"*Way* too long. Any preferences?"

"Anything with you in it."

I hung up the phone, smiling. Trina was still with her customer. I strolled to the back of the store and stopped in front of a large glass display case that featured celebrity lingerie. A pink, fur-trimmed sheer nightie from an Austin Powers movie. A purple nightgown from Naomi Judd. The green boxer shorts Tom Hanks wore in *Forrest Gump*. I still think *Shawshank* should have won.

To the right of the display case was a short flight of gray-and-white marble stairs that led to the museum. Here the items were more sedate: Frederick's of Hollywood catalogs dating back decades. The bra worn by Tony Curtis in *Some Like It Hot*. Judy Garland's nightgown from *Presenting Lily Mars*. Greta Garbo's black slip from *Camille*.

I was examining a black bustier with strategically placed gold tassels when Trina appeared at my side. Five-inch stiletto black heels made her a touch taller than me.

"That's the second bustier Madonna donated," she told me.

"The first one was purple, from her *Who's That Girl?* tour. It was stolen during the Rodney King riots."

Up close I could see freckles peeking through her pancake foundation. "Really?"

"Frederick's had to donate ten thousand dollars to Madonna's charity, the one that gives poor women free mammograms. My favorites are the crinoline from *Seven Brides for Seven Brothers* and Ava Gardner's slip from *Showboat*. That's my e-mail screen name. Ava Gardner." She smiled. "I'm Trina. Jonnie said you were asking for me?"

Her blues eyes were measuring my chest, and I found myself standing straighter and squaring my shoulders. "Molly Blume. I'm—"

"Thirty-six C, right?"

"B." They always flatter you.

"We have an Extreme Cleavage bra that's real popular. We also have a vinyl bustier that's really cool. Well, not *cool,* 'cause it's vinyl." She giggled. "Married or single?"

"I'm getting married in two weeks," I said, not sure why I volunteered the information.

"Wow! Then we have to get you something special." Her smile erased a few years and revealed almost straight teeth. "I know just the thing."

I would have preferred talking here, in private, but Trina's heels were already clacking on the marble. I followed her downstairs to a lingerie rack at the front of the store.

"How about a bridal teddy with a matching veil?" she suggested. "Or a maribou-trimmed baby doll? That comes with a veil, too, and matching slippers."

"I don't think that's me."

She flipped through the rack. "I know you'll like this." She pulled out a black corset with burnt black velvet detail. "Sexy, but elegant. Am I right?"

It wasn't bad. "Trina—"

"Come on," she coaxed, draping the corset against her body, then thrusting it at me. "Try it on, just for fun."

I took the corset. "Actually, I'm not here to shop. I'm a reporter." With my free hand I found a card in my purse and handed it to her.

She tucked it into the waistband of her slacks without glancing at it. "You're doing a piece on the museum?" The enthusiasm had left her voice, and her eyes were scanning the room for the next customer.

"I'm here about your brother."

She stiffened and took a step back. "I don't want to talk about my brother." Her hand went to the long silver chain that circled her neck.

"I know how painful this must be for you, Trina." I cringed at the platitude but didn't know what else to say.

She glowered at me. "Did you ever lose a brother?" She kept her voice low but the words were an assault.

Several people, including Jonnie, turned to look at us.

"No." Thank God.

"Well, then, you don't know anything!" She narrowed her eyes, which were bright with tears, and regarded me with suspicion and unease. "How did you find me, anyway?"

"Mrs. Lamont, the building manager. Is there somewhere we could talk for a few minutes?"

She dropped the chain. "The police told you Randy killed some woman years ago and you want to write about it, huh? I should've figured that out." Contempt had aborted the tears.

"I'd like to hear more about your brother before I write anything. I *do* have questions about what happened. About his girlfriend, for one thing. Doreen."

"Isn't it enough that he's dead? Can't you leave us *alone*?"

I felt sorry for her, but pity wasn't about to stop me. Oh, no.

"If Randy didn't kill that woman, don't you want to find that out? Don't you want to clear his name?"

"Like you care about my brother! He's just a story to you."

It wasn't quite the truth, but it was close enough. My cheeks burned. I *didn't* care about Creeley. For all I knew he *had* killed Aggie. And Porter was right. I was desperate for absolution, hungry for details and determined to get them even if it meant manipulating this woman's grief.

Jonnie had approached. "Everything okay here?" she asked with false cheer that sounded desperate.

"We don't seem to have what this customer is looking for," Trina said, her tone as sharp as the *V* of the toes of her shoes.

"Maybe I can help," Jonnie offered.

"Actually, I've decided to take this." I held up the corset.

Jonnie smiled. Crisis averted. Trina threw me a suit-yourself shrug and walked off. Ten minutes later I was standing under the famous pink awning with my purchases—the corset and a white lace-and-pearl-beaded teddy that I'd spotted on the way to the register. I headed toward Cherokee and had crossed Hollywood when I heard someone calling my name. I turned and waited for Trina to catch up.

"You didn't have to buy the corset," she said.

She hadn't put on a jacket, but she didn't seem to notice the cold that was nipping at my cheeks. Her face was flushed, and she was breathless—from exertion or urgency, I couldn't tell.

"I wasted your time and upset you," I told her. "I'm sorry on both counts."

"Well, you should be." She pushed a thick strand of blond hair behind an ear decorated with multiple studs. "You can return it. We don't work on commission."

"I really like it. It *is* sexy and elegant. I bought a teddy, too." I smiled, but Trina was all seriousness.

"You mentioned Doreen. Did you talk to her?"

"No. That's one of the things I want to talk to you about. Can I buy you a cup of coffee?"

She glanced behind her. "I have to get back to work."

"How about after work? Five-thirty? Six?"

Trina ran her chain across her lip. I sensed that she wanted to say yes, that she hadn't run after me to talk about corsets.

"Did you mean what you said, that you wanted to help prove Randy didn't kill that woman six years ago?"

"I want to find out the truth," I said, though Trina's truth and mine might not end up being the same. "The woman who was killed—"

A truck backfired. I was startled, but Trina jumped at the loud noise and jerked her head around. When she turned back, the color had drained from her face, making the rose blusher look like clown's paint.

Her hand went to the chain around her neck. "I have to go."

"Trina—"

"I don't want to talk about Randy, okay?" she said with some of her earlier belligerence. "I just didn't want you to be stuck with something you don't want."

I barely heard her. I had sucked in my breath and was staring at the locket Trina had pulled out, a locket with an image of Rachel's Tomb.

"That's an unusual locket." Buses were belching fumes, cars were honking. My words were pounding in my ears.

"Randy gave it to me. It's supposed to be good luck."

"Is there a red thread inside?"

Trina's eyes widened with surprise, which quickly changed to alarm. "Yeah. Why?" The *why* was defensive.

"A friend of mine has a locket just like yours, with the red thread."

"Randy didn't steal it, if that's what you're getting at." She glared at me and clamped her hand around the locket before dropping it out of view.

"I'm not saying that at all. I'd really like to talk, Trina. You have my card. Please call me."

"Don't hold your breath. Well, you might have to, if you want to get into that corset."

She gave a nervous little laugh and practically ran down the block on those killer heels. I watched her for a few seconds before climbing back up the hill to my car. Bird droppings had decorated my windshield and someone had left a series of red-lipstick kisses on the driver's window and side-view mirror.

Hooray for Hollywood.

CHAPTER NINE

THE LOCKET THREW ME.

If Randy had given his kid sister a locket identical to Aggie's, including the red thread inside, it couldn't be coincidence that he'd been in possession of Aggie's. And it wasn't likely that someone had planted it on him.

So Connors and Porter were probably right—Creeley had killed Aggie.

But why had he given his sister a locket like Aggie's?

Trina might have answers, but she wasn't talking. Maybe I'd fare better with her father.

I'd taken along the Google information, including Creeley senior's phone number, which Gloria Lamont had matched to the one she had.

I should probably phone first, I thought. With the funeral two days away, Creeley might not be in the mood to talk. But phoning ahead would ruin the element of surprise that is often vital in an interview. And what if Creeley, forewarned, *never* wanted to talk to me?

Wiping off the bird doo and lipstick with a towelette from the stash of emergency supplies my dad had stored in my trunk, I considered. Then I dialed Creeley's number on my cell phone, introduced myself as a reporter to the woman who answered, and asked to speak to Roland Creeley.

"I'm *Mrs.* Creeley," she said. "What's this about?"

She was clearly the keeper of the gate. "I heard about Randy's death, and I'm sorry for your loss, Mrs. Creeley. I know this is a hard time, but if it's possible, I'd like to talk to you and your husband about Randy."

"If this is about the dead girl, we don't know anything." She had the put-upon tone I use with telemarketers just before I hang up.

"The police are saying Randy's responsible, but I'm not so sure," I said quickly. "I have some questions."

"Well, we're not interested in talking to anyone."

"Talk to who?" I heard a man ask. "Who is that, Alice?"

"Hold on," Alice Creeley told me, annoyed again—either with me or with the man, who I assumed was her husband.

After half a minute or so of muffled conversation he came on the line.

"You're with the *Times,* right?" He sounded eager and pleasantly surprised. "I didn't think they'd get back to me. I asked them to check into my son's death. The police say Randy overdosed on drugs, but I don't believe it."

I felt a flutter of excitement, but I told myself that like many parents, Creeley was probably in denial about his son. "I'm not on the *Times* staff," I admitted, "but I freelance for them and several other papers."

"Oh."

"And I've investigated crimes. I write a weekly crime column and books about true crimes." I mentioned *Out of the Ashes.*

"Never heard of it. I don't read all that much. When I do, it's mostly magazines. So how'd you hear about Randy? What's your interest in him?" Suspicion had sharpened his voice and raised it a notch.

"From the police." I repeated what I'd told his wife. "I'd like to hear why you think your son didn't overdose."

"And you want to check into his death? The police aren't going to, they said as much," he told me again with some anger.

"Yes."

I took the silence that followed as a good sign.

"Well, if you want to come tomorrow morning, fine," Creeley said, his lack of enthusiasm indicating he was settling.

"I can do that. Or I can come now, or this evening." I'd have to postpone the florist, but I was eager to talk to Creeley and worried that between now and tomorrow morning he'd change his mind or have it changed for him by his wife. Or what if a *Times* reporter *did* call?

"Tonight's no good. I have to clear out Randy's apartment, pick up his car. And as soon as I hang up I'm leaving for the funeral parlor to finish the arrangements. They want us to pick flowers. Like Randy's gonna see the flowers, like he gives a damn. Vultures." Creeley grunted. "What's your name, by the way?"

"Molly Blume."

"I know that name. Is that the name you write under?"

"No. You're probably thinking about the fictional character. James Joyce's *Ulysses?*"

Throughout most of my adult life I've been teased about my name (most frequently, by Connors). I blame my mother, who teaches high school English and should have known better, but teasing aside, and though I'd practiced writing *Molly Abrams* in countless high school notebooks, my name has opened some doors and I've pretty much decided to continue using it for professional reasons after Zack and I are married, when I'm not writing under my pseudonym.

"I saw the movie years ago," Creeley said. "Didn't like it much. Your parents had a sense of humor, huh?"

"Apparently."

"Nine o'clock tomorrow morning. Family will be coming to the house from ten on, so if you're gonna be late, don't bother showing up."

CHAPTER TEN

THE CREELEYS—FATHER, DAUGHTER, AND SON—LINGERED in my thoughts while I did a load of laundry, and kept me company when I picked up my mother on the way to Flores Lindas, a flower shop on Third Street just east of La Brea. I'm pretty sure she sensed my preoccupation and its cause, but unlike my oldest sister, Edie, my mother doesn't push.

Raul, who owns the shop with his wife, Dani, greeted us with double-cheek kisses. He's a Brazilian charmer with sensual Latin good looks—dark, wavy moussed hair that brushes his shoulders; cheekbones so sharp they'd probably bruise your fingers if you touched them; black eyes that my mother, who's had one romance novel published (anonymously) and is almost finished with the second, would call "smoldering." A filigreed gold cross gleamed against the all-year-round-bronzed, hairless skin exposed in the deep V of the crisp white shirt he'd tucked into tight jeans, the kind of jeans Connors wears well and Zack used to before he became a rabbi, though I'm sure they'd still fit him just fine.

"If I didn't know better, Celia, I would think you are the bride," Raul told my mother. "You look like a beautiful flower."

His accent softened the words in the sexy way that only Portuguese does, in my opinion, and that makes me think of "The Girl from Ipanema" and other lazily sultry tunes on a Stan Getz–João Gilberto vinyl album (my parents') that Zack and I made out to in high school and that still gives me tingly memories.

"A *preserved* flower," my mother said, but I could tell from her flushed cheeks that she was pleased. She's almost fifty-six but looks younger, with only a few fine lines around the brown eyes she's passed on to me and most of my siblings, and a trim figure she maintains by taking evening walks with my dad, who still gazes at her the way he did in their wedding photos from over thirty-five years ago and tells you she is his world.

"Absolutely not." Raul tilted his head. "You should always wear that shade of brown. It brings out the copper in your hair. And I *love* the headband. Very chic."

I wondered if Raul was aware that the olive velvet band camouflaged the point where my mother's rich chestnut brown met her fall of the same color.

"And Molly." He turned his high-wattage smile on me. "You are going to be stunned with what I have done. *Stunned.* But why waste words? Come."

He waved us through a narrow hall perfumed with floral arrangements in various stages of construction to a table with a sample centerpiece formed of dozens of tightly packed, open red-black roses that sat on a bed of green hydrangea in a square black Lucite container.

"Is *magnífico,* yes?" Raul beamed. "Simple, elegant. And there will be tea lights, of course. Many, many tea lights. And white tablecloths, with embroidered organza toppers. Celia, I do for you and the lovely Molly what I don't do for other clients at twice the price."

Raul has provided flowers for numerous Hollywood galas (his keenest disappointment to date is losing the Brad Pitt–Jennifer Aniston nuptials), but he takes equal satisfaction in his creations for less spectacular events, including all the Blume bar mitzvahs and weddings. If he likes you, he'll throw in extras (and he's been known to donate flowers to brides who have no means), but if you don't set firm limits, you can end up spending the farm.

In this case, Zack's parents' farm. In Orthodox circles the groom often pays for FLOP—flowers, liquor, orchestra, and photography (still and video). The Abramses had given Raul a generous budget that he'd urged my parents to supplement for "this once-in-a-lifetime magical event," which he'd momentarily forgotten wasn't my "once." My dad, a contractor, had groused ("Six hours later, what do you have left? Put the money in the new kitchen"), but he had been ready to give in. I had nixed the extras.

"It's beautiful, Raul," my mother said. "Exquisite. It's everything you promised and more."

"Beautiful," I echoed. My mind had skipped to Creeley, who at this moment was choosing flowers for the funeral of his son. Aggie's killer?

My mother nudged me. I glanced at Raul. He looked crestfallen, his smile dimmed.

"I absolutely *love* it, Raul. It's *breathtaking.*"

Back in his office, Raul shoved stacks of magazines off chairs for us so that we could sit, and after taking his place behind his French desk, he showed us sketches for the chuppa and the pre-ceremony reception that culminates in the *bedeken,* during which the groom views the bride and lowers the veil over her face.

The veil originated with Rebecca, who veiled herself when she first saw Isaac. The rite, which assures the groom that he's mar-rying the woman he chose, stems from the experience of Jacob, whose crafty father-in-law Laban substituted his older daughter, Leah, for her sister Rachel on the wedding day. According to the commentaries, Jacob and Rachel, anticipating Laban's treachery, had exchanged secret signs so that Jacob would know if it was Rachel behind the veil. But Rachel, taking pity on her sister and wanting to spare her humiliation, revealed the signs to Leah. And in spite of that magnanimous gesture, Leah was jealous of Rachel and the love her younger sister shared with Jacob when he took her as his second wife. And it was Rachel who was barren for so long while Leah and Jacob's two other wives triumphantly bore many sons and daughters to their husband, Rachel who died young and was buried on the lonely roadside.

In my mind's eye I saw myself inside Rachel's Tomb, circling the sepulchre and pressing my red thread against the dark velvet. I saw Aggie slipping the locket, a snip of the red thread inside, around her neck. I saw Trina Creeley clutching an identical locket before she dropped it out of sight. I wondered again where Cree-ley had obtained the red thread and the locket, and why.

Raul was gesturing with his free hand and explaining while his pencil flew over page after page of his white pad. I forced my-self to focus. Soon thoughts of Aggie and the locket receded, and I was caught up in Raul's excitement. That's how I'd been since Thursday—grieving for Aggie one minute, giddy with anticipa-tion the next.

My mother asked about the *mechitza.* I would have been fine without the partition that would separate the men and women during the dancing throughout the dinner. So would the Abramses, who are less strict than their son, the rabbi. But we'd been overruled by Zack and my parents.

"The *mehitza* will be a grand surprise," Raul said, pronouncing the word without the guttural *ch*. "Gorgeous, fabulous, everybody will be talking about it for weeks."

And he would stay within the budget, he assured my mother.

"Even if I have to do this at my cost. But don't tell Dani." He cast a worried look over his shoulder and put his finger to his sensuous lips.

"Because you are family, you know," he said a moment later as he gave each of us a kiss and a long-stemmed yellow rose and ushered us out of the shop.

CHAPTER ELEVEN

I TOOK MY ROSE AND MY EUPHORIA TO THE HAIR SALON on Melrose near Sierra Bonita, where my mother and I were joined by my three sisters and my sister-in-law, Gitty, who had come to provide moral support along with coffee and mouthwatering cheese Danishes from the nearby Coffee Bean & Tea Leaf. We nibbled and giggled at silly jokes that caught the attention of a woman and the hairdresser cutting her hair, both of whom looked at us with curiosity—and envy, I think. Natalie, the anorexic Israeli salon owner who has been doing my hair for years, kept chiding me to face the mirror as she played with my curly blond hair and the lace-and-pearl headpiece until they came together in a soft updo I loved and so did everyone else, including Edie, who is tougher than a Russian judge at the Olympics.

I stole a glance at my mother, knew she was thinking what I was, that I'd been given a second chance and wasn't life wonderful. *Bli ayin hara,* I added silently to ward off the evil eye, certain that my mother was doing the same even though her prayers four years ago and the red thread she'd knotted around my wrist before I'd joined Ron under the chuppa had been no match for his adultery.

Natalie removed the headpiece and slipped a voluminous, almost-to-the-waist blond wig on top of my hair, which she'd gathered and fastened at the back with a clip.

"The cap fits good, yes?" Natalie said, her Israeli accent still strong after twelve years in L.A. "It's going to feel even lighter after I cut the hair."

"The color's a perfect match," Edie said. "Maybe I'll borrow it in an emergency."

My sisters and I all have different shades of brown hair, which Edie and I have transformed with highlights into streaked blond. She wears hers in a short, blunt cut that suits her height (five feet) and personality.

"Touch it," Natalie invited. "*Maksim,* no?" she said, using the Hebrew for *enchanting.* She caressed the silky strands as though they were spun of gold, which they might as well have been, considering the two thousand dollars I'd spent on the wig, with its custom-fitted cap into which the color-blended hairs had been hand-sewn. "A hundred percent European."

"More like Nashville." I stared at my reflection and swallowed hard. "I look like Dolly Parton."

"Only from the neck up, unfortunately," Mindy said, and we all broke into laughter.

The other hairdresser had left, along with her client, and the salon was quiet. Natalie had gone to the rear to shampoo my wig. My mother was fanning her flushed face with the magazine she'd been reading. Mindy had taken off her hat and slipped on the wig she'd had Natalie style for the wedding. Edie and Gitty were at the front of the shop, trying on hats. I swiveled in my seat and watched Liora, who had moved to a table piled with wigs and was trying on several close to her own rich brown. Liora is eagerly committed to covering her hair when she marries, and I've overheard her discussing the costs and merits of the newest *sheitels* (wigs) and the *sheitel machers* (stylists) who create the illusion that foreign hair is growing right out of the wearer's head.

Aggie had planned to cover her hair. I had, too, in high school, though my conviction hadn't been strong even then. We'd argued about it, me whispering on the phone so that I wouldn't wake Liora, with whom I shared a room until Edie and Mindy married; or lying on the pop-up trundle next to Aggie's daybed long after her parents were fast asleep and we'd finished our homework and watched TV and talked about which guys in school were cute and what it would be like to kiss them, about whom we would marry, how many children we would have, what we would name them. A woman's hair is alluring, Aggie would insist. Once she's entered into a holy bond with her husband, only he and close family are supposed to see her hair. It's about remembering that God is above you, that you're married. It's about privacy and modesty, don't you see that, Molly?

Later, when I abandoned Orthodoxy, Aggie didn't argue or try to sway me, certainly not about covering my hair, and not about keeping the Sabbath or keeping kosher or following other laws that were no longer part of my life.

I returned to Orthodoxy a few months before she was killed. It was a tenuous, gradual return that pleased my family but made them tiptoe around me, since they didn't know what had sent me running, and in truth, neither did I. Aggie's death rocked my faith and my resolve. She was deeply pious, pure of heart and pure in action. If she had been killed, what chance was there for me? But instead of bolting again, I married Ron, which I suppose was a different kind of bolting, though I didn't recognize it at the time.

And now I was marrying a rabbi. I was happy to align myself with the many Orthodox Jewish women—like my grandmother, who is a role model of piety, and my sister Edie and Zack's mother and some of my friends—who deal with the custom more in the breach than in the observance. I was doing this for Zack, who had asked but hadn't insisted that I cover my hair, and not wear pants in public, and lengthen my skirts and sleeves, which were shorter than strict Orthodoxy allowed and had no doubt raised the brows of several of his congregants, all of whom would be looking at me even more critically from now on.

How I dressed, what I did, what I said and didn't say. I had a flash of panic and wondered what had made me think I could be a rabbi's wife.

Natalie placed the stick-straight wet hair back on my head, securing the wig with a thin elastic strap that she clipped to the tabs on either side. The strap dug under my chin.

"Now you look like Cher," Mindy said.

"How long do you want it?" Natalie asked.

"Like my hair. A little below shoulder length." I would be under a congregational microscope, I thought. Every day, for the rest of my life.

"I'll leave it a little longer," Natalie said, misreading my frown. "I can always cut it, but it won't grow back." She raised a length of hair and performed the first snip. "You want me to cut in a few layers, or leave it one length?"

"Layers," Edie said. "And wisps, not bangs."

"One length," I told Natalie, mainly to counter Edie, who is usually right.

GRAVE ENDINGS

77

"That's for twenty-year-olds," Edie said. "It doesn't look natural on anyone older. Too flat."

"Gitty's are one length," Mindy said.

My twenty-three-year-old sister-in-law has custom wigs that match her gorgeous red hair, which she'd covered with a black snood tonight.

"I don't mean Gitty." Edie sounded flustered, which is unusual for her. "Your *sheitels* always look great," she told her.

I caught my sister-in-law's eye in the mirror and winked at her. She smiled.

"It's Molly's decision," my mother said. "Natalie can always cut layers later."

Half an hour later the linoleum around the pedestal of my chair was carpeted in blond hair (about three hundred dollars' worth, I figured). Natalie finished blow-drying and flat-ironing the wig into a sleek waterfall, the kind you see in L'Oréal commercials and that I'd always envied.

"*Nehedar, nachon?*" Natalie said. "Shake your head. Don't be afraid. See how the hair moves like it's your own?"

I shook my head vigorously and told her the wig *was* gorgeous. It was—nicer than my hair, thicker. "No more bad hair days. And it won't frizz, right?"

"You don't like it." Natalie frowned. "I can fix it."

"It's a great cut. Perfect."

The wig was beautiful, but my hair and I were a team. We'd weathered close to thirty years and the occasional falling out over its mercurial temperament, and neglect or abuse on my part.

"You're not used to seeing yourself in a wig, honey," my mother said. "You look great."

It wasn't about how I looked. The Molly in the mirror was an imposter, taking on a commitment for which I wasn't ready and everything it represented. I could work up to the wig, I decided, start with the hats or berets I'd bought, though I couldn't picture myself conducting an interview in a hat. Or I could wear nothing at all. . . .

"Maybe if you put in a body wave," Gitty suggested. "It'll look more like your hair."

"Layers," Edie said.

But was it such a big deal, really, to commit to something that would make Zack happy and to which my objections were not theological but personal?

My cell phone rang. I was grateful for the distraction, and though I didn't recognize the number on the display, I pressed a button and said hello.

It was Trina Creeley. "I've been thinking about what you said," she told me, a whispery quality making her sound nervous. "If you're still interested, I can meet you tomorrow at noon at Musso & Frank Grill. It's just a block from where I work."

I wondered what had changed her mind. "I know where it is." I'd eaten there once or twice in my nonkosher days.

"You have to enter through the back. So will you be there? I have to talk to you. It's important."

Her anxiety was contagious. "Musso & Frank's at noon," I agreed in a low voice, but not low enough so that Edie didn't hear.

"Who are you meeting at Musso & Frank?" she asked when I flipped my phone shut.

I dropped the phone back into my purse. "A woman I'm interviewing."

"Musso & Frank isn't kosher," Liora commented, as I'd known she would.

"I'm not planning to eat there. I'm just meeting her."

"A week before your wedding?" Edie said. "What's so important that it can't wait?"

"Two weeks." I turned to Natalie. "What about a headband? Can I wear one with this wig?"

She *tsk*ed. "You'd need to buy a band fall. I can get you one for five hundred. Human hair, good quality."

Edie narrowed her eyes. "This is about Aggie, isn't it? Don't do this to yourself, Molly."

My oldest sister is generous and kindhearted—she'll cheerfully do your car pool or marketing for as long as you need help—but she's a pragmatist. She understands why Connors's news upset me, but not why it has plunged me back into mourning, and she's been phoning me daily to make sure I stay on the wedding track.

My mother and sisters were looking at me. Natalie excused herself and walked to the rear of the salon.

"I'm not *doing* anything," I said. "I'm talking to the sister of the man who killed my best friend."

"Why?" Edie asked.

"To find out if he killed her."

"*If?*" Mindy frowned.

Mindy is an attorney, and I often bounce my theories off her. I explained what I'd learned. "For a while I thought maybe he didn't do it, but with Trina's locket . . ."

"Does Zack know you're pursuing this?" Edie asked. "Are you seeing him tonight? Or are you off investigating?"

"Edie," my mother warned. Her face was flushed again, either from another hot flash or from annoyance.

"Zack is studying with a bar mitzvah boy tonight. He knows what I'm doing, and he understands."

"He's probably just saying that," Edie said.

"I didn't choose the timing, you know. And I have all the wedding details under control."

"And your emotions?" She placed her hand on mine. "Don't

take this wrong, sweetie, but does it matter who killed Aggie? Knowing what happened won't bring her back."

I gripped the arms of the chair. "It matters to me."

"Okay. I won't say another word."

She didn't, not even after we all left the salon and walked to our cars. She was hurt, I was determined. In the morning she'd phone to tell me she loved me and wanted me to be happy, which I know is true.

"Speaking of Zack, Molly," Liora said in an undertone, so I figured she didn't want Edie to hear. "Aren't the two of you meeting with Galit at noon tomorrow to see the *ketubah*?"

I was glad that the darkness hid my blush. "Right. Thanks." I didn't know how I'd forgotten. I'd been eager to see the marriage contract the calligrapher was illuminating. "I'll have to reschedule."

"Galit, or Musso & Frank?" Edie asked.

"Cut it out, Edie," my mother said with unaccustomed sharpness. "Molly knows what she's doing."

You could laugh or cry, I thought, leaning toward the former. I turned around to say something to Edie and saw my mother's eyes. I could tell she was worried, too.

CHAPTER TWELVE

Wednesday, February 18. 10:32 A.M. Corner of Washington Boulevard and Kensington Road. Officers stopped a man riding a bicycle that turned out to be stolen, and wearing a backpack with $1,500 in burglary tools. The rider admitted he'd been arrested on burglary charges three times and used rock cocaine. The owner of the bicycle was contacted. He arrived and identified the bicycle. While the officers were talking to him, the suspect slipped into the driver's seat of the patrol car and drove off. The suspect has a tattoo of the word "Venice" on his stomach. (Culver City)

ROLAND CREELEY LIVED ON GOLDWYN TERRACE NORTH of Washington Boulevard in Culver City, which is south of Beverly Hills and sandwiched between Ladera Heights and Palms.

I'm only moderately familiar with the area—even less so with Ladera Heights or Palms. I *do* collect *Crime Sheet* data from the Culver City Police Department (it's not part of LAPD), and Zack and I have been pricing furniture and sighing over art we can't afford while browsing in some of the stores that took up residence years ago in the landmark Helms Bakery Building on Venice Boulevard when the official bread maker for the 1932 Olympics permanently shut its ovens.

With a Post-it on which I'd noted Creeley's address affixed to the center of my steering wheel, I drove south on La Cienega. Traffic was sluggish. It took me almost twenty minutes to drive to Washington Boulevard, another ten while I passed numerous car dealerships and Ince Boulevard, named for Thomas H. Ince, the pioneer filmmaker who moved his studio here from its beach location at the urging of Henry Culver, the area's developer, who had watched Ince film a silent Western on La Ballona Creek.

A few minutes later I parked in front of Roland Creeley's residence, a small, yellow clapboard bungalow within viewing distance of Washington Boulevard and the Grecian columns on either side of the old main gate that marks the entrance to what remains of Ince's former studio, now part of Sony Pictures. (Before that it was Goldwyn Studios, MGM, DeMille Studios, RKO, Selznick International, and Desilu. After Ince's sudden death, the studio had changed hands and names more often than Elizabeth Taylor.) I wondered if living in such close proximity to the studio had influenced young Randy and given him the acting bug.

"I can see where you'd think that," Creeley said when I asked him. "I grew up here, saw them filming *The Wizard of Oz* when I was a kid, and *Ben-Hur,* and lots of other movies that say 'filmed in Hollywood' on the credits but were made right here," he added with a touch of resentment. "Anyway, it didn't give *me* any ideas.

No, it was his mother. Sue Ann took him from one agent to another when he was in diapers, told him he was special, that he was going to be a star."

We were in a small, overfurnished, and overheated living room painted Wedgwood blue. Creeley and his wife, wearing black sweatshirts and gray slacks, sat hip to hip on a rose-colored velvet sofa opposite a matching armchair that practically swallowed me.

Alice Creeley was a solidly built woman with a thick neck and a broad face that looked even broader because she'd slicked back her graying hair against her skull. I don't mean to be uncharitable, but she was an unpretty woman, especially in contrast to the woman she'd replaced, and to her husband, who was clearly the author of his son's good looks. Roland senior had the same defined cheekbones and squared chin, and though the years had lined his face and silvered his still-thick hair, he was a man you'd look at twice.

He had the same deep brown eyes, too. Today they were somber and dull. I had seen the same vacant look in the eyes of the Lashers when they were sitting shiva for Aggie.

"Sue Ann was the actress," Alice said, the nostrils on her wide, flat nose flaring. "She sure played Roland for a fool."

"I thought she was happy," Creeley said with more sadness than anger. "I'm a carpenter by trade. I worked on the studio lots, building sets, doing odd jobs. There was always food on the table, and money for extras. Then one day I came home and she was gone. She left a roast in the oven and a note on the fridge saying she didn't want to be a mother anymore, didn't want to be a wife."

He said this with surprise, as though he had just come across the note, and it was in a foreign language or some code he was still puzzling out. There had probably been signs he'd overlooked, nuances, body language. I had overlooked signs, too, had felt that same shock when I'd learned Ron was cheating on me, had felt foolish afterwards.

"She left her little one crying and told Randy he was in charge," Alice said, indignation making her voice quaver like a violin. "He was nine years old. She cleaned out one whole bank account, too."

"To be fair, it was money she'd saved," Creeley said. "And she told Randy to go next door if he needed help."

"Sue Ann's parents didn't know where she went?" I asked Creeley, hoping to head off a diatribe from Alice, who had opened her mouth to say something.

"No, ma'am. Which isn't surprising. The Jaspers—that's her folks—gave her a hard time about leaving Minneapolis to come out here and be an actress. Whenever she talked to them, which wasn't often, they faulted everything she did."

"Don't go blaming them," Alice said. "They didn't make her walk out that door."

"I know that."

"That's what she did, walked out whenever things didn't go her way."

The tension in the room crackled. "What about her friends?" I asked Creeley.

"She didn't have many. And she didn't say anything to them about wanting out. Sue Ann was kind of closed. I figured she'd be back, you know?" he said with that same bewilderment. "I figured she'd run out of money and realize she'd made a mistake. She sent a postcard from Chicago and another one from Houston a month later. That was the last I heard from her. Well, except through the lawyer she hired to handle the divorce. He wouldn't tell me where she was. A year later Alice and I married, and after a while Trina, that's Randy's sister, didn't even ask for Sue Ann. But Randy—"

"He never gave me a chance," Alice said, those nostrils flaring again. I expected smoke to come out any moment. "He turned Trina against me, too."

"Trina loves you, honey." Creeley placed his large hand over his wife's.

"I tried my best."

"No one could've done more," Creeley said, and I knew they'd been down this particular road many times, had worn ruts that would never be filled. "Randy was pining for Sue Ann," he told me. "They had this bond."

"A bond of green," Alice said. "She only loved him because he was beautiful. He was her ticket to fame and fortune."

I disliked Alice. Maybe it was the spite that came out like pellets from a PEZ dispenser, or the small dark eyes that looked hard as onyx. Living with this tough, unbending woman couldn't have been easy for Randy.

"He *was* beautiful." Creeley's sigh tugged at my heart. "Everybody said so. He had buckets of personality. He was bright, too, so he didn't need coaching. The casting people loved him. But then he got too old for commercials, and there are lots of kids and only so many movies with big parts for them."

"Like the kid from *Sixth Sense*," Alice said. "He's doing other stuff. But the one who talked about how much a brain weighs in *Jerry Maguire*? I haven't seen him in anything lately, have you?" she asked her husband.

"No, I haven't." His voice was taut with controlled impatience. "Every time Randy lost out on a role, Sue Ann'd shut herself in her room and wouldn't talk to anyone for days," he told me. "And then one day she left."

"She knew Randy wasn't going to be a star," Alice said. "She figured she'd cut her losses and start over."

I tried to imagine young Randy, a child burdened with having to win each role to hold on to his mother's approval; a child who blamed himself for every failure that drove her into one of the temporary abandonments that foreshadowed a permanent one. He'd probably blamed himself for that, too. I felt stifled by his past, by this house, by the heat that was beginning to make me feel queasy.

"I think she loved the kids," Creeley said, braving the Dragon. "She just couldn't handle things. I see that now."

"You bring children into this world, you take care of them." Alice folded her arms beneath her breasts. "I can't believe you're soft on her."

"I'm not soft on her. I'm saying we don't know why she left. Anyway." Creeley shifted and left a space between him and his wife. "Randy started having trouble in school. His grades dropped. He was picking fights with kids, cheating on tests, playing hooky."

"She messed him up good," Alice said, her venom at a woman long out of her life making me wonder if she was the one who had ripped the photo I'd seen of Randy and his mother. "Randy kept pushing Roland to find her. That's why we did what we did." She nodded at her husband. Go ahead, your turn.

"I told the kids Sue Ann died in a boating accident and they never found her body," he said, not meeting my eyes. "We hadn't heard from her for over three years. Not a phone call, not a birthday card. *Nothing.* I figured maybe she *was* dead," he added with defensiveness that reddened his complexion.

"She might as well have been, for all the interest she showed her kids," Alice said.

"Did you ever hear from her?" I asked Creeley, wishing Alice would shut up. I suspected her husband shared my feelings.

He shook his head. "I hoped Randy would let go. I hoped he'd be the young man I knew he could be. But a year later he got into trouble with the police. Small stuff at first, and then . . . But I guess you know all that."

"The police think he killed a woman around six years ago," I said, forcing myself to sound casual about the event that changed my life and gives me nightmares. And what had it done to Aggie's parents, who had lost their only child?

Creeley bowed his head and sighed deeply. "It grieves me to think Randy came to that, that he took someone's life."

I'd hoped for denial, outrage, anything to bolster my own wavering doubts. "You don't sound surprised."

"Nothing about Randy surprises *me*," Alice said.

Anger flashed in Creeley's eyes. "I loved that boy. But I can't say I was proud of him. No, ma'am. I tried to teach him right from wrong, but he took what he wanted and lied his way through life. He was good at it, too. Then he got caught. I thought, Good. He'll learn a hard lesson. But a couple of years later he was back in prison."

"You reap what you sow," Alice said.

Creeley's cheek pulsed. "I'm not saying he didn't deserve to do time. But he didn't deserve to die like that. He was off drugs. He found God and peace. He asked my forgiveness a few weeks ago for the things he'd done wrong. He asked your forgiveness, too, Alice."

"Words are cheap," she said. "He was playing you like he played you so many times before I can't even count them."

I was liking Alice less and less, but I'd been thinking the same thing. "What about his girlfriend, Doreen," I said. "Where did he meet her?"

"One of his twelve-step meetings, or church?" Creeley looked at Alice. She shrugged, and for once didn't have an answer. "He talked about bringing her by so we could meet her, but he never did. A couple of days before he died I asked him how things were going. 'I'm doing fine, I'm clean,' he said. He sounded hopeful."

Alice huffed. "He told his parole officer the same thing, and that was a fat lie. He went to those Narcotics Anonymous meetings and lied to everybody there, too."

Creeley pursed his lips. "I know when he's lying, Alice. Someone killed him and made it look like he overdosed. I know that like I know my own name."

Alice rolled her eyes.

"Go ahead," he told her, his voice flinty with anger. "Roll your eyes. The police don't believe me, either."

I scooted to the edge of my chair. "Why would someone kill your son, Mr. Creeley?"

"Could be someone he wronged. I'm sure there's a long list. Or maybe it had something to do with that woman the police say he killed."

My heart skipped a beat. "She was killed almost six years ago, in July. I know that's a long time ago, but can you recall if Randy seemed upset then?"

"July, six years ago . . . ," he repeated. "That was about a year after Randy got out of prison. The couple of times we did see him, he was looking for a fight. I don't know why."

"Ask Trina," Alice said. "He told Trina *everything,*" she added with a childish whine.

I would be seeing Trina in less than two hours and I planned to do exactly that. "You didn't see him often?"

Creeley shook his head.

"Because I told him what he didn't want to hear," Alice said. "Because nobody wants an ex-con liar and drug addict hanging around their daughter."

"Let him be, goddammit!" Creeley seemed startled by his own outburst. He took a deep breath. "The boy's dead, Alice. Let him be."

Alice turned her head aside, but not before I could see the red that had worked up her thick neck and that Creeley would undoubtedly pay for after I left.

She pushed herself off the sofa. "I have things to take care of," she said in a wounded voice.

I would have bet money that Creeley would apologize and beg her to stay, but he said, "All right then," and ignored the hurt, angry look she tossed him before she stomped out of the room.

I pitied Alice Creeley. Sue Ann had walked out, but Alice was the other woman, scrabbling to maintain her position in this family, holding tight to the reins of her marriage, forever competing with the beautiful wife her husband couldn't bring himself to hate and their beautiful son. I wondered if she lay awake nights, worrying that Sue Ann would walk back into their lives.

"If he killed that woman," Roland said when we were alone, "and I'm not saying he did . . . If he killed her, he tried to make up for it with good deeds."

My heart hammered in my chest. "Do you think Randy killed her, Mr. Creeley?"

He examined his hands, as if they held the answer. Then he rubbed them on his knees. "Randy was troubled the last few months," he said in a low voice that made me lean closer so that I could hear him. "He said it was something from his past he couldn't fix. It filled him with despair—*his* word. I told him to talk to someone. I was afraid if he didn't, he'd start doing drugs again. See, I think part of the reason he used drugs and liquor was so he wouldn't have to think about what happened."

"So you think he killed her." It wasn't the answer I'd come for, but it was an answer.

"The police think so. They came here to talk to Trina. Randy told them he'd been with her the night that woman was killed. Trina said that was so, but she would've said anything to help him, she loved him that much."

I was confused. From what Connors had told me, the police had linked Randy to Aggie's murder through the locket they'd found in his possession *after* he'd overdosed. "Was this recently?"

Creeley looked at me as though I'd asked him if the Earth was flat. "Not unless you consider six years ago recent."

"The police questioned Randy six years ago about Aggie Lasher's murder?" I stared at him. "But why would they think Randy killed this woman? He didn't even know her."

"I don't know where you got your information. Of course, Randy knew her. He was working at the same place she was. I forget the name."

My chest felt as though someone had stomped on it. "Rachel's Tent?"

Creeley nodded. "Randy was a handyman and driver. He did other stuff there, too. He liked her a lot, you know. He told Trina all about her. But I guess something went wrong."

CHAPTER THIRTEEN

MUSSO & FRANK GRILL IS THE OLDEST RESTAURANT IN Hollywood, a legendary Rat Pack hangout that, unlike the Brown Derby and Romanoff's, has survived shifting economies and continues to be a favorite with screenwriters, actors, and other celebrities.

The restaurant is a block from Frederick's and just west of Cherokee. I parked my Acura up the street—I should probably claim a permanent spot, I thought—and passed through the back into the dimly lit front room (there is no front entrance) five minutes before noon. The few times I've been here I've come for inspiration and literary osmosis—F. Scott Fitzgerald ate (and drank) here, as did Raymond Chandler (he wrote *The Big Sleep* here), Dorothy Parker, Ernest Hemingway, and others, including Charlie Chaplin, who liked the martinis. That was the draw, along with the Postum, and the coffee that comes in small, individual pots, and the possibility of spotting a famous screenwriter creating magic on a laptop—David Mamet, maybe, or Anthony Minghella or Callie Khouri, none of whom I ever actually saw.

Today my mood was dark and I wasn't interested in stargazing. In any case, I didn't recognize any of the occupants of the high-sided red leather booths along the black wood-paneled wall to my right, or anyone seated along the bar facing the opposite wall and a brick fireplace large enough to grill a steer.

"I'm meeting a friend," I told the red-jacketed waiter who approached, menu in hand. I had scanned the diners but hadn't spotted Trina.

"Perhaps your friend is in our other room," he said, beckoning me to follow him to a far wider dining area where I saw a large mirrored bar on the left wall, but no Trina.

"Can I offer you something while you wait?" the waiter asked.

"Iced tea would be great, thanks."

I chose a booth instead of one of the small square tables in the center of the room. I generally carry a paperback mystery in my purse to keep me from becoming antsy while I'm waiting, but I didn't need a diversion. I was trying to digest what Creeley had told me.

Aggie had known Randy.

They'd worked together at Rachel's Tent.

He'd liked her "a lot."

I have to admit that my first reaction to Creeley's revelation had smacked of self-absorption: I was Aggie's best friend. We'd shared everything—our hurts, our successes, our hopes, our fantasies, the intimate details of our lives. Why hadn't she told me about Randy?

Maybe there had been nothing to tell. Maybe Aggie hadn't been aware that Randy liked her—and what, after all, did *like* mean? It wasn't necessarily romantic. But if it was? And if Aggie hadn't reciprocated, which of course she hadn't, if she'd rebuffed his advances, if she'd angered an ex-convict who did drugs and drank?

It had occurred to me, as I left the Creeleys' Culver City home and drove to Hollywood, barely aware of my surroundings or Bobby Darin, who was crooning "Dream Lover" on my favorite oldies station, that this connection between Randy and Aggie was the other evidence Connors had alluded to. It explained why he'd refused to share the information with me, why the police were certain that Randy had killed Aggie, why Porter had been so irritable and evasive, why he'd wanted me gone.

Why he'd hedged when I'd asked him where Randy had been working around the time that Aggie had been murdered.

Rachel's Tent.

Wilshire had screwed up. Maybe Porter was nervous that if I discovered the truth, I would make it public: The LAPD had let a killer slip through its fingers six years ago. And what if he'd killed again?

If I phoned Porter, which I had no intention of doing, he'd inform me in his snide way that Randy'd had an alibi. Some alibi, I'd tell him, his sister who adores him and obviously lied for him.

Yesterday I'd wanted to talk to Trina to confirm my suspicion that Randy hadn't killed Aggie. Now I wanted to find out why he had. *He told Trina about her,* his father had said.

I wondered if Aggie's parents were aware that Aggie had known her killer.

And I still didn't understand about Trina's locket. That was another thing I hoped she could explain.

It was five after twelve, not terribly late, but Trina had asked me to be prompt. I waited a few minutes before I retrieved the number she'd used when she'd contacted me last night. I placed the call, let it ring, and left a message.

Maybe she'd set me up, pretended to be anxious, pulled a fast one on the nosy reporter. Maybe acting ran in the family.

I finished my iced tea, declined a refill, and after another five minutes paid my tab and left.

Jonnie recognized me when I entered Frederick's. There was a wariness in her kohl-lined hazel eyes that hadn't been there yesterday, and I suspected that whatever Trina had told her about me hadn't been complimentary.

"She's not here," Jonnie said when I asked for Trina. "She phoned and said she had to help with funeral arrangements for her brother."

So Trina hadn't been playing me. I felt better but wondered why hadn't she phoned to cancel our meeting. I checked my cell phone again but found no messages.

Maybe she'd been overwhelmed with family and hadn't had a chance to phone. Or maybe she'd changed her mind about talk-ing to me, just as she had yesterday afternoon.

When the truck backfired. I replayed the scene in my head, saw her jump at the sound, saw her sudden pallor, the fear that hadn't registered because I'd been staring at her locket. The ner-vousness in her voice when she'd phoned last night and told me she had to talk to me, it was important.

Feeling somewhat anxious myself, I returned to Musso & Frank. Trina hadn't showed.

"Would you like to leave a message in case your friend shows?" the waiter offered.

"No, thanks."

Still thinking about Trina, I chugged halfway up the block to my Acura and was grateful to learn that it hadn't been decorated this time. I decided to pay Gloria Lamont another visit.

Someone was having a yard sale on the apartment building's patch of lawn. The seller, in his mid-to-late twenties with a two-day stubble on his chin and bleached blond hair cut in a severe buzz that from a distance had made me think he'd done a Bruce Willis, was wearing baggy tan cargo pants with enough pockets to store a small wardrobe, a skintight black sweater that revealed his ribs, and several earrings in his left ear. He was slouched in a green-and-white-webbed beach chair surrounded by a six-pack of Budweiser and assorted junk. Books, a toaster, rolled-up posters, a stack of framed artwork, a Starbucks mug, shirts, DVDs, video-cassettes, a piece of twisted metal I couldn't figure out. His eyes were shut, his head was bobbing to music only he could hear through black earphones the size of Frisbees.

"Slow day, huh," I said.

His eyes flickered open, a deep brown with long, thick, dark lashes that were wasted on a guy and that my double-action lengthening mascara doesn't come close to achieving.

"Kind of." He took a swig from a can of beer.

"I'm Molly. What's your name?"

"Mike." He squinted at me with one eye. "You were here the other day, right? Asking about Randy. I saw you."

"Funny, I didn't see *you*."

He grinned. "I'm the Invisible Man."

"Or maybe you saw me when you opened your door to listen in on my conversation with Mrs. Lamont."

"A guy dies in your building, you kind of want to know what's going on." He took another swig of beer. "So are you a private detective or something? Your card didn't say."

At least he'd kept it. "Reporter."

"So you ask questions. Randy's dad asked me a whole lot. Wanted to know if his son was doing drugs. The cops asked, too."

"Was he?"

Mike shrugged.

"When did you last see Randy?" I asked.

"That's another thing the cops asked. Why do you want to know?"

"Just curious."

He smiled. "*How* curious?"

I could see where this was going. "What's the going rate for curiosity these days?"

"Ordinarily it might be free, but my unemployment just ran out, and my agent hasn't phoned to tell me I'm costarring with Tom Cruise in his next film. Plus business has been slow, like you said." He nodded toward the lawn.

"How much?"

"Twenty dollars. I'll throw in something from my fine collection of wares."

I could hardly contain my joy. "First I need to know what I'm buying."

"More than what I told the cops."

I took a twenty from my wallet and handed it to him. "Tell me about Randy."

He folded the bill and tucked it into one of the large pockets on his pants. "We weren't best buds, but he'd invite me over to watch a game. You saw his TV, right? Cool, huh? We'd swap DVDs and stuff, grab a beer once in a while, shoot the breeze. Not so much lately, though. Lately he was one serious dude. He was an actor, too, did you know that?" When I nodded, Mike said, "We griped about the business, how hard it is to get a break nowadays."

I wasn't interested in hearing Mike's career woes and had a feeling I'd thrown out twenty dollars. "So you didn't know him well?"

"Well enough to know he was carrying around major guilt.

He killed a woman." Mike watched me to make sure I was prop-
erly impressed.

After talking to Roland Creeley, I wasn't surprised, but the
words went through me like an electric shock. "What makes you
think so?"

"We had drinks one night. He was wasted and told me. He
said he was going to hell for what he'd done, so he might as well
enjoy himself. I think that's why he overdosed. He couldn't take
the guilt, especially since he was into all this twelve-step stuff.
You're supposed to make amends, right? But how can you make
amends for taking someone's life?"

That was a good question. "When did he tell you all this?"

"I moved here three years ago. I'd say this happened about a
year later."

"And you never told the police?"

Mike snickered. "Tell them what? That a guy who was so
drunk he couldn't stand straight told me he killed some woman
years ago? I didn't even believe him. I thought it was the liquor.
But the other day the cops were here, asking questions about a
woman they think he killed six years ago, so I guess he really did
it." Mike sounded awed more than shaken. "Turns out he was
into some kinky stuff, too."

"Did Randy say why he killed this woman?" This was what
I'd wanted to know all these years. Not just who, but why.

Mike shook his head. "He was crying, said he loved her, that
he didn't mean for her to die, that things just got out of control.
And now he's dead, too. Strange, huh?" He crushed the beer
can. "His girlfriend found the body. The way she was screaming, you'd think someone was trying to kill *her*."

"What's she like?"

"Doreen? She seemed nice enough. Pretty, too, if you like
tall, skinny women with spiky black hair, which I guess Randy

did. He met her about five months ago, I think at one of his twelve-step meetings. I don't think Doreen was into it like Randy, though. I think she was using. That's just my take, I could be wrong." Mike shrugged.

I didn't know what else to ask, so I thanked him and entered the building.

Gloria looked as weary as she had the other day and not much happier to see me. She was wearing another black sweater, this one with a puppy design.

"I didn't hear from Doreen, if that's why you're here," she told me. "Too late for her now, 'cause I cleared everything out of the apartment, and the cleaning crew is comin' tomorrow."

"Actually, I wanted to ask you about Randy's other girl-friends. Did he ever talk to you about them?"

"*Brag* is more like it, honey. He had a new one every couple of weeks. He'd bring them by, make sure I'd meet them. 'What do you think, Mrs. Lamont?' he'd ask me later. Sometimes I thought he was playin' me, you know? Other times I thought, well, he doesn't have no momma, he's got to talk to somebody and maybe that's me."

"I was wondering if there was somebody he liked who didn't like him back, and he was upset about it. Maybe he told you about it." I didn't know why I was asking these questions, what answers I was hoping for. "It would be someone from around seven years ago."

"Seven years?" The manager snorted. "I can't hardly remember what I was doin' seven *months* ago, never mind what Randy was up to seven years ago, 'cept that it prob'ly wasn't somethin' he'd be proud to tell anyone, including me."

Probably not. "By the way, have you heard from Trina?" I asked.

"Not since last night. She came by, but her daddy and step-momma were here, so she left kind of quick. I got the feeling Trina doesn't like her. I can't say's I blame her. She has a mean face, that woman."

I thanked Gloria and left her standing in her doorway, her face scrunched in concentration.

"Hey, you forgot to choose your bonus," Mike said when I emerged from the building. "From my sale items," he added when I gave him a blank look.

"That's okay." I glanced at the junk-strewn lawn. That's when I noticed a bit of colorful print fabric peeking out from under a gray Old Navy sweatshirt. Crouching, I yanked on the sleeve and pulled out a Hawaiian print shirt.

"I saw this in Randy's closet yesterday," I said.

"I didn't *steal* it." Mike sounded offended. "Randy's dad took what he wanted. The manager said I could have what was left, she was going to give the rest to Goodwill. I did her a favor, cleaning out some of the junk."

I looked around. "What else did you take?"

He pointed to his left. "There wasn't much left. A couple of books, a few heavy-metal CDs, some shirts, a few chipped plates and cups, some videocassettes, DVDs. The dad wanted the movie posters, but his old lady said no. I kept the better ones for myself."

The crockery didn't interest me, but I examined the books. Mostly paperbacks with tattered covers, and *Alcoholics Anonymous.* Hoping the photos were still inside, I took the book and exposed the one lying underneath it. *A Practical Guide to Kabbalah.*

I picked up both and straightened my legs, which had begun to stiffen. I held up the Kabbalah text. "I didn't see this when I was in the apartment yesterday."

"It was on the floor between the nightstand and the bed. I guess it fell down."

"Did Randy ever talk about his interest in Kabbalah?"

"He was interested in a lot of stuff. Kabbalah, twelve-step programs, church. He went to a couple of twelve-step meetings every day."

"Do you know if he went to a Kabbalah class?"

Mike scratched the stubble on his chin. "He never mentioned that. He *did* wear one of those red threads around his wrist. He said it's supposed to protect you. He ordered lots of them online and e-mailed me the link, but I'm not into that. Although lately you hear about a lot of actors who are, so maybe you can hook up with some if you go to a meeting or something."

I could see from Mike's expression that he was considering the possibility. "Did he ever say anything about a locket with the image of Rachel's Tomb?"

"A locket?" Mike frowned. "No. What's Rachel's Tomb?"

I told him. "When was this? That Randy ordered the thread, I mean."

"A couple of months ago? It's funny, isn't it? I mean, if the thread was supposed to protect him, it didn't do the job. But I guess nothing protects you against yourself."

CHAPTER FOURTEEN

ZACK BROUGHT WEDDING GIFTS THAT HAD BEEN DELIV-
ered to his parents' house, and steak sandwiches with sautéed
onions that scented my apartment. Between taking bites of my
sandwich and wiping barbecue sauce from my chin, I described
yesterday's wig and florist sessions, imitating Raul's accent and
manner.

Zack barely smiled. Maybe he *was* upset that I'd postponed
our meeting with the calligrapher. But when I asked, he told me
he was troubled about a family whose son had been expelled
from the local Jewish high school for taking drugs.

"They're devastated, Molly. This kid had a promising future.
And now? I hope it's not too late to save him."

Randy had hoped for a promising future, too. It seemed like

ages, not days, since I'd first heard his name. The hate had been pure then, sharp, searing. Now it was complicated and diluted and muddied, and maybe it wasn't even hate. Maybe it was sadness.

"So let's see the wig," Zack said when we had finished the steak sandwiches. I think we were both eager to lift the gloom that had entered like an uninvited guest.

In my bedroom I twisted and reclipped my hair three times until I got it to lie flat against my head. Then I spent about ten minutes brushing the wig before deciding on a center part.

"It's exactly like your hair, but straight," Zack said when I returned to the breakfast nook. "It looks great."

"I wear my hair straight sometimes," I reminded him. "You don't like it straight?"

"This is one of those lose-lose questions, right? I love it straight. I love it curly. You look beautiful."

"Doesn't that defeat the purpose?"

"There's nothing wrong with a married woman being attractive. The idea is not to look seductive to anyone but her husband. That would be me." He smiled.

"I don't hate the wig," I admitted. "I just don't know if I want to wear it."

"I told you, it's your call. The board won't fire me if you don't cover your hair. Half the women in the shul don't."

"But you'd be happier if I did."

"Yes. But not if you're miserable. *Shalom bayit* is more important." Peace in the home.

"I love you."

"I know."

"I don't know if I can do this."

The kettle whistled. I went into my tiny kitchen and prepared two cups of coffee, careful to avoid the kettle's steam. Steam frizzes the hair, Natalie had warned me.

It was Zack who brought up Trina.

"She didn't show," I told him. "I'm a little worried, because she was anxious to tell me something important."

"She was probably too busy to cancel."

"Probably." I took a tentative sip of coffee. Too hot. "Randy knew Aggie, Zack. He killed her."

He put down his cup, eyes narrowed. "How do you know?"

"He worked at Rachel's Tent as a handyman and driver." I repeated what Creeley had told me. "At first I thought maybe Randy came on to Aggie. She rebuffed him, he got angry. He followed her that night. He was high, or drunk. So he killed her."

"And now?"

"Rachel's Tent must pay *really* well." I described the TV, the furniture, the expensive sound system. "And he has a Porsche. Suppose he was dealing drugs at Rachel's Tent and Aggie found out. She threatened to report him. He panicked—he couldn't afford a third strike."

Zack nodded. "Once an addict . . ."

I picked up a chocolate chip cookie from a batch Edie had dropped off in the morning. Her peace offering. "A couple of things still puzzle me."

"Like?"

"Randy gave Trina a locket just like Aggie's, with a red thread. He had a book on Kabbalah, and the neighbor said Randy ordered red threads online."

"As much as thirty-six bucks on some websites." Zack took a bite of his cookie. "These are good. Cheaper at your local Judaica store or Kabbalah center, even less in Israel. The thread, I mean. Not the cookies." He smiled.

Pennies if you buy the thread and wrap it around the sepulchre yourself, as I had done. "But why would Randy give Trina a locket with the red thread?"

"I told you, it's the latest spiritual fad. I heard that Britney

Spears posed for the cover of *Entertainment Weekly* wearing a red thread, and apparently not much else."

"Why the cynicism? I thought you said Kabbalah could fill a void."

"I said people are *turning* to Kabbalah to fill a void. There's nothing spiritual about wearing a red thread when you're almost naked. And many rabbis don't believe that the red thread has any meaning or power."

"Don't tell that to Bubbie G. She believes in it. So do I and most of my family."

"Mine, too. A lot of people believe in the red thread, and there are all those stories. Are they true?" He shrugged. "The major Kabbalists throughout the ages didn't wear red threads. The point is, Molly, Kabbalah isn't about the red thread, and it wasn't intended for the masses. You have to be married and at least forty before you read the *Zohar.* You have to be thoroughly versed in the Torah and Talmud, and on a superior level of observance."

From my Jewish studies I knew about the *Zohar,* Rabbi Shimon bar Yochai's fundamental text on Jewish mysticism. "That gives you ten years to get ready," I said.

Zack shook his head. "I'm light-years away from ever being ready. So are most people."

I dunked my cookie in my coffee and took a bite. "But aren't you tempted? I've heard that the Kabbalah holds secrets of Creation and the key to mystical powers."

"To be honest, the prospect intimidates me. It's an intense study, Molly. And it's risky. The Talmud talks about four of the greatest sages who attempted the mystical experience described as 'entering the orchard.' Rabbi Akiva and three of his disciples— Shimon ben Azai, Shimon ben Zoma, and Elisha ben Avuya."

"What happened?"

"Ben Azai's soul left his body when he was in a state of spiritual rapture. Ben Zoma became insane from the experience. Elisha ben Avuya abandoned his faith and became an apostate."

"And Rabbi Akiva?"

"Rabbi Akiva is the only one who emerged unscathed. But that's not the Kabbalah people are getting from some of the classes and centers springing up around the country and the world."

A hundred thousand people, and the numbers were growing, from what I'd recently read. "So what *are* they getting?"

"For three-fifty, a bottle of water that has supposedly absorbed the Torah reading." Zack's expression was wry. "They can buy red threads, jewelry, incense, candles, meditation cards, age-defying skin creams. And of course countless books on Kabbalah, and outrageously overpriced translations of the *Zohar* in English and Hebrew. Basically, it's a spiritual panacea."

I took another cookie. "What's wrong with something that makes you spiritually connected?"

"Nothing. Books and lectures that encourage introspection and tell you to be kind to your fellow man, that talk about the positive force of goodness and align it with light—those are great. But you don't need Kabbalah for that. And studying the authentic Kabbalah without a solid background in Judaism is like taking a class in calculus when you can't even count to ten. You may memorize a few terms, but you don't have a clue what they mean. It's worse, really. Because if you misuse the Kabbalah, the result can be disastrous."

I nodded. "Like the rabbis who died or became insane."

"Or people who tapped into its mystical powers to learn black magic, or used the combinations of the names of God for evil."

I grimaced. "Heavy stuff."

"And profitable. A friend of mine who works in a Judaica store had a customer who was anxious to get a copy of the *Zohar*. She heard that touching it would cure her illness. He couldn't talk her out of it."

"People desperate for cures aren't always logical. I know cancer patients who traveled to Mexico for laetrile even though there's no proof that it helps. I guess Randy was desperate to find a spiritual cure for his guilt. He tried everything—Kabbalah, twelve-step, church."

"And in the end none of it was enough." Zack sighed. "A sad life, a sadder ending. What a waste."

Bubbie G says life is like a child's undershirt, short and soiled. That sounded very much like Randy's life.

"His funeral's tomorrow morning at eleven, by the way, not ten." I was glad I'd checked with the mortuary.

"We're meeting Galit at eleven-thirty, Molly."

This time I'd remembered. "I'll reschedule for tomorrow night. I'd like to go to Rachel's Tent after the funeral."

"I'm giving a class tomorrow night."

"Saturday night then, or Sunday."

"What if Galit's not available? I don't want to leave this for the last minute, Molly. We have to make sure the wording on the *ketubah* is correct."

"Right." A rabbi would read the *ketubah* under the chuppa and the wording had to reflect my divorced status. Any error, even a misspelled word or name, would invalidate the contract—and our marriage. "I'll phone her now."

I stood and walked the few steps to the wall phone. Galit was in, and I rescheduled for Saturday night.

"She says she'll have plenty of time to finish," I told Zack. He was eyeing me over the rim of his cup. "What?"

"Anything else you want to reschedule?"

"Meaning?"

"I'm sure something else will come up." His voice was too quiet. "If you're having second thoughts—"

"No." I stared at him. "Why would you think that?" My face felt warm.

"You're busying yourself with this investigation, Molly. The wedding is taking second place." He shrugged. "I just wondered."

"You said you understood."

"I did. I do. But maybe you don't want to deal with your feelings. You keep telling me you don't know if you can handle being a rabbi's wife. Ten minutes ago you said you didn't know if you could do this."

"I meant covering my hair. Don't read into this, Zack."

He put his cup down. "You could've told Trina you'd meet another time. You believe that Randy killed Aggie, but you're still going to his funeral and Rachel's Tent."

I felt hurt that he'd doubted my feelings, guilty that I'd given him reason, alarmed that I was ruining the best thing that had ever happened to me.

"Trina sounded nervous, Zack." I sat down. "She had something important to tell me. So yes, I forgot about Galit. I'm sorry. And the funeral . . . I'm not sure why I'm going. If you're upset, I won't go."

"And Rachel's Tent?"

I had no answer.

"Go to the funeral," he said. "Go to Rachel's Tent. Do what you have to do. Just be honest with yourself, Molly."

"Here's honest," I said, leaning forward and brushing the wisps of someone else's hair out of my eyes so that he could read what was in my heart. "I love you. I want to marry you. I want to make babies with you and grow old together, and I am so, so sorry if you thought otherwise for even one second. Okay?"

"Okay."

"But I need to do this, Zack. I still have questions. Can you understand that?"

He nodded. "Sometimes it's better not to ask questions, Molly. You may not like the answers."

CHAPTER FIFTEEN

Thursday, February 19. 10:13 A.M. 10800 block of Jefferson Boulevard. While at the customer service desk of a department store, a woman placed her wallet on the desk. When she was finished, she walked away without the wallet. She did not report the loss for three days because she was out of town for a funeral. (Culver City)

ROLAND CREELEY HAD CHOSEN LILIES AND WHITE CAR-nations for his son's service, which took place in a small chapel darkened by stained-glass windows that filtered the light from this morning's crabby sun.

Between last night and this morning I'd changed my mind half a dozen times about attending the funeral. In the past year I'd paid my final respects to two people I'd hardly known because their stories had drawn me, and because I'd suspected foul play and had hoped to observe something that would help identify a murderer. A word spoken or omitted, a nuance, a telling glance, an unexplained presence or absence. It's what homicide detectives do, in real life as well as fiction. With Randy, I had accepted that there was probably no foul play, and I doubted I'd learn anything. But a little before ten I was in my car on the San Bernardino Freeway, headed for the downtown interchange that would take me to the Pomona and Downey.

I had arrived early and taken a seat toward the back of the chapel so that I could observe people as they entered. Creeley and his wife were both somber and stiff in black. Trina, in a pale blue suit and matching heels, had pulled her hair into a knot that exposed her face and the shadows under her eyes. I was relieved to see her. Since her no-show yesterday, my mind had presented me with several dire possibilities, none of which I'd really believed, each worrisome enough to make me contemplate phoning the Creeley home. I hadn't phoned—I'd felt foolish and hadn't wanted to intrude. Now I was glad.

Mike, the yard salesman, clean-shaven and wearing a brown sports jacket and slacks, sat with Gloria Lamont across the aisle from the Creeleys with ten or twelve men and women of varying ages who had walked in as a group. Probably Randy's friends, from one or more of his programs or his church group. A middle-aged man in a well-cut gray suit approached Creeley and rested his hand on the grieving father's shoulder before taking his seat a row behind him.

The photo of Randy and his mother from the copy of *Alcoholics Anonymous* was in my purse. Taking peeks at the photo, I tried aging Sue Ann two decades, but I'm no sketch artist, and I didn't see anyone who resembled her among the middle-aged blond women who passed by me. I also kept my eyes open for someone who matched Mike's description of Doreen. I noted a number of tall, skinny young women but none with spiked black hair.

One woman, around five-eight, with straight auburn hair that reached the middle of her slender neck, wore a coppery brown suit almost the same color as the eyes behind her black-framed glasses. She glanced around her when she entered, maybe hoping to sit with someone she knew, and took a seat in the middle of a pew across the aisle from me and a few rows up.

There was something about her. . . . I studied her, and when she bent her head, I realized she was wearing a wig. A good wig, but if you live in a community where women wear them all the time, you can tell.

Tall and skinny with a wig didn't mean she was Doreen. But if it *was* Doreen, why had she disguised her appearance?

I had been watching the redhead and was unaware of Connors until he was looming over me. He looked like a handsome imposter in a navy sports jacket, striped tie, and dark slacks instead of his trademark jeans and boots.

"Okay if I join you?" he asked.

It wasn't okay. Another time I would have welcomed Connors's company, but he'd withheld the truth about Randy. I didn't know if I was more angry or hurt. Scooting to the middle of the pew I'd had to myself, I gave him a wide berth and a cool glance.

"Still looking for Randy's murderer, huh?" he asked.

"Actually, I'm curious to see if Randy's mother will show." I wasn't about to volunteer my suspicion about the redhead. Connors had pooh-poohed my interest in Randy's girlfriend. He could do his own detecting.

"You're assuming the mother's alive," he said. "And that she knew about Randy's death and the funeral."

"There was a piece about him in yesterday's *Times.*"

"Doesn't mean she saw it, especially if she doesn't live in the L.A. area."

He was right, of course. That annoyed me. "There's been nothing in the media linking Randy with Aggie's murder. Strange, don't you think?" I watched him to see his reaction.

Connors shrugged. "I guess they have bigger stories than a six-year-old murder."

More likely, the police had killed the story to avoid embarrassment. "So why *are* you here, if the case is closed?"

"Keeping tabs on you," he said, treating me to a lazy smile that ordinarily I would have found cute. "Creeley keeps calling, insisting Randy couldn't have overdosed and what are we doing about it. I figure it's worth a couple of hours of my time if it makes him feel better."

"He's in denial. Randy probably killed himself because he felt guilty about Aggie."

"What happened to your Randy-was-framed theory?"

I was tired of the games. "I know he worked at Rachel's Tent, Andy. I figure you didn't tell me because you didn't want to get Wilshire in trouble, but I have to be honest, it hurts."

Connors scowled at me. "You figured wrong. Wilshire went by the book. Randy had a solid alibi."

"His sister," I said, accompanying my sarcasm with a snort. "How convenient."

"The prayer vigil started at nine. Randy and his sister went to an eight-thirty movie. He was able to tell the detectives details of the plot. He ordered the tickets by phone. With *his* credit card. He had his ticket stub, she had hers."

"She could've gone with someone else and given him the other stub," I said, pointing out the obvious. "Did they even bother to check him out?"

Connors gave me a withering look. "An ex-con who knew the victim? What do *you* think?"

"I think someone obviously screwed up." I lowered my voice, though no one was within earshot. "Why didn't you tell me he knew her, Andy? Why let me go on thinking it was a random mugging?"

"Like I said, it wasn't my case. And the truth isn't always helpful. Are you happier knowing that your best friend had something going on with her killer?"

I winced as though he'd slapped me. Anger flamed my cheeks. "You don't know that."

The organ music began. I edged away from Connors and faced forward. Out of the corner of my eye I saw him open a psalm booklet that he'd removed from the back of the pew. A moment later he put it back.

"I'm going to tell you something," he said. "I think you need to hear it. But it's just between us, understood?"

I nodded, though I couldn't imagine what he could tell me that would make a difference.

He moved closer to me. "We found the locket in a mailer addressed to the Lashers, along with a letter saying he was sorry."

"That doesn't mean—"

"He talks about how much he loved her, how she changed his life, made him want to be a better man. He says he hated her for making him think they had a future when all along she didn't think he was good enough for her. He wishes he could undo what he did."

I'd been shaking my head while Connors talked.

"Who's in denial now?" He sighed and ran a hand through his hair. "It explains why he kept the locket, Molly. I know it's tough, finding out there was a side to your best friend you didn't know anything about. I had a partner who was on the take. Even when they showed me the proof, I didn't want to believe it."

"I'm sorry about your partner, but that has nothing to do with Aggie. She would never lead anybody on, Andy. She was kind to everyone, caring, affectionate. Randy obviously made it into something else. He says so himself."

"Maybe."

"She would have *told* me, Andy. We told each other *everything.*"

"The way you talk about her, you had her on a pedestal. Maybe she didn't know how to climb down. Or maybe she was going to tell you, but then she was killed."

"There was nothing to *tell.*" I frowned. "You don't have to tell her parents about the letter, do you? It would upset them for nothing." From the expression on his face I could tell he already had.

"You're not the only one who needs answers, Molly."

The music stopped, and the minister stepped up to the podium. I was agitated but I forced myself to concentrate as he spoke with heart about a life tragically cut short. I sensed that he'd really known Randy, that he wasn't going through the motions. He was followed by Roland Creeley, who didn't cry but had to stop several times while he talked about the son he had loved and would miss terribly, the young boy with the golden hair and golden future, the troubled teenager, the adult who had worked hard to turn his life around.

Aggie's father hadn't cried at her funeral, though unlike her mother, he hadn't been sedated. I think he was numb. I think he hadn't absorbed the reality of his daughter's violent death two days earlier, or the further violation of her body and Orthodox law through the autopsy that the coroner's office had insisted on performing, despite entreaties from prominent members of the Jewish community.

Aggie's father didn't cry, but I could hear the heartache in his voice, the disbelief, each word dropping like a heavy stone into the absolute stillness of the auditorium that couldn't accommodate the more than two thousand people who came to hear him tell what they already knew. That Aggie was a loving daughter, an only child God had given them after they had stopped hoping; that she had brought joy into the life of everyone whose path she

crossed; that she exemplified *chesed,* loving-kindness, in her inter-
actions with her family and friends and with those less fortunate,
with whom she'd worked every day at Rachel's Tent, people to
whom she'd tried to give hope, people whose lives would be
emptier now that she was gone.

"She was Rachel," the rabbi who spoke after Aggie's father told
us, using the Hebrew pronunciation. "*Rachel mevaka al baneha.*
Rachel is crying over her children who are in distress and will not
be comforted. Like Rachel, Aggie cried over those in distress.
Like Rachel, Aggie would not be comforted until they were
helped. And now we cry for Aggie, for the young woman who
will never stand under a chuppa with her beloved, for the children she will never hold, whose tears she will never dry. And
we ask ourselves why. Why Aggie? We have no answer. Only
Hashem knows, and we have to accept His decree and trust in
His eternal wisdom. But if Aggie were here, I think she would
tell us: Do more *chesed.* Open your hand and your heart to those
who are troubled. Use soft words and shun *loshon hora,* because
gossip is a neighbor of the *ayin hora* that, once aroused, disrupts
the order of the world and brings calamity. I think that's what
Aggie would tell us."

I didn't realize Roland Creeley had finished speaking until I
heard the organ music. I looked to my right. Connors was gone,
and so was the redhead. Slipping out of my pew, I joined the
queue filing out of the chapel into the foyer and tried to find her,
but the room was too crowded.

I joined the end of a long line of people waiting to sign the
guest book and found myself in front of a large floral arrangement with a note card attached to one of those long-handled
plastic forks. I flipped open the card:

With deep sympathy from the Horton Family
and all of us at Rachel's Tent.

Sooner or later the media would link Randy with Aggie's murder. I imagined that the Rachel's Tent people who had chipped in for this offering would be filled with horror when they realized they'd sent flowers to the man who had killed one of their own.

It was my turn to sign the guest book. I wrote a short message and would have liked to check the other signatures, but the woman behind me cleared her throat several times, signaling her impatience, so I stepped aside.

The Creeleys emerged from the chapel and stopped to accept condolences. The man in the gray suit took Roland Creeley's hand in both of his, said something about Rachel's Tent, and introduced a man in his late twenties with thick dark hair and a serious, dutiful expression. I didn't hear the name, but Creeley looked almost pathetically grateful.

The younger man said something to Trina and put his hand on her shoulder. She nodded and gave him a wan smile. She was tense, her red-rimmed eyes darting around the room, her hands clenched. When I tried to make eye contact with her, she stared at me without recognition.

I roamed the foyer, and seeing no sign of the redhead, I returned to the guest book, which I now had to myself. Paging backward, I scanned the signatures and messages. Three people had written that they were from Rachel's Tent. Of course, there was nothing from Doreen or Mom.

Mike had signed, and so had Gloria Lamont. I saw Connors's signature and a few pages before that a name that raised goose bumps on my arms:

B. Lasher. "Our prayers are with you."

There was undoubtedly more than one Lasher in Los Angeles. And who said this Lasher was local? And the *B* wasn't necessarily for Binyomin, as in Aggie's father, who went by Benjamin outside the Orthodox community and whom I hadn't seen in the chapel. I wondered what Connors would think if he assumed that Aggie's father had attended the funeral of the man who had killed her.

A tap on my shoulder startled me. I turned around and saw Gloria Lamont.

"That was a nice service, wasn't it?" she said. "I feel for Randy's daddy. He sounds like a good man what did his best for his son, which wasn't easy, considering he had to do by hisself. But you never know how your kid'll turn out, do you? There's so much temptation in this world, and Satan works hard to put it right in your face."

I told her I agreed.

"I was gonna call you," she said. "The other day you asked me about Randy's ladies? There was this woman."

My heart lurched, though I don't know why.

"I wouldn't of seen her, but I was waitin' up for Shirrel to come back with Jerome. She was worried 'cause he was runnin' a high fever and cryin' something fierce, so she took him to the emergency? Anyway, one in the morning it was still hot as hell, I didn't have air-conditioning then, so I was sittin' on the stoop to get me some air, and up walks Randy with this woman. He didn't look happy to see me, unh-unh, whisked her inside before I could say how are you. She must've left after a few hours 'cause I didn't see her leave the next morning."

Not Aggie, I told myself. Someone else, another one of Randy's many girlfriends.

"I asked him about her the next day," Gloria said. " 'Is your lady friend married that you have to sneak around with her?' He gave me a hard look that said mind your own business, but an hour later he knocks on my door, asks me to promise I won't tell no one about the woman 'cause it would put her in a heap of trouble and Randy, too. 'Who's gonna ask, her husband?' I said, but Randy said, just promise. So I did. The next few days and for a long time he was in a bad state, all tucked into himself, so I guess she decided to end it, or *he* did."

My tongue seemed to be stuck to my palate. "This woman," I said. "What did she look like?"

It couldn't be Aggie, because Gloria hadn't recognized her when I'd showed her the photo; because Aggie told me everything, good or bad, the same way I told her; because that's what best friends do, they have no secrets.

"She had her head down, so I didn't get a good look at her face," Gloria said.

Aggie would never have gone to Randy Creeley's apartment. Aggie had planned to marry an Orthodox Jewish young man and cover her hair and live the life that I had temporarily thrown away.

"She had dark hair, I remember that," Gloria said. "Long and curly. Like your friend's, the one whose picture you showed me? And she had this locket. I didn't see a locket in that picture, but that's who you think it is, don't you, honey? Your friend, the one the police think Randy killed. That's why you look like someone just stepped on your grave." The woman clucked. "Poor thing."

I don't know whether she was referring to Aggie or me.

CHAPTER SIXTEEN

GLORIA PATTED MY ARM AND SAID SOMETHING COMFORT-
ing, but I couldn't tell you what, because the room was intensely
noisy and cloying, so many people talking at once, the over-
powering scent of the flowers making me queasy and aggravating
the dull pain that had started at my right temple and was gripping
my skull in a vise. I found the restroom and used cold water from
the faucet to splash my face and chase two Advil tablets.

When I returned to the foyer everyone had gone, probably
headed for the burial site. I walked outside and was leaning
against the cool granite of the building's exterior, inhaling fresh
air to calm the turmoil in my head and stomach, when the redhead exited the foyer and walked by me. She must have been in a

stall in the ladies' room when I was there, because I hadn't seen her in the foyer.

She headed for the parking lot. I followed her. My mind was a tangle of thoughts—Aggie and Randy, Trina's locket, B. Lasher. I couldn't sort it out now, but I could try to find out if this was Doreen and, if so, why she was wearing a wig.

She was walking at a rapid pace that I had difficulty matching in my Manolo Blahnik heels. I considered calling out "Doreen," to see if she'd turn around, but she disappeared behind a steel gray minivan.

Almost tripping as one skinny heel caught in the asphalt, I sped up, determined to reach her before she got into her car and drove off, but a second later she reappeared and continued walking in that steady pace. I figured she'd mistaken this car for hers—there were a number of gray minivans in the horseshoe-shaped lot.

Then she did it again—walked around a car and came back a couple of seconds later, first behind a beige minivan, then a black sport-utility vehicle, then a blue Suburban.

What on earth was she doing? No one could be that disoriented, and her purposeful gait said she wasn't drunk or stoned. I doubted that she was planning to steal a car and trying to see if a forgetful owner had left his or her key in the ignition.

Now she was at the bottom of the horseshoe. I was still following her, but I'd dropped back. With one eye watching her, I pretended to rummage in my purse as she walked around another black SUV and reemerged from behind another minivan several cars farther ahead.

That was when I figured it out: She'd been taking cover behind large vehicles that would prevent her from being seen.

By whom? And why?

I looked over my shoulder, but there was no one else in the parking lot.

My Acura was two cars up. Twenty seconds later I was inside, seat belt buckled, ignition on, my eyes glued to the rearview mirror so that I'd be able to watch her as she made her trek across the lot until she arrived at her car.

Ten seconds went by, then twenty. A minute. There was no sign of the redhead, but she couldn't have left the lot.

I kept my eye on the mirror. Another half minute passed. A black Lincoln Town Car with tinted windows pulled into the lot and glided to a velvet stop on the other side of the horseshoe, in front of a dark blue SUV.

In a fluid movement that would have done Jackie Joyner-Kersee proud, the redhead sprinted from behind the SUV to the Town Car, yanked the door open, and slid into the limo, which rumbled past me seconds later on its stately way out of the lot and afforded me a fleeting glance at a mustached driver with a swarthy complexion.

Backing out of my spot, I sped after the car, turned left when it did, and kept several lengths behind as the driver entered the Pomona Freeway heading west. Minutes later we merged onto the 10 toward Santa Monica.

I've never followed anyone in my life. The tension, and maybe the adrenaline, added to my headache, which was boring through my skull. With my right hand I found my pillbox, flicked it open, and downed another Advil with water from the bottle I always carry with me.

The Town Car was keeping pace with the traffic. I did the same. At one point it made a sudden lane change. I stayed in my lane but was able to track its progress, and five minutes later I changed lanes, too, though I allowed two cars to separate us.

It was a long forty minutes, which felt longer because I didn't know our destination and was unfamiliar with the area. At the National off-ramp the Town Car exited and so did I. We drove to Robertson, took that to Olympic, and turned left. My headache was subsiding, in part because I was more relaxed as we passed through familiar streets.

We were in Century City when the Town Car cut a diagonal to the right lane and made a sharp turn onto Avenue of the Stars. Muttering a curse, I did the same, eliciting several angry honks in the process, and found myself behind four black Town Cars. Two were in the lane to my left, two in front of me.

I'd memorized the license plate of the redhead's car and was able to eliminate the car in front of me and the one alongside me. Pulling forward until I was inches from the bumper of the car ahead, I read the license plate of the lead Town Car on my left.

That was the one. I allowed myself a satisfied smile that disappeared moments later when both Town Cars on my left turned into the drive of the Century Plaza Hotel while I had no choice but to continue to the intersection.

I made a right turn, and three more that brought me back to Avenue of the Stars and the hotel's semicircular driveway.

My Town Cars had spawned a fleet. A parking attendant dressed in a red-and-gold-trimmed Beefeater uniform complete with cap opened my car door.

"Okay if I leave my car here for a few minutes?"

His frown said my smile wouldn't do, so I handed him a five, which didn't bowl him over, but he pocketed it.

The redhead's Town Car was three cars up. I knocked on the driver's door.

He lowered his window. "Where you want go?" he asked in a thick Russian accent. He had unnaturally black hair and bushy eyebrows and a trim mustache below a nose with prominent capillaries that said he probably drank too much. I hoped he didn't indulge while he drove.

"I wanted to ask you about the woman you just drove here from the cemetery in Downey."

"Lady, you want driver, okay. I'm not lawyer. I don't make money talking."

I pulled a ten from my wallet and showed it to him. He rolled his eyes in disgust. I took out another ten.

He stretched his hand out the window and snatched both bills.

"Where did you pick her up?" I asked.

"Here." He pointed toward the hotel. "She wants go to Downey, wants I should wait, but not in lot. She will phone when she is ready to leave. I am thinking, this is crazy lady, but she says she will pay me two hundred dollars, so okay." He shrugged.

"What's her name?"

"Who gives name to limo driver? You?" He shook his head, as if he couldn't believe my stupidity.

"Anything else?"

"She brings big black bag and leaves it in car."

I peered into the back of the Town Car.

He followed my eyes. "In *Downey,*" he said, impatient. "Not now. Now she takes bag and goes back into hotel. Crazy lady."

I thanked the driver and took a few steps, then walked right back. I knocked on the window again and waited until he turned down his radio.

"You said she phoned you," I told the Russian. "So you have her phone number. Can you tell me what it is?"

"Why you are looking for this lady?" A crafty expression had narrowed his brown eyes.

"I want to ask her a few questions."

"Maybe she is not wanting to talk to you. When she is in car, she is nervous, turning head to look out back window."

"Do you have the number?"

"Fifty dollars."

"Twenty."

"Fifty."

He was literally in the driver's seat. I opened my wallet and pulled out three tens. "That's all I have. Unless you take Master-Card or Visa."

He grunted. "Funny lady. You should go on *Leno.*" He stuffed the bills into his pocket, then punched a few buttons on his cell phone. "You have paper?"

"I hope so, 'cause I'm sure that's gonna cost extra."

He gave me a dark look and rattled off ten digits. Between the speed and the accent, I had to ask him to repeat the numbers twice before I got them all down in sequence.

The prefix was 619. That was in the San Diego area.

I tucked the slip of paper with the phone number into my wallet. This time I didn't thank the driver. I don't think he was crushed.

I headed to the lobby, avoiding eye contact with my valet. I was out of cash and goodwill. Inside the elegant plant-filled room with a soaring ceiling, a guy at a black baby grand (his jeans said he was a hotel guest, not an employee) was playing the hell out of *The Phantom of the Opera* for a handful of people sitting on sofas who couldn't have cared less.

I've been there. I've done signings at chain stores where most of the customers look at me as though I'm wallpaper, or ask me for other writers' books or directions to the restroom. At a Valencia library where only one woman showed up for my reading, a man interrupted me to ask where he could find a book on Marco Polo and gave me a baleful look when I said I didn't know. The woman bought a copy of *Out of the Ashes.* "I probably won't read it," she told me. "But I felt bad for you, honey, you came all this way and had such a bad turnout."

My redhead, of course, was nowhere in sight. I've attended

weddings at the Century P but have never stayed here, so it took me a minute to find Registration, where I improvised my spiel for the brunette behind the desk:

A woman had come in five minutes ago, tall and thin with medium-length red hair, carrying a large black bag. Her first name was Doreen, I didn't know her last name, we'd just met at a prewedding brunch and the bride had asked me to give Doreen a ride to the Century, which I did and was about to drive off when I noticed she'd taken my day planner and left hers in my car. Her name wasn't in her planner, so I hoped the clerk knew who she was. Oh, and she was from somewhere near San Diego. I remembered that.

The clerk had listened patiently while I talked. "You could ask the bride for the woman's name," she suggested.

I nodded. "I would, but she's with her fiancé, doing a final inspection of the house they bought. It's in Hancock Park, and you can't get cell reception there, unless you have Nextel, which she doesn't."

"Well, then, you can leave the planner, and when you talk to the bride and find out this woman's name, I'd be happy to return the planner to her."

"Right. But in the meantime, she's probably frantic, thinking she lost it. And I *really* need mine," I added, hoping the anxiety in my voice would sway her. "Could you check to see if you have a guest named Doreen?"

The woman's smile was less friendly but still polite. "I'm sorry. I'd like to help, but I couldn't give out any information about any of our guests. I'm sure you understand."

It had been worth a try. On my way out of the hotel, I detoured to the restroom to use the facilities and get the most for my five dollars. Fifty-five, if you counted what I'd paid the limo driver.

I was looking in the mirror as I freshened my lipstick when a woman emerged from a bathroom stall.

It was my redhead.

I recognized her coppery eyes. She'd chucked the wig and the glasses, which had left reddened indentations on either side of her thin, delicate nose. Short black hair peeked out from under a floppy gray fleece hat that sat low over her forehead. She'd changed into jeans and a sheepskin jacket and a pink pair of the sheepskin Ugg boots that stores can't keep in stock. She'd probably stashed her funeral attire in the black tote she'd slung over her shoulder, the tote she'd left in the Town Car during Randy's service.

I shut off my cell phone and counted to ten. When I returned to the lobby, Piano Man was playing music from *Cats* and she was walking out past the large glass doors.

She turned left. My valet was busy and didn't notice me as I followed her down the wide boulevard. I stayed back while she waited for the traffic signal to turn green, and I stepped into the intersection after she reached the other side, when the Don't Walk sign started flashing red. She turned left again and slipped into the middle of a small group of pedestrians, but I was able to keep her gray hat in sight until she entered the Century City mall underground parking lot.

It's a huge, multilevel structure. If I didn't hurry, I was sure to lose her. If I did hurry, she'd hear my footsteps, louder in this echo chamber, and would confront me: What the hell was I doing, following her? The truth is, I didn't know. There was no reason for me not to walk up to her and ask her why she'd disguised herself, who she was hiding from. Unless she'd come here to meet someone. If that was so, I wanted to know who.

When I caught up with her, she was several hundred feet ahead of me and was leaving the parking area through a door that would take her to the escalator that, from my many visits to the mall, I knew was there.

Scurrying past rows of cars, I ran up the escalator in my damn heels, eliciting stares from people who moved aside to let me pass. I ran up the second escalator and was out of breath when I stepped off and found myself in the outdoor mall. I looked all around me.

She was gone.

She could have entered any of the stores surrounding me—Macy's, Pottery Barn, Talbots—or others farther down. If she had, I'd never find her. I was about to step onto the down escalator when I glanced to my left and saw her, several hundred feet up ahead.

I no longer cared whether she spotted me. I hurried to catch up, turned left when she did, and followed her to an escalator near Bloomingdale's, but by the time I reached it, she had descended and disappeared. At the bottom of the escalator were two exits to the parking structure.

Right and left.

I turned left and entered the structure. I didn't see her. I walked for a minute or so, searching in all directions for the gray hat. I had given up and was on my way back, intending to check the other side of the parking lot, when I felt something hard and cold against the back of my head.

"Don't move," a woman said.

CHAPTER SEVENTEEN

MY BREATH WAS SO TIGHT I COULD FEEL MY RIBS.

"Don't make a sound," she said. "Don't think about running, because I will use this gun."

I've never had a gun held against my head. She could have been faking, but I wasn't about to take the chance. I was nauseous with fear.

"If you want money . . . ," I said, knowing this wasn't about money. My eyes darted left and right. I strained to hear the mating call of chirping car alarms but heard silence. Where were all the people?

"Unzip your purse and hand it to me."

With shaking hands I slipped the strap of my Coach bag off

my shoulder. My hands were slick with sweat, and I fumbled with the zipper for an eternity before I got the bag open.

She yanked the bag from me. "Put your hands at the back of your head and keep them there."

I did what she said. A few seconds later I felt her hand inside the pockets of my peacoat, then in the waistband of my skirt, under my sweater, between my legs.

"You can put your hands down. See the black Suburban and red Explorer to your right?" She had a soft voice that under other circumstances would have been pleasant. "I want you to walk in between those cars. If anyone passes you, don't say a word. Go on."

She gave me a sharp shove and moved the gun from my head to the small of my back. My legs felt wobbly and heavy at the same time, Jell-O and lead. I was amazed they were working.

"Kneel and put your hands behind your neck," she said when we were standing between the cars.

I did as she directed, my knees flattening cigarette butts, popcorn, and gum wrappers floating in a puddle that oozed from a large cardboard soda cup nearby.

"Who sent you?" she asked, her tone conversational.

My heart drummed madly against the wall of my chest. "No one."

She rapped the gun against my head. I winced. Tears stung my eyes and I bit my lips. It occurred to me that this was how people were executed. My mind refused to stay with that thought.

"*Who sent you?*" Her voice shook with anger and nervousness. "You've been following me since I left the cemetery. I want to know why."

"I swear, no one sent me." I didn't want to make her more nervous. I didn't know whether the safety was off the gun. I licked my lips, which had gone dry. "I saw you at Randy's funeral. I wanted to talk to you about him."

I heard footsteps several hundred feet ahead. Laughter. Please, I thought. Come this way.

"If you yell . . . ," she said, leaving me to fill in the rest as she increased the pressure of the gun against my head. "If anybody approaches, put your head down. I'll say you're feeling faint."

I nodded. Sweat was trickling under my arms and between my thighs.

I heard a series of clattering sounds and realized she'd dumped the contents of my purse onto the concrete. A lipstick rolled past me.

"You don't mind if I look through your wallet," she said. "Molly Blume. Is that your real name?"

"Yes." In my wallet, I remembered with a jolt, was the slip of paper with her phone number.

"Who was that man you were sitting with at the funeral? Did he tell you to follow me?"

"No one—" My voice was raspy. I cleared my throat. "No one told me to follow you."

"Who is he, Molly?"

"A friend." I wasn't about to tell her Connors was a detective.

"He was whispering in your ear, Molly. You looked very chummy."

"A *good* friend."

"Do you work for them, Molly? You and your good friend?"

"I don't know who you mean."

"I don't believe you." Her breath was warm against my neck. "They sent you to follow me, didn't they? Just tell me. I need to know."

"No one sent me. I'm a freelance reporter."

"You're a liar, Molly Blume. Or should I say Morgan Blake? How many other names do you have?"

"Morgan is my pen name. I write books."

"Is that another lie, Molly?" She rubbed the cold barrel of

the gun against the side of my head, near my eye. "What kind of books?"

"About true crimes. That's why I wanted to talk to you about Randy. I saw you at the funeral. I hoped you could fill in some blanks."

"True crimes. I think that's funny. Don't you think that's very, very funny, Molly?"

Her voice had an edge of hysteria that frightened me more than her anger. I didn't know the right answer. I concentrated on the gun that was cold against my temple.

"Who's this?" She held a photo of Zack in front of me.

"My fiancé. We're getting married in two weeks." If you say it, I told myself, it will happen.

"And you want me to feel sorry for you, right? Does he know about your *good friend,* Molly?"

I tried to remember where in my wallet I'd put the slip of paper. With the photos? With a few receipts? Behind my business cards?

I heard the rustle of paper. Maybe it was a receipt, I thought. I shut my eyes. Please, let it be a receipt.

"Where did you get this?" She was rattled now, her voice a fierce whisper that made me shiver.

"Where did I get what?" I asked, desperate to buy time, hoping she'd decide it didn't matter that I'd copied down her phone number, she could tear it up and let me go.

"This." She thrust something in front of me.

I opened my eyes and stared at the photo of Aggie, the one taken in her backyard. Not the paper with the woman's number. I thanked God and felt weak with relief.

"It's mine. That's me on the left, with my friend."

"Aggie Lasher."

I swallowed hard. "Yes."

"She was murdered."

"Yes."

She moved the photo out of my reach. "This doesn't look like you." Her voice was sharp with accusation.

My heart was pounding. "That photo was taken six years ago. My hair was different."

She didn't answer. "You and Aggie were friends?" she said a long moment later.

"Best friends."

"Best friends," she repeated. She sounded thoughtful, calmer. Sad. Then she inhaled so sharply that her breath whistled. "You gave her the locket with the red thread!"

I almost turned my head around. "How did—"

"What do you *want* from me? Why did you follow me?"

Her voice had changed. The venom was gone. In its place was anguish and something I couldn't define.

"I thought you were Randy's girlfriend," I said. "Someone described you. He said you were tall and thin and had black hair. I could tell you were wearing a wig."

"Did he tell you my name?"

I hesitated. "Doreen."

"Did he tell you my last name, too?" Her tone was angry again.

I shook my head.

"What else do you know about me?"

"Nothing. I promise."

"What do you *really* want, Molly?"

"I want to know why Randy killed Aggie."

"Now *that* was a true crime, but I don't think you want to write about it, Molly-Morgan. I can tell you but then I'd have to kill you. Or they would."

"Who is *they*?"

"The ones who killed Aggie. The ones who killed me. If I leave you here, will you let me disappear?"

"Yes." God, yes.

"I want to believe you, Molly. I do."

I heard clicking sounds I couldn't identify and wondered what she was doing.

She tossed my cell phone onto the ground, in front of me. "I took the battery out. In case you're thinking of phoning someone so they'll be looking for me. I know where you live, Molly. On Blackburn." She recited the address. "I know where to find you if you try to find me."

"I won't try to find you." When I said it, it was the truth.

"People always lie to me, Molly. That's just the way it is."

"Did Randy lie to you?"

"He lied to everyone. But it was the truth that caught up with him and killed him."

Seconds later she was gone.

CHAPTER EIGHTEEN

I WAITED AWHILE BEFORE I MOVED, EACH MINUTE CRAWL-ing by like an hour. I wanted to make sure she wasn't just feet away, lurking behind a car, testing me to see if I would follow her.

I pushed myself to a standing position, my knees creaking and threatening to snap my legs in half. The movement intensified the throbbing in my head. I touched the area where she'd rapped me with the gun and I winced. Drawing in a hissing breath through my clenched teeth, I probed the area and felt a bump the size of a lemon. I looked at my fingers. No blood, so the skin wasn't broken.

After walking in place for a few seconds to get my circulation going, I squatted and gathered the items that had been dumped onto the concrete. Lipstick, car keys, batteryless cell phone, a contact lens case, pens, a handful of Hershey's Kisses, the pillbox with the Advil. An antique cloisonné compact, a gift from Bubbie G, had chipped. The mirror inside was cracked.

I dry-swallowed two Advil and hoped I wasn't overdosing. I checked my wallet. My driver's license was behind the plastic window, the smile on my face absurdly happy. My credit cards were all there, and the photos. Not the one with Aggie. I checked a few times to see if it had stuck to one of the other photos. I wondered why she'd taken it.

The slip of paper was where I'd stuffed it as I'd hurried toward the lobby, tucked behind a tiny laminated card with an abbreviated version of the Wayfarer's Prayer. Hebrew on one side, English on the other. "May You rescue us from the hand of every foe, ambush, bandits, and evil animals along the way. . . ." The card had arrived eleven years ago with my El Al ticket to Jerusalem. I use it whenever I travel far from home, which doesn't include following someone from Downey to Century City. Or maybe it does.

I had to use a credit card to pay the ten dollars to redeem my Acura, which had been valet parked.

"You were gone almost an hour, ma'am," the valet said. The *ma'am* sounded mocking, probably because of my skirt, which was wet and streaked with grime and reeked of root beer. I was clearly not Century Plaza material. "It's eight dollars for the first hour, two each additional. Twenty-three, max."

He didn't offer to return my five dollars. I considered asking him for a single to tip the driver, who brought my Acura to a screeching halt inches from my toes and dismissed my apology with a shrug and a look that said he didn't believe I had nothing to give him.

On the way home I stopped at the Verizon store on La

Cienega near Third, signed in, and waited over thirty minutes before someone sold me a replacement battery.

"If you bring in the original, maybe we can exchange it, no cost," my salesman said. "If it's defective."

I told him I didn't think so and thanked him for the offer. With the new battery inserted, my phone told me I had five messages. Two from Zack, wondering where I was. One from his mother, telling me how touched she was by the note I'd sent to thank her and her husband for the candlesticks.

Edie had phoned. She and Mindy wanted to know if the flower girls were going to wear wreaths, and if Zack and I had decided on the processional order.

The last call was from Connors.

"Sorry about today, Molly. Call me if you want to talk."

It was after two by the time I parked in my driveway. My head still hurt like hell, and I don't think I said more than ten words to my seventy-eight-year-old, thrice-widowed landlord, Isaac, who stepped onto the porch when he heard me arrive. He's a sweetie who wears his pants practically like a bib and is always full of neighborhood gossip that he loves to share with me.

"Terrible headache," I said when I saw his hurt look. "Talk to you later." I hurried past the porch glider to my door before he could stop me.

Inside my apartment I stripped out of my clothes, which I left in a heap on my bedroom floor, and filled the tub. I added jasmine bath salts, sat on the edge, and phoned Zack.

"How was the funeral?" he asked.

So much had happened, that I hadn't had time to assess my feelings. I told him about Creeley's eulogy. "You could tell he really loved Randy, no matter what Randy had done."

"I can't imagine anything worse than burying a child," Zack said. "I've counseled parents who have lost children, and I always feel so inadequate. Are you glad you went?"

"I suppose. Although now I can't help thinking of Randy as someone's son, not just Aggie's killer. I'm finding it hard to hate him."

"That's not a bad thing, is it? Maybe it'll help you get closure. What about Rachel's Tent? Did you learn anything?"

"I didn't go."

"Probably just as well. So where have you been?"

"Here and there. No place special." Maybe I would tell him later. Right now I didn't want to think about what had happened. "Your mom phoned to thank me for the thank-you note. She's so sweet."

"She loved your note. She loves *you*. She wants to take you to lunch before the wedding, but I told her you're swamped."

"Is she upset?" I liked my future in-laws, and the last thing I wanted to do was upset them.

"Not at all. She understands."

"That I'm preoccupied with Aggie, you mean." I wondered what Zack had told them.

"That you're planning our wedding and writing a crime sheet column and have a lot on your plate. Are you all right, Molly? You don't sound like yourself."

"I'm a little blue, and my head is killing me."

"Want me to come over?"

"I'm about to take a bath."

"I guess that's a 'no.' "

Despite my mood, I couldn't help smiling. "Baths always relax me. I'll call you later."

Minutes later I lay in the tub. With my eyes shut, I inhaled the jasmine fragrance and trailed my fingers through hot water that reached my chin and lapped gently against the island of my body. I felt some of the tension seep out, but my aching head was a constant reminder of what had happened earlier.

When I had toweled myself off and put on jeans and a sweater,

I sat on my bed and took out the slip of paper with Doreen's phone number. She was probably on the road now, on the way to somewhere in the San Diego area. In the safety of my home, the promise I'd made two hours ago, that I wouldn't try to find her, seemed unnecessary.

Not that it mattered. I had only her cell number. If I had her home number, and if she wasn't home, and if she had an answering machine, the message might reveal her last name. A lot of *ifs*, and I wasn't sure what I would do with the information.

I was way behind with my *Crime Sheet* column, which I had to e-mail to my editor tomorrow morning. I spent the rest of the day and most of the evening fine-tuning the data I entered and was only half done when Zack phoned after his meeting and offered to come over. He was disappointed when I told him I had work to do. I was, too. But unlike Ron, who never respected my work, Zack understands about deadlines.

At a quarter to twelve I was done. I went into the kitchen, where I celebrated by finishing half a pint of Baskin-Robbins Jamoca Almond Fudge. As I turned off my cell phone before plugging it into the charger, I wondered whether Doreen had turned off hers. If she had, I'd hear her voice message, and maybe her last name.

My home phone has call blocking, so if Doreen's phone *was* on, she wouldn't know I was calling. If she took the call, I could hang up. Still, I wasn't sure whether she could learn that I'd called, and the memory of the gun at my head and the fact that she knew where I lived recommended caution.

I was about to leave when I realized I was in my jeans. At that time of the night, I was unlikely to meet anyone I knew, but I'd made a commitment to Zack. Slipping on a skirt over the jeans, I grabbed a handful of quarters, dimes, and nickels and drove the few blocks to the Beverly Connection, where I found a phone booth. I dialed the number and inserted the necessary coins.

"You've reached Brian," a pleasant male voice informed me. "Leave a message and I'll call you back."

I cursed the Russian driver. He'd given me a wrong number— intentionally or accidentally, the result was the same. Or maybe I'd transposed the digits. I didn't have enough coins to sit there and play a Rubik's Cube of phone numbers. I was out fifty dollars and change and had no way of finding Doreen. A part of me, the part that throbbed at the back of my head, said maybe that was a good thing.

I wondered how Doreen knew about the locket and the red thread. Had Randy showed it to her? Told her it was Aggie's? But how would he explain having a locket that had belonged to a murdered woman?

And how had Doreen recognized Aggie in the photo? I hadn't seen a photo of Aggie when I was in Randy's apartment, but Gloria Lamont had been in a hurry for me to finish, and I hadn't checked every inch of the place.

I hadn't found any red thread, either. According to Mike, the yard salesman, Randy had ordered a large quantity of the threads online, had offered to e-mail Mike the link to the website. He could have used them all up, given them to Trina and to his friends.

Or maybe he'd stashed them somewhere. I replayed my visit to the apartment, mentally walked through the rooms. There was Randy's desk in the living room. I hadn't seen any red threads in the desk drawers, or in his bedroom closet, or in the bathroom or kitchen.

Something was nagging at me. . . .

I canvassed the place again: living room, dining area, bedroom, bathroom, kitchen. My mind kept taking me back to the desk in the living room.

I was halfway home when I realized why: Randy had ordered red threads online. His multipurpose fax machine no doubt served as a printer, but I hadn't seen a computer anywhere in his apartment.

"Sure, he had a computer," Gloria said when I phoned her early Friday morning. "One of them laptops. 'Pick it up,' he tol' me. 'See how light it is.' It weighed less than a gallon of milk, but I guess it cost a lot more." The manager chuckled.

"When was the last time you saw Randy's computer, Mrs. Lamont?"

"When?" She thought for a moment. "I know he had it the day before he died. Jerome was over at Randy's playin' games on it. Randy was nice like that. He showed Jerome how to use it, and not just games. Kids today, they know more'n their folks do 'bout computers. I wouldn't know how to turn the damn thing on."

I told her I hadn't noticed the laptop when she showed me the apartment, and asked her if she remembered seeing it the night she found Randy dead.

It took her some time to answer. "Well, now that you mention it, I don't think I *did* see it, no. But I was all shook up, you know? But you're right. It wasn't there when I showed you the place, huh." A grunt, not a question. "Could be Randy gave it in to be fixed."

"Could be," I said.

Chapter Nineteen

Friday, February 20. 10:04 A.M. 3800 block of Huron Avenue. A woman told officers her husband was in the garage smoking narcotics with a woman she didn't know. In the garage the officers found the two practically sitting in cocaine residue. The other woman said they had been smoking cocaine "in his religious office." The man said he had converted his garage into an office and shrine devoted to "black magic." The two were arrested for possession of cocaine. Both suspects had yellow teeth. (Culver City)

THE EXTERIOR OF RACHEL'S TENT, A TWO-STORY STUCCO building on Palms south of Pico, was a darker shade of sand than I remembered. I found a spot in front but sat in my car. Almost seven years had passed since I'd been here, long enough to weaken the threads of memory, but I was reluctant to enter the building where Aggie had spent so much time.

I'd been inside Rachel's Tent only once, a month after Aggie had organized her desk and hung her diplomas on the terra-cotta walls of her first-floor office. Five months shy of twenty-three, she had been the youngest social worker at the facility. I'm sure the hiring committee saw in her what we all did: wisdom beyond her years, determination, compassion, a yearning to help others. In high school, while I split my time between my studies and my social life and fared reasonably well in both, Aggie aced enough AP courses to eliminate a semester at an all-women New York college, where she received credit for her year of Judaic studies at a Jerusalem seminary not far from the one I'd attended. She eliminated another year and a half by enrolling in the accelerated track of a piggyback program with a social work school.

By the time she was twenty-two and a half, she had a BSW, an MSW, and a job she had coveted. I had graduated from UCLA and was figuring out what to do with my BA in English and with my life, which hadn't followed the path my parents had anticipated. I envied her single-mindedness, the passion she invested in the many twelve-hour days her work demanded of her, her absolute faith in God and His laws that gave her a clear blueprint and, for the most part, an acceptance of whatever life brought her way.

She wasn't a saint. She had a wicked sense of humor and a temper for which she was constantly doing penance. "I need Yom Kippur every day," she would tell me. She was intolerant of those less focused or efficient. She was enraged by injustice, dishonesty, and hypocrisy and quick to express her feelings. She worried about her weight and cried when the man she'd hoped to marry ended their relationship. But while I pined over Zack for more than a year, and other failed romances for months, Aggie was ready to move on after a few days.

"It wasn't *bashert*," she told me. "God obviously has other plans for me."

For a long time I wondered whether God's plans for Aggie had included having her murdered while she walked to the meeting hall.

Not *God's* plan, my father said. Man's plan. For God, time is a continuum with no past, no present, no future. He sees the video of your life, the beginning and the end. That's what pre-destination means, Molly. But God doesn't dictate people's actions. People have free will to choose between right and wrong, between compassion and cruelty, between good and evil. God knows what they will choose because He has seen the video.

The lobby of Rachel's Tent was large, with a domed ceiling painted an azure blue and the finish on the walls a textured pale yellow stucco. To my right was a reception area. I took a brochure from the stack, introduced myself to the youngish blond woman behind the teak desk, and told her I was writing a story about the agency.

"Monica Prince is our public relations person," she said. "Or you may want to speak to the director."

I opted for the director. While the receptionist checked to see if he was available, I crossed the entry and gazed at a mural of Rachel's Tomb—the way I'd seen it, before it had been enclosed by guard towers. In the foreground was the domed stone edifice. Behind the building, palm trees shot up from sandy mounds, their fronds scraping the robin's egg blue sky. Off in the distance two camels trudged along under heavy loads.

Printed in large, deep blue letters against the background of sky were verses from Jeremiah, one of which the rabbi had recited at Aggie's funeral:

> *Rachel is weeping for her children.*
> *She refuses to be comforted, for her children are gone.*

Restrain your voice from weeping and your eyes from tears
There is hope for your future.

A comforting message for the women who stepped into Rachel's Tent, I thought. But not for Aggie.

"Miss Blume? William Bramer."

I turned around and shook the director's hand. He had a firm grip and a pleasant smile and clear blue eyes enhanced by the blue of the shirt he wore with a gray pinstripe suit. A few lines around the eyes and touches of gray in his wavy brown hair put him somewhere in his late forties to early fifties. I can identify every designer shoe, but I'm not great with ages.

"You look familiar," he said. "Have we met?"

"I don't think so." He looked familiar, too. From the formality in his posture and tone I decided he didn't go by "Bill."

"Really? Because I'm almost sure . . . Well, it'll come to me." He pointed to the mural. "The stones look real, don't they? I've never been to Rachel's Tomb. Have you?"

"A few times," I said. "Years ago."

"It's dangerous there now. A terrible shame." He sighed. "Rachel is the universal mother. Everyone should have access to her resting place." A second later he brightened. "So you're doing a story about us. Is it for *Los Angeles Magazine*? They expressed interest a while back."

"That's one possibility." Randy's funeral—that's where I'd seen Bramer. He was the one who had approached Creeley. I hoped he didn't make the connection. "By the way, who came up with the name Rachel's Tent? It's so appropriate."

"That was my idea." The director smiled, pleased. "As I said, Rachel is the eternal mother. She spans generations and embraces all nationalities. And the image of a tent is informal. There's something private and intimate about a tent, something comforting and cozy."

"Unless you're hiking and it's raining."

"Well, yes." Bramer looked uncertain, then laughed. "I'm not a hiker myself. Why don't I give you a quick tour and you can ask your questions."

We started with the ground-floor counseling rooms, all variations on the one he showed me, which was painted a comforting pale yellow and furnished with a chintz love seat, upholstered chairs, an area rug, and a desk with French legs.

"The idea is to create a homelike, nonthreatening environment," Bramer said when I complimented him on the decor.

Also on the ground floor were a meditation room that served as a nondenominational chapel, a small exercise studio ("We offer yoga," Bramer said), a recreation room, and a kitchen and a large cafeteria filled with square tables that seated four.

"In addition to group therapy, we encourage activities like bingo and trips to malls, parks, and movies, for example," Bramer said. "The idea is to strengthen socialization skills. We teach developmentally disabled clients how to make a budget, how to market. Simple skills you and I take for granted."

On the second floor were bedrooms and bathrooms that provided temporary shelter for women who were abused or homeless. Each suite was small but cheerful.

"We're open to women of any race or religion," Bramer told me when we were in his office, which was decorated in masculine tones of gray and navy. "We treat prostitutes and judges, drug addicts and doctors, women who are homeless and those who shop at Barneys. We try to help homeless women achieve independent living and regain their dignity. We give victims of domestic violence tools to empower themselves. We teach pregnant women about prenatal nutrition and give them parenting classes and genetic counseling. If they don't want to keep the child, we can arrange for an adoption. As a matter of fact, Rachel's Tent began as a haven for unmarried pregnant women."

Most of this I knew from Aggie, but I figured I'd allow Bramer the pleasure of telling me about his "baby." "How long has Rachel's Tent been in existence?"

"It was founded nine years ago through a charitable trust set up by the Horton family. That's a picture of Mr. Horton with his wife, son, and daughter at the grand opening of Rachel's Tent." Bramer pointed to a wall behind me. "He's the one standing next to former Mayor Riordan."

I took a quick look at the photo, but from where I was sitting, I couldn't see much. "I think I've seen the Horton name in the paper several times and on the wing of a hospital." I recalled seeing it at the funeral on the card accompanying the floral arrangement.

Bramer nodded. "Mr. Horton donates generously to many charities and organizations, but he has a special connection to Rachel's Tent. If you like, Miss Blume, I'll ask him if he'll meet with you."

"Molly." I smiled. "That would be great. Why the special connection to Rachel's Tent?"

"You haven't read Mr. Horton's autobiography?" The look he gave me was a mix of surprise and disapproval. "It's a remarkable story, truly inspirational. Mr. Horton never knew his father. His mother was unwed. She had no education, no skills, no job. She put him in foster care and disappeared. Years later he found out that she had died, hungry and homeless."

Bramer paused—I think to give me an opportunity to acknowledge the tragedy of the woman's life, which I did. There's a Yiddish proverb that says the ugliest life is better than the nicest death, but this woman's life *and* death had been ugly. I wonder sometimes what it would be like to be born without the advantages I take for granted. A secure home, parents who provided material needs and education, comfort and advice, unconditional love.

"As you can imagine, Mr. Horton had a difficult childhood and adolescence," the director continued. "Eventually he ended up in prison. But in prison he read books he'd never appreciated in high school, and when he was released he was determined never to go back. He found a job and turned a small business into an empire. And he never forgot his beginnings. He founded Rachel's Tent because he wanted to help women like his mother who had nowhere to turn."

Bramer had spoken as though he was delivering a testimonial, but I had to admit it was quite a story. I couldn't help thinking about Randy Creeley, who had also been abandoned by a parent and had allowed that event to shape his destiny in a strikingly different way.

"Mr. Horton sounds like a remarkable man," I said.

"He is. Every month he invites one of our clients to his home for dinner with his family. He wants to get to know the women, to encourage them, to show them that their lives have promise. And he's setting a fine example for Jason and Kristen. His children."

A modern-day Daddy Warbucks. I didn't think Bramer would appreciate the comparison. And I wasn't sure whether being shown a grand home, which I assumed Horton lived in, was encouraging or daunting.

"What angle were you planning to focus on, Molly?"

Drugs, I thought. "I'd like to share success stories with my readers, stories about women whose lives have been changed by Rachel's Tent."

"Without names, of course." Bramer sounded wary.

"Of course."

He nodded. "We get letters all the time from women who entered Rachel's Tent at a low point in their lives. Women with no skills, with nowhere to turn. Now they're happy, functioning, contributing to society, leading worthwhile lives."

"You mentioned that you treat women with addictions," I said, angling for my opening. "I read that someone who worked here died of an overdose last week." I glanced at my notebook as if I had to refresh my memory. "Randy Creeley."

Bramer frowned. "I didn't see anything in the *Times.*"

"I don't think it was the *Times.* I saw the link on the Web when I looked up Rachel's Tent," I lied.

"Randy was a handyman and drove clients to activities and appointments," the director said with reluctance. "But he hadn't worked here in almost a year. I attended his funeral yesterday. Very sad. Of course, we didn't know he had a continuing drug problem when we hired him."

"Of course." I didn't blame Bramer for distancing himself from Randy and his drug problem. "It's wonderful that you hired him, considering that he was an ex-convict."

"So was Mr. Horton," Bramer reminded me, his tone a light slap on the wrist.

I managed to look contrite. "You're right. I'm sorry."

"Mr. Horton tries to help ex-convicts find employment so that they won't return to a life of crime. It's his way of showing gratitude to the person who gave *him* his first job when he finished serving his sentence."

"So Randy was referred by Mr. Horton?"

"Or one of his assistants. The point is, Rachel's Tent is about giving people second chances, about compassion. It would have been hypocritical for us not to give Randy one."

"In spite of his drug problem?"

Annoyance tightened Bramer's face. "His parole officer said he was clean. Randy attended Narcotics Anonymous meetings several times a week. That was a condition of his employment. He worked here for over six years, and I never knew."

I nodded and threw in a *tsk* to show sympathy. "Do you think he was selling drugs here at Rachel's Tent?"

"Absolutely not." Bramer leaned against the back of his chair. "We're getting off topic, aren't we, Molly? Unless you're doing an investigative piece on Rachel's Tent? Am I going to see myself on *Dateline?*" Underneath the humor was an edge of irritation.

"Sorry." I smiled. "No *Dateline,* I promise. I was just so taken with Creeley's story. And I have to say I'm impressed that you attended the funeral."

"The father asked me to tell people who were close to Randy. He sounded devastated, poor man." Bramer checked his watch. "We all talk about compassion. Most of the time we give it lip service. I felt I should set an example."

"Did Mr. Horton attend?"

"He was out of town. Jason represented him, and Mr. Horton sent flowers from all of us at Rachel's Tent."

I almost said "I know." The son was probably the twenty-something man Bramer had introduced to Creeley and Trina. No wonder Roland senior had looked so grateful. "Was Randy close to a lot of the people who worked here?"

"Some more than others. I'm afraid I have to cut our visit short. I know you want to hear our success stories. Let me see if anyone is free to talk to you now. If not, you'll have to come back."

"Thanks. I appreciate your help."

Bramer picked up his receiver. I walked over to the wall with the photo of the Horton family standing in front of the entrance to Rachel's Tent. Even nine years ago Horton had significant gray in his thick hair and looked several years older than his petite, dark-haired wife. The son and daughter were in their late teens and wore tailored suits and dutiful expressions, much like the one I'd seen on the son's face yesterday at Randy's funeral.

Next to the photo was an impressive grouping of Bramer's diplomas, including a doctorate from USC School of Social Work. On the adjacent wall was a bookcase crammed with large tomes. There were more books on the credenza, next to a stack of blue packets, the size seeds come in.

I picked one up. On the front was printed RACHEL'S TENT, above a color image of Rachel's Tomb that matched the mural in the lobby.

"You're in luck." Bramer put down the receiver. "Barbara Anik, one of our therapists, had a cancellation. Barbara's been here since Rachel's Tent opened, so she can give you a great deal of material for your story."

"Thank you."

The name sounded familiar, and a second later I remembered why. Dr. Anik had been Aggie's supervisor. But I hadn't met her the one time I'd been here, and I hadn't seen an Anik in the funeral guest book. So I was safe.

"This looks interesting." I held up the packet. "Okay if I look inside?"

Before Bramer could answer, I turned over the packet, opened the unsealed flap, and pulled out a length of red thread attached to a teeny gold-tone medallion imprinted with the agency's name.

"We give one of those to each of our clients when she leaves us," the director said. "We sell them in our gift shop, too. The proceeds help fund our programs. You've heard of the Kabbalah? The study of Jewish mysticism?"

I nodded.

"According to the Kabbalah, a red thread wound around Rachel's Tomb has protective powers. We thought it would be fitting, because of our connection with Rachel."

"It's a great idea," I said. "Who came up with it?"

Bramer hesitated. "Randy. He took care of ordering the threads from Israel and filling the envelopes, which we had printed. We handled the rest. Since he quit we've been making our own arrangements. He was a bright young man, enterprising. His death was such a waste."

The director checked his watch again and stood. "You can take that packet if you like. If you have any more questions, give me a call. Oh, and I'll ask Mr. Horton if he's willing to meet with you. Do you have a card?"

I handed him one.

"Excellent." Bramer peered at me. "You're sure we haven't met? Because I rarely forget a face, and you look *so* familiar."

CHAPTER TWENTY

THE FIRST THING I NOTICED ABOUT BARBARA ANIK WAS her eyes. They were kind eyes, perceptive eyes, almost the same shade of slate gray as the short hair that framed her full, relatively unlined face and set off the soft pink of her sweater.

"I'm definitely the *senior* staff person here," she said with amusement when I told her Bramer had told me she'd been with Rachel's Tent from its start. "I turned seventy-one last month. They had a cake for me—only one candle, thank goodness, or there would have been a conflagration."

I had put her in her mid-sixties and I told her so.

"I love what I do. Perhaps that keeps me young. And worrying about others doesn't allow me to spend time on my own concerns." She smiled. "The truth is, I dread the day they tell me I

have to retire. So does my family. I'll probably drive my poor husband and daughter crazy."

Her voice was rich and mellow, with a hint of an accent I
couldn't place.

"I'm a mutt as far as my speech goes," she said when I asked
about the accent. "I was born in Vienna and I lived there until I
was five years old, when my parents sent me to England on the
Kindertransport. That was just days before the Germans invaded
Poland and began the war. You know what that was? The Children's Transport?" When I nodded, she said, "I met my husband
Paul—he's American—when he was at Oxford. He's a professor
of economics. We lived in Atlanta and Chicago before settling
here."

"My maternal grandparents were survivors," I told her, not
with the intention of ingratiating myself. At least, I don't think so.

"Ah." She looked at me with interest. "Where are they
from?"

"Poland. They were in various forced-labor camps. They met
in Germany after the war and married, then came here a few years
later."

The words were shorthand for the harrowing period Zeidie
Irving talked about frequently, though I'm certain he spared us
many details. Bubbie G has talked about it less easily and less
often, so I hesitated before I asked the therapist whether she had
seen her parents again.

"No." Barbara sighed the word. "It took me a long time to
forgive them for sending me away, to understand their sacrifice."
She straightened a stack of papers on her tidy cherrywood desk.
"But you didn't come to write about me. Dr. Bramer said you
wanted success stories. Let's start with Cindy—that's not her real
name, of course."

She talked with affection and pride about her clients—a prostitute who had transformed her own life, a homeless woman who was now supporting herself and providing for her two young children, an attorney who had left an abusive boyfriend, a woman whose undiagnosed attention deficit disorder had prevented her from holding down a job. The stories were heartwarming, but my mind kept drifting to the packets in Bramer's office. Randy's idea.

"Thank you for sharing those wonderful stories," I said when the therapist had finished. "Dr. Bramer showed me one of the red-thread packets Rachel's Tent gives to clients when they leave. It's a lovely gesture."

Barbara smiled. "I have to admit I'm not a believer in red threads. I don't think it's healthy for our clients to rely on miracles. It gives them a false sense of security. But it's a popular item, and the proceeds from those we sell help Rachel's Tent, so I suppose everyone benefits."

"Dr. Bramer told me about the man who came up with the idea. Randy Creeley? He said Randy died of a drug overdose. It's so ironic and sad. He worked here in Rachel's Tent and didn't get the help you provide for so many others."

"Very sad." She nodded. "His death was a shock. But of course we didn't know he needed help."

"Of course not. He was a handyman, not a client. Was he close to any of the staff?"

The therapist fixed those gray eyes on me. I had the squirmy feeling that I'd tipped my hand. "I'd love to hear more of your successes," I said to fill the silence.

She linked her fingers and tapped them against her lips. "You're Aggie's friend," she said, without a trace of accusation or anger. "I thought I recognized your name. She had your picture on her desk, you know. She talked about you all the time. Did we ever meet?"

"No." I slid my hands along the leather arms of the chair and felt as though I were in my high school principal's office, where I'd been a frequent visitor.

"I didn't think so. Aggie was lovely, truly special. When she was killed we all felt the loss—the staff, her clients. I still think about her." Barbara rested her folded hands on her desk. "Why are you here, Molly? What can I do for you?" Her voice was gentle, soothing.

I started to cry. Fat tears rolled down my cheeks. I caught them with my tongue and tasted salt. I wiped my eyes with the tissue Barbara handed me.

She left the room and returned with two china cups and saucers, plastic spoons, and packets of sweetener. She placed a filled cup in front of me and resumed her seat, waiting patiently until I was cried out.

"I hate Styrofoam," she said, with a nod at the cup. "That's lemon-flavored tea. There are other flavors—or coffee, if you prefer."

"Lemon tea is perfect. You sound like my grandmother. She thinks a *gleyzele* tea is the answer to most problems."

"She may be right." Barbara smiled.

I added a packet of sweetener, stirred, and took a sip. The warm liquid was a balm to my throat. "Aggie talked about you, too. She said you were kind and honest. She said she learned a great deal from you."

"I learned a great deal from *her*. Do you want to tell me why you're here, Molly?"

I finished my tea. "The police found Randy with the locket I gave Aggie."

I hadn't planned to blurt that out or try to gauge the therapist's reaction, but I couldn't miss the shock in her eyes and the tremor in the lined hands that held the dainty cup. A second later she gazed at me without expression.

"Go on," she said.

"They think he and Aggie were involved. They think he killed her because she ended their relationship."

"But you don't believe it."

"No."

"The fact that he killed Aggie, or his motive for doing so?"

I was tempted to tell her that Randy's computer was missing; that his girlfriend had come to his funeral in disguise and had made incomprehensible comments about men who were following her. *The ones who killed Aggie. The ones who killed me.*

"His motive," I said.

"Because she was an observant Jew and Randy wasn't Jewish? Or because she didn't tell you?"

I took a moment to consider. "Both." Even if he *were* Jewish, why would she become involved with an ex-convict with a high school education and a drug addiction?

"Did you ever meet Randy?"

"I saw a photo. I know he was handsome, if that's what you're getting at."

"It was more than that. He had a magnetic personality, irresistible charm. He worked that charm on *me* a few times, and I should have known better," she admitted with more melancholy than regret. "From my experience, Molly, people don't always behave logically when it comes to matters of the heart. Perhaps Aggie was momentarily infatuated."

I shook my head.

"What if it was true, Molly?"

I flashed to the woman Gloria Lamont had seen sneaking into Randy's apartment. "It's not."

"All right, it's not." Barbara nodded. "But if it *were.* How would that make you feel?"

"Shouldn't I lie down on your couch?"

"If you prefer." She wasn't smiling.

I twisted the tissue. "Hurt. Sad that she didn't let me help her. She probably felt very lonely, isolated. *If* it were true."

"Do you feel responsible for Aggie's death, Molly?"

"In a way." I told her about turning down Aggie's request to accompany her to a prayer vigil. "I had therapy after Aggie was killed. I know I couldn't have predicted what happened."

Tell me how you feel, Molly.

I feel empty. I feel guilty. I wish I could turn back the clock. I don't know what you want me to tell you.

Whatever you want to say. There are no right or wrong answers, Molly. Whatever you tell me stays in this room.

I was angry at her.

When?

That night. I knew if I'd asked her to go somewhere with me, she would have. Anytime, anyplace. So I was angry that she asked, because it made me feel inadequate.

That's understandable.

I envied her. I wished I could be more like her. Focused, successful.

Envy is a human emotion, Molly.

If you envy someone, you can cause the person harm.

The evil eye? The ayin harah? Is that what you mean?

It's a powerful force. I read that if you envy someone, you cause that person's life to be judged, and your own, too.

Do you think your envy caused Aggie to be judged?

I don't know.

Did your envy put the knife in the hand of the person who stabbed her? . . .

"The police asked me about Randy after Aggie was killed," Barbara said. "I told them he was very respectful to Aggie, that I had no reason to believe he'd killed her."

"So there was nothing between them," I said, vindication flushing my face.

"Not then, no. Randy was friendly to everyone—*too* friendly sometimes." She hesitated. "But he was drawn to Aggie. I could tell from the way he looked at her, the way he reacted when she smiled at him. One time I entered her office without knocking. She was between clients and I needed a file. Randy was there. They weren't touching, but I sensed a sexual tension, as though I'd interrupted something."

"They could have been having an intense discussion," I insisted.

"Perhaps." Barbara regarded me with sympathy. "This happened months before Aggie was killed, and I never saw anything between them again. I didn't tell the police. I was afraid they would twist nothing into something."

"What about closer to the time she was killed? Was there friction between them?" I asked, moving to more comfortable ground.

"Not that I saw. But Aggie was troubled. She said she was concerned about a client, but given what you've just told me, it may have been about Randy."

"What makes you think that?"

The therapist was studying her hands, probably deciding what, if anything, to tell me. "I caught him going through her files. She phoned me from the field. She needed an address she'd left on her desk. When I entered her office Randy was standing next to an open filing cabinet."

I felt a prickling of interest. "What did he say?"

"He made up a silly explanation for his being there. He begged me not to tell Aggie, but of course, I did. She asked me not to tell Dr. Bramer. She wanted to do it herself. I thought Randy was just nosy. But if you're right, and he had a drug habit to support . . ."

Blackmail? "Did you tell the police?"

"I assumed Dr. Bramer would do that." She played with the strand of pearls at her neck.

"But then the police would have asked you to confirm what happened," I said, thinking aloud. "They would have asked you for details."

A flush spread up her neck. We had switched roles.

"He told me he was with his sister when Aggie was killed," Barbara said. "He had proof, but he was terrified the police wouldn't believe him, because he was an ex-convict. To me he was like a puppy that digs up the garden, always getting into mischief. He wasn't a pit bull. I didn't think he was capable of murder. And why would he kill Aggie?" Her accent had become more pronounced, her tone imploring. "She didn't say anything to you about Randy?"

The police had questioned me. I was her best friend, I would know things she hadn't told her parents. Was there a boyfriend she had dropped? A jealous rival or coworker? Had Aggie been upset about anything? Worried? Afraid of anyone? Connors had posed the same questions days ago. My answer to everything had been no.

Now I wondered. "Did you tell the police Aggie was worried about a client?"

The therapist shook her head. "They would have subpoenaed her files. Women confide their darkest secrets with the assurance that those secrets will stay inside Rachel's Tent. I couldn't subject them to a police inquiry that would violate their privacy and possibly endanger them. And what would the police find, after all?"

"What if one of Aggie's clients killed her?"

Barbara frowned. "I never believed that for a minute. Aggie had a wonderful rapport with all her clients."

"But you said she was worried."

"About a *client's* safety. Some of our women come from abusive relationships. Aggie asked me how far she should push a client to go to the police, whether the police could really ensure the woman's safety."

"When was that?"

"Sometime in early July, two or three weeks before she was killed. It was after the holiday party at the Horton residence. They invite all the staff and clients twice a year. July Fourth and Christmas. Aggie was jittery at the party. She spilled food on her dress—a pastel silk, so everything showed. She was mortified. She would have gone home, but she had come with another staff member. Mrs. Horton loaned her something."

Aggie hadn't mentioned anything about the weekend, or ruining her dress. It was the kind of thing we would have laughed about. "Was Randy there?"

"I'm sure he was. I can't recall seeing him."

"How many clients did Aggie handle?"

"Between fifteen and twenty." Barbara was losing patience. "I can't discuss any of them with you."

"But what if—"

"A client's expectation of confidentiality is sacrosanct." The gray eyes flashed. "Aggie would have been the first to agree. She would not have wanted her clients' confidentiality violated."

"I think she'd want her killer caught," I said.

"She was your best friend, and you are grieving for her. You want answers, you want justice. Don't presume to think you know what Aggie would have wanted." In a gentler voice she said, "In the end it didn't matter, did it. The client Aggie worried about left Rachel's Tent. And the police found Aggie's locket with Randy."

I wondered how much of Barbara Anik's attitude toward the police had been shaped by her childhood. I wondered, too, what would have happened if Aggie had reported Randy to Bramer— I was convinced that she hadn't—or if Barbara had done so.

I'm sure the therapist wondered the same thing.

She sighed. "I'm too old for this." She sounded weary and sad, and looked all of her seventy-one years.

★ ★ ★

I was in the lobby, taking another look at the mural, when I heard Bramer bellowing my name.

He'd figured out where he'd seen me, I thought, forcing a smile as I turned to face his anger.

"I'm glad I caught you," he said when he was at my side. "Mr. Horton will meet you Monday morning at nine-fifteen." He handed me a business card. HORTON ENTERPRISES, with a Wilshire address. "If you can't make it, be sure to let him know. He's a very busy man."

Bramer sounded as though he'd arranged a visit with royalty. I wondered if he expected me to curtsy when I met the man.

"Mr. Horton is delighted that you're doing the story," the director said. "But I wouldn't bring up Randy or his drug addiction. Mr. Horton had high hopes for Randy, so it's a painful subject."

"I understand."

"Excellent. I hope you enjoyed your talk with Barbara. Was she able to give you what you needed?"

"She gave me a great deal to think about," I said.

CHAPTER TWENTY-ONE

Saturday, February 21. 9:35 A.M. 6100 block of Sepulveda Boulevard. A woman took a cab to UCLA. The cabbie pressed her to pay him. "I'll pay when we get there," she said. "You are so beautiful," the cabbie replied. "I bet it's good." The woman told him she wasn't comfortable with him talking to her like that. The cabbie persisted in demanding payment. The woman refused. The cabbie stopped at a gas station, pulled the woman from the cab, and began yelling at her. The woman told the station's employees to call the police. The cabbie pushed her, causing her sandals to come off, then kicked her in the small of her back. The woman finally reached a pay phone and called the police. The cabbie left, taking the victim's sandals. (Culver City)

I SAW AGGIE'S MOTHER AT B'NAI YESHURUN, THE LARGE Modern Orthodox synagogue where Zack has officiated as rabbi for the past seven months. The shul is well attended on most Shabbats, a testament to its growing membership and to Zack. This Saturday the number of congregants was swelled by family and guests who had come to celebrate his *aufruf,* the calling up of the groom to the Torah, usually on the Shabbat before his wedding.

In our case, two Shabbats before the wedding. Zack and I had wanted to share the happiness and import of the day, but Ashkenazi Orthodox tradition says the bride and groom don't see each other during the seven days before the wedding. The idea is to heighten the anticipation, and maybe to ward off bad luck. Not everyone is strict about the custom, and my anticipation didn't need heightening, but after one failed marriage, I was taking no chances.

Yesterday, after leaving Rachel's Tent, the *aufruf* had been the farthest thing from my mind. I had sat in my car, trying to make sense of what I'd learned, and had been startled when I looked at my watch. Ten to twelve. Sunset in February arrives early, and I had a lot to do in the five hours before Shabbat would begin.

I stopped at the florist's to okay the linen for the dinner reception and make sure Raul had the correct delivery address for the floral arrangement my parents had ordered for Zack and his family. I shopped for groceries. I packed a suitcase for my weekend at my parents' and picked up my new suit from the dressmaker. Then I picked up Bubbie G and two loaves of the challa she had baked. Bubbie, who will turn eighty this May, is thin and looks frail but is surprisingly spry. Even with her cane, which she uses grudgingly, she had me hurrying to keep up with her as she walked to my car.

The house smelled like Shabbat. Chicken soup with dill simmered on the stove. A French roast warmed in the oven, along with a potato kugel and one of Bubbie's challas, which are the best. Zack phoned to wish me a good Shabbos and thank my parents for the flowers. My mother, Bubbie, and I lit our Shabbat candles, and they worked their magic, ushering in a heavenly stillness and quiet that soothed my soul.

My father and two younger brothers went to shul. After setting the dining room table, Liora and I joined my mother and Bubbie G in the family room, where we recited the Shabbat and Friday evening prayers, singing parts and saying the rest aloud to include Bubbie, who is having difficulty even with the large-print siddur we bought her. I had a wave of nostalgia for the Friday evenings when all four of us Blume girls would harmonize prayers and other songs we'd learned in school or camp. Sometimes my mother joined in. Other times, like tonight, she would watch us and smile. She looked wistful now, and I sensed she was remembering those Friday nights, too, maybe wondering how long before Liora would marry and leave this big house that suddenly had so many empty rooms. Probably within the year, considering how often people call to set up my youngest sister. And my brother Noah has been dating someone for six months. . . .

An hour or so later my father and brothers returned. My father is almost fifty-seven, tall and broad-shouldered, and though he has more gray in his dark brown hair than he had a year ago, he still looks young, at least to me. My friends say he reminds them of Harrison Ford, without the scar and the earring. Noah and Joey are lankier. Noah is twenty-five, an overachiever and second-year law student at UCLA keenly aware that he's following in the able footsteps of my sister Mindy. Joey, two years younger and two inches shorter (I'm not sure which bothers him more), has a BS in computer science but no job because of the glut of unemployed programmers following the dot-com crash. He's been helping my dad, who hopes Joey will like the construction business and take over when he retires, something my dad talks about but the rest of the family agrees won't happen anytime soon.

My father always blesses us on Friday night. He usually goes from oldest to youngest, but tonight he saved me for last and rested his large, calloused hands on my head longer than usual. His lips lingered against my forehead.

"Mazel tov, sweetie," he murmured, and we hugged each other tightly. "Happy?"

"So happy."

"*Bli ayin hara,*" my grandmother said.

My mom joined our little circle. Liora did, too. I was waiting for Joey to make a flip comment—he's tenderhearted but uncomfortable with sentimentality. But he didn't say anything, and when we took our seats, I saw that his hazel eyes were misty.

Noah noticed, too. "Joey's all mushy."

"Don't tease him," Liora said.

Joey's face had turned red. "I'm worried that with all the money Dad's shelling out for Molly's wedding, there won't be anything left for mine."

"You mean in twenty years when you're all grown-up?" Noah said.

"A hundred bucks says I get married before you do. What's *taking* you so long, anyway?"

"*Za nisht kayn k'nacker,*" Bubbie said.

"I'm *not* a big shot, Bubbie. Noah started it."

"Cool it," my dad said. He likes decorum at the Shabbos table.

"They're just joking, Steven," my mother said.

My father made kiddush over the wine and recited the blessing over Bubbie's challa. Between courses we sang *zemirot* and discussed the week's Torah portion and neighborhood news. Someone had become engaged, someone had given birth, someone was moving to Baltimore because housing here was so outrageously high. Mr. Friedland was in rehab, recovering from hip surgery, and had struck up a romance with Mrs. Goldowski.

"Maybe you should go out with Zack's grandfather, Bubbie," Joey teased. "He's a cutie."

"And he's a *greeneh*—like you, Bubbie," Noah added. An immigrant.

My grandmother shook her head and smiled. Even before the macular degeneration, some of the sparkle had gone out of her blue eyes when Zeidie Irving died.

At one point my dad's walkie-talkie crackled with static from the kitchen counter. My father and my brothers belong to an L.A. Jewish emergency-response organization that serves the Hancock Park–Miracle Mile area. Zack belongs, too. My dad went into the kitchen and returned a minute later to tell us the call had been answered. Joey looked disappointed.

Zack usually walks over on Friday nights, but he had a house full of company. After dinner Noah took a stack of texts to the breakfast room, and my dad fell asleep on the family room sectional sofa reading the local Jewish paper. Bubbie dozed next to him, snoring lightly, while my mom, Liora, and I ate sunflower seeds and played Rummy Q with Joey at a game table in the corner. Joey almost always wins, unless Edie plays, but tonight he was distracted and Liora won.

"I was just kidding, Molly," he said when everyone else had gone upstairs and we were putting away the tiles. "About Dad spending too much for the wedding."

I smiled. "I know that."

"Zack's a cool guy."

"Very cool," I agreed. Something was on Joey's mind. I wondered what it was.

"Ron phoned the other day," he said a moment later. "He

knows I've been looking for a programming job, and he wants to
set up an interview for me at a company he deals with. Would
that be a problem for you?"

"Ron and I aren't enemies, Joey. If he can help you, that's
great. But I thought you liked the construction business."

"I do. I love working with Dad, and I have ideas about ex-
panding the business. But I'd like to give computer programming
a try. It's why I got the BS. I told Dad, and he's fine with it."

I nodded, and wondered if that was so.

"Ron asked about you, by the way. He sounded sad, Molly. I
think he's sorry he blew it."

A year ago that might have given me pleasure. "Divorce *is*
sad, Joey. Ron's dating several women, so you don't have to worry
about him."

I kissed my brother's cheek and said good night.

I didn't think about Aggie or Randy and the packets of red
thread until I was lying in my bed in what used to be my bedroom. Staring into the dark, I wondered what Barbara Anik had
interrupted when she entered Aggie's office unannounced, wondered about the client Aggie had encouraged to go to the police,
wondered why Aggie had been so nervous at a party she had told
me nothing about.

I thought about her again when I awoke this morning. How
much I missed her and wished she were with me today, how
happy she would have been for me, how senseless and tragic her
death was. Now I was in the front pew in the high-ceilinged
sanctuary, surrounded by my family and Zack's, and I was focused
on the man on the other side of the wood-panel *mechitza* that
separated the women's and men's sections, the man who had
stolen my heart twice.

The morning service was over, and the Torah reading was about to start. I opened my text to this week's portion. *Mishpatim.* Laws.

" 'And these are the ordinances. . . ,' " the shul's official reader, Simon, began.

I paged ahead, calculating how long before Zack would be called up. Out of the corner of my eye I saw my mother watching me, amusement in her warm brown eyes. I'm always amazed at how easily she can read me.

"Lost my place," I mouthed.

She smiled and pointed to the line Simon was reading. I ran my index finger right to left beneath the Hebrew words to anchor my attention, but I was still only half listening when a verse jolted me into awareness.

"One who strikes a man, so that he dies, shall surely be put to death. . . ."

I had a name for Aggie's killer, but no clear motive. Had she rebuffed Randy's advances? Had she discovered that he'd been blackmailing her clients, and possibly those of other social workers? That he'd been selling drugs?

"If a man shall act intentionally against his fellow to kill him with guile," Simon continued in the ancient traditional cantillation, "from My Altar shall you take him to die."

Had Randy followed her from her house that night? Had he planned to talk her out of reporting him to Bramer? Or had he left his apartment intending to kill her? And if I had been there with her . . . ?

In a large, close-knit family like mine, a sigh is never just a sigh. Mine had drawn the attention of half the pew except for Bubbie G, who probably hadn't heard me, and Liora, who was absorbed in the reading. Mindy and Gitty flashed me sympathetic smiles. Edie was frowning at me.

Zack's mother, Sandy, was gazing at me, a question in her blue eyes, which were hooded by the brim of her black velvet pillbox.

"I'm just a little emotional, because of the day," I told her, though she didn't ask. I felt a little guilty when she hugged me and said, "Me, too."

My mother's look said she knew better. She squeezed my hand and held it. I forced myself to return my attention to the Torah portion and safer ground: laws dealing with lesser crimes and civil torts; the commandment to extend free loans and show sensitivity to the helpless and abandoned; instructions for maintaining the integrity of the judicial process and dispensing justice.

I supposed justice had been dispensed. Creeley was dead. But why had Doreen disguised herself? Who were the people she feared? And what, if anything, did they have to do with Aggie and with Randy Creeley?

Edie was watching me. Pushing Randy from my mind, I concentrated on the reading. At one point Mindy left the pew to help her two little girls, who were staggering under the weight of an enormous, beribboned wicker basket as they tottered up the aisle and handed out the blue voile bags Zack's mom had filled with Jordan almonds and fruit gems and other candy. The candy symbolizes the wish for a sweet life. The almonds represent fertility, although if the Torah reading didn't conclude soon, I thought, I'd probably be too old to conceive.

Ten long minutes later Simon finished.

"Let's go." Edie stood.

With a swishing of clothes we all filed out of the pew and crowded in front of the five-foot-high *mechitza*. Parting the panels of the ivory lace curtain at the top, I stole a glance at Zack, sitting on his high-backed chair on the platform at the front of the room. I was hoping he'd look my way, but he was facing the congregation.

Ron was staring at me. He winked when we made eye contact. In spite of what he'd told Joey, I wasn't surprised by the wink, or by his presence. As I mentioned, he's on the shul board. Plus his ego probably hadn't let him stay away. *Look at me, see how cool I am even though my ex-wife is marrying my high school pal.* I cast a quick glance behind me and was relieved to see that my ex-mother-in-law wasn't there.

I was reflecting on how difficult this day must be for Ron's parents, who have always been pleasant to me even after the divorce, and for Ron, too, despite his bravado, when the cantor bellowed Zack's Hebrew name with the pomp you'd use to introduce a Vegas headliner.

My heart racing, I watched as Zack, looking oh so debonair and sexy in a navy suit and Zegna tie I'd helped him pick, made his way to the center of the room and the bima, the elevated table where the Torah scroll is read. Once there, he turned toward me. Our eyes met. For one moment it was as though the world had stopped and we were alone in the large sanctuary. Then he unfolded the fringed white *tallit* I'd bought him, draped it around his broad shoulders, and recited the blessing.

A minute or so later, he recited another blessing. The room reverberated with cries of "Mazel tov!" and the rapid-fire *thunk*s of the voile bags we all hurled over the *mechitza* at Zack, who had ducked and taken cover behind the *tallit* to deflect the sweets-filled missiles, much to the shrieking delight of the kids who swooped down like locusts to claim them. He didn't escape completely. I'm pretty sure I got him, and Edie did, too. Bubbie G landed one on Ron. I think he was her target all along.

Zack was dancing around the bima with his father and mine and other men, including my brothers and brothers-in-law. I was flushed with exhilaration, grinning and kissing family and friends and some people I didn't even know, when I turned to accept a hug and was startled to see Aggie's mother in the entrance to the women's section.

We exchanged smiles. I don't know if mine showed my sudden awkwardness. Hers looked fragile, and I was touched that she'd come to share in Zack's and my happiness. I was also saddened by the ghost of Aggie that she'd brought with her, and embarrassed by the conspicuousness of celebration. The white roses along the walls and at the four corners of the bima, the vines draped along the top of the *mechitza*. The squeals of the children, the laughter, the jubilant singing and dancing.

I'd tried phoning the Lashers during the past few days. The line had been constantly busy, and I'd assumed they'd left the receiver off the hook. On Thursday I'd passed their Mansfield Avenue house on the way to Edie's, but I didn't stop. I'm not sure why.

In the months after Aggie was murdered, I'd visited her parents at least once a week, usually more often. When my family expressed concern that my involvement in their lives wasn't healthy for them or me, I was defensive: Aggie was an only child. I had spent countless hours and many nights in the Lashers' home. It was a mitzvah to comfort those who have lost loved ones, and what better comfort could I provide than filling some of their lonely hours and telling them stories about Aggie that would preserve her memory and lighten their pain?

I didn't tell the Lashers everything. I didn't tell them that on that fateful July night, Aggie had asked me to accompany her to the prayer vigil. I didn't tell them that I'd been too lazy to change out of my shorts; that I'd had little interest in prayers, or faith in their power; that I'd preferred staying home and watching a rerun of *Will & Grace*. I didn't tell them that at the time Aggie's lifeless body was being tossed like garbage into a Dumpster miles from where she was last seen, I was flirting on the phone with a guy whose last name I can't recall.

I made my way through the throng of women and children toward Mrs. Lasher. I didn't know what to say, how to juggle grief and joy. When I reached her, she hugged me and kissed my cheeks. Without lipstick or blusher her face looked pale against the dark brown of the wavy, shoulder-length wig she had left in her closet for a year or so after Aggie died. She had always reminded me of a butterfly—pretty in a delicate way, sunny, a little restless as she flitted from room to room. She was subdued now, dormant, her color hidden inside her folded wings.

She clasped my hands. "Mazel tov, Molly. Binyomin and I are so happy for you."

There was something brave about her tremulous smile, something wistful and painful and hopeful. Her smile said that she saw Aggie when she looked at me, that she was struck again with the realization that she would never walk her daughter to the chuppa, would never see grandchildren, that despite her heartache she genuinely wished me well in this second chance at joy.

Tears filled my eyes. "Thank you so much for coming, Mrs. Lasher. I wish . . ."

"I know." Her brown eyes glistened. "We almost didn't come. We didn't want to make you sad, Molly. But how could we *not* come? You're like a daughter to us. You were a sister to Aggie."

She leaned closer. "The detective told us he talked to you," she said in an undertone, although with the noise in the room no one could have heard her. "Knowing won't bring Aggie back, the pain will always be there. But now we can move on. We *have* to move on, Molly."

Someone grabbed me by the waist and spun me around. Lola, one of my grandmother's Amazonian friends. She pressed me into her pillowy chest and kissed me with gusto, and when I turned back, Mrs. Lasher was gone.

I thought about her as I recited the blessings for the month of Adar that would begin on Sunday—a month distinguished by great rejoicing, which was why Zack and I had chosen it for our wedding. I thought about her and her husband as I prayed that the month would be filled with goodness and sustenance, with "peace, joy and gladness, salvation and consolation."

I didn't see Mrs. Lasher or her husband at the buffet kiddush Zack's parents hosted in the shul's reception hall. To be honest, I tried not to think about them or Aggie during the kiddush and the family lunch that followed.

Later, in my apartment, at the end of a wonderful day of celebration, I thought about them and wondered again why Binyomin Lasher had attended the funeral of the man who killed his daughter. I wondered how they had reacted to news of the letter Creeley had written.

I had changed into a skirt and sweater and was freshening my makeup when my cell phone rang. Zack, I thought, telling me he was on the way to pick me up for our appointment with the calligrapher.

It was Trina Creeley.

"He trashed my apartment," she said, her words a crescendo of wailing, like an approaching siren. "The front-door lock is broken. Everything's a mess. I can't stay there tonight."

I put down my lipstick. "You know who did this?"

"A man phoned a day after Randy died. He said his name was Jim. I don't know if that's his real name. And his voice sounded funny, like he was using something to change it. He said Randy had a package that belonged to him. I told him I didn't know what he was talking about, but he didn't believe me."

"Maybe it was burglars," I said, leaning against the sink.

"He phoned tonight right after I got home, so I know he's watching my apartment. He said he wouldn't have had to do that if I'd looked for the package. I told him again I didn't have any package. He said I'd better find it. He killed Randy, and now he's going to kill me!"

My heart beat faster. "Did you call the police?"

"He said no police. He said he'd know if I called them. I need to get some things from my apartment and find a place to stay until I figure this out. I can't call my father. He— I just can't. Can you help me?"

"Trina—"

"I'm sorry about the other day. I don't blame you for being angry. I thought maybe he sent you."

"Where are you now, Trina?"

"In the ladies' room at Grauman's Chinese. You said you wanted to help. Will you come? Please? Because I don't know who else to call."

CHAPTER TWENTY-TWO

ZACK PARKED IN A LOADING ONLY ZONE AROUND THE corner from the theater.

"I don't want you going inside," he said again. "What if it's a setup? Why doesn't she want you to phone Connors?"

I had relayed Trina's explanation when I'd phoned him, and again when he'd picked me up. I repeated it now. "She's waiting in the restroom for a change of clothes, Zack. Obviously, you can't go in there."

"Well, come right back. Then I'll go and bring her to the car." He didn't look happy. "Buy a ticket, Molly. If this Jim followed her, he'll be looking for anything unusual. You don't want to draw attention to yourself."

I nodded. "Why don't I just wait for her to change, Zack? She's terrified. At least she knows me."

"If this guy was at the funeral, he may have seen you and may recognize you if you walk out with her. He won't be looking for a woman leaving with a guy wearing a yarmulke. Tell her who I am, what I'm wearing. Tell her I'll meet her at the concession counter."

I got out of the car and rounded the corner. The sidewalk was packed with people waiting in line for one of several new films, including the new Hugh Grant romantic comedy. The forecourt was crowded, too. Crowds are good, I decided. Then I wondered if Jim was hiding among them, watching.

I imagined eyes on me as I bought a ticket and handed it to a man inside the lobby. He tore it in half and glanced at my large tote, probably suspecting that I was trying to sneak snacks inside. I kept smiling and he waved me through.

Trina had told me she would be in the women's restroom to my left. I found the restroom but didn't see her. Stood up again, I thought with a surge of anger. Or maybe she was playing games. I phoned her on my cell and was surprised when she answered on the first ring.

"Where are you?" she whispered.

Her fear made me shiver. "In the restroom. Where are you?"

The door to a stall squeaked open and out she came. I gave her my tote and reached for her black vinyl one. She hesitated, then handed it to me. It was heavy.

"Don't lose that," she said.

"My fiancé's wearing navy Dockers and a gray sweater over a white T-shirt." I kept my voice low, though I doubted that any of the other women in the restroom were interested in our conversation, or that they could hear us over the sonata of flushing toilets and groaning faucets. "Phone me when you're ready. He'll meet you at the concession stand."

"Why can't you wait?" Her tone was plaintive.

I told her. She blanched, then nodded and disappeared into a stall.

A minute later I was back in the forecourt. I sauntered along the sidewalk, rounded the corner, and got into the car.

"She's there," I told Zack. "She'll phone me when she's ready." I put Trina's bag at my feet and resisted the temptation to unzip it and peek inside. "Thanks for not being upset about all this."

"She needed help, Molly. Why would I be upset?"

"I forgot to cancel Galit," I said, just now remembering.

"I phoned her on my way to your place. We're tentative for tomorrow afternoon, assuming you can leave Trina. If not, I told Galit we'll figure something out."

I wished I could kiss him. "Have I told you recently how much I love you?"

"Twice in the last hour. But keep it coming." He smiled.

Ten minutes passed. I wanted to phone Trina, but Zack said to wait. A minute or so later my phone sang "Für Elise." I flipped it open and handed it to Zack.

"So she'll know your voice," I said.

He put the phone to his ear. "Trina? This is Zack. I'm with Molly. Are you ready? Okay, I'm on my way." He shut the phone and handed it to me.

"Keep it," I said. "In case she needs to reach you."

Zack gave me his phone and left. I maneuvered myself around the gear stick on the center console into the driver's seat in case the driver from Parking Enforcement who had been circling the block ordered me to move the car.

With my hands on the steering wheel, I waited and checked my watch for seven minutes that seemed like a hundred before Zack appeared with Trina. They were walking close together and looked like a couple. She had switched her black leggings for my denim skirt and wrapped my Burberry shawl around her neck. The streetlamp gleamed on the European hairs of my straight blond wig.

Zack opened the back door for Trina, then slipped into the front. She gave me her address, on Selma.

"I'll drive around in case someone's following us," I said. The words sounded ridiculous to my ears.

I drove to Vine, then to Sunset, then back up to Hollywood and the address on Selma.

I circled the block slowly. Zack didn't see anyone lurking near Trina's two-story building, so I parked. He took a flashlight from the glove compartment and told us to wait while he made sure no one was in the apartment.

"I don't want you going in there," I said, but he was already sprinting up the walkway to the front door. A moment later he was inside.

I had many questions for Trina and exercised great effort not to ask them. I didn't know what she was thinking. We waited in silence for Zack to return, which took about five minutes but felt considerably longer.

"All clear." He handed me the flashlight. "Molly, go with Trina. I'll watch from here. Make it fast. Don't turn on any lights."

I put my phone on vibrate mode and told Trina to do the same with hers.

Inside the apartment, I shut the door behind us and switched on the flashlight. We were in the living room.

"That bastard!" Her face was pinched with anger and fear.

Even with only the light of the narrow beam, I could see that someone had done a thorough job of ransacking the place. The sofa had been overturned, its underside and cushions ripped. The backings of several framed posters had been slashed. The contents of the wood-tone TV stand—DVDs and videocassettes—were on the floor.

"I need stuff from my bedroom," Trina said.

I handed her the flashlight and followed her down a short, narrow hall. Her mattress had suffered the same fate as her sofa, and the contents of all six drawers of her dresser had been emptied onto the carpeted floor.

She gave me the flashlight. I focused it on mounds of clothing, which she pawed through. She stuffed a pair of sweats, underwear, and sweaters into a suitcase she dragged out from the closet, then added slacks and two pairs of shoes.

The contents of her medicine cabinet had been dumped onto the tile floor. Trina took a makeup bag and a vial of sleeping pills ("I've been having trouble sleeping," she told me) and left the remainder.

The kitchen floor was a puddle of egg yolks, sugar, and flour. A recipe for heartache.

"I had four hundred dollars in that canister," she told me, pointing to a shattered ceramic jar shaped like a hen. She started to cry.

"I can lend you money," I said.

She shook her head. "I have a credit card and enough in the bank. It's not the money, it's the violation." She picked up a piece of the jar and put it on the counter. She hugged her arms. "I don't think I can live here again."

Michael Jackson said the same thing after police searched Neverland last November. I guess it doesn't matter whether you're a salesperson at Frederick's living in a one-bedroom apartment on Selma or an international celebrity with a multimillion-dollar home in Santa Barbara.

Trina took a last look around.

Then we left.

CHAPTER TWENTY-THREE

WHEN WE ARRIVED AT MY APARTMENT TRINA WAS AL-
most catatonic, staring at nothing and answering in monosyllables. She was shivering, too. Shock, Zack and I agreed. After
moving stacks of gifts off the sofa bed in my spare room, I made
up the bed while he prepared a cup of hot chocolate that Trina
finished without seeming to realize she'd had anything to drink.
I gave her towels, and a new toothbrush I'd bought for my wedding night, and sent her to bed in a pair of my pajamas and an
extra comforter when her shaking wouldn't stop.

In the car Trina had asked us to take her to a nearby hotel,
but Zack and I had worried about leaving her alone in her panicked state. And to be honest, I wanted to talk to her about
Randy and Aggie. I still felt I'd made the right decision, but I had

reservations. Yes, I felt sorry for her and wanted to help her. I hadn't heard the phone call from Jim, but the condition of her apartment proved she had good reason to be frightened. She couldn't stay there with the front door unsecured even if she did call the police, which she refused to do even after I told her about Connors—that he was smart and trustworthy and would know how to handle Jim.

Her refusal bothered me. It made me wonder if she had another reason for not calling the police. And the fact that someone had trashed her place and threatened her with bodily harm made me nervous. I was fairly certain no one had followed us here, but what if I was wrong? And in spite of her explanations, I didn't understand why she'd turned to me instead of family or friends.

Zack voiced similar concerns. "You don't know anything about her," he said when we were alone in my breakfast nook. "She could be running from the police."

"It's just for tonight," I said, though I had no idea what to do with her tomorrow. Then I thought about Norm, Mindy's husband, and the nursing home he leases.

I phoned Mindy, explained about Trina, and asked if Norm had an empty bed Trina could use for a few days.

"Why did she contact *you*?" my sister asked. "She has family."

"She doesn't want to involve them."

"But it's okay to involve you?"

I sighed, mainly because Mindy was right. "She didn't ask to stay here. That was my idea. Can you ask Norm? Please?" I was hungry. I took a bag of popcorn and placed it in the microwave.

"Hold on." A moment later Mindy was back. "Every bed is filled. Good news for us, not so good for your guest. What about Rachel's Tent?"

"No."

"Why not? It's perfect."

"Randy Creeley worked there." I filled her in on my conversations with William Bramer and Barbara Anik, aware that Zack was listening. I couldn't tell what he was thinking, but I could guess. "What if Randy was blackmailing one of Aggie's clients, Min? And Aggie found out, and threatened to expose him, and he killed her?"

"I don't see what that has to do with Trina staying at Rachel's Tent. Did you sense they were trying to cover up Aggie's murder?"

"No." I told her about Randy snooping through Aggie's files, and the packets with the red thread. "Maybe Randy was using the packets to distribute drugs."

"A clever idea, if it's true. If it *is,* do you think Bramer knew what was going on?"

"He didn't seem concerned. And he let me keep one of the packets." The microwave *ping*ed. "Of course, Randy hadn't worked there in almost a year."

"Most likely it's just business, sweetie. Randy figured out how to make a few extra bucks. Everybody sells the red threads. Why shouldn't Rachel's Tent, considering the agency's name? Suggest Rachel's Tent to Trina, Molly. Let her decide."

"Maybe I will." I hung up and faced Zack. "I was going to tell you. I was there yesterday morning, and after that the day got so crazy, I didn't have a chance."

He nodded. "Why didn't you go Thursday, after the funeral? Because of your headache?"

"In a way."

I was relieved that he sounded curious, not angry. I emptied the popcorn into a glass bowl and took it to the table, along with two tumblers and two bottles of Diet Peach Snapple.

"Remember Randy's girlfriend, the one Gloria Lamont tried to phone?"

"Doreen." He took a handful of popcorn and tossed a few kernels into his mouth.

"I saw her at the funeral. I know it's crazy, but I followed her."

Zack stopped chewing. He listened intently while I told him everything that had happened. Almost everything—I down-played my fear and omitted the blow to my head.

"You could have been badly hurt, Molly." His gray-blue eyes were grave. "You could have been killed."

"I don't think she wanted to hurt me." The bruise on my head throbbed in protest. "She was frightened. She thought people were following her."

"Who?"

"She kept saying 'they.' She said they killed Aggie, and they killed her."

"Maybe she's paranoid."

The thought had occurred to me, too. "What if someone *is* following Doreen—like this guy Jim? Randy is the common de-nominator between Doreen and Trina, and he's dead."

Zack didn't answer. I was debating whether to tell him Doreen knew my address when I realized he was looking at something behind me. I turned and saw Trina in the doorway. Without makeup, she looked like a young girl. A sad, frightened young girl.

"I can't sleep," she said. "I keep seeing what he did to my apartment, hearing his voice. It was so . . . nasty. So cold." Her hand had crept to the chain around her neck.

I pulled out the chair next to me and patted the seat. "Do you want something to eat?" I asked when she was sitting. "Other than popcorn, I mean."

She shook her head. "I heard you mention Doreen. Where did you see her?"

"At the funeral."

Trina looked puzzled. "She was there?"

"She was wearing a red wig, but I figured out it was her. Randy's neighbor described her. At least, I think it was her."

"I saw all the gifts on the floor." Trina had apparently lost interest in Doreen. "When are you two getting married?"

"In eleven days." I threw in a silent *bli ayin harah* even though Bubbie wasn't there to prompt me.

"You must be excited, huh?" She tried a smile, but looked pensive. "I can go to a hotel, it's no big deal. I don't want to put you out."

"You're not putting me out," I assured her.

"I'm sorry I stood you up. My dad said you'd been by, asking lots of questions. And at the funeral you were sitting with that cop. Jim said no cops. Can I change my mind about food?" she asked shyly. "I'm really hungry."

I warmed up half a frozen pizza and some cream of broccoli soup that comes in a carton and tastes pretty good. Cooking for one isn't much fun, and aside from preparing the occasional meal, since my divorce I've been relying on takeout and lots of broiled fish and chicken.

The aroma of tomato sauce, mushrooms, and broccoli filled my tiny kitchen and gave it a cozy feeling that belied the evening's drama and the reason Trina was here. She devoured the soup and two slices of pizza, eating as though she hadn't seen food in days.

"That was perfect," she told me. "Thanks."

I had refrained from engaging her in conversation, but I had so many questions. I began with Doreen.

"I met her a couple of times," Trina said, nibbling on a third slice of pizza, cold by now, but she didn't seem to care. "I never thought she was good for Randy. She met him at NA. Randy didn't trust her. Not at the end."

"Why not?" Zack asked.

"She was a snoop. One time he came home and found her there, reading his journal."

"She had a key to his apartment?"

Trina nodded. "Another time he found her using his laptop. She said she was surfing the Web, but he knew she was trying to read his files."

So Doreen had lied to Gloria Lamont. "Where *is* his laptop? It wasn't in the apartment when I was there with Mrs. Lamont."

"Randy took it to my place the morning before he died. His journal, too. He didn't want to leave them around with Doreen coming over all the time. He told her he was having the laptop repaired. Now it's gone." A flash of anger sparked in her eyes. "He took it."

"Jim?"

She nodded. Her hand was at her neck, sliding up and down the chain.

"What about the journal?" I asked.

"He took it, too. I had it under my mattress." She opened a Snapple and sipped straight from the bottle, ignoring the glass I'd given her.

"Why didn't your brother just end things with Doreen?" Zack asked.

"He wanted to. But Doreen told him she was pregnant with his baby. I told him she was lying. I said, go with her to the doctor next time, get a paternity test. But then he died." Her eyes filled with tears. "I think she knows who killed him. That's why she disappeared. She's scared."

"The police say he overdosed, Trina." I said it gently, not wanting to upset her.

"No way! He was through with drugs. He thought he was going to be a father. Why would he kill himself?"

It was a good question. I could see that it had Zack thinking, too. "Did you tell that to the police?"

"Your cop friend said he'd check into it." Trina sniffed. "He said maybe Randy didn't mean to kill himself, maybe the stress of having a kid, blah, blah, blah. He said he'd talk to Doreen. Then he said he couldn't find her. How hard did he try?" She took another swig of the Snapple. "You asked why I don't want the cops involved? They didn't give a damn about Randy, if he lived or died. They don't give a damn about me." Tears spilled down her cheeks. She wiped them with her hand.

I wanted to tell her that Connors wasn't like that, that he would care. I knew she wasn't ready to hear it. "Why would someone kill Randy?"

"Maybe it had something to do with what he had on his laptop. He had all his business stuff on it. And he was writing letters to people he knew years ago."

I wondered if the letters had anything to do with his snooping through Aggie's files. "Do you think he was planning to blackmail people?"

Trina frowned. "Why would you think that? No, he was writing to say he was sorry. It was part of his NA program. He was working his fourth step, where he writes down all the people and things he resents, and how he played a part in those resentments? He wrote all that in his journal. The fifth step is where you read everything to someone else. I don't remember what six and seven are, but your eighth step is when you write down everybody you've ever done anything wrong to, and your ninth step is making amends. Randy wasn't even finished with his fourth step, but he skipped to nine, 'cause he felt bad about a lot of stuff he'd done. He said it was like having a pile of bricks on his chest, day and night."

Randy making amends wasn't what I'd expected, although his father had mentioned that Randy has asked forgiveness several weeks ago, from him and from Alice.

"So your brother wrote letters on the laptop to people he'd wronged?" Zack said.

Trina nodded. "He said he could think better, and change things around without having to start all over. Why would you think he was going to blackmail people?" she asked me again, this time indignant.

I told her about my conversation with Barbara Anik, but didn't mention the therapist's name. "How did he afford his expensive furniture, and the TV and sound system? And the Porsche?" Blackmail or drugs, I thought. Or both?

"I guess Randy might have done that six years ago." She sounded embarrassed. "I loved him, but I knew he didn't always do the right thing. He was trying to make up for it with the letters, though." She ran her hand along the edge of the table. "Doreen didn't want him writing the letters. I was on the phone with him one time and heard her yelling, 'You don't know what the hell you're doing, you'll be opening up a can of worms.' I told him to go for it if it made him feel better. Get the bricks off, I said."

"Did he talk to you about Aggie Lasher?" I asked, wondering how many bricks Aggie's death had contributed to Randy's weighty guilt.

"The woman who died?" Trina nodded. "All the time. I was only sixteen, but he didn't have anybody else to talk to. He wasn't close to my dad, because of Alice. My stepmother? That's why I couldn't go to them tonight. My dad cares, but Alice . . ." Her voice trailed off.

"What did Randy tell you about Aggie?"

It took Trina a moment to focus. "He thought she walked on water. He stopped drinking for her. He got serious about his NA meetings. He even signed up for a computer class and talked about getting a college degree. Anyway, they went out a couple of times, but she told him it wouldn't work. One day he was flying. The next day you couldn't talk to him, he was so angry. He started drinking again, and probably doing drugs." She shrugged.

"My dad wouldn't let me see him much after that. Alice wouldn't let him into the house."

"How do you know he was angry about Aggie?" Zack asked.

"Because I asked, and he yelled at me and said not to mention her name again." Trina faced me. "I know what you're both thinking, that he killed her. That's what the police think. But it's not true. Randy wasn't a killer."

"Maybe he was drunk that night," I said. "Or stoned."

She shook her head. "I was with him when he heard Aggie was dead. He punched a hole in a wall. Then he sat on his bed and couldn't stop crying. He cried so much it scared me."

I pictured Randy in his cramped bedroom, crying over Aggie's death. I tried to reconcile that image with the man in my dreams wielding the knife. Which one was true? Or were they both true? Had he been so stoned when he killed Aggie that he didn't know what he'd done until he heard she was dead?

"And everything that happened with Aggie?" Trina said. "That was over months before she died. He was interested in someone else."

That agreed with what Barbara Anik had told me. "You were with Randy the night Aggie was killed?"

Trina nodded. "We went to Century City to see *The Truman Show*. Randy saw it twice before. He said he was like Jim Carrey's character, because Truman learns that his life is one big lie, and Randy's life was a lie, too."

I'd seen the poster in Randy's apartment. If Randy had watched the film twice, that would explain how he knew the plot details. "So Randy was with you the entire time?"

"I just said he was." Trina picked up the Snapple cap. " 'Lizards communicate by doing push-ups,' " she read aloud. "How do they know that?"

I know defensiveness when I hear it.

She put down the cap and set it spinning. It dropped off the table and clattered onto the floor. "He didn't kill her, okay?" Trina's tone was belligerent. "I guess it doesn't matter now if I tell, because he's dead."

I nodded. It was Trina's story. I wasn't about to rush her.

"He dropped off my ticket and said something came up," she said. "If he could make it, he'd meet me there. He didn't show. He called later that night and said he was sorry, he couldn't get away. And after the police talked to him, he asked me to tell them he was with me. He was afraid they wouldn't believe him otherwise, because of his record. But he didn't kill her. My brother wasn't a killer. Just because he had her locket doesn't mean he did it."

"How do you think he got it, then?" I asked.

"I think he stole it," Trina admitted, her face flushed. "To get even with her, you know? I saw it in his room. There was writing on the back in some language. I guessed it was Hebrew. I figured it was hers. When I asked him about it, he said she gave it to him."

"What about *your* locket?"

"Randy bought it for me a couple of months ago." She pulled the locket out of the pajama top and opened it. "He said this red thread is supposed to protect me. He made me promise I'd wear it all the time."

I asked her about the red threads Randy had ordered for Rachel's Tent.

"I don't know about that. Randy didn't like to talk about his work." She slipped the locket back under the pajama top. "I don't want to talk about Aggie anymore. I can tell you don't believe me. I don't know why it matters so much to you, anyway."

I felt I owed her the truth. "Aggie was my best friend. I'm trying to understand why she didn't tell me about your brother."

"You didn't tell me that." It was hard to miss the accusation in her voice, the sudden edginess. She looked as if she wanted to bolt from the room.

"I wasn't sure you'd talk to me if I did. Or tell me the truth. Did you read Randy's journal?"

Trina blushed. "I thought maybe something in it would help me figure out who killed him. But he didn't write all that much. Mostly about the family. My dad, my mom, me, Alice. There were a couple of pages about her." She snickered. "He wrote about Doreen, too, and I can see why he didn't want her reading *that* part."

She gave us her first smile of the evening, but it disappeared quickly, a sliver of sunlight poking through clouds on a gloomy day.

"Did he write anything about Aggie?" I asked, ignoring Zack, who was shaking his head. *Let it go, Molly.*

"A little. He wrote how he loved her, how hurt he was when she told him it wouldn't work because he wasn't Jewish and she was real religious. He wrote about her parents, too. He blamed them for making Aggie break up with him."

That startled me. "Aggie's parents knew about Randy?"

"That was one of the letters he wrote. There were other letters, mostly to people I don't know. He wrote a list at the back of the journal. He put a check next to some names, I think the ones he already mailed letters to."

She was obviously referring to the letter Connors had mentioned, the one he'd found with the locket. He'd made me promise not to mention it or the locket to anyone, but Trina knew about the letter. I asked her about it.

She narrowed her eyes. "That must be a second letter. He mailed one to her parents, saying he was sorry about what happened to Aggie, because he'd never told them. He wrote that he knew they were good people, that they'd raised their daughter the way they thought was best."

This letter didn't sound like the one Connors had found. "Maybe Randy rewrote the letter."

"He showed it to me before he mailed it. It was the same day he mailed a letter to our mom."

It took me a second to react. I exchanged a look with Zack. "He knew that your mother was alive?"

"He's known since he got out of prison. Alice let it slip. I was in my room and heard her ranting. 'You think your mother's so grand, why did she leave you and your daddy and sister? I'll tell you why. Because she was sick of you. She had the right idea. She's living it up somewhere, thrilled to death people don't know her son is a drug addict, an ex-con.' She went on and on."

I pictured Alice Creeley. I pictured the words coming out of her pinched mouth, a ribbon of hate and resentment, saw the ribbon twist itself around Randy's neck.

"She tried taking it back," Trina said. "She said she meant *if* my mom was alive. Randy didn't believe her. He made me promise not to say anything to my dad, and I don't think he ever told him. It wasn't a big deal to me. I hardly knew my mom. But Randy never got over her. I think things would have turned out way different if she'd stayed."

I had more questions, but Trina was talked out. She took one of her sleeping pills and went back to bed. Zack helped me with the dishes. I didn't bring up Trina or Aggie, and neither did he.

"If you're at all scared," he told me when he was leaving. "If you hear a noise, or anything worries you, call 911. Then phone me, no matter what time. Promise?"

I promised. I dead-bolted the door and watched through the front window as he walked to his car. He turned and waved at me. I waved back.

I checked on Trina. She was sound asleep, curled into a fetal position. I shut the door to the room and prepared for bed. I thought about Randy, what he had felt when he'd learned that his mother was alive but hadn't cared to see him all these years.

Maybe that had changed him, given birth to anger, turned him into a man who would hold a knife and use it. Trina insisted that her brother wasn't a killer, but Roland Creeley had talked about his son's despair. Something from his past that he couldn't fix, Roland had said. And in the letter Connors found, Randy had asked forgiveness from the Lashers and said he wished he could undo what he'd done. And Randy had told Mike he'd killed a woman.

I couldn't fault Trina. She was trying to hold on to an image of her brother, just as I had been trying to hold on to an image of my best friend.

Sometime before I fell asleep I realized I'd forgotten to ask Trina about the package.

CHAPTER TWENTY-FOUR

Sunday, February 22. 9:02 A.M., 1200 block of Horn. During the afternoon, persons unknown burglarized an apartment and stole a laptop computer, cash, jewelry, a video camera, and miscellaneous items. The preliminary estimate of the loss was $20,500. (West Hollywood)

TRINA CAME INTO THE LIVING ROOM WHEN I WAS RECITing the Amidah, a unit of eighteen blessings toward the end of the weekday morning prayers. You're not supposed to talk during the Amidah, or interrupt the prayers in any way, but I acknowledged her with a nod before genuflecting.

"Sorry," she said, with an awkward smile.

She backed out of the room. I resumed my prayers, a mo-

ment later beseeching God to bring a speedy recovery to a number of people, including Bubbie G, whose Hebrew names I keep
on a slip of paper at the front of my siddur. I tried hard to focus,
but Trina's voice carried from the kitchen, and I heard her say,
"Hi, Dad," and then, with impatience, "No, I'm not home. I'm
okay, I'll call you."

"Do you pray every day?" she asked me later over breakfast.

Two pieces of French toast for her, one for me. You wouldn't
know from the way she fit in her tight jeans that she had such a
hearty appetite.

"I try to," I told her. "Sometimes I skip. Sometimes I rush
through the prayers, which isn't the idea. Zack is much better."

Trina poured syrup over her toast in a lattice pattern that
quickly lost its shape. "He's a rabbi, right? I figured he was, 'cause
he was wearing a skullcap."

I nodded. "But not all men who wear skullcaps are rabbis."

"Randy went to church a lot the last year. He wanted me to
go with him, but I never did." She ate a few bites of toast. "So
you guys probably aren't allowed to have sex until you're married,
huh? How do you know you'll be good together?"

It was an unusual conversation to be having with a woman I
barely knew. "I'm not worried. We have a lot of chemistry."
Zack and I had never slept together, but we'd had some steamy
moments in high school that make my face hot when I let myself
think about them, as I did now.

"Aggie wouldn't have sex with Randy," Trina said. "He wrote
that in the journal. He was okay with it, though." She gazed at
me. "Do you not want to hear this?"

"I'm not sure." I sensed she was testing me. I did feel strange
and uncomfortable hearing her talk about an Aggie I hadn't known.
A little jealous, too, if I'm totally honest.

"Some people have sex when they're dating but stop a week
or a few days before the wedding," Trina said. "I kind of like that.

I used to talk to Randy about stuff like that. I couldn't talk to my dad, or Alice. You met her, so you know." Trina grimaced, as if she'd caught a whiff of a noxious odor. "It would've been nice having a real mom. Do you get along with yours?"

"Pretty much." I have a remarkable relationship with my mother and father and siblings, but felt the need to downplay my embarrassment of riches. The *ayin harah*, I thought. "Did you try to get in touch with your mom?"

"I thought about it a couple of times but decided not to. What if she didn't want to see me? And that's cool. I don't have much to say to her anyway." She twirled a chunk of toast in the syrup that had pooled at the side of the plate.

She was trying to sound tough. I could hear the hurt in her voice and I wanted to give her a hug, but sensed she wouldn't appreciate it.

"How did Randy find out where she lives?" I asked.

"He wouldn't say. I don't think he planned to tell me he found her, but I guess he had to tell someone."

"When was this?"

Trina thought for a moment. "A couple of months before Aggie died? He was real tense. I thought it was because Aggie dumped him. I told him, 'When are you going to get over her?' That's when he said he found her. Our mom, I mean."

"Did he tell you where she lives?"

"No. But he said it's half an hour's drive from his apartment."

That was a surprise. "Your mother lives in Southern California?"

"Can you believe it? Alice would croak if she knew." A look of spiteful amusement hardened Trina's face.

"Do you know what was in the letter he wrote her?"

"No. But he was saying he was sorry about something. That's what all the letters were about."

I wondered what Randy had done that would require mak-

ing amends when it was the mother who should be asking forgiveness. "You said Randy wrote a list of names at the end of the
journal. Do you remember any of them?"

"Like I said, aside from our family and Aggie and Doreen, it
wasn't people I knew. But I have—"

Her cell phone rang. She flipped it open, cutting short a
jaunty tune, and listened. The color left her face.

"I told you, I don't have any package," Trina said.

Jim. My stomach muscles curled.

"You can threaten me all you want," Trina said with amazing
cool. "I don't have it. If you call me again, I *will* phone the police!" She shut the phone and slammed it onto the table. Her
hand was trembling.

"That was Jim?"

She nodded. "My home phone service forwards calls to my
cell. So does Randy's." She ran both hands through her hair.
"Maybe I shouldn't have said that, about calling the police." She
looked at me for reassurance.

"You *should* call them, Trina. Talk to Detective Connors
again. I know he'll help you. I'll talk to him too, if you want."

She shook her head. "I have to tell my landlord about the
door. They have to fix it, right?"

"Yes, but they'll want to file a police report. And if they decide to report it to the insurance company, the insurance company will want a police report, too."

"So I'll fix it myself."

"Trina—"

"Let me think about it, okay? I need to figure some things
out."

I couldn't imagine what she meant by "things," but the warning in her voice told me to back off. "Trina, do you have any idea
what the package could be?"

"None. Randy was into a lot of stuff he didn't tell me about."

"Drugs?"

"Maybe," she admitted. She sounded unhappy.

"Aside from his laptop and journal, he didn't leave anything with you?"

"I have his cell phone. The cops were busy in the bedroom, looking at . . ." She bit her lip. Her eyes filled with tears. "I saw it on the coffee table, under a stack of newspapers. I put it in my purse. I'm not sure why, and then I was afraid to tell them."

"Do you have it with you?"

"You want to see if Jim phoned Randy, right?" She nodded. "I don't have caller ID at home, but now that he called me, maybe the same number will show up."

She left the room and returned with a phone similar to hers. Flipping open her own phone, she accessed a screen that showed the numbers for the ten most recent incoming calls. Jim's would be the top one. I glanced over her shoulder as she punched buttons on Randy's phone. There was no match on the screen of incoming calls, or on the screen showing outgoing calls. Three of the calls were listed by name, not number: TRINA, DAD, and MAX.

"Max was Randy's NA sponsor," Trina said.

On her own phone, she selected Jim's number and pressed SEND. Ten or fifteen seconds later she shut her phone. "No one answers, and there's no answering machine."

"He probably used a pay phone. That's what I would have done." That's what I *had* done when I'd tried phoning Doreen.

I took another look at Randy's outgoing calls. The eighth one, at the bottom of the screen, had a 619 prefix.

"Don't shut that off," I told Trina.

I fished in my purse for the slip of paper with the numbers the Russian limo driver had dictated. I found it and compared the numbers to the 619 call on Randy's phone.

No match.

"Whose number is that?" Trina asked, pointing to the one on my paper.

"I'm not sure. Did you try any of these numbers?"

"I was going to, but then I got nervous that if one of them was Jim's, he'd know it was me. Dumb, huh?"

"I don't blame you for being careful. Okay if I check?"

She nodded. I picked up Randy's phone, selected the 619 call, and learned that he'd placed the call on Wednesday at 9:29 A.M. I was about to press SEND but stopped.

"If I use Randy's phone, I'll be eliminating the earliest call he made."

"Use mine," she said and handed me her phone.

I placed the call. After three rings a man answered. He sounded like the person who had identified himself as Brian.

"Is this Brian?" I held the phone between Trina and me so that she could hear, too.

"That's me. Who's calling?"

So the Russian had given me the correct number. "A friend of Doreen's. Can I talk to her, please?"

"There's no Doreen here. Sorry."

"This is the number she gave me."

"Well, she gave you a wrong number. I guess you have the wrong Brian, too."

"Is this the Morgan residence?" I asked, hoping he'd supply his last name.

"Not even close." He hung up.

Either my redhead wasn't Doreen, or she'd given Randy a false name. But why? And if she wasn't Doreen, who was she?

Trina hadn't recognized his voice. "Who was that?" she asked.

I gave her a brief, edited explanation.

"She probably lied to Randy from the start," Trina said, anger and fear darkening her blue eyes. "She's probably with Jim."

I didn't see the logic to that. The woman's terror had been convincing. She was the pursued, not a pursuer. *If* she was telling the truth, I reminded myself.

With Trina watching and a pen and paper in front of me, I checked the other outgoing calls and wrote down the information. The most recent, number ten, listed at the top of the screen, had been to a pizza shop. I recalled the congealed leftover lasagna I'd seen in Randy's kitchen. Randy had placed the call at 6:42 the Wednesday night he'd died. The ninth call, to TRINA, had been an hour earlier.

"He sounded fine when I talked to him," she said. "I told that to the police, too."

The eighth and sixth calls were the same, with a 310 prefix and digits that looked familiar. Both had been placed after noon that Wednesday. I dialed the number.

"Rachel's Tent," a woman said. "How can I help you?"

"Sorry, wrong number." I hung up. Bramer hadn't mentioned that Randy had phoned him shortly before he'd died. Then again, I hadn't asked.

The seventh call had been to DAD. The fifth, sent at 10:08 on Wednesday morning, had been to MAX, Randy's sponsor. The fourth call, sent at 9:43 A.M. Wednesday, had been to a number with a 626 prefix. That was in Pasadena, I knew. I tried the number. There was no answer, no voice message.

The third call was to Brian.

I scrolled down to view the first two phone numbers Randy had called. I sucked in my breath and stared at the bottom number. Trina was watching me.

The second number had a 213 prefix. Randy had placed the call Wednesday morning at 9:01. I dialed the number and listened to seven rings before I ended the call.

"Nobody named Jim." I put her phone on the table. "I didn't think there would be. And nothing from Doreen."

"What about the incoming calls? Shouldn't we check those, too?"

My head was throbbing again. "Right."

I accessed the screen for received calls. The most recent call was from the 619 area, at 12:38 Thursday morning. After Randy was dead, I realized. The thought was macabre.

I tried the number. No answer, no voice message. I scanned the numbers and saw that he'd received another call from the same number at 9:17 Wednesday morning.

Several calls matched the outgoing calls—one from Rachel's Tent, one from the 626 number I hadn't identified.

And two calls from DOREEN. I felt a flicker of excitement as I selected her name and pressed SEND.

"Leave your number, I'll call you back."

I couldn't tell if the voice belonged to my redhead. It sounded a little different, but a woman talking in the safety and comfort of her home might not sound the same when she's in an underground parking garage confronting someone who has been following her.

"Didn't you just eliminate the oldest outgoing call?" Trina asked.

"Sorry." In my excitement at seeing Doreen's name, I'd forgotten. "I wasn't thinking. I was anxious to hear her voice and find out if she's the redhead I saw at the funeral. Anyway, I don't know Doreen's number. You don't either. So the only way I could do that was by replying to her call."

"But now we won't know about that other call Randy made," Trina said.

She sounded petulant, or maybe I was being defensive. I apologized again. "There are other calls we don't know about, Trina. Let's concentrate on the ones we have. We can try the unidentified outgoing calls later, or tomorrow. If it's a business, it wouldn't be open on Sundays."

"Business" made me think of Horton Enterprises. I found

the card Bramer had given me and compared the 213 phone number with the 213 call on Randy's phone. A match.

I told Trina. "Do you know why Randy would have phoned Anthony Horton?"

"Randy liked him. He said Horton was a cool guy. Horton gave Randy a job when he got of prison. He was like a father figure, you know? Randy was close to the son, too. The son was at the funeral. He said I should let him know if I need anything, and he called to see how I was doing. That's nice, don't you think? He didn't have to do that."

There was another number with a 310 area code. Using my own phone, I dialed the numbers and listened to a message from Jerry Luna.

"I think that's Randy's agent," Trina told me.

When I returned to the main screen, I noticed the blinking envelope icon. Randy had two voice messages, I learned.

"I saw that, but I don't know his password." Trina sounded dejected. She looked at the pad on which I'd made notes. "That's not twenty phone calls."

"There were doubles, and some of the phone numbers were yours and your dad's."

"Plus the one you wiped out," Trina reminded me. "I wonder who that was."

I knew who it was. I'd dialed the number hundreds of times and knew it by heart.

Aggie's parents' number. I had been stunned to see it, had felt sick.

I hadn't written the number down. Trina would probably think I'd deliberately eliminated the call, and that wasn't true. At least, I didn't think it was, although a little voice in my head said, "There are no accidents."

CHAPTER TWENTY-FIVE

I DIDN'T TELL ZACK, WHEN HE PICKED ME UP TWO HOURS later, though I was tempted. I did tell him about the other calls Randy had made and received.

"Two calls to Rachel's Tent, huh?" he said. "That's interesting."

"Maybe he wanted his job back."

"Did Bramer mention that?"

I shook my head. "Could be Randy didn't call for Bramer. Maybe he phoned Barbara Anik to make amends for lying to her all these years."

"Ask her."

"Maybe I will."

I switched the radio to an oldies station and caught the middle of "Return to Sender." "Address unknown," I sang. I thought about "Doreen." No such number? No such phone?

"I don't understand how the redhead had Brian's phone," I said.

"Maybe she stole it. You can try his cell number later and see if he answers—or I can do it, since he's heard your voice."

"She's probably from the San Diego area, Zack. Those unidentified calls must be from her."

"How does that help you?"

"It doesn't."

We rode awhile without talking. The Beatles were singing "Let It Be." I wished I could.

"The pizza shop call bothers me," I said. "If Randy was depressed the night he died, why would he order lasagna?"

"As opposed to a calzone?"

"Be serious."

"You said he got a call from his agent. Maybe it was bad news. Now he's going to have a child to support, with a woman he doesn't trust. More pressure. That plus his guilt. . . . He orders food, has a beer to go with the lasagna. Another beer, then the Jack Daniel's. Next thing, he's shooting up."

"Trina's convinced he was killed, Zack."

"And the neighbor told you Randy confessed. How *is* your houseguest, by the way?"

"Restless. She keeps apologizing for being there, saying she doesn't want to put me in any danger. Speaking of which, Jim called."

Zack whipped his head toward me, then returned his eyes to the road. "You promised you'd phone me right away."

I could see his stern expression from his profile. "There was no reason. He doesn't know where Trina is. She handled it well. She warned him to leave her alone or she'd call the police."

"Which she won't do," Zack said. "Maybe she *does* have the package, and doesn't want to give it up."

I'd considered that, too.

Minutes later Zack pulled up in front of Galit's house. The *ketubah* was beautiful, more beautiful than we'd imagined when we'd given the calligrapher a rough idea of what we wanted: a chuppa motif with flowers in shades of mauve, green, and blue. The text was perfect, too, including the wording that indicated I'd been divorced. Galit told us the *ketubah* would be ready on Wednesday.

"Do you want to grab some lunch?" Zack asked when we were in the car on our way back.

I reminded him that Trina was in the apartment. "She's so sad, Zack. She lost her brother, someone trashed her apartment. I don't want to leave her alone for long."

"And you want to ask her about the package, right?"

"That, too," I admitted.

But Trina was gone.

I called her name when I stepped into my apartment. I looked in the kitchen. I knocked softly on the door to the guest room, in case she was taking a nap, and louder on the bathroom door. I looked in the small yard, though it was too chilly to sit outdoors. I checked my bedroom, too, thinking she might have wanted to use my computer, not sure how I felt about that. But she wasn't there, and nothing had been disturbed.

What if someone had followed us to my apartment, had waited until I wasn't home . . . ?

I hurried back to the guest room, and that's when I noticed that the sofa bed had been made and Trina's suitcase was gone.

And on my kitchen table I saw Randy's cell phone, on top of an envelope. Inside were two folded sheets of lined paper and a note.

Molly, thanks for everything. You and Zack are great, and I hope you have a fabulous wedding. I feel bad that I called you last night. I didn't know who else to call, but I don't want to put you in any more danger. I'm going to a hotel while I figure out some stuff. I should of done it in the first place.

I'm leaving Randy's cell phone. You can give it back to me later, whenever. You said you wanted to help prove Randy didn't kill Aggie, so maybe you can try those numbers again. I also left you a couple of pages from his journal that I tore out. I didn't tell you about them because I wanted to talk to you first and see if I could trust you. He has names and addresses, and some of them sound like the ones I saw on his computer files, but I'm not sure. I was going to check them out, but I'm afraid to go anywhere. And I'd probably mess things up, I wouldn't know what to say to people and get them to talk to me. You're a reporter, you'd know. I don't know if any of those names will help. Maybe it's nothing.

I'll call you in a couple of days. Don't worry, I'll be okay.

P.S. The newspaper clippings were in the journal.

P.P.S. You can give Randy's phone to your cop friend. You'll probably do it anyway, even without my okay. I guess I should of given them everything right away. Maybe they'll listen to you and treat this serious.

Trina

I reread the note and debated showing it to Zack. I knew what he'd say: Trina was using me. She'd phoned me instead of contacting family or friends and involved me in her drama because she'd counted on my persistent interest in Randy. Now she'd left his phone and a list of names and addresses to investigate. *I'd probably mess it up. . . . You're a reporter, you'd know.*

It occurred to me that she could have trashed her own apartment as bait, that she'd invented Jim, whose voice I'd never heard, not even this morning when he'd phoned her. That could have been someone else, someone she'd called "Jim" for my benefit.

In my mind I played back the past few days. I saw the terror in her face. Last night, this morning. On the street a few days ago when the truck backfired. Her terror was genuine, I decided. And so were Jim and his threats.

I wasn't as sure about Trina herself. Either she was completely ingenuous and had left the phone and the list because she was out of her league and needed my help, or she was playing on my ego and sympathy to sucker me into doing her work for her. The truth, I thought, was somewhere in between. And it didn't matter, because I was hooked.

Tucked inside the folded pages were three yellowed newspaper clippings. I caught my breath when I saw Aggie's face on the grainy paper of the first clipping. The article was dated July 24, the day after she was killed:

> The body of a twenty-four-year-old woman fatally stabbed last night was found. . . . The victim, Aggie Lasher, was a social worker at Rachel's Tent. . . . If you have information, please call the Wilshire Division at . . .

Twenty-four years reduced to three paragraphs, I thought now, as I had six years ago.

The second clipping, dated July 28, was only one paragraph and asked again for the public's help in identifying Aggie's killer.

The third clipping, a July 14 column from the *Times* "Metro" section, which has since been renamed "California," was a digest of crimes that had taken place the previous day. An ATM robbery in Glendale; a police-involved shooting in Alhambra; the discovery of the torso of an unidentified woman in a freshly dug grave in Griffith Park; a drug bust in Hollywood resulting in a third strike and probable life sentence for a thirty-year-old male; a gang shooting in Compton; a domestic violence arrest in the Wilshire area.

I read the column again and tried to see it through Randy's eyes, but I had no idea why he had kept it. Trina might know. I would ask her when I talked to her.

Or maybe this clipping was part of the lure. I reminded myself that I had to maintain a healthy skepticism about anything she had told me, including Randy's letters.

Setting the clippings aside, I scanned the entries on both pages: Some were names accompanied by addresses—street name and city; some names with only phone numbers; some addresses without name or phone number. Several addresses were just street names, with no city or other identifier. Some had initials. None of the complete addresses was in the San Diego area.

There were close to fifty entries, but I recognized only a few:

Roland Creeley
Alice Creeley
Benjamin and Ann Lasher
Barbara Anik
Anthony Horton
William Bramer

Randy had placed check marks next to all these names except Horton's. Check marks appeared next to many of the other names on both sides of the pages.

I wondered which name, if any, belonged to Randy's mother.

CHAPTER TWENTY-SIX

I THOUGHT I HEARD A TRILL OF SOMETHING DARKER THAN surprise in Mrs. Lasher's voice when she looked through the privacy window of the front door and said my name.

It could have been my imagination. Even if there *was* something, it disappeared by the time she opened the door and welcomed me with a warm smile and hug, and led me into the large kitchen that had been my second home.

Before Aggie's death, Mrs. Lasher had planned to remodel the kitchen and had spent hours poring over magazines, gathering samples and showing them to Aggie and me ("my two girls"), laughing ruefully because she couldn't make up her mind. She had laughed easily then, and often, and had sounded more like a schoolgirl than a fifty-eight-year-old mother. A year or so after

Aggie died she had talked about resuming her project as though
it was a chore she needed to cross off her list. "Dr. Lasher thinks
it's time," she told me.

But almost five years later the cabinets were still oak, and the
flooring, an off-white linoleum with a brick pattern, was un-
changed, as were the marbled beige Formica counters on which
Aggie and I had prepared countless midnight snacks. I don't
know if Mrs. Lasher wanted to preserve Aggie's memory or had
simply lost interest.

She insisted on serving me a glass of milk with a slice of fresh
banana cake warm from the oven. When we were teenagers,
Aggie and I used to drizzle Hershey's chocolate syrup on top of
the cake. I'm sure Mrs. Lasher remembered that, too.

The walls in the kitchen and breakfast room were still sponge-
painted in cream with accents of apricot and, if you looked close,
a little blue. I had first noticed the blue after staring at the walls
during the night that had turned into morning with no word of
Aggie. At a quarter after eleven I'd been polishing my nails while
talking on another line when my brother Judah yelled, Pick up
the phone, Molly, it's Mrs. Lasher. Was Aggie at our house? Mrs.
Lasher asked me. Had I heard from her? She's probably with
friends, I said, fanning my nails, impatient to return to my other
call. She'll be home soon, you know she loses track of time. That
girl, Mrs. Lasher said, not really worried about the daughter to
whom she had given birth late in life after multiple miscarriages,
the daughter she had tried not to smother. I wish she'd remember to turn on her cell phone, that's what it's for, she added with
a note of exasperation that would probably stab at her forever, a
sliver of glass beneath the skin, too small to find but always there.

"It's so sweet of you to stop by, Molly," she told me now.
"You must be so busy preparing for the wedding." She was wearing a navy kerchief with a paisley design on hair that had turned
quite gray.

"It's a little hectic," I said. "Zack and I are so happy that you and Dr. Lasher are coming."

"We wouldn't miss it. I'm sorry we didn't stay for the kiddush on Shabbos, but the last few days . . ." Her voice trailed off. "It was good news, but still, a shock."

An hour after Mrs. Lasher's call on that July night, Dr. Lasher had phoned. He always speaks softly and slowly, weighing his words, but his voice was heavy with dread, each sentence more ponderous than the one before, a bowling ball gathering momentum as it rumbled along the lane. Aggie wasn't home, they hadn't heard from her, they'd contacted a number of women who had attended the vigil, no one had seen her, but there had been over five hundred women, so maybe . . . Did I have any idea where she might have gone? If you know something, Molly . . .

My father drove my mother and me to the Lashers'. There had been no police report of an accident involving Aggie's white Honda, Dr. Lasher told us when we arrived, no record of her having been admitted to a hospital. My mother and I sat with Mrs. Lasher in the sponge-painted breakfast room while my father accompanied Dr. Lasher in his dark olive green Infiniti to the Pico-Robertson synagogue where the vigil had been held. Mrs. Lasher set a bowl of fruit on the table and served coffee and cake that no one touched, and we said, five hundred women, maybe they just hadn't *seen* Aggie, or maybe she's in the ER, you know how disorganized Admissions can be, maybe she's hurt but not badly, God forbid, five hundred women, hurt but not badly, repeating it over and over like a mantra, until my father phoned and told my mother they had found Aggie's car a few blocks from the hall, her keys weren't in the ignition, there was no sign of foul play. That became our new mantra. No sign of foul play.

"I know this is such a hard time," I said to Mrs. Lasher now, the burden of inadequacy as heavy today as it had been almost six years ago.

Mrs. Lasher sighed. "*Hashem firt der velt,* Molly." God runs the world. "We can't ask questions. But at least now we have some answers."

When the men returned that night, Dr. Lasher phoned the police, who told him a missing-person report isn't filed until someone has been missing twenty-four hours. Maybe your daughter met someone, a boyfriend, she'll probably show up in the morning, it happens all the time. My mother held Mrs. Lasher's hands while Dr. Lasher, in the careful, solid, unexcitable way that makes him an excellent internist, explained about the prayer vigil and five hundred women who hadn't seen his daughter, a daughter who had never been out this late, ever, who didn't have a boyfriend, whose car was parked two blocks from where she was supposed to be. What did they say, Benjy? Mrs. Lasher asked after her husband hung up the phone. They're checking out the car, he told her. An hour or so later two uniformed police showed up at the house and left with a photo of Aggie.

My parents and I stayed with the Lashers as the hours ticked by, though by now we were not alone. Dr. Lasher's sister and brother-in-law had arrived at some point, and Mrs. Lasher's brother. Mrs. Lasher fell asleep with her head on the breakfast room table, her hand on the phone receiver. When the first light of dawn stole through the slats of the wood blinds, the men went into the living room to recite morning prayers and began putting on their phylacteries. From the breakfast room I could see Dr. Lasher kissing the little leather boxes, with attached straps, that contained parchment with handwritten Torah verses. Fastening one box onto his left upper arm, he wound the straps around his arm and palm, secured the other box on the center of his forehead, then finished winding the first straps around his fingers. He had kissed the fringes of his *tallit* and wrapped himself in it when the police returned. We found your daughter, they said, words of hope hijacked almost before they were airborne, *We're so sorry to tell you . . .*

Dr. Lasher, tears streaming down his face, said, "*Baruch Dayan ha'emet.*" Blessed be God, the Righteous Judge. I think he had known when they found the car.

Mrs. Lasher's mouth opened in a wide *O* but for a second no sound emerged. Then she covered her ears so she wouldn't hear herself screaming Aggie's name. Her husband took her in his arms, stroked her back, murmured Chavi, Chavi, Chavi, rocked her until her shrieks subsided into groans, Chavi, Chavi, lowered her onto the sofa and administered a sedative from the black bag he asked my mother to bring from his study.

The other men resumed their prayers, but Dr. Lasher removed and folded his *tallit* and slipped it onto a large blue velvet bag. (My father later told me that from the time Dr. Lasher heard that Aggie was dead until after her funeral, according to Jewish law he was an *onen,* absolved of all ritual observance and mitzvot.) He unwound his teffilin and, with tears streaming down his cheeks, kissed the leather boxes before winding their leather straps and tucking them into a small velvet bag that he placed into a larger one. Then he knelt at his wife's side, adjusted the blanket someone had spread over her, held her hand, and whispered to her for a few minutes before he left with the officers to identify his daughter's body.

I have wondered over the years whether Dr. Lasher kissed the boxes that morning out of habit, or acceptance of God's will. I remember being awed by and envious of the rocklike faith that enabled him to get through those first days. The urgent but quiet phone calls to his rabbi and others when the coroner's office insisted on an autopsy; more calls after the autopsy to the director of the Chevra Kadisha burial society, who assured him that all the organs had been returned to the body before it was transferred to the mortuary, where the body was ritually prepared by women for burial. The funeral. The burial, where Dr. Lasher rent his garment and threw shovelful after shovelful of red dirt onto the grave. I think he found more solace kissing those little black boxes than his wife did from the sedatives in his black bag.

"I hear that everyone at B'nai Yeshurun is very happy with Zack," Mrs. Lasher said now. "He looks like a fine young man. And the Abramses seem very nice. What are their first names? I forgot."

"Larry and Sandy."

"Very, very nice. My husband said so, too. They're both attorneys, my husband said. Zack was going to be a lawyer, too, wasn't he? And then he learned in Israel. Everything is *bashert.* Which yeshiva?"

I told her. "Is Dr. Lasher home? I'd like to talk to him."

"Your throat hurts?" She smiled. "How many times did he check your throat? Twenty? Thirty? And your brother—I think Dr. Lasher gave him stitches. Twice, I think. Which brother was that? Noah?"

"Joey." She knows I'm here about Aggie, I thought. "Is Dr. Lasher busy?"

"He's learning. I hate to interrupt him when he's learning, Molly. He's so busy all week, late into the night, and sometimes weekends, too. When he finds a few hours for Torah, it's a luxury."

"Mrs. Lasher—"

"Remember how sad you were when things didn't work out with Zack? And now they did. Everything is *bashert.* I heard your sister Edie made the *shidduch.*" The match. "She has three children, right? I was thinking of taking one of her Israeli dance classes. My friends tell me she's a terrific teacher. And Mindy? How many children does she have, *bli ayin hara?*"

"Two girls and boy." *Bli ayin hara,* I echoed silently.

"Beautiful, *kenehoreh,* beautiful." She smiled again. "I'm sure your parents have a lot of *naches* from all of you. And Liora?"

"She goes on dates all the time. She hasn't met the right person yet." There was a desperate quality to Mrs. Lasher's small talk, to her smiles. "I need to ask Dr. Lasher one or two questions, Mrs. Lasher. I won't take much of his time."

"Maybe I can help you?"

I hesitated. "I just wanted to know what the detective told him."

"You're a good friend to worry so much." Mrs. Lasher took my hands. "He told us about this man Creeley. He needed money for drugs. He saw our Aggie walking. . . ."

Was it possible that she didn't know? Had Connors showed the letter that accompanied the locket to Dr. Lasher? *Don't tell my wife, she won't be able to bear it.*

"I really need to talk to your husband," I said.

She nodded and released my hands. "I'll tell him. I'm so glad you came by, Molly."

CHAPTER TWENTY-SEVEN

DR. LASHER WAS SITTING BEHIND HIS DESK WHEN I ENtered the study, a wood-paneled room lined with built-in mahogany bookcases filled with a collection of medical and Judaic texts. It's an impressive collection, and Dr. Lasher is an impressive man. He's tall and somewhat hunched, and he has a narrow face and high forehead and gold-rimmed bifocals that he wears low on his nose. He's in his mid-sixties, but looks older, because of his thinning hair, which has more white than gray, and because of the beard he decided not to shave after the thirty days of mourning for Aggie were over.

"It's been a long time since you've been here," he said when I was seated. "You look wonderful, Molly. You're happy?"

"Very."

"Good." He nodded. "I spoke to your *chossen* at the kiddush. I can see why you picked him." He shut the text that had lain open in front of him. "Mrs. Lasher says you came to talk to me about Aggie?"

"Yes." Aggie's father had always been direct. Now I was the one who craved small talk. On the way here I'd rehearsed my opening, but it had flown out of my head.

"You're nervous, Molly? Don't be. What do they say—'I'm a doctor, you can tell me anything'?" He smiled briefly, a forced effort. "Detective Connors told me you're bothered about this man who killed Aggie. You want to know more about him. You want to know what happened."

"I was at his funeral," I said. "I was surprised you came. I saw your name in the guest book."

Dr. Lasher nodded. "I surprised myself. I almost didn't go. Mrs. Lasher and I don't know the family, they don't know us. But we're connected, whether we like it or not. Our daughter, their son. A terrible link, but a link. I wanted to show them I don't hold them responsible for what he did. Why were *you* there?"

"I'm not sure." Randy's mother, Doreen. It was too complicated to explain. "I didn't see you at the service."

"No." He shook his head.

"I talked to Randy's father and sister, Dr. Lasher. They told me Aggie knew Randy, from Rachel's Tent. Did you know that all these years?"

He picked up a letter opener and ran his fingers across the blade. "When Aggie was killed, the police asked us about Creeley. We told them the truth. Aggie never said anything about him. We'd never even heard his name."

"Why–?" I stopped.

"Why didn't we tell you the police asked us about him? There was nothing to tell, Molly. Creeley had a solid alibi."

Not so solid, I thought. I licked my lips. "The sister told me Aggie and Randy had a relationship."

Dr. Lasher put down the letter opener. "And you believed her?" His wise eyes were full of reproach.

My face was warm. "She said they dated a few times. She said Randy wrote to you about it before he died."

"Detective Connors showed us the letter Creeley wrote to us, and the locket they found on him. The one you gave her, Molly. But you know that." He cleared his throat. "He was infatuated with Aggie. He probably told her he had feelings for her. . . ."

"Not *that* letter," I said, wishing I were somewhere else, hating the fact that I'd caught my best friend's father in a lie. "The one he mailed a week before he died. The one where he talked about his relationship with Aggie."

Dr. Lasher's face was flushed. "There was no relationship," he said firmly. "The letter wasn't signed. It had just the initial *R.* The writer was sorry for our loss. He meant to write to us when she died. He knew we were good parents, that we wanted what was best for Aggie, that we must have been very proud of her."

This sounded like the letter Trina had described. I was relieved to know she'd told the truth, at least about that. But I was surprised Randy hadn't signed the letter. "Did you tell the police about the letter?"

"About a condolence letter six years after the fact? I tossed it out."

"Then why did Randy phone you, Dr. Lasher? I have his cell phone," I added before he could deny it. I had no interest in trapping him in another lie. "I recognized your phone number."

Dr. Lasher removed his bifocals and set them on his desk. "You've been in this room many times, Molly. There are hundreds of books here. Medicine and Torah. You think they're just books? They're my *life,* Molly. You think I would spend forty years trying to heal people, you think I would study the Torah for over fifty years, that I would study God's laws and violate them, that I would take a man's life?" He sounded more sad than angry.

"I need to know about the phone call."

"You *want* to know. You don't *need* to know. All you need to know is that I didn't kill Randy Creeley."

I thought about the gentle, caring man sitting five feet away from me, about the way he'd kissed the black leather boxes, about the black bag with its syringes and vials.

"About the phone," I said. "It shows other calls Randy received, and some that he made. They might be evidence."

"Evidence of what? The police say he overdosed."

"I have to give the phone to the police, Dr. Lasher. I wanted to tell you before I call Detective Connors."

"Are you asking me or telling me, Molly?" He put on his glasses. "If you're asking, my answer is: Do what you think is right."

What was right? I'd been agonizing for hours over giving Connors the phone and subjecting Dr. Lasher to police scrutiny. I'd eliminated the call to the Lashers, but Connors could get a complete list of Randy's calls from the cell phone company. In a way I'd tampered with evidence—accidentally—but the call was evidence only if there was a crime, which Connors kept telling me wasn't the case. But if Dr. Lasher had nothing to fear . . . ?

"Did you talk to Randy, Dr. Lasher?"

"Will my answer help you decide?" He sounded as close to sarcastic as I'd ever heard him. "Creeley phoned the house the Tuesday evening before he died. Thank goodness I answered the phone, not Mrs. Lasher."

"What did he say?"

"He told me he was the author of the letter I'd received. For a second I didn't know who he was. Then he said he'd worked with Aggie at Rachel's Tent. He was trying to make amends for things he'd done wrong. He had something of Aggie's and wanted to return it. It wasn't his to keep."

My heart thumped. "The locket?"

"He didn't say. That's what I assumed. He told me how much he had liked Aggie, how sad he was about what happened. He'd written another letter, but he needed to see me. I told him I'd think about it and said I would call him back. My mind was reeling. How did this man get Aggie's locket unless he killed her? But maybe it wasn't the locket? Maybe he'd taken something from Aggie's desk. Creeley had a solid alibi. He sounded genuinely upset about Aggie. He was almost crying when he talked about her."

"And then you phoned him back," I said, phrasing my guess as fact.

Dr. Lasher nodded. "Early Wednesday morning. I was catching up with paperwork at home. He sounded nervous and said he couldn't talk long. He told me again that he felt terrible about Aggie's death. I asked him if he had her locket. He said yes. I asked him, 'Did you kill my daughter?' It was a surreal conversation, Molly. He swore he didn't. He asked me to give him one day and he would tell me everything. He had to take care of something first, to make sure he wouldn't be putting someone in danger."

The package, I thought, with a thrill of alarm.

"I didn't know what to believe. I thought, if he *did* kill Aggie, maybe he would confess to me more easily than to the police. Because he phoned me, right? He wanted to talk. Thursday morning I phoned Detective Porter, but he was out. I didn't leave a message. I was going to ask them to put a wire on me, you know? Like in a detective movie. Crazy." Dr. Lasher shook his head. "A few hours later Detective Connors came here and told my wife that Creeley was dead, and that he had killed Aggie. I suppose Creeley was trying to do *teshuvah*." Repentance. "I have to give him credit for that."

"Did you tell Detective Connors about the phone calls?"

"To what end? Creeley was dead."

"What if he didn't kill Aggie? You said he sounded genuinely upset."

"That doesn't mean he didn't kill her, Molly. Just the opposite. He couldn't live with the guilt. Connors showed me the letter. Creeley said he wished he could undo what he did. *Halevai.* I wish it, too."

"But what if he didn't?" I don't know why I was fighting Creeley's guilt. Because of the package, I think. And Trina's trashed apartment, and the redhead in the parking lot. "Don't you want her killer to be caught?"

Dr. Lasker looked stricken. "Can you even *ask* that, Molly?" he said with a profound sadness that shamed me and made me wish I could retract the question. "The first year that was my waking thought, and my last before I fell asleep. I davened to Hashem, 'Let the police find the man who did this and bring him to justice.' And after that I davened, 'Let me sleep one night without nightmares, or if not a night, a few hours. Let my wife laugh again. Let her walk into our daughter's room without crying. Let her go to someone's *simcha* and be able to share their joy with a full heart.' "

I blinked back tears. "I'm sorry."

"Do I want Aggie's killer caught? I think Hashem caught him. You know how I know? Because Thursday night I slept, Molly. And the next night, and the next. And Shabbos my wife said, 'Let's go to Molly's *chossen*'s *aufruf.*' So we went. And she's thinking about getting a new dress for your wedding. So I *know.*"

I should have left the room then, but I had one more question. "When you phoned me that night, Dr. Lasher, you told me no one had seen Aggie at the vigil."

"Right." He sounded cautious.

"You said something I never thought about till now. You asked me if I had any idea where Aggie might have gone. And then you said, 'If you know something, Molly, please tell us.' And I was just wondering, why would you say that?"

"I don't know what you mean."

There was a warning note in his voice, my last chance to back off. "Why would you think there was something I would keep from you and Mrs. Lasher? Unless you suspected that Aggie was seeing someone you wouldn't approve of, that she told me what she couldn't tell you."

Dr. Lasher was looking somewhere beyond me. Then he smiled, and shook his head.

"I always told my wife, 'Molly is bright, she doesn't miss anything.' " Now he was looking at me, and I could see deep pain in his eyes. "A few months before she died, Aggie wasn't herself. I asked her what was wrong. She said the job was making her stressed. But one night I picked up the phone and heard her talking to a man, laughing with him, arranging a date for Saturday night. I waited for her to tell us about the date. She always told us. But she didn't say anything, not to me, not to my wife. Saturday night she said she was going with a friend to the movies. Which friend? I asked. Oh, you don't know her, another social worker. *Her*, not him. The next week she had to stay late for a meeting at work. How was it? I asked when she came home. Again, I knew she was lying, she was dating a man she couldn't bring home. And then all of a sudden it was over, and Aggie was Aggie again. I don't know what happened, why it ended. I didn't ask. She never said anything to you?"

I shook my head.

"Two dates, three dates—that's not a relationship. In the end Aggie knew what was right for her. She made her own decision. Creeley is dead, it's over. I'm not interested in finding out why he killed her. He loved her, he hated her." Dr. Lasher shrugged. "It doesn't make a difference. I don't want Aggie's name in the papers. It's a good story. A sheltered, beautiful young woman falls in love with a handsome drug addict who kills her because her Orthodox Jewish parents forbid her to see him and six years later kills himself because he can't live with the guilt. It's not exactly the truth, but it's a good story. Maybe they'll write a book, or make a television movie. Is that what you want, Molly? For Aggie, for her mother?"

CHAPTER TWENTY-EIGHT

Monday, February 23. 9:12 A.M. 1200 block of North Vermont Avenue. A man walked up to a woman on the street and said, "You're gonna be sorry, you and your wonderful family," then fled. The suspect is described as a 49-year-old African-American man standing 5 feet tall and weighing 165 pounds. (Northeast)

HORTON ENTERPRISES OCCUPIED THE TENTH FLOOR IN one of those large office buildings on Wilshire east of Vermont, halfway to downtown and a block from the old Bullocks Wilshire where my mom bought the Priscilla of Boston wedding gown that none of us Blume girls would have worn even if it hadn't turned yellow in the garage.

The reception area was sleek—gray leather chairs, glass-and-chrome coffee and end tables, abstract art on walls papered in pale gray with a subtle burgundy stripe. The receptionist, an attractive woman in her thirties with shiny auburn hair and cognac-framed glasses so narrow that I wondered what she could see through them, offered me magazines and a cup of coffee.

"It might be a while," she said.

From the apology in her voice I sensed I'd be in for a long wait, but after five minutes and only a few sips of very hot, very good coffee that I would have liked to finish, she told me Horton was ready to see me.

In person Horton was taller than he'd appeared in the photo in Bramer's office. Nine years had added lines and jowls to a face with a ruddy complexion and had thinned his silver-gray hair, which had been styled to camouflage the thinning. But he had an electric energy—his voice, his smile, the spring in his step—that a photo couldn't capture and that made him appear much younger.

After pumping my hand as though it were an oil derrick, he introduced me to his son, Jason, who was several inches shorter than Dad—around five-ten—with a slimmer face and dark hair. I had a moment of nervousness, but Jason didn't recognize me from the funeral. Both men were wearing navy suits that fit so perfectly they must have been custom tailored.

There were two burgundy leather armchairs. I took one, Jason took the other. Horton sat behind his desk, a beveled sheet of thick glass resting on a charcoal granite base as large as my kitchen which held a computer, a phone, pens, a Rolodex, a notepad, and a framed photo. Other office equipment and photos sat on a black-and-gray granite credenza, in the center of which was a simple tall glass vase with bloodred roses that explained the heady fragrance I'd noticed when I entered the room. Above the credenza hung a portrait of a young woman with curly brown hair and soulful eyes.

"My mother Katie, may she rest in peace," Horton said with a catch in his voice when I asked him about the photo. "That's a blowup of one of the few pictures I had of her."

I told him how inspired and moved I was by his story.

Horton looked pleased. "I've had my share of rough times. Some people call it bad luck, but I think you make your own luck. And a little help from the good Lord doesn't hurt." He smiled. "That's why I wrote the book, to give people hope. My mother didn't even have enough food to feed herself, let alone me. I think she would've been amazed and proud to see how I turned out. I just wish she'd lived to know my family. We had this taken Christmas."

He turned the frame on his desk toward me and identified the people in the photo. His wife, Pam; Jason and his wife, Angie, and their year-old son, Tyler; his daughter, Kristen, and her husband and their two daughters, Nicole and Lisa.

His eyes lit up when he talked about his grandchildren. "They're my future," he said, gazing at the young faces before he turned the photo around. "So you're writing about Rachel's Tent. I apologize that I'm not familiar with your work, but I did look you up on Google. Well, Jason did." Horton smiled again. "I have this new computer, but I still prefer pen and paper, and most of what I know I keep up here." He tapped his temple. "I read that you write true-crime books and a crime column. I'll have to get a copy of your latest, have you sign it for me. I hope you don't think there's anything criminal going on at Rachel's Tent." He laughed.

"Dad." Jason laughed, too, but he sounded embarrassed, as though his father had propositioned me.

"Miss Blume knows I'm kidding. Isn't that right?" he asked me.

"Absolutely. And I left my handcuffs at home." I smiled. "I

also write for several papers, including the *Times,* about all sorts of topics. Health, politics, gardening."

Horton nodded. "Well, I hope your article reaches all the women who don't know about Rachel's Tent but could use help. Jason oversees the funding for the agency, so I thought you'd like to talk to him as well. What would you like to know?"

To tell you the truth, I'd come fishing. Bramer had set up the appointment, which hadn't interested me much until he asked me not to bring up Randy and drugs.

"Background information, for starters," I said. "I Googled you, too, but I'd like to hear your story in your own words. Tell me about Horton Enterprises."

"It's an umbrella company for a number of—well, I guess you'd call them enterprises." Horton chuckled. "I started in property management, found out I was good at it. I'm a saver, Molly. I'm still driving the same Mercedes I bought seven years ago. I saved every nickel I earned, every dime. When I had enough, I invested in a property, then in another. When I had more, I bought a company that sold sports caps. I found out I could cut the price if I imported them. That led to importing other items, and then to other businesses. Jason?"

"We have land investments, an import-export business, oil wells, a printing company, medical supplies," the son said, like a waiter informing me of today's specials. "We've invested in several tech companies and we're looking into fiber optics and genetic testing."

Horton beamed. "Jason's my right-hand man. We're a team. Everything I know, he knows. You want to know the two most important rules in business, Miss Blume?" He nodded at his son.

"Diversification, and knowing when to cut your losses," Jason said, a pupil who had learned his lesson well.

"Diversification, and knowing when to cut your losses," the

father repeated. "That's in my book, but I don't mind giving you a freebie. I've lived by those rules my whole life and I've never been sorry."

"So you built up this business empire, and then you founded Rachel's Tent," I said, trying to make a smooth segue. "I've heard some of the success stories. They're wonderful."

Horton nodded. "It's all about giving back to the community, isn't it? That's what I've tried to teach my children. Pam shares my vision. She's very involved with a number of charities. So are Kristen and Angie."

"I was interested in the red-thread packets I saw at Rachel's Tent," I said. "Does one of your companies handle that?"

Horton turned to his son. "Jason?"

I felt as though I were watching a ventriloquist act. Horton pulled the strings, the dummy talked. I wondered if Jason felt the same way.

"We import the threads from Israel and do the packaging," Jason said. "Our printing company does the envelopes. Rachel's Tent handles the sales."

"To be honest, it's not a moneymaker," his father said. "But not everything is about money. That's in my book, too."

"Dr. Bramer mentioned that a man who worked at Rachel's Tent came up with the idea," I said. "Randy Creeley?"

Horton looked as though I'd thrown cold water at him. Jason didn't look much happier.

"That's right," Horton said, subdued. "Randy set everything up and handled it for a while. Then it got too big, so we took over."

"You must have taken his death especially hard, since you helped him get the job."

"It's painful," he said quietly. "I had high hopes for that boy. I help a lot of people, but there was something about Randy. . . . I felt a connection because his mother abandoned his family. I even loaned him money to hire someone to find her. I spent more time with him than with some of the others, had him over to dinner often. I hoped Jason would be a good influence." He nodded in his son's direction. "But you can't fight drugs. Randy's death is a tragedy for his family and friends. A goddamn waste."

He sounded genuinely upset, and there were tears in his eyes. I debated, a little nervous to broach the next subject, but if you don't stir the pot . . .

"I talked to the manager of the apartment building where Randy lived," I said. "Apparently he had expensive tastes. Beautiful furniture, a big-screen projection TV, a Porsche. I can't imagine he was earning enough at Rachel's Tent to afford all that."

Horton tilted his head and stared at me as though I was a dartboard and he was aiming for a bull's-eye.

"I guess I should've paid attention to what I read on Google," he said with the kind of quiet that's more intimidating than shouting and that told me I didn't want him as an adversary. "I thought you were interested in the women of Rachel's Tent."

"I am. But I'm intrigued by Randy's story. Do you think he involved anyone else in his drug use?"

Something twitched in Horton's cheek. "Off the record?" he said after what seemed like a minute but was probably only seconds.

Jason had turned white. "Dad—"

Horton silenced his son with a look—the dummy was talking without permission. Then he turned to me. "Well?"

"Off the record." I would have agreed to pretty much anything if it meant I'd finally be getting information.

"Around a year ago Dr. Bramer came to me in a panic. Someone left him an anonymous note saying Randy was selling drugs at Rachel's Tent. Randy denied it, of course. I was madder than hell. I'd given the guy a chance to make something of him-

self, taken him into my *home*." Horton sounded pained. "Bramer
worried that if we went to the police, they'd investigate everybody Randy came in contact with, and that would be the kiss of
death for Rachel's Tent. And a third strike for Randy, so he might
have been in prison for life. As angry as I was, I didn't want that
on my head. So we let him go, and said he could tell people he'd
quit. We didn't report him, but as far as I was concerned, Randy
Creeley didn't exist."

"You cut your losses," I said.

"Exactly." Horton nodded.

I told him that according to Gloria Lamont, Randy had made
his major purchases, including the car, around five years ago.

Horton looked thoughtful. "Five years, huh? So he was
probably dealing long before Bramer found out. You want to
know the truth? Aside from the fact that Randy was jeopardizing
Rachel's Tent—and that really hurt—I felt like a fool. I thought I
was a better judge of character. I guess I was a bigger fool than I
realized."

I thought about the newspaper clipping. There had been an
item about a drug bust that had resulted in a third strike for the
offender. Had Randy kept that as a warning to himself? If so, the
warning hadn't kept him from reverting to his old ways.

"What about the red-thread packets?" I asked. "Is that how
Randy distributed the drugs?"

Father and son looked at each other.

"That's what we suspected," Horton said. "We never found
out for sure. But we took over the whole operation. Like I said,
that was almost a year ago. I can promise you that the only thing
in those packets now is red threads from the Holy Land. Does
that answer your question?"

"Pretty much. I appreciate your candor."

"Candor, hell." Horton grunted. "If I didn't tell you, you'd
go digging and find out anyway. I care about Rachel's Tent, Miss

Blume. It took years of hard work and a lot of dollars to make it what it is today. All it takes is a couple of questions, a raised eyebrow, and the place is history. And then where do all those women go to get help?"

I reiterated that I wouldn't include what he'd told me in an article. A safe promise, since I didn't plan to write one. "Did Randy ever mention a man named Jim?"

Horton shook his head. "Doesn't ring a bell."

Jason looked equally blank.

We talked awhile about Rachel's Tent. Horton hoped to establish two more centers, one in the San Fernando Valley and one in Southeast L.A. Under different circumstances I probably *would* have wanted to write about the agency.

"By the way," I said as I was ready to leave, "Randy's sister told me he was trying to make amends for things he'd done wrong. Did he contact you?"

There had been no check next to Horton's name on the list Randy had written, so I assumed that if Randy had written a letter, he hadn't sent it. But there had been the phone calls. I wanted to see if Horton admitted to them.

"I'm glad you told me," Horton said. "As a matter of fact, Randy phoned the office a couple of weeks ago. I couldn't take the call, and when I returned it, he wasn't in. That was the day he died. What day was that, Jason? Tuesday?"

"I think it was Thursday."

Horton waved his hand. "Doesn't matter. The point is, when I heard he died, I felt terrible that we didn't have a chance to talk. I guess he wanted to go with a clean conscience. I have to give him credit for that. And maybe I wasn't completely wrong about him after all."

CHAPTER TWENTY-NINE

GLORIA LAMONT WAS WEARING DUCKS TODAY. I KNEW MY stock had risen when she invited me into her living room and offered me a seat on a green velvet sofa while she took the beige armchair that looked worn, in a comfortable way. I was happy to sit. After leaving Horton Enterprises a little after ten, I'd spent two hours collecting *Crime Sheet* data from the Northeast and Wilshire Divisions, and my feet ached from the high heels I'd worn to go with the black power suit I'd decided would impress Horton, though I can't say he even noticed.

"You doin' okay?" Gloria asked, her brown eyes filled with concern.

"Pretty okay. I have a favor to ask, Mrs. Lamont. I know you keep files on all the tenants, and I'm wondering if I could take a peek at Randy's."

The manager frowned. "I don't know that I can do that. What would you be needing to see it for, anyway?"

"I'm trying to help his sister."

"That poor girl." Gloria *tsk*ed. "She looked something awful at the funeral. How is she?"

"I haven't heard from her since yesterday."

I'd phoned Frederick's and learned that Trina had taken a leave of absence. I'd left a message on her phone but wasn't surprised that she hadn't returned my call. She probably didn't want a babysitter.

"Trina gave me Randy's cell phone." I took the phone from my purse, turned it on, and showed it to the manager. "See the message box? There are two voice messages, and Trina wants to hear them, in case they're important."

Gloria eyed me, dubious. "Important how? Randy's dead, honey. It don't matter who called him. An' why isn't Randy's sister here askin' me? Why did she send you?"

"Somebody trashed her apartment. She's staying in a hotel, I don't know which one, until she figures things out. She thinks the person who did it killed Randy."

"Randy *killed*?" Gloria put her hand to her mouth. Then she narrowed her eyes and dropped her hand. "Is this one of your *stories*?"

"No, ma'am." I told her about Trina's Saturday-night call for help.

"So what all do you need from Randy's file?"

"His Social Security number. If I have that, I can call the cell phone company, change the password, and listen to the voice messages."

Gloria chewed on her lip. "It don't seem right."

"Like you said, Randy's dead. It's not as though his social se-curity number means anything to him anymore."

"You really think someone killed him?"

"I'm not sure," I admitted. "Trina thinks so. Did you see any-body coming to his apartment the night he died, Mrs. Lamont?"

"I was asleep before nine o'clock. I had a cold and took some of that NyQuil. I was dead to the world. Randy's girlfriend had to ring my bell twenty times before I heard her and dragged my-self out of bed."

"So can I take a look at his application, Mrs. Lamont? No one will even know. I promise."

Gloria tugged on the sleeves of her sweater. I could see the uncertainty in her eyes and was surprised a moment later when she nodded.

"I've got a box full of files. It'll take me a few minutes."

While she was gone, I looked around the room. There was a small brown spinet and some framed photos, one of a pretty woman who looked like a younger version of Gloria. Probably the daughter, Shirrel. Several more of Shirrel's son and daughter. Cute kids.

"Well, here it is," Gloria said as she came back to the living room. She handed me the application form.

I took out my notepad and pen and wrote down Randy's so-cial security number. "I can't thank you enough, Mrs. Lamont."

"I hope you're wrong about Randy being killed," she said as I was leaving. "I don't like thinkin' something like that could happen right here."

She shut the door. I heard the sound of a dead bolt as I walked down the hall to Mike's apartment. I rang his bell.

"Hey," he said when he opened the door in shorts and a black T-shirt. "What's up?"

It was almost one o'clock, but from his tousled hair and rumpled appearance, I could tell I'd woken him up. "Sorry to bother you. The night Randy died, Mike, did you see him?"

It was the first question I'd asked days ago when we were talking on the front lawn. I'd been sidetracked when he told me about Randy's drunken confession and hadn't realized until an hour ago that he'd never given me an answer.

"Yeah, for a minute," he said. "I was leaving to grab a bite and catch a movie when the Domino's guy showed. I invited him to come. Randy, not pizza man." Mike's smile stretched into a yawn. "He said he was meeting someone at eight, and Doreen later. He looked uptight. I thought maybe they weren't getting along."

"What time was this?"

Mike scratched his head. "Seven-ten, -fifteen? The movie was nine-thirty. That was the last time I saw him. But his Porsche was in his spot when I came back before midnight."

From Hollywood I drove to Burbank and barely got there in time for my one-thirty next-to-final fitting for my gown—a simple, full-length ivory satin slip dress with echoes of Vera Wang and a modest jewel neckline and long, fitted sleeves.

"You lose more weight." My dressmaker, a tiny Asian woman who made me look tall, clucked. "Okay. I take in here and here." She pinched the fabric at my waist and hips and inserted a few straight pins, which she pulled from her mouth. "I don't want touch here, line is beautiful." She ran her hand across my chest. "You bring two padded bras Thursday, okay? We see which one better. Length is good?"

The length was fine. Two or three millimeters too short for the three-inch-heel ivory satin pumps I was wearing, but no one would notice. And after the chuppa, I'd be wearing the new white tennis shoes Liora had dressed up with pearls, rhinestones, and lace appliqués. It's what many Orthodox brides do, and their mothers and other women in the bridal party. I love my heels, but they're not made for the high-energy Israeli dancing we'd be doing throughout the dinner reception.

"You eat," the dressmaker instructed as I was leaving. "But not too much."

Back in my apartment I changed into comfortable clothes and fixed myself a tuna sandwich. I phoned Trina and left another message.

I contacted Randy's cell phone service. I gave them Randy's cell number, told them I'd forgotten my password and couldn't access my voice messages, and supplied the necessary ID: Randy's Social Security number and his mother's maiden name, which after some hard thinking this morning, I'd remembered was Jasper.

When I hung up a minute later I had Randy's new password, and a problem. If I accessed the voice mail via my phone, I'd be eliminating a received call, the one at the bottom of the screen.

I accessed the screen and scrolled down to the last number. That was the call from Max, the NA sponsor. At least I didn't have to identify the caller. I jotted down Max's name and the time of the call.

I shut off Randy's cell and dialed his number on my phone. I felt eerie listening to his message, but when he was finished, I pressed the pound button, then the new password, then 1.

"You have two unheard messages," a recorded voice informed me. *"First message, sent on Wednesday, three twenty-two P.M."*

"Randy, I'm asking you to reconsider before you do something you'll be sorry for later. Call me."

"End of message."

Alice Creeley. That was a surprise.

"To erase this message, press seven. To save the message, press nine."

I pressed 9.

"Next message, sent on Thursday, 12:41 A.M."

"Randy, why aren't you answering? Randy? Do they know?"

"End of message. To erase this message—"

I pressed 9. I would have liked to play the message again, to listen to the woman caller's voice, but I didn't want to erase any more phone numbers. Even without hearing it again, I was fairly certain the caller was my redhead.

CHAPTER THIRTY

"YOU DIDN'T CALL BACK, BUT I FIGURED YOU'D HAVE TO talk to me today or tomorrow," Connors said when I was sitting next to his desk. "Give me a minute, and I'll get you the DO sheets."

Connors is one of the detectives who make my life easier by giving me sanitized photocopies of the Daily Occurrence sheets for my column. At many police stations, including Wilshire, I have to copy the data.

"Thanks, but that's not the only reason I'm here." I took the cell phone from my purse and placed it on his desk.

"A little early for my birthday," he said. "Plus I have my own, thanks."

"That's Randy's. His sister took it from the apartment the

night he died. She gave it to me. I figured you might want to know who Randy talked to before he died."

Connors leaned way back in his chair and linked his hands behind his head. "And why would I be interested in that?"

I told him about Trina's trashed apartment and the threatening calls from Jim. "I kept pushing her to contact you, but Jim warned her not to. She's convinced that someone killed Randy—maybe Jim. She says the police don't believe her, and that they don't care about Randy because he was an ex-con, or about her. I tried to tell her otherwise, but she wasn't buying it."

Connors had listened with interest. His hands came down. "My guess? The package is drugs, Molly. Randy was dealing, Jim was his supplier. Now that Randy's dead, Jim wants his stuff back. That doesn't mean Jim killed him. Just the opposite."

"Randy was in NA."

Connors shrugged. "He got sucked back in. Doesn't take long. He didn't have money to buy the stuff. His pal Jim says, Why don't you sell, you'll have money."

I had to admit that sounded plausible. "So you're not interested in knowing who Randy talked to?"

"Doesn't hurt to find out. I assume you already know?" Connors said wryly.

"Trina and I checked out the calls yesterday. It wasn't evidence, Andy," I said before Connors could object. "Just a phone belonging to a dead man who overdosed."

Connors turned on the phone and accessed the screens of incoming and sent calls. "Can I assume you know who these unidentified numbers belong to, Miss Marple?"

I handed him a copy of the revised list I'd made.

CALLS RANDY MADE:
Wednesday, 9:01 A.M.—Horton Enterprises
Wednesday, 9:29 A.M.—San Diego Brian (last name?)

Wednesday, 9:43 A.M.—626 call (?)
Wednesday, 10:08 A.M.—Max
Wednesday, 12:03 P.M.—Rachel's Tent
Wednesday, 12:19 P.M.—Dad
Wednesday, 1:17 P.M.—Rachel's Tent
Wednesday, 5:33 P.M.—Trina
Wednesday, 6:42 P.M.—Domino's Pizza

CALLS RANDY RECEIVED:
Wednesday, 8:12 A.M.—Max
Wednesday, 9:17 A.M.—619 call (?)
Wednesday, 2:33 P.M.—Jerry Luna, Randy's agent
Wednesday, 3:14 P.M.—Rachel's Tent
Wednesday, 4:42 P.M.—626 (?), same as sent 9:43 A.M.
Wednesday, 5:17 P.M.—Dad
Wednesday, 5:44 P.M.—Trina
Wednesday, 9:16 P.M.—Doreen
Thursday, 12:14 A.M.—Doreen
Thursday, 12:38 A.M.—619 same as 9:17 above (unknown)

Connors studied the list. "What's Randy's connection with Horton Enterprises?"

"They fund Rachel's Tent. Anthony Horton is the founder." I repeated the business mogul's story. "I met with him and his son this morning. Randy phoned Horton the morning he died, but Horton wasn't able to take the call. Now he feels bad."

"Does Horton have any idea why Creeley wanted to talk to him?"

"He didn't, but I did."

Connors gave me a crooked smile. "Why am I not surprised?"

"According to Trina, Randy was making amends to people

he'd wronged over the years. He was writing them letters. I know he asked forgiveness from his father and stepmother."

"Like the letter he was writing the Lashers." Connors nodded. "But why would he ask forgiveness from Horton?"

"Horton got him the job at Rachel's Tent. Maybe Randy wanted to thank him again, and apologize for not living up to Horton's expectations. Horton said Randy disappointed him." I didn't feel right telling Connors about Randy's drug dealing. That had happened a year ago, and I'd promised Horton to keep it off the record.

Connors glanced at my list. "Ditto for the calls to Rachel's Tent, huh? Who's Brian in San Diego?"

"I don't know. At the funeral I saw a redheaded woman who I thought might be Doreen. I followed her." I ignored Connors's sigh and told him what had happened, watched his interest darken to annoyance, then anger.

"I should lock you up for your own good," he said when I was done. "Do you have a death wish or something?"

"I got caught up in the thing, Andy. I had no idea she'd pull a gun." The memory of the cold steel was still vivid. I suppressed a shudder. "She thought people sent me to follow her."

"Which people?"

"She didn't identify them. She said, 'The ones who killed Aggie, the ones who killed me.' "

Connors grunted. "Sounds like she was stoned or missing a few screws."

"I don't know. I *do* know she was terrified. And she knew who Aggie was—she identified her in a picture she found in my wallet—and that I'd given Aggie the locket."

"Things Randy's girlfriend might know," Connors said. "I don't get this redhead's connection to the 619 Brian."

"I tried reaching her on her cell phone and got a voice message: 'Hi, this is Brian.' Then, when I tried the 619 call on

Randy's cell, the guy who answered said he was Brian. Same voice, same guy. He didn't know a Doreen."

"How did you get her cell number?" Connors asked.

I told him about the Russian limo driver.

"Very enterprising," he said. "The driver, I mean."

I figured he was too annoyed to give me points. "I don't understand how this woman got Brian's cell phone, Andy. Unless she stole it. She probably lives in the San Diego area, because someone made two calls from the 619 area to Randy, and she had Brian's phone."

"If she stole his phone, she didn't necessarily do it when she was in San Diego. And anybody could have made the 619 calls. For all we know, Randy had business dealings with someone in San Diego, and with Brian. Or Brian could be a friend. Did you ask him if he knew Randy?"

I shook my head. Dumb of me. "I was focused on finding out about Doreen."

Connors drummed his fingers on his desk. "So Randy made calls. To his dad, his sister, a pizza shop, his agent, his girlfriend. Nothing unusual. You're probably right about the calls to Rachel's Tent and Horton. He wanted to make amends. And the calls verify what the girlfriend said, that Randy didn't show for their date and she got worried. Thanks anyway, Molly. I'll hold on to the phone and get it back to Randy's sister."

I could leave now, I thought. If Connors was interested, he could obtain a list of all the calls Randy had made and received. . . .

"Something else?" Connors asked.

"I accidentally eliminated a call Randy made to the Lashers," I said, the color and heat rising in my face like one of my mother's hot flashes. "I didn't include it on the list I gave you. Randy phoned the Lashers the Tuesday night before he died, but I don't have the exact time."

Connors was quiet for half a minute or so, swiveling back and forth in his chair. "Were you considering not telling me?" he asked when the chair had come to a stop.

"I *did* tell you, didn't I?" Not really an answer. "I spoke to Dr. Lasher last night, Andy." I repeated what Aggie's father had told me. "He thought Randy might talk more openly to him than to the police, but Thursday morning he phoned Wilshire anyway. Porter wasn't in. And then you showed up at their house with the locket."

"I have to talk to him, Molly." Connors looked unhappy. "You know that. I wish he'd told me right away."

"He didn't see the point. You told him Randy had over-dosed."

Connors sat up straight and leaned toward me. "The *point* is, Molly, and you know it as well as I do or you wouldn't have had second thoughts about telling me about the call, the *point* is that Lasher had two conversations with the man who killed his daughter, and he had the last one a few hours before the man died."

"Of a self-inflicted overdose," I said. "It's what you keep telling me."

Connors gave me a hard look, I think to see if I was mocking him, which I wasn't. Then he sighed.

"I know it wasn't easy for you to come here with this, Molly. I think you know you did the right thing."

I hoped so. "I told Dr. Lasher I had to tell you about the phone call. He didn't try to talk me out of it."

Connors nodded, but I could tell he wasn't impressed, or focused. His mind was elsewhere, probably on Dr. Lasher.

"I have a few questions, Andy, and a favor to ask."

He grunted. "So the phone is gonna cost me, huh?"

"And the list," I said. "You have to admit it'll save you some time."

"What do you want to know?"

"Randy killed Aggie somewhere between Alcott, where she parked her car, and the synagogue hall, which is on Pico off Livonia. Why did he move her body to a Dumpster behind a restaurant a mile away? And don't tell me to ask Porter. He won't give me a straight answer."

"You and I are friends, Molly, not partners."

"What difference does it make if you tell me? Aggie's dead. Creeley's dead."

Connors swiveled again in his chair. "I'll talk to Porter and see what he says. That's the best I can do. What else?"

"I want to know who made the 619 calls to Randy."

Connors shook his head.

"I'm not asking for the address. Just a name."

"Can't do it."

"What about Brian? Can you find out if his cell phone was stolen?"

"Let me think about it. If I can, I'll let you know."

"One more thing? Randy has two voice mails and—"

"And you want me to tell you what they are?" Connors sighed. "Again, I can't do it, Molly."

"Actually, I heard them. One is from his stepmother, Alice," I said before Connors could make a snippy comment. "The other one is from my redhead."

That perked Connors's interest. "How'd you get the password? Scratch that," he said. "I don't want to know, or I might have to arrest you." His eyes said he was only half joking. "You're sure it's the redhead?"

"Pretty sure. I wanted to compare her voice with Doreen's, but I didn't want to eliminate any more calls on Randy's phone."

"Very considerate," he said dryly. He picked up Randy's phone, glanced at my list, and accessed the screen for received calls. He selected DOREEN and pressed SEND.

"Leave your number, I'll call you back."

Using his desk phone, which he placed on speaker, he dialed Randy's cell, waited for the prompt, and pressed the pound button. "What's the password?" he asked me.

I told him.

He punched in the four numbers, waited for a prompt, and pressed 1. We listened to Alice Creeley. Connors saved the message. A moment later we heard the woman's voice.

"Randy, why aren't you answering? Randy? Do they know?"

Connors played it again and looked at me.

"It's not Doreen," I said.

He nodded.

CHAPTER THIRTY-ONE

MAX PALEY LOOKED JUST THE WAY HE'D DESCRIBED HIM-
self over the phone—tall, brown hair with a severe crew cut, a
goatee, tortoiseshell glasses. He was wearing jeans and a blue shirt
over a black T-shirt, and it took me a moment to realize that I'd
seen him at the funeral.

It was five to seven. I had been waiting ten minutes and had
just about decided that he wasn't planning to show when he entered the kosher deli on Pico near Robertson, which I'd chosen
because it was close to where he worked.

I had found Max's name and phone number among the entries on the pages Trina had left. A good thing, because otherwise
I would have been tempted to use Randy's phone to reach the

NA sponsor, which would have erased another call and necessitated another apology to Connors.

"Thanks for coming," I said after the waitress left with our orders. A steak sandwich with fries (a nod to my dressmaker) and a Diet Coke for me, a pastrami burger and a Dr Pepper for Max. Mushroom barley soup for both of us. My treat, I told him.

"I almost didn't," he said. "I'm still not sure I should be here. The relationship between a person and his sponsor is totally private. That's what makes the program work."

He'd been suspicious after I'd identified myself, not happy that I'd found him, even after I told him it was through Randy's sister.

"I wouldn't have asked you to meet with me if wasn't vital, Max. As I said, the police know you phoned Randy the morning before he died. So you'll probably have to talk to them. You weren't Randy's lawyer or minister."

"That doesn't mean I have to talk to *you*."

I nodded. "True. But I'm hoping you will. I'm trying to find out who killed him."

"I don't know."

I took a sip of water.

Max pulled on his goatee. "You really think someone killed Randy?"

"The police are looking into the possibility." Connors planned to talk to Dr. Lasher, so it was true. "The evidence points to Randy overdosing, but his sister doesn't believe it. Neither does his father. Do you know if Randy was clean?"

"What day?"

That startled me. "Wednesday, the day he died."

"Do you know anything about addiction, Miss Blume?"

"Molly."

"Molly. Do you?"

"I know it's hard to beat. Are you saying Randy was doing drugs on and off?"

The waitress brought our soups.

"You don't *beat* an addiction, Molly," Max said when she left. "It's with you every day for the rest of your life. Whether it's smoking or gambling or drinking alcohol or spending or over-eating. Or using drugs. You have a day where you abstained, that doesn't mean you're going to abstain the next day. You have a month of abstaining, or five months, or five years, the next morning you get up and thank God for helping you. You acknowledge that you still have an addiction, that you're powerless to control it, that you need help. Randy was beginning to understand that. So if you ask, Did Randy shoot up Wednesday night? I have to say I don't know. He could have."

"Was he clean on Tuesday?"

"Yeah, but it was a struggle." Max took a spoonful of soup. "He had a lot on his mind."

"Trina said he was writing letters, asking forgiveness. She didn't know specifics." Or she wouldn't tell me. Instinct told me Trina had been holding back about a few things.

"He was working the program way too fast. It's not something you rush. But it was like he had a premonition he wouldn't be around, and he had to do as much as he could in the time he had left."

"Did he ever mention someone named Aggie Lasher?"

Max shook his head. "He didn't talk about people by name. Why?"

"The police think he killed her around six years ago. You don't look surprised," I added.

Max ate more soup. I think he was stalling, trying to figure out how much to tell me. My own bowl of soup was steaming my face, but I hadn't touched it.

"Randy asked me how a person would go about making amends to someone who died," Max said. "Be of service to other people, I told him. Work the program. Then he asked, What if that person was responsible for the other person's death? Hypothetically, he said."

"What did you tell him?"

"That deep inside he knew what he had to do, that he didn't need me to tell him. About a week before he died, he told me he had a huge dilemma. In making amends, he'd be involving people who would be facing legal and financial repercussions. Did he have a right to do that? To be honest, that was too big for me. Aren't you eating your soup? It's good."

I took a spoonful, but barely tasted it. I wondered if Randy had told his supplier—Jim?—that he was no longer willing to deal drugs. Worse—that he was planning to turn himself in to the police. Was that why he'd been in such a rush to make amends to all the people he'd wronged—because he knew he could be in prison for life?

"Do you think Randy was dealing drugs?" I asked Max.

"No way."

His anger made me flinch. "What if he couldn't get a supply any other way?"

"I talked to Randy every day, usually more than once. I would have known. Now his girlfriend . . ." Max sniffed. "They met in NA, but she was definitely using, at least the last time she came to a meeting, a month ago. I don't know where she got the money. Randy said she wasn't working."

"Did Randy know she was using?"

"I told him. It's much easier to slip with a partner. And she was nosy. She called me, said he sounded troubled, she wanted to help him but he wasn't opening up to her." Max grunted. "I think she was afraid he was going to dump her." He finished his soup and pushed the bowl away.

"So if it wasn't drugs, Max, what do you think Randy was involved with?"

"No clue. I know he was worried about protecting someone. If he made amends, if he told the truth about something. He was vague. I thought he was talking about protecting his kid sister, but I could be wrong."

That would have been my guess, too, especially since Trina's apartment had been trashed. "There was a woman at his funeral who lives down in the San Diego area. And a man named Brian. Did Randy ever mention either of them?"

Max shook his head. "I told you, he didn't use names. Is someone meeting you here?"

"No. Why?"

"There's someone at the counter who's been turning around every few minutes and looking at you."

I felt a shiver of fear and turned around. I didn't see anyone. "Who?"

"That guy, there," Max said, pointing. "The one wearing the hat and walking out the door."

"What did he look like?" I asked, still looking at the door.

"Average. Medium height, brown hair. He probably thought you were someone else. Or her," Max added. "It could've been a woman. I couldn't see the face."

The waitress brought our main courses. Max attacked his burger with gusto, but I had lost my appetite. When he was finished, I asked the waitress to box my sandwich and asked Max to walk me to my car and wait until I had locked myself inside.

CHAPTER THIRTY-TWO

I KEPT MY EYE ON THE REARVIEW MIRROR ALL THE WAY TO my sister-in-law Gitty's apartment on Detroit Street, where we were playing mah jongg tonight. I didn't think anyone was following me, but I made extra turns and doubled back a few times to make sure. I was still shaking when I ran up the stairs to the upper story and rang the bell.

I hadn't been in the mood to play. I adore mah jongg and value its therapeutic qualities, which helped me get through many lonely nights after Ron and I divorced, but I had too much on my mind, so many errands I should be taking care of before the wedding. My sisters had insisted that I needed the break.

"It's your last game as a single woman," Mindy had said.

Now, as I worried whether someone was following me and

why, the thought of being with family was reassuring and I was glad they'd insisted. I looked over my shoulder, rang the bell again, and was about to ring a third time when my brother Judah opened the door. I stepped into the small entry and stood on tiptoe to give him a kiss. His trim beard tickled my cheek.

I took a step back and peered at him. "What's up? You look strange."

"Nothing's up. I'm just happy for you. One more week, huh?"

"Are they throwing me a shower?" I had told everyone, no shower. I was too old, and this was my second time. I still had shower gifts from my first marriage that I'd never used.

"It's not a shower," he said, and grinned.

Judah doesn't grin. At twenty-eight, he's the oldest male sibling, but number four in the Blume totem pole. I suspect he always wanted to be the firstborn, which explains his friendly rivalry with Edie, and probably the beard, and his tendency to take himself too seriously at times, though he does it less often since he married Gitty. She has mellowed him and so has their one-year-old son, Yechiel, who is starting to talk and calls me "Ahwee." Works for me.

I followed Judah through the large living room, still furnished only with bookcases and books, and into the kitchen, where my sisters and sister-in-law were standing, along with my mother and Bubbie G. They were all wearing long, stick-straight wigs in bright colors—red, green, turquoise, orange, purple.

"Edie got them on Hollywood for the Purim play at school next week," Liora said. Her wig was orange. "Aren't they fun?"

"They're great," I said.

"Here's yours," Edie said, handing me a purple one. "No layers," she added, and a moment later Bubbie wanted to know why we were all laughing.

Gitty had set out our usual mah jongg nosh—popcorn and

potato chips, trail mix, and soda. And water, crudités, and fruit, because she's a nutritionist. Bubbie G had baked a preview batch of hamantaschen, the three-cornered cookies filled with poppy seed, prune butter, or apricot (I like the prune the best) that we eat on Purim, which was a week from this coming Saturday night. In between munching, Edie took us into the living room to practice the new dances we still hadn't mastered though she'd given us private instruction.

"Thank goodness we're all wearing long gowns," Mindy said.

We reminisced and watched old family videos of when we were kids. I was a little worried about Bubbie, but she was smiling and nodding at our young voices, probably filling in from memory what she couldn't see. We ate too much of the assorted chocolate candy Liora had bought at Munchies, and laughed so hard we were breathless and the tears streamed down our faces, and my mother wasn't the only one who had to run to the bathroom.

It was a wonderful evening. For three hours I forgot about the man who had been watching me at the deli, and Aggie and Randy Creeley, and financial and legal repercussions—of what? And when I got home after eleven I was almost sorry to find that Connors had phoned.

"Call me at home if you want," he said, "I'll be up late."

He answered on the second ring. I heard noise in the background and thought he had company, but he told me it was the TV.

"So where were you?" he said. "Out with your rabbi?"

"Mah-jongg with my sisters, and a miniparty."

"Two more weeks, huh?"

"Actually, a week from Wednesday."

"You ready for this?"

"I'm ready." I don't know much about Connors, aside from the fact that he has an ex-wife in Boston, something he let slip once. I do know he's not much for chitchat, which meant he was procrastinating. "Did you talk to Porter?"

"Yeah, I did. You asked why Creeley moved the body. He didn't."

"I don't understand."

"Aggie wasn't killed near the synagogue, Molly. She was killed about a hundred feet from the Dumpster. Creeley saw her somewhere between her car and the synagogue—on Livonia, probably. She got into his car—willingly or unwillingly—and he drove her to the site where he killed her. Okay?"

I was seething. "No, it's not okay."

"You know what I mean, Molly."

I realized I was still wearing my purple wig. I yanked it off. "All this time Wilshire knew Aggie was abducted and killed somewhere else? That's not a mugging, Andy. That's not a random act. No wonder Porter didn't want me to know."

"Hindsight is always twenty-twenty, Molly. She could have been abducted by a stranger. Happens all the time. By the way, I checked the 619 calls. They were made from a pay phone in San Diego."

"Is that my consolation prize?"

"Don't shoot the messenger." Connors sounded annoyed. "You wanted to know. A thank-you would be nice."

"*Thank* you. Did you find out about Brian's cell phone?"

"Not yet. I *did* learn that Doreen hasn't been living in her apartment since Creeley died. She picked up her mail twice and told the landlord she's moving."

"Doesn't that tell you she's frightened, Andy?"

"Or that she's had her fill of Hollywood."

"She was in NA, but I spoke to someone who told me she's still using."

"Call the *Times*," Connors said. "They'll run a special edition."

I restrained my impatience. "She wasn't working, Andy, so how did she buy drugs?"

"I'm assuming you have a theory."

"I think someone paid her to spy on Randy. His sister told me she *did* have a key to his apartment. Randy found Doreen snooping through his things. His journal, his laptop files. This person I spoke to told me Doreen called and tried to pry information out of him."

"Who is this person?"

"It doesn't matter. The point is, someone was worried that Randy was planning to make amends. I think they wanted Doreen to find out what he was writing, and to whom."

Connors didn't answer.

I stroked the purple hair. "Trina told me Doreen yelled at Randy about the letters, told him he was making a mistake. But Randy told her he had to do the right thing. Suppose Doreen told this person that Randy was ready to mail the letters. The guy has to kill Randy."

"And he does that how?"

At least Connors wasn't laughing. "He meets with Randy and gets him drunk so that he passes out. You said he had enough alcohol to open a bar, right? The guy shoots drugs into Randy's arm. He doesn't find the package or the laptop—he wants to see who Randy's been writing to. So he breaks into the sister's apartment and takes the laptop. But he needs the package. He thinks Trina knows where it is."

"Does she?"

"I don't know. She said she didn't have Randy's journal, but she does."

"When did you last talk to her?"

"Sunday morning. I left a few messages on her cell phone. She said she'd get in touch in a day or so."

"She didn't tell you which hotel she was going to?"

"No."

Connors didn't respond. I figured he was thinking.

"I still think Creeley overdosed," he said, "but I'll check around. By the way, I spoke to Dr. Lasher. He doesn't have an alibi for Wednesday night. He says he was at the hospital, but that was early in the evening."

"Lots of people don't have alibis, Andy."

"Lots of people didn't just talk to the guy who killed their daughter. Lots of people aren't doctors with medical knowledge and syringes and access to drugs."

I debated telling Connors that I thought someone had followed me to the deli, and wouldn't that rule out Dr. Lasher, but he said good night and hung up.

I phoned Trina and left another message. Then I talked to Zack, who had known about the wig party all along.

"You're not supposed to keep secrets from your fiancée," I said. "You're supposed to tell me everything."

"Like you tell me everything?" he teased.

I thought about that as I filled him in about my meeting with Randy's sponsor but didn't mention that someone may have been following me. Not the same thing, I told myself. Because if it wasn't true, I would be worrying Zack needlessly.

"Don't forget about dinner tomorrow night," he said before he hung up. "I'll pick you up at seven-thirty."

I washed off my makeup and put on pajamas, then entered the *Crime Sheet* data I'd collected today until it was after two and my contact lenses were fogging. After saving my files, I shut my computer.

The list I'd made from Randy's phone was on my desk. I was tempted to call Brian. At worst, I told myself, he'd pick up and yell at me for waking him up in the middle of the night.

And at best . . .

I dialed the number.

"The party you called does not accept calls from blocked numbers . . . ," a recorded voice informed me.

Maybe it was a sign. I hesitated, then pressed star 82 to un-block my phone, and punched Brian's number again. One ring, two, three. After four rings, the answering machine picked up.

"You've reached the Warfields." Brian's voice. "Please leave a message."

CHAPTER THIRTY-THREE

Tuesday, February 24. 11:54 A.M. corner of Braddock Drive and Harter Avenue. Officers stopped a man for riding a bicycle on the sidewalk. The man said he had been arrested twice for possession of cocaine and methamphetamine. He showed signs of drug use and failed a field sobriety test. "I haven't smoked rock since this morning," the man said. During a search, one of the officers found a cocaine rock in the man's pocket. "Damn, I forgot that was in there," the man said. (Culver City)

"AS A MATTER OF FACT, I RECEIVED A LETTER THREE weeks ago," Margaret Hobbs told me. "Randy was in my history class. A bright young man, but headed for trouble, anybody could see that. He wrote to ask forgiveness for plagiarizing two term papers. Can you imagine, after all these years?"

Margaret was in her sixties, with the beautiful silvery blue hair you see in commercials. She lived in a Venice apartment a few blocks from the boardwalk and the mystery bookstore where I had my first signing when *Out of the Ashes* was published two years ago. She was the fifth person from Randy's list that I'd visited this morning, only the second I'd talked to (two hadn't been home, one had received the letter and tossed it, unread), and she was saddened to hear of Randy's death. So was the Santa Monica mom-and-pop grocery store owner for whom Randy had worked one summer and from whom he had now admitted stealing.

"A little late, but it's something," the man said, referring to the two hundred dollars Randy had included with his apology. "My wife suspected him all the time, but he had me fooled. What's he up to now, anyway?" he asked, and sighed when I told him. "A shame."

I had written down the addresses Randy had checked off and grouped them by location. I'd started with Santa Monica and Venice and moved east to Culver City, where Randy had grown up. During the next three hours I talked to over a dozen people whose lives Randy had touched, as in the case of a nurse who lived a block away from the Creeleys.

"He was thirteen," she told me. "I hired him to paint a room, and he took forty dollars from my wallet. He denied it, but I knew it was him. I could've reported him to the police. But he was such a sweet boy, and so heartsick about his mother. I couldn't bring myself to do it. It's nice that he wrote, don't you think? And he sent forty dollars, too."

I talked to other people who had suspected that Randy had stolen items or money but, like the nurse, were loath to report

him. From one couple, Randy had asked forgiveness for intro-
ducing their son to marijuana. From another, for sideswiping
their car. For some, Randy's letter had rekindled anger, but most
people were sorry to hear he'd died and smiled wistfully when they
talked about him. I wondered if Randy's life would have taken a
different course if one or more of these kind, forgiving people had
taken a tougher line with him. Maybe not. They had played their
roles in the video of Randy's life, and he had played his.

Everyone I talked to told me Randy had changed almost
overnight after Sue Ann left. And almost everyone hinted that
Alice hadn't improved the situation.

"She's not an easy woman," a neighbor said. "But I have to
say she tried hard to make a home for Roland and those kids."

I had a clearer picture of the sad pattern of Randy's path to
prison, but nothing I'd learned implicated anyone else or provided a motive for Randy's murder. I couldn't imagine anyone
seeking revenge after so many years over a minor theft or a dent
in a car. The encouraging news was that Trina had told the truth
about Randy's letters, which suggested that she may have been
honest about other things she'd said.

Like Jim. Since last night I'd been looking over my shoulder
and in the rearview mirror, not really expecting to find someone
following me. Still . . .

After my last stop in Culver City I found myself on Goldwyn
Terrace. I slowed when I passed the Creeley house, but neither
the Mazda nor the Ford Explorer that I'd seen last time was in the
driveway. I would have liked to ask Alice about her phone call to
Randy the day he died, but even if she'd been home, she probably wouldn't have talked to me.

It was past two and I hadn't eaten anything since the English
muffin and mozzarella cheese I'd had for breakfast. I drove to a
restaurant on Pico and ordered a veggie burger. From there I
drove to South Pasadena. With traffic it's over an hour's drive, but

Randy had checked off several addresses in the area, and there had been two calls with a 626 area code on his phone.

Pasadena (Chippewa Indian for "Crown of the Valley") is about nine miles northeast of downtown Los Angeles and is nestled at the foot of the 10,000-plus-feet-high San Gabriel Mountains, which make a magnificent backdrop if you're driving along the 210 freeway. Originally settled by the Tongva Indians, Pasadena was a Spanish mission before it attracted a group of Indiana residents who wanted to create the "California Colony of Indiana" and relocate there for the warm climate. It was a peaceful city (probably even more so after it became incorporated in 1886, primarily to get rid of a saloon), and for a long time it was known for its citrus groves and vineyards and as a winter resort for the wealthy.

Pasadena still has a quaint, sleepy flavor. I've been there several times, most recently with Zack. We walked around Old Town, caught an exhibit at the Norton Simon Museum, and toured one of its many historic homes. When I was younger my family and I camped out several times at three in the morning in the biting cold on New Year's Day to get a good look at the magnificent floats in the Rose Parade. And now that I'm a published writer, I always drop in at Vroman's, a local independent, to see if my book is in stock and faced out, and say hi to the people at BOOK'em Mysteries. The city has a growing Jewish population, though only a small Orthodox one, and you can get a kosher meal at nearby Cal Tech, which has a kosher kitchen, or a snack at the Coffee Bean & Tea Leaf on Fair Oaks in South Pasadena, where I stopped now for a vanilla latte.

Fair Oaks was also one of the addresses from Randy's list. It belonged to a blond woman in her forties whose face turned a shade of eggplant when I mentioned his name.

"I don't care how many letters he sends," she said. "He's scum."

One night over ten years ago, she told me, Randy had hidden behind bushes in front of her house and leapt out as she walked up to her door. He'd taken her wallet and her peace of mind and she'd never been the same. The letter had revived the nightmares.

"The fact that he sent the letter to my house, that bothers me," she told me. "What if it's some game?"

I told her he'd died, and saw her startled expression. She didn't do a pirouette, but she wasn't unhappy.

"Well, I guess I won't be getting any more letters," she said, and shut the door.

My next stop was in San Marino, a small, wealthy enclave near South Pasadena that is home to the Huntington Library, where my mother and I have spent many enjoyable hours admiring art and old folios and strolling through its botanical gardens. Driving through the well-groomed neighborhood, I admired stately homes set back from golf course–size lawns and made two wrong turns before I found Cambridge Road.

After parking my Acura, I made my way up the long brick walk to the front door of a graceful two-story white Colonial. Before I could ring the bell, the door was yanked open by a lanky, towheaded teenager who looked startled to see me on the doorstep.

I was startled, too. He was strikingly handsome, with eyes the color of walnut.

"Hi." He sounded uncomfortable, probably because I was staring.

"Hi." I pulled my lips into a smile. "Is your mother home?"

"She's inside. Mom, somebody's here," he called and dashed toward the driveway and the silver Audi parked in front of a dark green sport-utility vehicle.

It was Randy—the way he would have looked at sixteen or seventeen. I watched the boy as he pulled open the front door and got inside the Audi. I was still watching as he backed out of the driveway and drove off too quickly, the way my brother Joey does.

"Can I help you?"

Maybe I was wrong, I thought, but my heart raced as I turned toward the woman who was speaking, and when I saw her, I knew.

Sue Ann Creely.

She must have been fifty or close to it, and there were fine lines around her brown eyes and grooves running from her delicate nose to the corners of her pink-lipsticked mouth, but she didn't look all that different from the young mother in the photo whose face I had memorized. She looked elegant, composed. That was different, and so was her chin-length hair, a rich blend of blond and brown. She was wearing cream slacks and a fawn-colored sweater with a matching cardigan whose sleeves she'd looped in front.

"My name is Molly Blume. I wonder if I could speak to you a minute, Mrs. Richardson." The name had been next to the address on Randy's list.

"What's this about?" She had a smooth, cultured voice.

"Your son."

She glanced toward the driveway. "You just missed him." A frown darkened her lovely face. "Is something wrong?"

"I meant your other son. Randy." If I hadn't been watching, I wouldn't have seen her jaw stiffen.

She moved several strands of hair behind her ear. "I don't have another son. You must have the wrong Richardson. Sorry."

"He wrote down your name and address. That's how I found you. And your phone number is on his cell phone." It was a reasonable guess.

She shook her head. "There's some mistake."

Her face was a well-crafted balance between annoyance and confusion, but I could see alarm in her eyes. Eyes, I have learned, find it harder to mask the truth, although Ron's had fooled me often and for some time.

"I'd like to talk to you, Sue Ann."

"My name isn't Sue Ann." She took a step back.

"I'll leave my card in case you change your mind."

She slammed the door shut, but I didn't hear footsteps. I had the feeling she was on the other side, waiting to make sure I would leave.

I dropped my card into the brass mailbox and walked to my car. I was tempted to drive home—I was too wound up to think straight—but I had three more Pasadena addresses and I wasn't keen on coming back tomorrow to check them out.

One was an old address. "He moved," the homeowner told me about the man whose name Randy had written down. "The post office probably forwarded the letter."

The woman at the second address wouldn't discuss the letter. "It's personal" was all that she would tell me.

My last stop, at twenty after five, was a small, tidy house near Washington Avenue, so close to the San Gabriels that they looked as if they were in the backyard of the petite young woman with short brown hair who opened the door and smiled pleasantly after I showed her my card. She was my age, I thought, give or take a few years, and she was wearing a gray skirt and royal blue sweater that overwhelmed her small frame.

I did my thing—introduced myself and gave her my credentials, told her I was writing an article about Randy Creeley, asked her if she'd received a letter from him recently and would she mind telling me about it. I was prepared for strike three, would almost have welcomed it because it was getting dark and chilly and home was beginning to sound awfully good.

"I *did* get a letter," she said. "I met Randy at Rachel's Tent around six years ago. I remember him well."

CHAPTER THIRTY-FOUR

HER NAME WAS CHARLIE—SHORT FOR CHARLOTTE, SHE TOLD me when we were sitting opposite each other on camel-colored love seats in a small living room that smelled of fresh paint. I'd conducted most of today's interviews on doorsteps, but Charlie had invited me inside and insisted on serving coffee and Pepperidge Farm cookies, which happen to be kosher, so I had a few.

"I haven't talked to Randy for almost half a year," she said. "I meant to phone him when I got his letter. So what's the focus of your piece?"

She obviously hadn't heard about Randy's death, and I decided to postpone telling her. "The letters he sent. Apparently, he was trying to make amends to people he'd wronged. Most people don't take responsibility for their actions. That makes Randy unique and interesting. I'm hoping my readers will think so, too." If she'd heard about his death, I would have thrown in "poignant."

"I would read it." Charlie took a sip of coffee.

"You mentioned that you met Randy at Rachel's Tent," I said. "I'd be interested to hear about your experiences there, if you feel comfortable talking about them."

She hesitated. "I wouldn't want my name in your article."

"Then I won't put it in."

That and my smile must have reassured her. She set her cup on the coffee table and settled against the sofa cushion. "My story's not all that unusual. I ran away from home because my step-dad was molesting me and my mom wouldn't do anything about it. I tried getting a job, but didn't have any skills or a high school diploma. So I hooked up with some guy I met. He was an alcoholic, and I became one, too. It doesn't take much. Then he started beating me."

She said this without drama, as though she were telling me the plot of a movie she'd just seen. She'd probably told her story numerous times, and maybe this was the best way she could get through it without reliving painful memories.

"I wanted to leave," Charlie continued, "but I was afraid. Of what he'd do, of how I'd survive. I'd probably still be with him if not for Rachel's Tent. Or dead. Have you been there?" When I nodded, she said, "That was the best day of my life, the day I walked in those doors." There was a catch in her voice.

She had found her way to the agency six years ago. A year and a half later she had moved to Pasadena to work as a secretary for a real estate company, a job she'd found through Rachel's Tent's placement service. The agency had given her the vocational training that had prepared her for the job. The staff had coached her for the interview and the agency had provided the suit she'd worn, along with a modest starter wardrobe. Most important, Rachel's Tent had given her the tools and courage to escape an abusive relationship and enter a recovery program for her alcohol addiction.

"Five years ago I figured I'd be living on the streets," she said. "Now I'm leasing this house with an option to buy it. I'm studying for my Realtor's license, and I'm dating a wonderful man." She said this with pride and some wonder, as though she couldn't believe it herself. "And if things don't work out between us, that's okay, too. I know I can handle things on my own."

I asked her if she had known Randy well.

"Everybody knew him well." Charlie's smile lit up her face and crinkled the corners of her green eyes. "He was easy to talk to, and he made you believe he really cared about you. Like when he talked about his own battle with addiction."

I nodded. "One on one, you mean?"

"That, and in group. They always had different people come to talk to us, people who went through what we did and could understand what it's like. You don't get that from a textbook."

Randy lecturing about drug addiction was high irony—like Yasir Arafat getting the Nobel Peace Prize, which still amazes me—and an embarrassment to everyone at Rachel's Tent who knew the truth about his drug dealing. No wonder Bramer and Horton hadn't mentioned it.

"Was he a good lecturer?" I asked.

"One of the best. Well, he was an actor, so he had that extra edge, you know? He certainly fooled me." Now her smile was wry and not amused.

I wondered if Charlie was referring to his drug use. "In what way?"

"High school stuff, really. I thought he had a thing for me." She blushed. "He used to drive us in the agency van to special activities, and he spent a lot of time with me. The recreational therapist didn't like it. Anyway, Randy told me he thought I was special, that he wanted to get to know me. Can you believe I fell for that?" Charlie laughed, but I could hear the hurt in her voice.

I had fallen for similar lines, so I knew how she felt. "How do you know it wasn't true?"

"Because the next day he was cozying up to someone else. And a couple of days later, he dropped this other woman and went on to the next."

"Playing the field, huh?" Barbara Anik had said Randy was too friendly with the clients.

"I guess. Except he never tried anything, you know? It was more like, 'Tell me what's bothering you, Charlie, I really care.' Or, 'I'm a good listener, anything you tell me stays right here.' "

Had Randy been soliciting information? If so, I didn't think it was for blackmail purposes, because whatever these women told him, they'd told voluntarily. Or had he planned to blackmail other people in their lives? Like Charlie's stepfather?

"How many women did he do this with, Charlie?"

She pushed at a cuticle. "Six or seven that I knew of. There could've been more. A couple of us talked about it later, which is how I know Randy gave them pretty much the line he gave me. Well, all except one woman. Randy spent time with her, too, but she left Rachel's Tent kind of sudden."

Aggie's client? The one Aggie had been encouraging to go to the police? "Do you know her name?"

Charlie furrowed her brow. "It's at the tip of my tongue, but I can't remember. Don't you hate when that happens?" She smiled and shook her head.

I told her I did.

"Right after that, one of the social workers was killed," Charlie said, her voice somber now. "Randy changed. No more kidding around, no more flirting. I could tell he was real shook up."

"Was this your social worker?" I asked.

Charlie shook her head. "I heard she was really nice. She was only twenty-four. I remember thinking how lucky I was. I mean, the way my life was going six years ago, it could easily have been me who was killed."

I thought about my redhead and described her to Charlie. "Does that sound like someone Randy was friendly with?"

"Could be. Like I said, he was friendly with everyone. And there were a lot of women at Rachel's Tent." She was working the cuticle and seemed lost in thought.

"Tell me about the letter Randy wrote," I said. "By the way, how did he have your address?"

"We stayed in touch. Well, *I* did." She laughed and her face took on a tinge of pink. "I always kept hoping he'd get interested in me. He's so good-looking, don't you think? He's probably dating some Hollywood actress now."

"Charlie, I'm sorry to tell you that Randy died."

"Randy's dead?" She stared at me and blinked rapidly. Tears filled her eyes. "You're sure?" she asked, her voice husky.

"The police think he overdosed. I'm sorry."

She sniffled and picked at the fabric of her skirt. After a moment, she said, "I'm glad I have his letter. That's something."

"Do you think I could see it, Charlie?"

"It's kind of personal. I can tell you what it said. It came a few weeks ago. I thought it was an invitation or something, but it was an apology."

"For leading you on?"

She nodded. "He said he knew he hurt my feelings. He wrote about other stuff, too." She wiped away her tears.

"Did he say anything about dealing drugs at Rachel's Tent?"

Charlie's eyes widened. "No. Was he?"

"I don't know."

"Well, all I can tell you is that he sounded real sincere when he talked to us about staying clean. But you never know about people, do you? Huh," she added, as if she'd just absorbed the possibility.

"So that was it? In the letter, I mean."

"Actually, mostly he wrote about this." Charlie raised her arm and pushed back the sleeve of her sweater to show me the red thread tied around her wrist.

"You got that when you left Rachel's Tent, right?"

"Not this one. This is the one Randy just sent, with the letter. He said the first one wasn't from Israel. There was nothing special about it. He said it was all his doing. He'd fooled Dr. Bramer and everyone else, and now he wanted to make everything right. I wonder how many other women he wrote to saying the same thing."

CHAPTER THIRTY-FIVE

NIGHT WAS FALLING QUICKLY WHEN I LEFT CHARLIE'S house. The sky was changing from feathery gray to solid charcoal as I drove down Lake to Colorado, and by the time I made a left onto Arroyo Parkway, only a few stars relieved the inky blackness.

I couldn't stop thinking about Randy and the red threads he'd sold to (or through?) Rachel's Tent. All fake. In retrospect, I shouldn't have been surprised. Even people who liked Randy suspected that he'd been a liar and manipulator most of his life, and while Anthony Horton's prison experience had infused him with the desire to improve his life, from what I've read about prisons and rehabilitation, Horton was the exception, not the rule.

It was possible that Randy had entered Rachel's Tent determined to make a fresh start. But it's easy to slip, and when he saw an opportunity to make extra cash at Rachel's Tent, he seized it. No one would know. No one would be hurt. Thread is thread. Or maybe he'd been the actor all the time, giving a winning performance to Horton and Bramer, looking for the best venue to continue his life of petty crime. I knew what Alice Creeley would say, and maybe she was right.

In either case, after six years or so, a close brush with death had shaken him and done what prison hadn't. Randy had been determined to repent, and not just in words.

This wasn't what I'd come to Pasadena to learn, but it was intriguing and troubling, and maybe it explained the two calls Randy had placed to Rachel's Tent the day he died.

I had been lost in thought and hadn't noticed when the street had turned into a freeway. Running eight miles between Pasadena and L.A., Arroyo Seco (Spanish for "Dry Stream") is the oldest freeway in California, a serpentine byway with three lanes in each direction that wasn't built to accommodate today's heavy traffic and speeds and has more curves than Anna Nicole Smith, and buckled side rails that give testimony to the numerous accidents that have taken place here. It also features beautiful bridges that form overpasses, though their beauty is lost at night, and it's been designated a historic highway, which probably explains the disrepair.

I stayed in the middle lane, avoiding the rails on my left and the merging traffic on my right. I was fine for now, but in ten minutes or so, when I passed Dodger Stadium and approached downtown L.A., two other freeways would converge with the 110 (Arroyo's other name). At that point I'd have to get into my right lane because two exits later I'd have to cross several lanes to access the Hollywood Freeway, which would take me home. The setup is the epitome of ridiculously dangerous engineering and is, I'm sure, the cause of many accidents. It's the reason I dislike driving the 110 even in daylight, when I can see the signs more clearly and plan my move. One time I inadvertently exited on Sunset and ended up in Chinatown, which isn't bad if you know your way around, but this happened at night, and I'd had to phone my dad and have him talk me through the streets until I was back on a street I recognized.

My thoughts returned to Randy and the phone calls, and the letter he'd sent Bramer. I knew that he had from the check next to the director's name on the list Trina had left with me, and if I'd learned nothing else today, I'd verified that every person whose name had been checked off had received an apology from Randy.

Until now I had assumed that Randy had asked Bramer's forgiveness for selling drugs at the agency and betraying his trust. Maybe not. Maybe he'd sought forgiveness for selling the bogus threads and asked Bramer to send letters of apology on Randy's behalf, along with genuine threads, to all the women who had received or bought fake ones. And if Bramer had refused?

Then I'll have to do it myself, Dr. Bramer.

According to the director, Randy had ordered the threads and filled the envelopes. Rachel's Tent had taken care of the rest. Which meant that Randy wouldn't have had mailing addresses for the people who had received the threads.

If you won't help me, Dr. Bramer, I'll have to figure out something else. I have to do what's right, make amends.

A newspaper ad?

All speculation.

Arroyo was doing its thing, winding back and forth. Unlike the oncoming Pasadena-bound traffic, a stalled parade of bright headlights that glared at me, the L.A.-bound traffic was moving at a decent pace. I glanced in my rearview mirror and noticed that the twin dots of light from the car behind me were becoming larger. A few seconds later the car—an SUV, I now saw—was too close for my comfort.

I looked right and left, but there were no openings in either lane. With my eyes on the mirror, I honked and pressed my brakes several times, hoping the SUV driver would get the message. A moment later he dropped back. I watched him for a few seconds and relaxed when I saw that he was maintaining a safe distance between us.

I wondered if Randy had offered to pay for the replacement threads. According to Mike, he'd ordered "lots" of threads a few months ago on the Internet, where on some sites, Zack had said, the threads were selling for thirty-six dollars each.

Thirty-six dollars multiplied by X number of women a year, multiplied by six or seven years.

Even at half that price per thread, that could add up to a hefty chunk of money in reimbursements, especially for someone who hadn't been working steadily during the past nine months and had been doing odd jobs just to pay the rent and get by. Of course, for all I knew, Randy had a healthy bank account. Or maybe he'd offered to pay off his debt over time.

Bramer must have been livid when Randy confessed, but I suspected that Randy's betrayal had hit Horton even harder. He'd been emotional when he talked about Randy, maybe because of their shared history of abandonment. And concerned about his passion, Rachel's Tent.

It took years of hard work and a lot of dollars to make it what it is today. All it takes is a couple of questions, a raised eyebrow, and the place is history.

But what if Horton didn't know about Randy's scam?

Suppose Bramer had discovered nine or ten months ago what Randy had been doing. Bramer may have been afraid to tell Horton that his dream had been defiled. Maybe, I mused, he'd fabricated the anonymous note that accused Randy of dealing drugs at the agency. If Randy had been dealing drugs, removing him from the agency would have resolved the problem, and any clients he'd involved would have been eager to remain anonymous. But if clients learned that their hallowed red threads had come directly from a five-and-dime store . . .

People don't like to be scammed. And this wasn't just about money. This was about faked spirituality, about the abuse of faith. Charlie hadn't been upset with the agency, but she was staunchly loyal to the people who had saved her life, and maybe she hadn't been invested all that much in the red thread and what it signified. Some of the women Randy had duped might not be so forgiving.

I'm not a legal expert, but I assumed that Randy's actions had rendered the agency liable for multiple lawsuits, or even a class action suit. I could see the newspaper headlines:

RACHEL'S TENT COLLAPSES AS THREADS OF DECEIT UNRAVEL
SCAMMED CLIENTS SEE RED

And the lawyers' fees would no doubt be steep. They always are. Was this what Randy had meant when he'd talked to his sponsor about the financial and legal repercussions that could affect someone else if he made amends?

I passed under the Via Mirasol bridge and checked my rearview mirror. The SUV was kissing my butt again. The left lane was crowded with cars. So was the right lane, which also had two huge trucks. I was already doing sixty, five miles over the speed limit, which would be slow on other freeways, but not on the 110 with its hairpin curves. And I was closing in on the car in front of me.

I glared at the SUV through the mirror, as though he could

see me. Jerk, I thought. I honked and signaled with my brakes again, but the SUV was coming closer. When the left lane opened ten or twenty seconds later, I moved into it to allow the SUV to pass and wondered where Highway Patrol was when you needed them.

I thought again about the two calls Randy had made to Rachel's Tent the morning he died. Had he given Bramer an ultimatum?

Send the letters or I'm going public with what I've done. I'll tell Mr. Horton.

But even if the director was furious and faced potential embarrassment and a PR fiasco . . . Even if the agency had to reimburse everyone who had bought the fake threads, or replace them with genuine ones, even if they had to deal with lawsuits and legal fees . . . Even if all that was so, did that constitute a motive to kill someone?

But what if Bramer thought his job would be jeopardized by Randy's campaign of penitence? What if he thought Horton would make him the scapegoat?

This happened under your watch, William. Sorry, but I have to cut my losses.

One of Horton's golden rules.

I passed the Avenue Twenty-six exit. Next was Academy Road, which I'd taken several years ago when Connors had given me a tour of the Los Angeles Police Academy. In the distance I could see the lit-up skyline of downtown. Dodger Stadium was next, and not much farther up, the broad diagonal swerve that lay in store for me after the Sunset exit. I turned on my blinker and prepared to move into my right lane, but the SUV inched up so that it was blocking me.

There was an empty stretch of several hundred feet between my Acura and the car in front of me. I took the next curve, then sped up to pass the SUV. The driver sped up, too. I honked. He kept the front of his car alongside the middle of mine so that I couldn't make eye contact.

Fine, I thought. Let the jerk show me he's king of the road. I slowed down. He slowed, too, and a few seconds later, as my faithful Acura took another harrowing curve, I had a moment of panic when I saw that the SUV was creeping into my lane. I blared my horn again, but instead of correcting his position, the driver was narrowing the distance between his large car and mine, and I realized with alarm that set my heart racing that he was forcing me closer to the rails.

There were cars in front of me and behind me. I had no room to move, and the SUV was inches from the passenger side of my car. Still sounding my horn, I turned left with the next curve and heard the shriek of steel against steel. I had a brief reprieve of straight road, then another bend, this one to the right, but the one after that, only seconds later, was to the left again. I gritted my teeth at the screech of metal and felt the impact as my car grazed the rails.

The veins in my neck were pulsing madly. My muscles were rigid. My cell phone was in my purse, but I couldn't take my hand off the wheel to dial 911. I could only hope that some other driver had noticed what was going on and would alert the police, whose training grounds I'd passed only minutes ago.

The side of my car was scraping the rails. With my right hand gripping the steering wheel, I honked the horn repeatedly. Finally the Toyota in front of me moved to the right, in front of the SUV. My heart in my throat, I accelerated to eighty and urged the Acura forward as if it were a stallion. With only feet between me and the small car that now loomed in front of me, I passed the Toyota and made a sharp diagonal into the right lane.

Ahead of the Toyota, whose driver was honking furiously at me, ahead of the SUV.

Seconds later the Toyota returned to the left lane. Now the

SUV was behind me again, closing the gap between us with each curve.

I had passed the Dodger Stadium and Hill Street exits. Sunset was next. Ahead of me were the large green signs for the Santa Ana and Hollywood Freeways, and for the Harbor, which is the 110, renamed once you reach downtown.

Another sign indicated that the on-ramp to the Hollywood was approaching. It would be all the way to my right, I knew, on the other side of a triangular median.

The driver of the SUV didn't know which freeway I would be taking. I debated staying on the 110 or taking the Santa Ana and finding an alternate route home once I lost the SUV.

If I lost him. And if I didn't? I could be driving around for hours in unfamiliar territory.

I checked my gas gauge. The icon for the tank was blinking.

I passed Sunset.

If I turned off the 110 to access the Hollywood, the SUV driver could follow me, but I could lead him to the Hollywood police station.

Unless something happened before I got there.

I had seconds to decide. If I waited too long, I wouldn't be able to cross over because of the median.

If I *did* cross, I ran the risk of colliding with traffic speeding along lanes I couldn't yet see.

My hands were slick with perspiration. My heart thudded. There was the Hollywood Freeway sign.

I looked quickly to my right. The lane next to me was clear. The lane to its right was a line of barely moving cars.

The SUV was on my bumper.

Biting my upper lip, I made a sudden turn and drove onto the widest part of the median. The SUV sped by. I braked, but for a second or two my Acura bounced along the median, and my body bounced with it. Two seconds can be a long time. The wheels dropped and touched asphalt again. The impact jarred my teeth, which I hadn't realized I'd clenched.

My head whipped forward and backward and forward again. My palm was still on the horn when my car came to a shuddering stop and smacked the rear of a black BMW.

CHAPTER THIRTY-SIX

I WAS NAUSEOUS AND DIZZY. MY HEAD WAS POUNDING, ES-
pecially where the redhead had struck me with the butt of her gun.

The driver of the BMW, a short, wiry man with curly brown
hair, was rattling my car door.

"What the hell!" he yelled. "Are you crazy, lady?"

Even in the dark I could see that his face was red, his eyes
manic. I lowered my window a few inches.

"Someone was trying to crash into me," I said. "I'm sorry
about—"

"Sorry doesn't do it, lady. You could have killed me!"

He said the same thing to the California Highway Patrol
motorcycle officer who had witnessed my maneuver. The officer,
whose name was Lansing, checked to see that I was all right.

Then he radioed for help, which arrived a few minutes later in the form of another motorcycle CHP officer, who set flares and began to clear the traffic I'd brought to a halt. He moved my car so that it was blocking only one lane.

Lansing was medium height, well built and handsome. Most Chippies are—I suppose they have to be, since Erik Estrada set the bar. He took notes while he talked to me and to the driver of the BMW, who drove off after he and I exchanged insurance information.

Lansing had listened without expression while I explained about the SUV that had been chasing me.

"Were you feeling all right when you started driving, ma'am?" he asked now.

"I was fine."

I knew he was assessing me to see if I was under the influence of liquor or drugs. I had calmed down somewhat, but I was shivering from the blasts of cold air caused by the cars that were speeding by on all sides. I hoped he wouldn't mistake my shivering for symptoms of withdrawal.

"Did you get the license number of this SUV, ma'am?"

I could barely hear him over the roaring and high-pitched whining of the cars. "No. I didn't have time. I was too scared. I was just trying to figure out how to get away from him."

He nodded. "What about the make of the car, ma'am?"

"I couldn't tell." Most SUVs look alike to me, especially at night. "It could have been black, or a dark blue or dark green." I hugged my arms against the cold, which was going right through my peacoat.

"Was the driver a male or female, ma'am?"

"I don't know. I couldn't see, because of the way he positioned the car. I honked at him a few times, because he was crowding me. I used my brakes to try to signal him. Maybe I upset him. Maybe it was road rage."

"Anything else I should know?"

I debated telling Lansing that someone may have been following me. Even if it was true, I had no idea who that someone could be, but the dark green SUV in Sue Ann's driveway popped into my mind.

Maybe I would tell Connors. "No. Can I leave now?"

I assumed the Acura would start. The bumper was scraped and dented, but aside from a small buckling in the hood, I hadn't noticed much damage. The BMW hadn't looked bad, either, but even minor damages would probably translate into several thousand dollars in repair costs.

He handed me a card. "You can give this to your insurance company and ask them to get you a copy of the traffic report."

I dropped the card into my purse. "And that's it?"

"Unless you get a letter telling you to appear in court. This will go on your driving record, though. Nothing you can do about that."

I reined in my frustration. "I was trying to lose the SUV. I didn't do this on purpose, you know."

"You're lucky you didn't kill someone, ma'am, or yourself. To be honest, we have only your word that someone was following you. I'd like to clear this lane, ma'am."

"*You* were following me. Didn't you see the SUV on my bumper?"

"No, ma'am. I was too busy watching you. People have accidents all the time. Sometimes they make a wrong turn, or their hand slips. Sometimes they jump the median because they decide too late they want to take the 101."

"That's not what happened."

"I'm not saying it did. But you can't tell me the license plate number or car model or color. You can't tell me anything about the driver. And no one called in anything about an SUV involved in a noncontact hit-and-run."

"Check out the scrapes on the driver's side of my car, Officer Lansing. He was trying to force me over the rails."

"I don't mean to be insulting, ma'am, but I have no way of knowing when those marks were made. I'd take photos if I were you, in case you need them for court. Have a good night."

Have a good night?

Someone had tried to run me off the road. My car was damaged. Even if the traffic court judge let me off and I didn't have to pay any fines, I had a permanent mark on my record and my insurance rates would go up. I reminded myself that I should be grateful to be alive, but I felt like a child with a badly scraped knee. The Band-Aid with Disney characters that the doctor had slapped on was cute, but the scrape hurt like hell, the iodine had stung, and I still felt like crying.

I tried starting the Acura. It made cranking sounds, rebuking me for what I'd put it through. I was worried that I'd damaged something by driving over the median, but Lansing said I'd probably flooded the engine.

"Don't pump the pedal," he said. "You want to floor it and keep it all the way down while you turn the key in the ignition."

I can't say for sure, but I think he looked amused.

"Have a good night," he repeated minutes later when my engine purred. He patted my hood as if it were a pet. *Good car, nice car.* "And drive safely."

CHAPTER THIRTY-SEVEN

Isaac had left a yellow post-it on my door, telling me he'd taken in the packages UPS had delivered this afternoon. I hadn't talked to my landlord in days and knew he was probably hurt. I knocked on his door and thanked him.

"Wait right here," he said, and disappeared. A moment later he was back.

"What do you think?"

I wasn't sure what I was supposed to be looking at. He was wearing his usual outfit, a plaid shirt and dark slacks pulled up well past his skinny waist.

"Here." He pointed to the black suede yarmulke on his almost bald head. "I bought it on Fairfax for the wedding."

I told him it looked great.

He grinned. "I have a white satin one from my grand-daughter's bat mitzvah, but I wanted one like your dad wears, and Zack, so I'd fit in. Anyway, I'm breaking it in."

He helped me take the packages to my apartment, and we made a coffee date for tomorrow morning.

I would have loved to soak in a hot tub, but Zack would be here in less than half an hour, so I settled for a shower and let the water beat against the back of my neck and my shoulders, which were beginning to feel stiff. Whiplash, I realized.

I had just stepped out of the shower when Trina phoned.

"I was beginning to worry," I told her. "I left several messages. Where are you?"

"I told you, a hotel." She sounded edgy. "Did you find out anything from the list I gave you?"

"I spent the day talking to people who knew Randy. He was selling fake red threads at Rachel's Tent."

"That's it?"

"So far." You get what you pay for, I thought, a little miffed. "You said Randy was interested in someone after Aggie. Did he tell you her name?"

"That was six *years* ago. Why?"

"I'm wondering if she's the redhead I told you about. She's not Doreen."

"Randy didn't want to tell me her name. I remember that. Let me think. It was with a Dee," she said a moment later. "Donna? Dina? No, *Diana*. I teased him about her. 'How's Princess Di?' "

Diana Warfield? "Thanks. Are you okay, Trina?" I had the feeling she was upset with me.

"No, I'm not okay! I feel like a prisoner. I want to go home. Look, I know I asked you to help, but I changed my mind. Forget the list. Forget everything."

"I don't understand. Did you hear from Jim again?"

"He called today. I hung up on him."

"If you went to the police—"

"How will they find him? He'll wait until they stop looking and then . . . I have to figure out what this package is and where Randy hid it. I have to figure out who killed Randy."

"The police can help you, Trina."

"I don't need their help. A friend is helping me."

"You have no idea what the package could be? Did Randy have a bank safe-deposit box?"

"I wish everybody would stop asking me! He didn't have a safe-deposit box. The only *things* he left me were his laptop and journal. Those aren't packages."

"Trina—"

She had hung up.

I was upset by the phone call, but I couldn't blame her for being agitated. I would be, too. I finished toweling myself and put on a long-sleeved V-necked cream cashmere sweater and a flared black wool skirt that stopped an inch above my knee (my compromise length). After eating a few Hershey's Kisses, I swallowed three Advil tablets, which you're not supposed to do on an empty stomach, hence the chocolate. I was applying lipstick when Zack arrived.

"You're all right," he said with relief as he helped me on with my coat.

It felt good to be cared for. "Didn't you believe me?" I had phoned him on the way home and told him I'd been in a traffic accident but was unharmed.

"I thought you didn't want to worry me. You're sure you're up to this, Molly?"

"I'm sure."

I was exhausted and achy, but I'd canceled too many dates and appointments in the past week. Tonight was the last time we'd see each other until the wedding, and I wanted the evening to be special.

On the way to his car we stopped to look at my Acura.

"It doesn't look too bad," he said when we were in his Honda. He buckled his seat belt. "How did you get the front and side damaged at the same time?"

I told him what had happened and saw his lips tighten, the way they had when I'd narrated my run-in with the redhead.

"You must have been terrified," he said quietly.

"Pretty much." In my mind I saw the SUV barreling toward me, pressing the Acura against the rails. I heard the screech of metal against metal. "I haven't told my family, so don't say anything."

"You should probably *bentch gomel,*" Zack said, referring to the special prayer you say to thank God when you've survived a dangerous situation or journey. "It's ridiculous how many lunatics there are on the road," he added, with a surge of anger that shook his voice.

I could have left it at that. "I'm not sure it *was* road rage. Last night at the deli, Randy's sponsor, Max, thought someone was watching me. When I turned around to see who it was, the person was walking out the door."

"The person?"

He sounded calmer than I'd expected. "Max couldn't tell if it was a man or a woman. He or she was wearing a hat."

"And you think this person may have followed you to Pasadena today?"

I shrugged. "It sounds crazy when you say it, doesn't it? That's why I didn't mention it to the cop. I don't think he believed there *was* an SUV. I plan to tell Connors tomorrow, though."

Zack nodded. "Good."

"It *could* be road rage."

He inserted the key into the ignition slot but didn't turn it. "Suppose someone *did* follow you and try to run you off the road. Why would anyone do that?"

"I was thinking about Bramer, the director of Rachel's Tent. Or Randy's mother. Her name is Richardson now. I met her today." I told Zack how I'd found her. "She has a dark green SUV. I didn't notice the make, because the son's car was parked in front of it, and I was watching him."

Zack drummed his fingers on the steering wheel. "So she tried to kill you to keep her ex-husband from finding out she's been living half an hour away all these years? I can't see that as a motive, Molly. It's not that big a deal. And if *you* found her, someone else could."

"But no one else is looking. And maybe she's not worried about her ex-husband. Maybe she doesn't want Richardson to find out that she walked out on her first husband and two kids."

"It's more of a motive," Zack agreed. "*If* the new husband doesn't know about her past. But would she kill you for that?" He shrugged. "What about Bramer?"

I explained about Charlie and her new red thread and my theory. "Maybe Bramer is worried that I'll discover the truth and make it public."

"You could say the same about Horton. From what you said, Rachel's Tent is very important to him."

"His baby." It was a valid point. "But Horton has a hundred businesses, Zack. Bramer has only Rachel's Tent and his reputation."

"Talk to Connors. Let him check it out." Zack turned on the ignition.

"I found out Brian's last name, by the way," I said as we pulled away from the curb. "From San Diego? It's Warfield. I Googled him last night and got a business address for a real estate company. But I have no way of knowing whether he's the right Brian Warfield. And I still don't know his connection to the redhead or how she had his phone."

"Maybe they're married, and she borrowed it that day you met her."

"Why would she do that?"

Zack shrugged. "Because hers wasn't working, and she was driving up to L.A.? Because she didn't want to be traced? You said she was terrified that someone was following her."

I thought about that on the way to the restaurant.

"You know what I can't figure out?" I said when Zack was parking the car. "Even at thirty-six dollars each, Randy would have had to sell an awful lot of threads to afford the Porsche and everything else I saw in his apartment."

He looked at me. "Meaning?"

"He was getting money from something else."

"So we're back to drugs?"

"Or something else. But I have no idea what."

We didn't talk about anything connected to Randy or Aggie during dinner, and I welcomed the respite. A number of people we'd invited to the wedding came over to wish us mazel tov, but for the most part we were left alone in a corner booth that gave us privacy and a sense of intimacy. The steak-for-two topped with caramelized onions was delicious, and my mood was mellow, enhanced by the soft glow of the candles and the chocolate torte I had for dessert and two glasses of champagne that flushed my face—or maybe it was the way Zack kept looking at me all night and the things we said.

But by ten-thirty, when we were standing in front of my apartment door, the Advil was wearing off and I craved a hot bath and sleep.

"It's just as well," Zack said. "I promised I'd help my parents with the seating arrangements."

"The *S* word." I yawned. "I can't imagine not seeing you for seven days. Who made up this rule?"

"Not me." He leaned in close enough to kiss me, close enough so that I could smell the musk of his aftershave and see flecks of gold in his gray-blue eyes. "We can still see each other tomorrow."

"Until four-something tomorrow, right?" I felt like Cinderella at the ball. "Can you get away for lunch?"

"I have a noon meeting. How about breakfast?"

"I'm seeing another man." I told him about my date with Isaac. "You're sure you don't want to come in?" Suddenly I wasn't so tired.

"I should let you sleep. We'll figure out something for tomorrow."

Inside my apartment, I locked the door and slid the dead bolt. The packages UPS had delivered were on the living room sofa, where I'd left them. I picked them up and was about to take them to the guest room when the doorbell rang.

Zack, I thought. I dropped the packages and opened the door and saw Ron slouching in the doorway. My ex-husband is tall and blond and handsome—an Adonis, according to his parents. They probably told him that often enough so that he believes it, which I think accounts for his assumption that the world revolves around him and that he can do no wrong.

"So are you going to let me in, babe?"

I never particularly liked being called "babe" when we were married and had told him so. I like it less now.

"It's kind of late, Ron. I've had a rough day."

"I won't stay long. I was in the neighborhood and saw Zack leave. I wanted to drop off the response card."

That's why there are mailboxes. I stepped out of the way and let him into the apartment we had shared for fourteen months, some of them happy. I'm sure he was thinking the same thing as he glanced around.

"Everything looks pretty much the same," he said. "We had good times here, didn't we, babe?"

"Ron—"

"I didn't fill this out yet." He removed an envelope from a pocket of his black leather jacket. "I figured I'd let you do it." He extended the card toward me.

I shook my head. "It's your decision, Ron. I can understand that you might feel uncomfortable. But if you want to come, we're happy to have you."

"What about you, Molly? What do you want?" He put the card back in his pocket. "Remember in The Graduate, when Katharine Ross is about to tie the knot, and Dustin Hoffman yells, 'Elaine! Elaine!' And she leaves Mr. Perfect at the altar and runs out of the church with Dustin Hoffman. Dustin stopped her from making the biggest mistake of her life, Molly."

His speech sounded a little slurred, and I wondered if he'd had a few drinks. "You're not the Dustin Hoffman character, Ron. I'm not Elaine."

He put his hand on my shoulder. "You don't want to be a rabbi's wife, Molly."

"It comes with the package, Ron. I want to marry Zack. I am marrying Zack." I moved his hand away. "I think you should go home."

"I've changed, you know. I realize I blew it big time. I hurt you badly, and I'm very sorry about that. You don't know how sorry."

I nodded. I was sure he meant what he was saying. He'd said it often in the past, and had meant it then, too, every time. But as Bubbie G says, you can't put sorry in your pocket.

"The point is, Molly, I'm not that guy anymore. I could make it work this time."

"I'm sure you will, Ron. You'll find someone special and make her very happy," I said, though I wasn't sure at all.

He moved closer, until his face was inches from mine. "Are you saying you never think about me, Molly? Don't you miss what we had?"

I could have told him that my memories were mostly sad and painful, that what we had was probably an illusion from the start, that I had fallen for his looks and his quick humor and a zest for life that had temporarily filled the void left by Aggie's murder. I don't know what Ron had fallen for. Whatever it was, it hadn't been enough to hold his interest.

"I'm moving on, Ron. You should, too." I walked to the door and opened it. "Let me know what you decide about the wedding."

He nodded slowly and followed me to the door. "Hey, *I'm* moving on, babe. I moved on long ago." He put his hand on the doorknob and smiled. "I was just kidding around, Molly. You knew that, right?"

"Right." For the first time in years I felt sorry for him.

"I'm glad you're happy. I really am." Before I could protest, he leaned over and kissed my cheek. "So if I come to the wedding, can I bring a date?"

With Ron, it's always about appearances, although in this instance I couldn't blame him. "Let me know her name and I'll have a place card for her."

After he left, I took two Advil tablets and checked my answering machine. My mother had called, and Edie. I had shut off my cell phone so that Zack and I wouldn't be interrupted during dinner. I turned it on now and learned that Charlie had left a message.

"You can call me till eleven," she'd said.

It was five after eleven now, but I placed the call.

"Her name is Iris," Charlie told me. "The woman at Rachel's Tent who left suddenly? I phoned a friend that I met at the agency, and she remembered. It was really bugging me."

"Would your friend be willing to talk to me?" I asked.

"I'm not sure. She doesn't like to talk about her past, and—"

"And what?" I prompted.

"She never said, but I think she had a bad experience while she was at Rachel's Tent. Not with the agency. She loved the agency. We all did." Charlie sounded eager to get that point across. "Anyway, I'll ask her and get back to you."

Drugs? I wondered.

Still thinking about Charlie's friend, I sat at my desk and wrote notes about what I'd accomplished today. I had found Randy's mother. I had learned about his scam. I wondered if one of those discoveries was connected to the SUV that had tried to run me off the road tonight. Or maybe it *was* road rage, or something else.

I went online and tried to find a Diana Warfield in San Diego, but there was no listing. I wasn't surprised. People who disguise themselves to attend funerals and are terrified that someone is following them have unlisted phone numbers. And maybe Diana's last name wasn't Warfield.

The clippings were on my desk. I looked at them again and focused on the one with the crime digest.

An ATM robbery, a police shooting, a body found in a grave, a drug bust, a gang shooting, a domestic violence arrest. Different types of crimes that had taken place in different parts of the city. Something in the digest had been important enough to make Randy hold on to it. I had thought that it was the drug bust that had resulted in a third strike for the offender, but maybe not.

I turned on my computer and went online. Then I accessed the L.A. *Times* archives and typed in variations of key words related to each of the crimes mentioned in the digest.

An hour later I went to bed, tired but no wiser.

CHAPTER THIRTY-EIGHT

Wednesday, February 25. 10:45 A.M. 5900 block of Green Valley Circle. A Los Angeles man told police that he got a hotel room for his daughter whom he had just met three months earlier. The woman told the man that she had left her pager in the car and wanted the keys to go out and get it. Three hours went by and the woman still hadn't returned. The man, 55, reported that the woman took his 2003 Cadillac Escalade without his permission. (Culver City)

"OF ALL THE POLICE STATIONS IN ALL THE TOWNS IN ALL the world, she walks into mine," Connors said.

"Enjoy." I tossed a box of Krispy Kremes on his desk.

Connors glanced at the box. "Is this a bribe?"

"Half a bribe, and it's not even from me. My landlord bought them for our coffee date this morning and insisted I take the rest." Isaac doesn't keep kosher, but he makes sure to buy kosher goodies when he invites me to his place.

"Two-timing the rabbi a week before the wedding?" Connors smiled.

"If you recall, my landlord is seventy-eight, although he *is* kind of cute. Do you have a few minutes, Andy?"

"*Few* is the operative word. I have a court appearance at one, which is why I'm wearing a suit, and the D.A. wants to meet with me before that. I'm going to get coffee to go with the doughnuts. Want some?"

I'd had two cups with Isaac, so I declined. While Connors was gone I pulled over a chair and eyed the labels on the spines of the "blue books" on his desk. One of them said ROLAND CREELEY.

Connors returned and settled himself in his chair. "I take it this has to do with Randy Creeley." He selected a doughnut from the box and took a bite.

"I'm not sure." I told him about the incident with the SUV, watched his expression turn grave. "I'd like to think it was road rage, Andy. It doesn't thrill me to know that someone is after me. But it's a little coincidental, don't you think?"

"I think you're lucky to be alive," he said quietly. "What were you doing in Pasadena?"

"Checking out some people Randy sent letters to. Trina gave me a list."

Connors eyed me over the rim of his cup. "You didn't mention a list when you were here Monday."

"I figured I'd check things out first." Not quite the truth, but not a lie, either. "In case it turned out to be nothing, I didn't want you to waste your time."

"Thoughtful of you," he said, his tone droll. "So what did you find out?"

"Randy was running a scam at Rachel's Tent." I explained about the red threads. "Bramer must have been nervous when he found out Randy was planning to send letters to everyone he'd scammed. Suppose he wanted to shut Randy up, permanently?"

"What makes you think Bramer knew Randy's intentions?"

"There was a check next to Bramer's name on Randy's list. Everyone else I talked to whose name was checked had received a letter. Plus Randy made two phone calls to Rachel's Tent on the morning of the day he died."

Connors chewed on the doughnut and took a few sips of coffee. "It's interesting, Molly, but we don't know what was in the letter, or why Randy called Bramer that morning. We don't even know *who* Randy called."

"A lot of the clients might have sued the agency if they found out they'd been scammed, Andy. Bramer could have lost his job."

"What about the woman who told you Randy confessed about the fake thread? Is she planning to sue?"

"No, but she feels indebted to Rachel's Tent. She says the agency saved her life." I hoped Charlie's friend was willing to talk to me. I was curious to find out about her "bad experience" at Rachel's Tent.

"My guess is that most of the clients would feel the same way," Connors said. "They'd be angry with Creeley, not Bramer. Also, for all Bramer knew, Randy had already mailed his letters, so killing him would be pointless."

"How would Randy have the names and addresses of all the people who bought or received threads from the agency?"

"He had the address of the woman in Pasadena."

"Because she stayed in touch with him. Randy told a friend he wanted to make amends for something he'd done, but if he did, he'd be making someone else financially and legally liable."

"Which friend?"

"I can't tell you." I'd given Max my word. And Connors had Randy's phone. He could track Max down just as I had. "Who else would Randy phone at Rachel's Tent if not Bramer?"

Connors wiped his mouth. "So what do you want from me?"

"Can you find out what kind of car Bramer drives?"

"You think *Bramer* was driving the SUV?"

"It's one possibility."

"So is road rage. You honked at the driver a couple of times, Molly. You braked on and off. Drivers have gone ballistic over less."

"I asked Bramer a lot of questions about Randy. They made him uncomfortable. I also talked about Randy to one of the therapists and to Horton. I'm sure Horton must have told Bramer, and the therapist may have, too."

"So Bramer spent the day following you around?"

"The other night, I thought someone was following me." I told him about the person in the deli. "I didn't think anyone was following me yesterday, but that doesn't mean someone wasn't." I nodded in the direction of the "blue book." "I see you haven't closed Randy's case."

Connors scowled at me. "Did you look at that?" he said in a tone that would have made me squirm if I had.

"No. Not that I wasn't tempted."

He held my gaze for a few seconds, probably trying to see if I was telling the truth. "You said Bramer is one possibility. Who else?"

"Randy's mother. She lives in San Marino. She wasn't thrilled that I found her. In fact, she denied that she's his mother, but I know she is. Maybe she didn't want her new husband to find out about her old life."

"Interesting." Connors's tone was noncommittal. "What about Dr. Lasher? Maybe *he* followed you."

"I'm glad you think this is funny. I could have died last night."

"I'm being serious, Molly."

I stared at him. "That's ridiculous. Dr. Lasher wouldn't try to run me off the road. In fact, this whole incident with the SUV proves that he's *not* involved with Randy's death. He would never hurt me."

"Maybe he was trying to scare you, Molly."

"Why would he do that?"

"To shift suspicion from himself by making you think exactly what you *are* thinking, that he'd never hurt you, so someone else obviously killed Randy. He figured you'd tell me what happened, which you just did, and have me thinking the same thing."

"For your information, Dr. Lasher drives a green Infiniti."

"There was a navy SUV in the driveway when I went to talk to him the other day. Maybe it was *Mrs.* Lasher."

"She doesn't drive freeways," I said, but I had to admit the excuse sounded lame.

Connors shrugged. "They know where you live, right? One of them could have followed you from your house and stayed on your tail all the way to Pasadena."

"Why would Dr. or Mrs. Lasher wait until I was headed home to scare me?"

"You could ask the same thing about Bramer. Because it was dark, and there was less of a likelihood that the driver or car would be identified. You couldn't even tell if it was a man or a woman."

I tried reading his eyes but couldn't tell what he was thinking. "You don't really believe that the Lashers are involved, do you?"

"It makes more sense than Bramer. I know it's hard for you to be objective, Molly, but if we're talking motive, they just found out that Randy killed their daughter."

"Just because Dr. Lasher doesn't have an alibi—"

"It's more than that, Molly, but I can't go into it."

I clenched my hands. "I'm the one who told you that Randy and Dr. Lasher spoke. I didn't have to do that."

"Yes, you did." Connors nodded. "It was the right thing to do."

"What else do you have, Andy? You owe me."

"I can't tell you, Molly. Sorry." He checked his watch. "I have to go. Thanks for the doughnuts."

I opened my purse and handed him a photocopy of the newspaper crime digest.

"Trina left this with me, along with clippings Randy kept about Aggie's murder. I figure if he kept them, they were important. I checked the Web but couldn't find anything about any of those crimes. Maybe you can."

"What am I, your personal detective?" He scanned the photocopy and dropped it on his desk. "Next time bring a whole box, and Starbucks coffee."

I left my Acura at the body shop my family uses, on La Brea south of Olympic. I had given the name of the shop to my insurance company early in the morning when I notified them about the accident, and they had promised to send someone late this afternoon or tomorrow to appraise the damages, which the body shop owner estimated would run to over two thousand dollars. After I had filled out the necessary paperwork, one of the mechanics gave me a ride to a car rental agency closer to Beverly, where I rented a Ford Taurus.

I had made an appointment with Mindy's chiropractor. My neck didn't ache as much as it had this morning, but maybe that was the Advil. I kept the appointment with the chiropractor, who gave me an adjustment and ultrasound therapy and told me he could tell from my muscles that I was under a great deal of stress.

"Try to relax," he told me.

A half hour later I was following his advice in a steamy tub when my cell phone rang. It was a 626 area code. Charlie, I thought.

But it was Serena Richardson, aka Sue Ann Creeley.

CHAPTER THIRTY-NINE

WE AGREED TO MEET AT TWO-THIRTY AT A COFFEE SHOP on Third near La Cienega. I arrived a few minutes early, but she was already sitting at one of the small tables, elegant again in a pale gray cashmere sweater and darker gray slacks. We made eye contact and exchanged quick, uncomfortable smiles that we repeated a minute later after I paid for my coffee and sat down across from her. Her face was composed, but the back-and-forth swinging of her right leg betrayed her nervousness.

"I appreciate your coming here to talk with me, Mrs. Richardson."

"Please call me Serena. May I call you Molly?"

I nodded, surprised that she wanted to be on a first-name basis. Yesterday she'd slammed the door in my face.

"I was unprepared to talk about Randy yesterday, Molly," she said, as though reading my thoughts. "I'm not eager to talk about him now, especially to a reporter. I'm still coming to terms with the fact that he's dead."

"I'm sure this is difficult for you."

"Quite honestly, I resent having my privacy invaded. I came because I'm hoping I can persuade you not to make this whole thing public. Have you told my ex-husband?"

I shook my head and heard her puff of relief. I wondered again whether she was the driver of the SUV that had tried to force me into the rails. First the stick, then the carrot?

"How did you know you had the right address?" she asked. "Or were you just guessing?"

"Your son looks just like Randy. And I had an old photo of you." I took the photo from my purse and placed it in front of her.

"This was one of my favorites," she said as though she was admiring a work of art in a gallery. "I remember when it was taken."

She ran her fingers across the jagged seam. She must have felt some emotion when she looked at the face of the child to whom she had given birth, a child who now lay in a grave. She must have speculated, as I had, about the anger that had pushed someone to mutilate her likeness. But her face was a mask.

She slid the photo toward me. "Whatever I tell you is off the record and strictly confidential. Agreed?"

"I won't print anything you tell me unless I have your permission. I can't promise that I won't discuss what you tell me with the police."

She nodded. "Randy was in trouble again?"

As of this morning, there had still been nothing in the media linking him with Aggie, and I doubted that Randy had confided anything to the woman who had given birth to him and disappeared from his life.

"They think he killed my best friend. I've been trying to find out why."

Her brown eyes widened in shock. "I never thought Randy was capable of killing anyone," she said after a moment. "But I can't say I knew him. When was this?" She took a sip of her tea.

"Almost six years ago."

"And you think I'm to blame, because I abandoned him." The cup rattled as she set it down. "Randy had choices. It wasn't as though I left him on the street." Her voice was prickly with anger and defensiveness.

I wasn't interested in validating her self-justification. "Trina says Randy found you over six years ago. I'm surprised he never told his father."

"I convinced him not to."

She busied herself with a packet of sweetener. I thought about the Porsche and the projection TV.

"You paid him to keep quiet."

I could tell from the anger that pinched her lips that I was right, but I didn't know if the anger was directed at me or at Randy.

"We made an arrangement."

"How much did you pay him?"

"I don't see how this is your concern." She was definitely angry now. "Five hundred dollars a month. I can afford it, and it was a small price to pay for anonymity."

Not *so* small. Six thousand dollars a year, forever. And what if she'd grown tired of paying, or explaining the withdrawals to her husband?

"Is that why you didn't attend his funeral?" I asked.

"I couldn't risk being seen by Roland or other people who

might have recognized me. I didn't need a service to grieve for Randy. I did that in private."

She didn't seem to be grieving now. "But you must have been angry at Randy."

"Randy and I were fine. Four months ago he returned my last check and told me he didn't want any more money. Recently he sent a letter asking forgiveness. He said he would repay me, but it would take time. When we spoke a few weeks ago, I told him to consider the money a gift. That was the last time I talked to him."

No tears or other visible sign of emotion, but she sounded sad, and her fingers were making crumbs of the blueberry muffin on her plate.

"When was the last time you saw him?"

"Several months ago. We met for coffee not far from where he lived."

"And before that?"

"Almost six years ago." Her face turned pink. "It was a difficult situation, Molly. Randy understood that."

Did he? "So you walked out on him twice," I said, deciding to risk her anger.

"I did everyone a favor," she said coolly. "I thought about leaving for a long time before I did it. I felt suffocated. Every day another part of me died. Every day I told myself the same thing: Tomorrow you can leave, if you want to. Roland will manage. And he has, hasn't he? He married a solid, sensible woman who took excellent care of his children."

His children, not *my* children, or *ours.* "What made you pick that day?"

"The roaster. I had scrubbed it for twenty minutes, but there was a ring that wouldn't come off. So I filled it and let it soak. I was helping Randy with his homework and heard Trina scream. She'd pulled the roaster off the counter. There was water and bits of gravy and onions all over the floor and over Trina. She was hysterical. I slapped her and started shrieking at her and couldn't stop. And then I saw their faces. They were staring at me as if I were a madwoman. They were cowering, terrified at what I would do next. I mopped up the water and changed Trina's clothes. I finished helping Randy with his homework. And the next morning I had a neighbor baby-sit while I went to the bank and closed my account. I packed a bag, and when Randy came home from school, I told him I was going on a trip and his daddy would be home soon, and everything would be all right."

From listening to my sisters, I know that there have been days when the frustrations of motherhood have taxed their nerves and depleted their strength. But to leave your family? To walk out and never look back?

"All those years," I said, "weren't you curious to see your family? Didn't you have any regrets?"

"Randy asked that, too. I thought about writing to Roland, sending birthday cards. I decided it would be better if I stayed out of their lives. But regrets?" She shook her head. "The first night I almost turned back. I was lonely and scared. I had no idea where I was going. I missed the kids. I missed having Roland next to me in bed. But every night became easier, because I knew I'd done the right thing. I should never have married Roland. I should never have had those children."

I had agreed to a limited confidentiality, and I like to think I'm a good listener, but I was surprised by Sue Ann's candor. People often feel relieved to share their untold stories and end up revealing more than they had intended, but Sue Ann struck me as a controlled woman. I assumed she was trying to create an intimacy between us so that I would find it harder to turn down her request.

"Why *did* you have children?" I asked.

"It's the American dream, isn't it?" She took a sip of tea.

"You get married, you buy a house, you have children. You live happily every after. Roland is a good man, Molly. When he proposed, I told him I liked him but didn't love him. He said he had enough love for both of us. And for a while, it *was* enough." She sounded wistful. "And the kids . . . I was fine with one child, but Roland thought Randy should have a sibling, and he was so good to me, always trying to make me happy. So we had Trina."

After leaving Los Angeles, Sue Ann had traveled to Chicago and then Houston, where she decided to stay. When the divorce was finalized, she changed her name officially to Serena Henderson. She bought an expensive wardrobe and rented an apartment in an exclusive neighborhood, where word spread about the well-to-do widow.

"It was the role of my life," she told me with some irony. "I bet everything I had on it."

Her bet paid off. At a benefit months later for a charity to which she had made a generous contribution, she met Cornell Richardson, a wealthy investment banker. She married him. And when Richardson's widowed mother died a year after that, and he wanted to move back to his childhood home in San Marino, Sue Ann was nervous but told herself San Marino was leagues away from Culver City. She made friends, became involved with different charities. She had a child, and there was a nanny to help care for him.

And then one morning six years ago Randy knocked on her door.

"He thought I had drowned in a boating accident," Sue Ann said. "But his stepmother told him I was alive. Somehow he got the money to hire a detective to find me."

Horton, I thought.

"He had papers, he had proof. I didn't want the neighbors to hear my sorry past. My son was in school, Cornell was at his office. So I invited Randy inside."

Her leg was swinging faster now. "Over the years I had fantasized about what it would be like to see him. He was a beautiful child, and he had grown into a beautiful young man. Looking at him took my breath away." She paused. "He was seething. He refused to sit. He paced in my living room, picking up vases and bowls, asking me how much everything cost. I thought he was going to smash them. Then he stood in front of me and told me how much he hated me. He said I ruined his life, that I was a selfish bitch and he wished I *had* drowned."

She spoke as though she was narrating someone else's story—cool, detached. I wondered if that was a protective defense she'd built up over the years, or whether she was as unfeeling as she sounded.

"Randy expected a Hollywood ending," Sue Ann said. "He was waiting for me to cry and beg his forgiveness and tell him I wanted to make up for lost time." She sighed. "You can't go back, Molly. I had a son and husband to protect."

And a life based on lies. Cornell Richardson probably wouldn't have been eager to hear that the lovely widow he married had deserted a husband and two children, or that one of those children was an ex-convict.

"I tried explaining that to Randy," Sue Ann said. "I told him it would be better for everyone if he didn't come to the house again. We could still have a relationship. I would phone him and arrange to meet him in Los Angeles from time to time. He said he wasn't a bastard son I could hide. He said he wouldn't leave until he met my husband and son. He said he would tell Roland."

"That's when you offered him money?"

This time she flushed. "He said he deserved compensation. I suppose he did. I gave him five thousand dollars and agreed to pay him five hundred a month."

The price of motherly love, I thought.

"So that's my story, Molly. You may think I'm a terrible person who deserves to be exposed. Maybe that's true. I can't stop you from telling Roland that you've found me. But you'll be ruining many lives, Molly, not just mine. Before you do anything, I hope you'll think about my son and husband, and Roland and Alice and Trina. Nobody will benefit, Molly. No one will thank you. Trust me."

She was probably right. Something she'd said earlier had been nagging at me. Now I remembered. "You said Alice was solid and sensible. Did Randy tell you that?"

Sue Ann didn't answer right away. "I drove to the house once after we moved to San Marino. I parked across the street and watched Trina playing on the front lawn. She was a toddler when I left, and I didn't recognize her. I wanted a closer look." She had formed a small mountain out of the muffin crumbs. "I got out of the car and crossed the street. I was trying to get up the nerve to talk to Trina when Alice came out of the house. She wanted to know who I was, why I was watching her child. She had seen me through the front window. I was flustered. I told her I used to live in the neighborhood. I didn't know what else to say. But she recognized me, probably from photos."

I had a squirrelly feeling in my stomach. "How can you be sure?"

"She told me. She was furious. She said I had abandoned my family and had no right to come back into their lives. She said Roland had worked hard to rebuild his life, and that my showing up was the height of selfishness. I never went back." Sue Ann took her spoon and flattened the mound of crumbs.

"Did you ever tell Randy about your visit?"

Sue Ann nodded. "A few weeks ago, after I received his letter. Alice was right, you know. I should never have gone back."

CHAPTER FORTY

SEVEN LONG-STEMMED YELLOW ROSES AND A ROMANTIC note from Zack were waiting for me at my door when I arrived home. So was the copyedited manuscript of *The Lady From Twenty-nine Palms,* the true-crime book I had completed three months ago.

The letter that accompanied the manuscript, which was flagged with dozens of green Post-its, informed me that I had two weeks to review the copy editor's comments and make all necessary changes. I enjoy the editing process and am grateful to my copy editor, someone whose name and gender I don't know, who reads every word and has caught numerous errors, large and small, and spared me embarrassment. But I hadn't expected the manuscript for another few weeks—*after* the wedding. I would e-mail my editor in the morning and ask her for an extension. In the meantime, I would take a first look.

I phoned the shul, but Zack wasn't in. I left a message and placed the vase with his roses on my desk so that I could look at them while I did a first read of the manuscript. I tried to concentrate, but after reading fifteen pages and responding to two Post-it queries, I set the manuscript aside.

My mind was on Randy and his discovery, days before he died, that his stepmother had known all these years that her predecessor was living in Southern California, and had sent her packing.

I no longer had his cell phone, but I remembered the basics of Alice's message: Don't do something you'll regret, Randy. I might have paid more attention, but her message had been overshadowed by the redhead's cryptic one. Now I wondered whether Randy had told Alice that he planned to tell his father what he had recently learned.

You tell him, Alice, or I will.

That wasn't in the spirit of making amends, but Randy must have been furious. And Alice must have panicked, wondering how Roland would react. I recalled my impression of her, a woman threatened by the memory of the beautiful wife she had replaced.

Before talking with Sue Ann (I couldn't think of her as Serena), I had suggested to Zack and then to Connors that Randy's mother might have been desperate to keep her old and new lives separate. I had even wondered whether her desperation had driven her to kill her own son.

I hadn't ruled her out as the driver of the SUV, which is why I had waited in the coffee shop so that I could leave after she did. But if she was telling the truth—a big *if*, I knew—she and Randy had made peace, and she had no reason to fear him. And if she had planned to do anything, she would have done it long ago.

But Alice Creeley . . .

I pictured the black Ford Explorer I'd seen in her driveway last week. I had been in Culver City yesterday for more than three hours, talking about Randy to the Creeleys' neighbors, one of whom could have phoned Alice. . . .

My cell phone rang. I hurried to the kitchen counter where I had left it and looked at the LCD display. PRIVATE CALL. I pressed the green button and said hello.

"Are you Molly Blume?" a woman asked.

"This is she."

"Charlie said you wanted to talk to me." She had a soft, tentative voice.

"Right." The friend from Rachel's Tent. I pulled over a pad and pen. "Thanks for calling. Can we meet for coffee somewhere? What's your name, by the way?"

"I'd rather do this over the phone. What exactly did you want to know?"

I wondered why she was avoiding telling me her name. "Charlie mentioned that you had a bad experience while you were at Rachel's Tent. I'd like to talk to you about it."

"I don't want to get anyone in trouble."

"I understand. Was it drug related?"

"Is that what Charlie told you?" She sounded jumpy.

"Charlie didn't tell me anything. It would be easier if I could call you by your name. I won't use it."

"You can call me Melinda."

I assumed that wasn't her real name. I leaned against the counter. "Did you know Randy, Melinda?"

"We all did. He was around all the time."

"Charlie mentioned that he played the field with a lot of the women at Rachel's Tent."

"Right."

Richard Nixon had probably been more forthcoming. "Were you one of those women?"

"For a while," she admitted. "It was over before it started. I realized later that he was pumping me for information."

She sounded resentful, and I couldn't blame her. "The bad experience you had, was it with Randy?"

"Look, this happened six years ago. I don't want to rake it all up, okay?"

"Rake what up?"

"Why are you interested in this, anyway?"

"I thought Charlie told you. I'm writing about Rachel's Tent, and Randy. If you didn't want to talk to me, Melinda, why did you call?"

For a few seconds I thought she'd hung up. "It was after one of Mr. Horton's dinners," she said. "You know who Mr. Horton is?"

I told her I did.

"Every month he invites someone from Rachel's Tent to his house to have dinner with his family. When Randy was working at the agency, he'd drive us there and back and stay for dinner. He was close to Mr. Horton and the son. When it was my turn to go, I was excited, and nervous. I didn't want to embarrass myself and use the wrong fork. It was funny when Julia Roberts did it in *Pretty Woman,* but in real life, people laugh *at* you, not with you."

The vulnerability in her voice saddened me. I wondered if the "bad experience" had been the lingering humiliation of a faux pas she'd committed that evening.

"Anyway," she said. "Dinner was easier than I thought it would be, and Mrs. Horton made me feel comfortable right away. She's very sweet. It's what happened *after* dinner. The thing is, I'm not even sure anything *did* happen. Even if it did, there's nothing I can do about it."

In person, I could have encouraged her with a nod or a smile. Now all I could do was wait.

"They didn't serve wine during dinner, just fancy water. Some of the clients at Rachel's Tent have problems with alcohol. But in the car on the way home I had a beer. Except I don't think he took me home right away. I think—" She stopped. "I think he raped me."

I was chilled to the bone.

"I think he put something in my drink," Melinda said. "I remember feeling a little dizzy and real hot. I thought I was going to throw up. And the next thing, I was in my bed in my apartment, but my clothes weren't on right."

She could have been describing the effects of alcohol and Rohypnol, a drug frequently used in date rape and also called a "roofie" or a "forget pill," for obvious reasons. The tablet has no taste and no odor and costs less than five dollars, which is why it poses such a danger to unsuspecting women.

"Did you tell anyone, Melinda?"

"They wouldn't have believed me. With my background, and all. Plus I had that drink."

I couldn't see her, but I had the feeling she was blushing. "What about your family?"

"I haven't seen my family in years. I've been on my own since I was fifteen. I didn't want to make trouble. I was afraid I'd be thrown out of Rachel's Tent, and then where would I go? Back on the street?"

I wished I could offer some comfort, say something that would alleviate her pain and bitterness. "Couldn't you tell your therapist?"

"There was this girl at Rachel's Tent," Melinda said. "Iris. I don't know her last name."

"Right." I was puzzled by the non sequitur. "Charlie told me about her. The one who left the agency?"

"That's what they said. I don't know if that's so."

I had a prickly feeling at the base of my spine. "What do you mean?"

"We were in group together, and we got to be friendly. I talked to her the day before she left, and she didn't say *one word* about leaving. The same thing happened to her, after she had dinner at the Hortons'."

"He raped her?"

Randy was a liar and a manipulator, a thief and probably a murderer. I hadn't pictured him as a rapist. He was handsome, charming. He could have had any woman he wanted. But rape isn't about sex, I reminded myself. It's about control, and rage. Rage at his mother?

"She thought he put something in her drink, just like with me, but it wore off," Melinda said. "She woke up in his room, but pretended she was out. She was afraid of what he'd do. He was making a video. Anyway, Iris told her social worker."

I tensed. "Aggie Lasher?" It had to be Aggie.

"Right." Melinda sounded surprised. "Ms. Lasher was pushing Iris to go to the police, but Iris was afraid. She said no one would believe her unless she had proof. And then a few weeks later she told me she *had* proof, and she was going to the police. And then she disappeared."

"Melinda, even without proof, why wouldn't the police believe you and Iris over Randy? He was an ex-convict, a dope addict."

"Not *Randy*," she said. "Mr. Horton's son. Jason."

CHAPTER FORTY-ONE

THE UNDERGROUND PARKING GARAGE AT RACHEL'S TENT had assigned slots for staff. Driving slowly, I passed the empty spot reserved for DR. WILLIAM BRAMER and spotted Barbara Anik's, a hundred feet from a door above which a sign said EXIT. I found a visitor's spot and, sitting in my rented Taurus, glanced at the door every time it opened.

At a little after five-thirty Barbara stepped into the garage. Behind her was a bearded young man. He turned left. Barbara turned right.

I caught up with her just as she was opening the door to her silver Volvo.

"Dr. Anik?"

She whirled around and pressed her hand against her chest. Her face was mottled with red. "You scared me to death!" She dropped her hand. "What are you doing here, Molly?"

"I'm sorry. I didn't mean to startle you. I need to talk to you, Dr. Anik. It's urgent."

I had been nervous about confiding in her and enlisting her help. But Aggie had respected and trusted her. And I suppose I felt a bond, because of her past and my grandparents'.

"Then you can phone for an appointment," she said, her voice taut with irritation or anxiety, maybe both. She turned back to the car.

I put my hand gingerly on her shoulder. "This can't wait, Dr. Anik. *Please.*"

She turned to face me, her keys in her hand, indecision in her gray eyes. "All right," she finally said, her reluctance echoing in the dark garage. "Five minutes. My husband is waiting for me."

"Can we talk in your car? I don't want Dr. Bramer to see me."

She looked at me as though I'd lost my mind, but after a brief hesitation she unlocked the passenger door and walked around to the driver's side.

"What's so urgent?" she asked when we were both inside.

"The client Aggie was concerned about, the one who left Rachel's Tent? Her name—"

"I can't discuss any client with you, Molly." She pinched her lips. "I thought I made that clear."

"Her name is Iris," I said. "What I'm going to tell you is confidential, Dr. Anik. You can't tell anyone, not even Dr. Bramer."

"I *work* with Dr. Bramer," she said sharply. "I can't be put in this position. And I can't see why you would want to keep information from him."

"He has close ties to the Horton family, Dr. Anik, and the Hortons are very involved with Rachel's Tent."

She looked at me quizzically. "Dr. Bramer admires Mr. Horton a great deal, and with good reason. I don't see the problem."

There was no easy way to say this. "Six years ago Iris was raped by Anthony Horton's son, Jason. She's not the only one."

It took a few seconds for my words to register.

"I don't believe you." Barbara stared at me. "Where did you hear this?" she demanded.

I relayed my conversation with Melinda and saw the therapist's certainty crumble. "Melinda says she knows three other women who think they may have been raped by Jason." Women who were vulnerable, easy prey. "The pattern was the same. Jason offered to drive them home. In the car he would give them a drink laced with Rohypnol and wait until it took effect. Then he would take them to his room, rape them, and drive them home. They weren't sure what had happened, and were afraid to say anything. They had no proof."

"Dear God." Barbara shut her eyes for a moment and exhaled deeply. "He did this in his parents' home?"

"That's what Iris told Melinda. Jason has his own suite in a wing that's away from the rest of the family. He counted on the drug working until he got his victims home, so they wouldn't remember anything. But with Iris, it wore off too soon. She knew where she was. She was aware of what was going on but didn't let on. Iris said he videotaped what he was doing. I'm assuming he videotaped everyone."

Jason, the ventriloquist's dummy, speaking only when spoken to. Jason, an emasculated, pale copy of his charismatic, controlling father. Maybe he had violated women from Rachel's Tent to violate his father's dream. Doing so in his father's home, virtually under his nose, must have given him a perverse pleasure and a measure of control.

Barbara sat awhile without speaking. "Why did Melinda tell you this *now*?" she asked, the skepticism back in her voice.

"A week ago she heard that Randy died, and then she heard I was looking into his death. . . . When Iris disappeared, Melinda suspected Jason was responsible. She was terrified that if she said anything to the police, something would happen to her, too. She's still afraid, and she doesn't want to be involved, but she couldn't keep quiet any longer."

Do you think they can really get Jason? she'd asked.

"You have to tell Dr. Bramer," Barbara said. "If this is true—"

"He's too close to the Hortons, Dr. Anik. Melinda and the others think he suspected something was going on but didn't want to know."

The therapist shook her head. "I can't believe that. Rachel's Tent is his life."

"What if he worried that the agency would be shut down if this came out?" I waited to let her digest that. "Melinda talked with Iris the day before she left Rachel's Tent. Iris didn't say anything to her about leaving the agency."

"That's not unusual. I've had a number of clients who terminated therapy without warning. And I seem to remember Aggie telling me she received a note from the client a week or so after the woman left the agency."

"Anyone can write a note," I said. "Melinda said Iris had proof she was planning to take to the police. I think she got hold of the videotape." That was probably the package Jim wanted. "Do you remember when she left Rachel's Tent?"

"Not exactly." Barbara considered. "I think it was a week or so before Aggie was murdered."

"If you could take a look at Iris's records," I said. "Maybe Melinda is wrong. Maybe there'll be contact information and you can find out if Iris went back to her family."

"You know I can't do that." The therapist sounded anguished.

"What if Jason killed her, Dr. Anik? Or maybe Randy did, or

they did it together? And no one knows that Iris is dead because no one is looking for her."

I told her about the clipping Randy had kept. "They found a woman's torso in a grave in Griffith Park ten days before Aggie was killed. What if that's Iris?"

The stairwell from the parking garage led to the first floor. In the darkened lobby the mural of Rachel's Tomb looked somber, the blues almost black. There was no one at Reception or in the offices on the way to the storage room where I followed Barbara.

Barbara turned on the light. I had offered to help, but she made me wait just inside the door while she searched through banks of files that contained records of clients who were no longer with Rachel's Tent. Dead files, she called them. The term took on an ominous note.

Some time later—a half hour or more—she turned to me and shook her head.

"It's not there."

"Could it have been misfiled?" I asked.

"The records are filed by year, then by name. Last and first. I checked all the files for that time period and couldn't find anything for a client named Iris."

"Could the file be in someone's office?"

"After six years?" She brushed the dust off her hands. "I'm afraid someone must have taken it."

"Would Aggie have taken it home?"

"It's possible. Although why would she have kept it after the client left Rachel's Tent?"

On the way back to the parking garage, I asked Barbara again about the parties Horton hosted twice a year.

"One to celebrate July Fourth, the other around Christmas," she said. "Why?"

The body had been found July 13, just over a week later. "I'm trying to figure out how Iris got hold of the videotape. Were all the clients invited?"

Barbara nodded.

"So she could have sneaked upstairs to Jason's room that night," I said. "No one would have noticed her."

"It's possible. There's always a crowd at the Hortons' holiday parties. I always enjoy myself. Everyone does."

"Except Aggie," I remembered. "You said she seemed nervous at the last party. She dropped food on her dress?"

"Meatballs and duck, all over the front of her dress. It was a mess. The next day at work she laughed about it, but not that night."

Aggie wouldn't have eaten meatballs or duck. She kept strict kosher. I told that to Barbara. "Someone else must have bumped into her and spilled the food on her."

"There were meatballs and pieces of duck on her plate," Barbara said. "I don't know whether she had a chance to eat them before they landed on her dress. Some people keep kosher at home, but not when they're out."

Not Aggie. "You said she changed her clothes?"

"Mrs. Horton gave her something to wear. Aggie was gone for some time. She told me it was such a huge house that she got lost and almost didn't find her way back."

The green Infiniti was in the driveway, but I didn't see a navy SUV. Dr. Lasher opened the door and greeted me with his usual warmth. He didn't seem angry or uncomfortable. I was the one who felt awkward, and I was relieved when he told me Mrs. Lasher was at the market.

"I don't recall that Aggie had any work files in her room," he told me. "If there had been any, we would have returned them to Rachel's Tent right away."

"Could you take another look, just in case?"

"We cleared out everything a few years ago, Molly. I turned Aggie's bedroom into a project room for Mrs. Lasher. Sewing, crafts. She's thinking of taking art lessons." He peered at me through his bifocals. "Why are you interested in the file?"

I hesitated, but decided that he had a right to know. "Aggie had a client who left the agency a week or so before Aggie died. Her file seems to be missing."

Dr. Lasher frowned. "You think there's a connection?"

"I don't know. It could be nothing. Well, thanks anyway. Please give my regards to Mrs. Lasher," I said, as though this were a normal visit.

"I will. I'm sorry I couldn't be of any help, Molly. By the way, I met with Detective Connors. He seems like a fine man. Honest, straightforward. I explained about the phone calls. I think he believes me."

"I hope so." I know I sounded nervous. From the way Dr. Lasher was looking at me, he must have picked up on it, and maybe I wanted him to.

"Did Detective Connors say something to you?" he asked.

"He told me you don't have a solid alibi." My face was flushed. "There was something else, but he wouldn't say what. If you're keeping something back from him, Dr. Lasher, tell him now. He's very bright and very good at what he does."

"I didn't kill Randy Creeley, Molly." His mouth twitched with impatience.

"I believe you. But Detective Connors doesn't know you the way I do. And if he finds out you lied to him . . ."

"He knows I was there that night," Dr. Lasher said, not quite meeting my eyes. "At Creeley's apartment. I knocked on the door, but no one answered. When he didn't answer the door, I thought, it's just as well. I didn't go with vengeance in my heart, Molly. I wanted to talk him. But who knows what I might have done? Hashem protected me. I told all that to Detective Connors."

He walked me to the door. "About the file," he said. "Someone else asked about it, but that was a short while after Aggie was killed."

"Who?"

"The director. What's his name? Kramer? No, Bramer."

Aggie had ruined her dress so that she could search Jason's room for the tape.

I was certain of it and had thought about little else on the way to the Lashers'. I thought about it now as I sat at my desk, Zack's flowers just inches away.

Iris must have described the layout and told Aggie how to find Jason's room. I pictured Aggie standing among the guests, not having to feign being nervous and jittery because she was waiting for the right moment to drop food on her dress and set her plan in motion. I heard her self-conscious laugh as she followed Mrs. Horton up a wide staircase. *This is so kind of you, I'm so embarrassed, I'm never this clumsy.* I watched her as she walked down a hall and maybe made a wrong turn before she found Jason's room, felt the rapid beating of her heart when she shut the door carefully behind her, too late to turn back now, and rifled through drawers and closets and bookshelves, jumping at every unexpected sound, her palms clammy, nerves jangled even after she found the videotape and bundled it in her soiled pastel silk dress that she put in the trunk of the person who had given her a ride to the party.

Jason must have panicked when he realized the tape was missing. A day after the party? Two days? Not much later, because Iris disappeared a week or so before Aggie was killed. He probably assumed that one of the women he'd raped had taken the tape during the party. Or maybe he'd heard about Aggie's clumsiness and suspected that she had taken the tape for one of her clients.

But which one?

He asked Randy to find out. *Help me out, man. You're there all the time. Find out.*

Barbara Anik had caught Randy snooping through Aggie's files. Maybe he'd tried to search through other therapists' files, too. And when that failed, he'd invited clients to confide in him. Like Iris, who had disappeared.

Jason probably paid him to do it. *Find the girl, Randy. Find the tape. Get rid of her. I'll make it worth your while.* Maybe Randy was desperate for money. Maybe he felt a twisted sense of loyalty and gratitude to the Hortons, who had treated him almost like family.

Not *quite* family. I was certain that Jason had killed Randy. To stop him from implicating him in the murders. To get back the copy of the tape Randy had made as insurance. Randy would have been stupid not to make a copy.

And Aggie?

She probably suspected what had happened to Iris. Maybe she said something to Randy that worried him. I didn't think he *wanted* to kill her. Trina said he punched a hole in the wall when he heard she was dead.

Then again, Randy was an actor.

And Diana Warfield, if that was her name. She must know something about the murders. That would explain her paranoia. She had probably been terrified when Randy told her he was going to turn himself in.

Do they know, Randy?

Where was the tape? Something in the back of my mind teased at me, something I had heard, something I had seen. . . .

I had to warn Trina about Jason. She had mentioned that a friend of Randy's was helping her figure out what the package was and where Randy hid it, and I wondered with a quiver of alarm whether that friend was Jason. She'd been impressed by his offer of help, by the fact that he'd called to see how she was doing. *Wasn't that nice?* she'd said. *He didn't have to do that.*

What if she'd taken him up on his offer? What if he'd trashed her apartment so that she would turn to him for help and lead him to the tape?

What if I was building something out of nothing?

I phoned Trina, but she didn't answer. Feeling a little silly, I phoned her father.

"She's staying at some hotel," Roland Creeley told me. "She wouldn't tell me where. I asked her how she could afford that, but she said not to worry, a friend was taking care of it for her."

"By the way, did Randy leave any videotapes with you?"

"No. We're not into that, Alice and me. It's funny, because Trina asked me the same thing. And so did Mr. Horton's son. He was a good friend to Randy."

I left another message for Trina, asking her to call me immediately. I marked the message URGENT. I debated saying something about Jason—but what if she confronted him? I could see her doing that.

"Don't trust anyone," I said.

CHAPTER FORTY-TWO

Thursday, February 26. 12:03 P.M. Corner of Pico Boulevard and Wetherly Drive. The victim and an assailant were arguing. "This is the beginning," the assailant said. "If you go to jail, I'm gonna bail you out and kill you." The suspect is a male standing 5 feet 10 inches and weighing 180 pounds, with brown hair and brown eyes. (West Los Angeles)

BUBBIE G SAYS A FOOL MAKES TWO TRIPS WHERE A WISE man makes none. I don't know if I was a fool, but when Anthony Horton phoned and asked me to come to his office, I went.

The receptionist was away from her desk when I arrived, which suited me fine. I found my way around the corner to Horton's office and heard a raised voice on the other side of his door.

". . . do something . . . once in your life . . . tired of cleaning up your mistakes." Horton's voice.

Jason replied—at least, I assumed it was the son—but he spoke too low for me to hear to make out what he was saying.

". . . too late . . . she'll figure out what's going on . . . shut her up . . ."

So Horton was hoping to do some damage control.

I heard the click of the door. Hurrying along the carpeted hall, I made it around the corner and was walking back toward the office, as though I'd just arrived, when Jason emerged. He looked startled to see me, and after giving me a curt nod, he strode down the hall.

Horton stood in the doorway. He had bags under his eyes and looked as though he hadn't slept well. He definitely wasn't happy to see me.

"My receptionist didn't tell me you were here."

I wouldn't want to be in *her* shoes. "I didn't see her. She must be in the restroom. I hope I'm not too early?"

"Not a problem."

Pulling his face into a smile as flat as Enron stock, he invited me inside. There were fresh roses on the credenza, but it would have taken more than roses to diffuse the lingering tension in the room.

If flowers could speak, I thought as I sat down.

"You've been talking to people about Randy and Rachel's Tent." Horton wagged his finger. "I thought we had an understanding, Molly."

"I agreed not to write about the drug dealing. I didn't say I wasn't going to ask questions about Randy."

"What did you find out?"

"Why don't *you* tell *me?*"

He leaned against the back of his massive chair. "I think you found out what Dr. Bramer and I learned yesterday, that those red threads Randy was selling were fake. Am I right?"

"Yes."

"What can I tell you?" Horton sighed. "I'm disappointed. I'm saddened. We both are."

"Are you planning to reimburse all the people Randy scammed?"

Horton laughed, but the sound was hollow. "I like you, Molly. You're direct. I am, too. Yeah, we're going to make good to everybody. It's the right thing to do, and honesty is always good business."

"And you don't want to face lawsuits."

"Find me someone who does and I'll show you a lawyer." He grunted. "Speaking of honesty, you didn't tell Dr. Bramer you were at Randy's funeral." Horton wasn't smiling now. "You also didn't mention that the police think Randy killed one of our staff, which I'm having a hard time believing. I had to read that in the paper this morning."

I had seen the short write-up in the "California" section. "I had concerns about what was going on at Rachel's Tent. I had to be cautious. Is that why you asked me here?"

"That's part of it." He made a ball of his hands and leaned forward. "I need to know if I can trust you. I need your promise that what I'm about to tell you stays in this room."

I felt a quiver of excitement. "That depends on what you have to tell me."

He held my gaze for a moment. "It's a tough world, Molly. You're a reporter. You probably see more ugliness than most people. I worked hard to build a good life for my family. I tried to protect my kids, but it doesn't work like that, does it? Drugs, alcohol. You can't get away from them."

He looked up at the ceiling as if it held the escape he sought, then back at me. "My son came to talk to me last night. He had something hard to tell me, something he's been keeping in for some time. He told me because he knew you were asking questions, talking to women who had been at Rachel's Tent. He wanted to prepare me. I think you know what I'm talking about."

I nodded. Charlie had probably phoned the director after my visit. And Bramer had phoned Horton.

"He had inappropriate relationships with one or two of the women from the agency," Horton said. "Six years ago. They came here as our guests, to spend an evening with my family. That's what makes it particularly upsetting. I don't approve of casual sex, especially under my roof. That's not how I raised my son."

Was this the spin Horton was planning? "Jason didn't have _inappropriate relationships_ with these women, Mr. Horton. He raped them."

Horton flinched. "There was no rape. It was consensual. Maybe they felt obligated, because of my relationship with Rachel's Tent. Or maybe they were impressed by who he was. Young people today don't think twice about having sex outside of marriage."

"He didn't _have sex_. He raped them, Mr. Horton."

"Did any of these women file charges? No, they didn't. If they had been raped, they would have told someone. The police. A parent. A friend. They woke up in the morning and regretted what they had done. That happens all the time, Molly, but it's not rape."

I clenched my hands. "They didn't report the rape because they didn't think anyone would believe them, and your son knew that. They didn't report it because they had no self-esteem, because they'd spent years being told they were worthless."

"And that's my son's fault?"

"He drugged them with Rohypnol, Mr. Horton."

"Rohypnol?" Horton grunted. "Jason wouldn't do something like that. If those women were drugged, Randy did it."

"It's easy to blame a dead man," I said.

"You and I know Randy had a problem with drugs, Molly." He was making me part of his team. "He introduced drugs to Jason, and liquor. I should have seen it, but I didn't. I should never have brought him into our house. That was my fault. I felt bad for him. I trusted him."

Cut to the chase, I thought. "Why are you telling me this, Mr. Horton?"

"I'm asking you to keep this quiet. Don't ruin my son's life for something that happened six years ago, Molly. I'm willing to compensate these women generously for their emotional suffering. I will make a substantial donation to a rape center. You name the place and the amount. You'll have a check today."

"This isn't a business transaction, Mr. Horton."

"Everything in life is business. Everything has a price. It's his word against theirs, Molly. There's no evidence. There never was."

"There's a videotape," I said.

Horton pursed his lips. "*Stolen* from Jason's room. That tape probably wouldn't be admissible in court, even if it showed up. But we're not talking about legalities, Molly. My son was stupid. He's the first one to admit that. You shouldn't ruin a man's life because of stupidity."

I wondered how much Jason had admitted to his father. "What about the lives your son ruined, Mr. Horton?"

"How are their lives ruined, Molly? They're all doing better than they were before they came to Rachel's Tent. One of them was a prostitute. Another woman lived on the streets before we took her in."

"So did your mother," I said. "Are you saying her life wasn't worth as much as someone else's?"

"Don't talk about my mother." Horton's face was dangerously red. His cheek twitched. "You're putting words in my mouth, Molly. That's not what I meant. I'm talking from a practical point of view. This is never going to court, but it could make things uncomfortable for me and my family, and Rachel's Tent. And if you write anything about rape, as much as I respect you, Molly, I'd have no choice but to sue you for libel." He paused. "I could make their lives so much easier, Molly. Think about it."

I thought about it on the way home. I felt soiled by our conversation. Six roses from Zack helped lift my spirits, but not enough, because when I phoned to thank him, he asked me what was wrong.

I told him about my meeting with Horton. "And Trina hasn't called me back, Zack. The last time we talked, she sounded annoyed and told me she didn't need my help."

"Maybe she doesn't like you checking up on her all the time, Molly."

"She called *me* Saturday night. She was hysterical, she needed help."

"Did you see her face when you told her you were Aggie's best friend? If she could have left right then, I think she would have."

I remembered. "But Sunday she was chatty, Zack. She left me Randy's phone, and the list and the clippings. She asked me to check things out."

"Maybe she decided you're the wrong person to ask for help. You're convinced that Randy killed Aggie. She's trying to prove that he didn't, and that someone killed him."

I supposed he was right. "She said a friend is helping her find Jim. What if the friend is Jason?"

"What makes you think that?"

I told him.

"She probably has a lot of friends, Molly. Anyway, you warned her about him, right?"

"Not specifically. She's a little headstrong, Zack. I didn't want her to confront him."

Connors was sympathetic when I phoned him, but unhelpful. "Horton's right, Molly. We don't have a case."

"I could talk to Melinda again. Maybe she'd be willing to press charges."

"With what? She never told anybody about the rape. There were no lab tests. We don't have any body fluids. As far as the law is concerned, there *was* no rape. If we had the videotape and the victim, that would change everything."

If pigs had wings, I thought. "Horton said if the videotape was stolen, it wouldn't be admissible."

"Horton should stick to his enterprises. If *I* stole it, or someone else working for the state did, it wouldn't be admissible. If a private party stole it, we could use it. But we don't have a tape. We don't even know that it exists."

"It exists," I insisted. "Iris told Melinda that Jason taped her. Aggie took the tape. I know she did."

"You can't *know* it," Connors said. "I'm not saying I disagree with you. But I have nothing to take to the D.A."

"Maybe Jason has other tapes, Andy. You could get a search warrant."

"If he had other tapes, I'm sure he got rid of them. And if he didn't, his daddy did. Plus I don't have probable cause for a warrant."

"What if you could tie Jason to Iris's murder?"

"Molly, we don't know that there *was* a murder. We don't even have a torso, because it was cremated years ago. We don't have a rape victim. We don't have a missing woman. We have a client who left Rachel's Tent and may have gone home to her parents, but we can't check because her file is missing. Suppose she took the file herself?"

"Assume that Jason raped her and she was murdered. That's not enough of a connection?"

"Not if you can't prove conspiracy. We can't prosecute a rapist because he benefits from the death of the victim."

I felt like screaming. "Randy just decided to kill Iris on his own?"

"Look, I'm as frustrated as you are. You think I don't want to haul this guy in?"

I e-mailed my *Crime Sheet* column to my editor, then drove to the dressmaker to pick up my wedding dress.

"Very nice," she said when I had put on the gown. "Bra is very good. Now you have good breasts, yes? You see? Nice line. You should wear this bra all time."

I dropped off the gown at my parents' and invited myself to dinner—scrambled eggs with toast, but it beat eating alone. I helped with the seating arrangements for the wedding. When I left at half past eleven, my mom and dad were still hunched over the dining room table, moving three-by-five-inch index cards like Rummy Q tiles.

I had been leaving messages for Trina all day. When I arrived home I tried her again. After three rings her voice mail picked up.

I tried it again. And again. Finally, she answered. I could tell from her hello that I had woken her, but I was relieved.

"I'm sorry I woke you, Trina. I was worried, because you didn't call me back."

"Molly?" Her voice sounded groggy, and she drew out my name.

"Trina, are you okay?"

"Tired."

"Okay. Will you call me in the morning?"

"Have to . . . sleep."

"Did you take some of your sleeping pills?"

"Pills."

"How many did you take?"

"Tired."

"Trina, how many pills did you take? Trina?"

"Talk . . . later."

I was beginning to feel alarmed. "Trina?"

No answer.

"Keep talking to me, Trina."

Still no answer.

"Trina, are you there?"

I called her name a few more times, then phoned Connors at home. I grabbed the Yellow Pages from under my desk.

"If she took sleeping pills, Molly, of course she'd be sleepy."

I flipped to HOTELS. "Something's wrong, Andy. She sounded lethargic."

He yawned. "You have no idea where she's staying?"

"Saturday night, she wanted Zack to drop her off at a hotel near her apartment. She mentioned the hotel, but I wasn't paying attention."

"Did she say where it is?"

"On Sunset." I ran my finger down the list.

"That narrows it down."

"I think she said it's near Crescent Heights." I turned the page, and there it was. The Suncrest. "It's the Suncrest. I'll call you back."

I dialed the number.

"Suncrest Hotel," a man said. "How can I help you?"

"I just spoke to one of your guests, and she didn't sound well. Can you please check to see if she's all right?"

"The guest's name?"

"Trina Creeley."

"I'm sorry," he told me a moment later. "We have no one by that name registered here."

"I just spoke to her." My heart was pounding. "Could you please check again?"

"No Trina Creeley. No Creeley at all, for that matter. Sorry."

I thanked him and hung up. I had no idea what other hotel she might have chosen.

I was about to call Connors when I realized she had probably used an alias. Something she'd told me the first day we'd met . . . Her screen name. What was it?

I thought for a moment, then phoned the hotel and spoke to the same clerk. "Can you try Ava Gardner?"

"Excuse me?"

"Do you have an Ava Gardner registered?"

"Let me check."

I tapped my fingers on the counter.

"That line is busy. Do you want to leave a message?"

CHAPTER FORTY-THREE

THE PARAMEDICS ARRIVED BEFORE I DID. SO DID CON-
nors. I recognized his gray Cutlass as I raced past it into the lobby.

The clerk behind the desk was reluctant to give me Trina's
room number even after I told him I was the one who had contacted the police. I don't think he believed me when I told him I
was her sister, but he probably decided arguing with me wasn't
worth the effort.

The rickety elevator seemed to take forever, and Trina's room
was all the way at the end of a long hall. The door was open, and
the room was crowded.

"You can't go in," a uniformed policeman told me.

I bit my lip. "Is she okay?"

"Don't know yet."

"Can you tell Detective Connors that I'd like to see him? My name is Molly Blume."

A minute or so later Connors stepped into the hall.

"She's lucky you called her," he said. "But she's not out of the woods."

"Can I see her?"

He shook his head. "You don't want to. Her blood pressure is dangerously low. They're working on getting her breathing going and starting an IV. They may have to do a trache."

I shuddered. He was right. I didn't want to see that. "Do they know what happened?"

"We found an empty vial of sleeping pills on her nightstand and some booze. You can connect the dots."

"She wasn't depressed, Andy."

"I'm not saying she was depressed. She was anxious, she had a lot on her mind. Her name's on the vial, by the way. Did she have pills when she came to your place?"

I nodded. "She said she was having trouble sleeping."

"How many pills were in the vial, do you know?"

"No, I don't. Jason did this, Andy."

"We don't know that."

"This morning, at Horton's? I was in the hall outside his office and heard him talking to his son. He said he was tired of cleaning up the son's mistakes. He said something like, it was too late, and she'd figure out what's going on, and he had to get rid of her. I thought he was referring to me—that he wanted to get me off his back and do some damage control. Now I think he told Jason to get rid of Trina."

I should have warned Trina about him, I thought. I shouldn't have been vague.

The paramedics were wheeling out the stretcher. Connors and I stepped out of the way. I caught a glimpse of Trina as they rolled her through the doorway. She looked gray, and I could see the blue veins beneath the skin on her eyelids. An oxygen mask covered most of her face.

"Here's the thing," Connors said when the paramedics had left. "The room was locked, from the inside."

"There are usually connecting doors."

"Really? Hotels have those?"

"I'm sorry. I'm a little tense."

"The rooms on either side of this one were occupied from eight o'clock on, Molly. If she took booze and pills before eight, she would have been dead by now."

"Can I go inside now?"

He nodded. "Don't touch anything."

I entered the room and looked around. The natty maroon-and-beige spread for the king-size bed had fallen to the carpet. On the nightstand were a vial, a glass, and a bottle of scotch.

On the desk were newspapers and a several white Styrofoam boxes that had probably contained meals. The suitcase Trina had packed Saturday night was on the floor at the side of the bed. Her black vinyl tote was next to it.

"She had her brother's journal," I told Connors. "In that tote." I pointed to it.

Connors slipped on latex gloves and crouched next to the tote. He unzipped it and looked inside. "No journal."

"They took it."

"Who?"

"Whoever drugged Trina, and killed Randy. Come on, Andy. This is too pat. Randy dies of an overdose. His sister takes too many sleeping pills."

"Genetic stupidity," he said. "It *is* too pat. But we have a locked door. We're on the fourth floor, no fire escape. Windows are locked from the inside. When you figure it out, tell me."

I turned and glanced at the door. "I know how he did it, Andy."

"Faster than Houdini," he said. "He used a string, right? I was just thinking about that."

"Last year, when I was on a book tour in Indianapolis? I locked myself out of my room. That security latch at the top? The one that you flip over when you're in the room? I didn't open it all the way and lay it flat against the wall, the way you're supposed to. When I left the room and pulled the door shut, the movement jostled the latch and made it fall across the door. They had to call maintenance to get someone to remove the hinges."

Connors looked at the door.

"Maybe he left fingerprints," I said.

I had to wait until Connors lifted several sets of prints with the kit he kept in his car before he allowed me to demonstrate. Five times. Three out of five, when I positioned the latch so that it was just shy of touching the edge of the door, it flipped over the door when I pulled the door shut behind me.

Connors tried it a few more times himself.

"We know how," he said. "We still don't know who."

I didn't agree, but I liked the *we*.

CHAPTER FORTY-FOUR

Friday, February 27. 9:45 A.M. 1100 block of North Vermont Avenue. During the night, a burglar used a passkey to enter the victim's hotel room and took $27,300 in money and jewelry. The room was still locked in the morning. (Hollywood)

TRINA WASN'T WILLING TO PRESS CHARGES AGAINST JASON.

"She can't remember much after dinner in the hotel restaurant," Connors told me when I was at the station. "She barely remembers getting to her room. She says she must have locked the door."

"I'll bet Jason put Rohypnol in her drink. People usually revert to habit. Didn't he think it would show up in an autopsy?"

Connors leaned back in his chair. "A, we don't know that the lab tests will show Rohypnol. B, if she *had* died, and we found Rohypnol in her system, we couldn't have proved that Jason put it in her drink."

"Why would she put it in her own drink?"

"Welcome to the real world, Molly. People use roofies all the time for a high. Jason will say Trina knew what she was doing. Like brother, like sister."

"But the Rohypnol shows a *pattern,* Andy."

"What pattern? We have no proof that Horton ever used Rohypnol on anyone. We have a twenty-three-year-old woman who took sleeping pills after she mixed beer with a drug."

I rolled my eyes. "She was tired, so she took something to sleep?"

"I agree with you, Molly, but Horton's lawyer will argue that Trina was disoriented, so she took sleeping pills, which she usually does. This time she took too many."

"You know he tried to kill her, Andy. You know he had Iris killed. What kind of drugs did they find in Randy?"

Connors hesitated. "Cocaine, and roofies."

I stared at him. "And there's no *pattern?* What if he tries to kill Trina in the hospital?"

Connors should his head. "He knows I'm watching him. I spoke to him. He has an alibi for the night Randy died. I told him we were looking into the disappearance six years ago of a client from Rachel's Tent. He said that on the dates in question— meaning July thirteen, six years ago, when they found the torso of that unidentified woman—he was with his family in Europe. The father corroborated, said he could provide hotel informa- tion, et cetera."

"Nice for them." I sniffed. "I never said Jason killed Iris. I said he paid Randy to do it for him."

"I suggested that. Horton told me that after yesterday's *Times* linked Randy with Aggie's death, he began to wonder about

Randy. Apparently, Jason had confided in Randy about his sexual relations with clients from Rachel's Tent and told him that one of them stole a videotape. Horton now believes that Randy may have been overzealous in his attempt to help Jason out of an uncomfortable situation and took it upon himself to kill Iris."

"Uncomfortable situation? Overzealous?"

"That's what he said. And, of course, Jason is in no way responsible for what Randy did."

"Of course not." Talk about spin. I was infuriated. "But if you can prove that Jason or Horton paid Randy money to 'help'?"

"We can't prove it without having access to Horton's books. We can't get access without a subpoena, which a judge won't give us, because there's no probable cause. And if Jason paid cash, we'd have a harder time tracing the money. And Randy's not alive to tell us what happened."

"So we need the tape."

"Even if we had it, we couldn't use it without Iris."

I frowned. "You said it was admissible."

"It's admissible. But Jason's lawyer will argue that the sex was consensual, and Iris isn't around to say otherwise."

"So we need a resurrection," I said.

"It wouldn't hurt. Two would be better."

Roland and Alice Creeley were outside Trina's fifth-floor hospital room when I arrived. Creeley looked as though he'd aged ten years in two weeks. Alice, uncharacteristically silent, gripped her husband's arm and avoided my eyes. She'd probably heard from her neighbors that I'd been asking questions, and was anxious about what I'd learned, what I planned to do with the information.

"Trina's doing better," Creeley told me. "She was up, talking to the detective. She ate something, too. I think she's sleeping, but you can go in. He said you saved her life. He said if you hadn't . . ." Creeley tightened his lips, and his shoulders heaved.

I gave him a hug and went inside the room. A nurse was adjusting the IV flow. On the window ledge facing the courtyard was a huge floral arrangement. I looked at the card. *So glad you're going to be okay. Jason.*

"Can I stay a few minutes?" I asked the nurse.

She nodded. "She's been in and out of sleep. If she wakes, you can talk to her, but don't tire her out."

I sat at Trina's bedside and watched the rhythmic movement of her chest, heard the *whoosh* of oxygen running through the tubes. She looked fragile, but her skin had lost that frightening gray pallor.

I stroked her hand and was about to leave when her eyes fluttered open.

"How are you, Ava Gardner?"

She smiled weakly. "My throat hurts. They pumped my stomach." Her eyes filled with tears. "You saved my life, Molly."

My eyes teared, too. "Anytime. I'm just glad you're okay." I squeezed her hand.

"I guess I took too many pills." She sounded sheepish.

"You don't remember taking more than one?"

"No. But I must have. I've been so stressed."

"Did something upset you last night, Trina?"

She hesitated. "I had a fight with a friend. He's been trying to help me, and I thought he was getting too nosy. I hurt his feelings."

That explained why Horton had told Jason that "she" had figured it out. "The other day you said someone was helping you. Was that Jason Horton?"

Her hesitation was longer this time. "Yes. We're okay now.

He said he was sorry." She licked her lips. "Can I have some water?" She propped herself up on her elbows.

I filled a plastic cup from the yellow carafe on her nightstand and handed her the cup. "Didn't you get my messages, Trina? I must have phoned ten times."

She shifted her eyes and sipped the water. "I didn't get around to calling you back. I'm sorry."

I didn't believe her. "What happened last night?"

"I don't know. I was nauseous and cold. I thought I was coming down with the flu. I was very tired." She yawned, as if to prove her point.

"Where was Jason?"

She set the empty cup on the nightstand and lay down. "I guess he was home."

"Did you have anything to drink?"

"One beer with dinner. Another one later. But that was before the sleeping pill. I *know* you're not supposed to mix pills with liquor."

I could tell my questions were annoying her. I took her hand. "Trina, I know this isn't the best time, but I have to tell you something. Jason isn't your friend."

She yanked her hand away. "Jason *is* my friend. He was Randy's friend, too. So was Mr. Horton."

"That's why Randy helped Jason, Trina. He felt grateful."

Trina looked puzzled. "Helped Jason with what?"

"Getting information about people." Now was not the time to tell her about Iris. "Trina, Jason raped some of the women from Rachel's Tent."

Color blotched her cheeks. "You're lying!"

"I talked to one of the women he raped. He drugged her, and raped her. I think he drugged you, too."

She clamped her lips into an angry line. "Jason wouldn't hurt me. He's trying to find the package. He's trying to find out who Jim is. He said you would make up lies about him, just like you're making up lies about Randy."

"Trina—"

"You hate my brother!" She glared at me. "You think he killed your best friend, but he didn't. Jason believes me. He's the only one." She turned her head to the side. "I don't want to talk anymore. I want you to leave."

"He took your journal," I said. "From your black tote? It's not in your hotel room."

Her hands pleated the white sheet. "Maybe he borrowed it so he could read it, to see if I missed something. That's why I was upset with him, because he took it out of my tote once. But he's only trying to help."

She was determined to hold on to her perception of Jason. I suppose she'd substituted Jason for the brother she had lost. Even if I'd been more specific in my warning the other night, she wouldn't have listened.

"Trina, you didn't tell me at first you had Randy's journal. Is there anything else you haven't told me?"

Something flickered in her eyes. "No."

"I think there *is*," I said.

She frowned. "You're going to think worse of Randy. That's why I didn't show it to you."

"Show me what?"

The nurse came in. "How're you doing, Trina?"

"I want to rest now," she said.

CHAPTER FORTY-FIVE

SOMETIMES THINGS ARE RIGHT IN FRONT OF YOUR FACE
and you don't see them.

Five roses were on my doorstep when I arrived home a little
after eleven. I took a larger vase and added them to my growing
collection. Then I called Zack. I wished he could come over, but
hearing his voice was comforting.

After straightening up the house and washing a few dishes left
from breakfast, I packed a suitcase for the weekend and remembered to take an extra outfit for the Shabbat Kallah my mother
was preparing for our family and a few of my close friends. My
last Shabbat before the wedding, the last time I'd be going to my
parents' as a single woman. Zack and I would be staying in a hotel

the night of the wedding. After that, we'd be here until the house was ready. I hoped Isaac would respect our privacy.

In my bedroom I worked for an hour on my manuscript, but thoughts of Trina intruded. I had located her mother. I had located Charlie, who had put me in touch with Melinda. Now Trina was in a hospital bed, refusing to believe that Jason had tried to kill her. I had accomplished nothing and I still had unanswered questions about Aggie's death.

I looked at the books I'd picked up at Mike's yard sale. *Alcoholics Anonymous* and *A Practical Guide to Kabbalah*. I leafed through them, wondering if I had missed anything. I turned the texts upside down and shook them.

Of course, there was nothing there, aside from a sprinkling of dust.

I drove to Santa Monica, where a sweet young Iranian woman chatted while she brought me close to tears as she waxed my legs and other parts. From there I drove to a nail salon near my apartment and relaxed with a magazine while my feet soaked in a tub of warm water.

There was an article about Britney Spears and her recent, short-lived marriage. The upcoming Michael Jackson trial. Another Hollywood celebrity divorce and speculation about kinky revelations. The upcoming Martha Stewart trial. The prospects for John Kerry in next week's Super Tuesday primary races . . .

Kinky . . .

Mike had said something that first day. What was it?

I shut my eyes. He'd been talking about his relationship with Randy. He liked Randy's TV. They exchanged DVDs. He hadn't really believed that Randy had killed anyone, but then the police asked Mike questions about Randy and a woman he may have killed six years ago.

Turns out Randy was into kinky stuff.

I opened my eyes and removed my feet from the tub. Grabbing a towel, I wiped my feet and slipped them into my shoes.

"Something wrong?" the manicurist asked me. "Water too cold? Too hot?"

I told her the water was fine, gave her five dollars, and promised I'd be back.

Mike was scraping old paint off the frame of the front window when I arrived. He was wearing his headphones and I had to yell to make him hear me.

"I figured I could make a few bucks until my agent gets me something," he told me after he'd climbed down from the short ladder. "What's up?"

"When I talked to you the other day, you mentioned that Randy was into some kinky stuff. What did you mean?"

Mike laughed, but his face reddened. "He had this tape. A good thing Randy's dad didn't take it. He would've had a heart attack, or his wife would've killed him. It wasn't exactly PG rated, if you know what I mean."

"How did you happen to have it?"

"It was with his other stuff, things his dad didn't want. In a bag of clothes Randy was probably getting ready to give to the cleaners. I guess he didn't want Doreen to see the tape."

"You watched the tape?"

"A couple of days ago. I thought it was *The Truman Show*. That's what the cover said. But that ain't Jim Carrey." He laughed again. "Some guy, some woman. The woman looks drugged. I only watched a minute. It's not my thing. To be honest, I was surprised Randy was into that. He never struck me as the type."

I tried to keep my voice calm. "Do you have the tape?"

Mike nodded. "I'll probably toss it."

"Would you mind giving it to me?"

He looked surprised. "Yeah, sure."

I'd been cautious on my way here, checking my rearview mirror and executing several extra turns to make sure no one was following me. Now I felt exposed and vulnerable. Following him into the building, I waited outside his open door and caught a glimpse of general slovenliness.

He returned a minute later and handed me the tape. "What do you want it for, if you don't mind my asking?"

"It may be evidence of a rape."

"Jeez." His face turned pale.

"You mentioned a bag of clothes? What kind of clothes?"

"T-shirts, socks, a couple of shirts. One of the shirts has a bunch of rust stains. It's a nice shirt. I was thinking of taking it in to the cleaners to see if they can get the stains out."

Trina was sitting up and eating Jell-O when I saw her. She had phoned me just as I was leaving the Hollywood station after dropping off the videotape and the shirt. Connors was on his way downtown to have the shirt tested for blood and other trace evidence.

She was feeling better, she told me. The doctors thought she might be able to go home later today or tomorrow.

"I've been thinking about what you said, Molly. About Jason. Were you telling me the truth, that the journal is gone?"

I nodded.

"I really thought he liked me." She sounded forlorn.

"I'm sure he did, Trina. But he was manipulating you."

She played with the Jell-O. "He phoned me when I was at your place, about an hour after you left. He felt terrible about Randy and wanted to help. I told him about Jim, and my apartment, and he offered to put me up in a hotel until we found Jim and the package. I thought he was so kind."

"Randy never said anything negative about him?"

She shook her head. "Why would he drug me?"

"He was afraid you'd figure out what was going on. He needed the package, Trina. He probably thought you might remember, and then he'd be able to get it." I touched her hand. "I think he killed Randy."

"Why?" It was a wail, not a question.

I told her. "You said you found something else with Randy's things. What?"

She hesitated. "He had a driver's license and credit cards that belonged to a woman. I don't know who she is. The newspaper clippings were with the license."

"And you thought he stole the ID and cards?"

She looked miserable, burdened with her brother's guilt. "I wanted to return everything to her. I drove to her apartment, but she doesn't live there anymore, and I don't have her phone number."

"Do you remember the name on the license?"

"Iris. I don't remember the last name."

It was what I'd suspected, but now I had confirmation. I felt a wave of sadness for the dead woman.

Trina lowered her eyes. "You think he did something terrible, don't you? I saw it in your face. I shouldn't have told you."

"Did you tell Jason about this?"

"No. Why would I?"

"Did you keep the ID in your hotel room, Trina?" If so, Jason had probably found it.

A half smile tugged at her lips. She shook her head. "I put it in a safe place."

Jonnie looked skeptical, even after I showed her the note Trina had signed.

"I have to talk to Trina first," she said.

"She's in the hospital," I told her. "She had a problem with her medication."

I gave her the phone number and checked out a rack of teddies while she made the call.

A few minutes later I followed her across the store and up the short flight of steps to the glass-encased exhibit that held Jane Powell's crinoline. *Seven Brides for Seven Brothers.* One of Trina's favorites.

Jonnie unlocked the glass case, opened the door, and reached underneath the crinoline.

When she stood up, she was holding a small white envelope. "Is this what you want?"

I was anxious to open the envelope but waited until I was in my Taurus. I opened the flap, emptied the contents onto my lap, and picked up each item, careful to hold it by its edges.

Iris Strand. That was the name on the MasterCard and the gasoline and ATM cards.

It was the name on the California driver's license.

I looked at the photo. An oval face, thin nose, long, curly black hair. Brown eyes, five feet four inches, 118 pounds.

She was my redhead.

CHAPTER FORTY-SIX

Sunday, February 29. 10:15 A.M. 5700 block of Carlton Way. A man invited a woman to his house and gave her a beer. The victim suddenly felt woozy and lay down on a bed, where the assailant proceeded to attack her. The suspect is described as a 33- to 34-year-old man standing 5 feet 10 inches tall and weighing 150 pounds, with black hair and brown eyes. (Hollywood)

SHE WAS SITTING ON MY GLIDER WHEN I RETURNED FROM the weekend.

"Your landlord told me it was okay," she said, getting to her feet as I pulled my roll-aboard overnighter up the steps to the porch. My free hand was holding a vase with the four roses Zack had asked his father to drop off at my parents' on Saturday night.

She was wearing jeans and the pink Ugg boots and a rust sweater that brought out the copper in her eyes that the word *brown* doesn't come close to describing. Her hair, without the gray hat or red wig, was just below her chin. The shoulder-length dark curls that I had seen in the driver's license photo and that Gloria Lamont had mistaken for Aggie's were gone.

"It's fine," I said.

If I had checked my pulse, I wouldn't have been surprised to learn that it was a little rapid. Excitement, and some fear because it's not easy to forget a gun held to your head. It was a strange, somber reunion between two unsmiling women who were neither friends nor adversaries. She didn't say she was sorry she'd struck me. Maybe she wasn't.

"Thank you for not telling my husband," she said. "Brian doesn't know."

I had reached him on Friday and told him I was looking for a mutual friend from high school, Iris Strand. Could he give his wife the message?

"I don't want to complicate your life," I said.

I unlocked the door and invited her inside. She sat in my breakfast nook, lost in her own thoughts, her foot tapping to some internal song. I put up a kettle of water and filled a plate with the cookies my mother had sent with me. I wondered what had happened to the jittery, terrified woman who accosted me in the parking lot.

Her hands gave her away. They shook as she picked up one of the mugs I brought to the table.

"How did you know?" Iris asked.

I told her about the driver's license. "I figured Randy kept your ID to show Jason, that he helped you disappear."

She nodded. "That wasn't his original plan."

The plan, he told Iris after he abandoned it, the plan for which he'd been paid ten thousand dollars, had been to find the tape and arrange to have someone prevent Iris from going to the police. He hadn't anticipated that he would come to care for Iris and Aggie, that he would cringe at the thought of Aggie looking at him with horror and disgust. He hadn't anticipated being burdened by a conscience born in Rachel's Tent, having remorse.

On July 10 he hadn't yet coaxed the truth out of Iris, and she had been leaning toward pressing charges when she borrowed the locket.

"I asked Aggie why she always wore it," Iris said. "She told me you gave it to her. I asked her what was inside, and she showed me the red thread. 'It's not the thread,' she told me. 'It's the friendship. But if it gives you courage, I want you to take it.' "

Iris had been wearing the locket two days later when she confided in Randy and told him she had decided to take the tape to the police. He offered to drive her.

"But we never went to the station. He drove me to a wooded area and told me the truth. He'd manipulated me to confide in him, and he'd told Jason I had the tape. Even if I didn't press charges, Jason wanted me dead." She bit her upper lip, and her eyes glistened with tears.

I imagine that even after six years it would be hard to talk about someone wanting you dead.

"I didn't believe him. I thought he was crazy. But he grabbed my shoulders and kept saying it, over and over. 'Jason wants you dead, Iris. You have to disappear, now, Iris. I'll tell Jason you're dead, Iris, or he'll never stop looking for you.' " She wiped her eyes. "So I died."

The ones who killed Aggie, the ones who killed me.

"And Randy told Jason he took care of everything," I said. I'd had the weekend to puzzle it out. "He sent Jason the clipping about the woman's torso as proof. He stole your chart and destroyed it." Jason had no reason to doubt Randy. He was an ex-convict, a drug addict. He was indebted to the Horton family. "But whose torso did they find?"

"We had no idea. Randy waited days for the right clipping. He said that one was perfect, because the police probably wouldn't be able to identify the victim, and after a while they cremate the remains."

Grave endings, I thought. For the unidentified woman who had been someone's wife, daughter, mother, sister. For Aggie, for Randy. For Iris, too.

"And the timing was right," Iris said. "I'd been staying in Randy's apartment while he arranged to get me new ID from someone he knew from prison. The next day he saw the item about the torso."

That was when Gloria Lamont had seen her. "And Aggie?" I asked. "Randy didn't kill her, did he?"

She shook her head. "Aggie told Bramer she was worried that something had happened to me. And she was concerned about the women going to dinner at the Horton home. Bramer mentioned it to Horton, Horton told Jason. Jason told Randy."

A sinister game of telephone, I thought.

"Randy assured Jason that Aggie didn't pose a threat," Iris said. "He'd planned to return the locket to Aggie and tell her I'd asked him to do it for me. He told Jason he'd send Aggie a letter from me, saying I'd terminated therapy. Jason seemed fine with that. But one night not long after I disappeared, Jason phoned Randy."

My chest tightened. "July twenty-third." All these years I'd wanted to know. Now I wasn't sure.

"July twenty-third," she repeated. "He said he'd been in a bar brawl and needed fresh clothes and Randy's help in cleaning up the blood in his father's car. His father would have a fit if he found out. Randy helped him. He always did. When he heard the next day that Aggie was dead, he knew Jason had killed her. But the police would never believe him. He was heartbroken. He couldn't stop crying, blaming himself."

Iris had wanted to come back, but Randy had convinced her to stay away. Your showing up won't bring Aggie back, he told Iris. You have no evidence that Jason killed her.

"He told me I'd be in jeopardy again, that everything he'd done to save me would be pointless. He said he would be in danger, too, if Jason knew he'd deceived him. To be honest, I was relieved."

Guilt about Aggie plagued Randy. He started drinking again, doing drugs. Then he had a scare. He joined a church and became serious about dealing with his addiction. He wanted to make amends.

A month ago he'd told Iris he was planning to go to the police.

"After all these years I was still terrified," she said. "Maybe more, because I was beginning to feel safe. I knew Jason would find me."

And then Randy died. She had thought about going to the police after the funeral, but had been too afraid. And she told herself that nothing she said would bring Randy back.

But she hadn't stopped thinking about him, or Aggie. He had saved her life, and Aggie had tried to.

She had planned to drive up even before I phoned. She had been trying to find the right time to tell her husband, had realized there would be no right time.

She was still afraid. "But I'm tired of hiding. I'm tired of worrying every time the phone rings."

CHAPTER FORTY-SEVEN

Tuesday, March 2. 4:45 P.M. Corner of Sunset Boulevard and Vine Street. A 34-year-old man approached two men and asked for directions to a homeless shelter. The men told the victim to go "south on Vine," and then followed him as he began walking. They then attacked the victim, grabbed his crutches, and beat him with them. The suspects are males in their early twenties. (Hollywood)

A FOOL MAY MAKE TWO TRIPS WHERE A WISE MAN MAKES none, but I would have made a third trip to watch Jason's face when they arrested him early Monday morning.

"Maybe in the movies," Connors told me, "but that's not

how it works in real life. I could compromise the case by having you there, and suppose you got hurt?"

Connors told me Jason didn't seem bothered that the police had the tape. I think he'd more or less expected that it would surface, and not end up in his hands. But he turned white as flour when they told him Iris Strand was alive and willing to testify, and he didn't look much better when Connors said the police were examining Horton's Mercedes. According to the complaining witness, Connors told him when they were in the interrogation room at the station before the attorney arrived, that's the car you used to transport her. It's a good thing for us your daddy's a frugal man. Not so good for you.

Did you know it's almost impossible to get bloodstains out completely, Jason? You could use solvents and bleach, but there's this product called Luminol. You spray something with Luminol, and blood that's years old will fluoresce in the dark. I wonder whose blood they'll find in your daddy's Mercedes. What do you think?

The next morning Horton and the attorney joined Jason. A night in jail will take the starch out of most people. Jason was subdued and glassy-eyed. Connors thinks he realized this was something his father couldn't fix. I wondered at what point Horton would stop covering up for his son. Maybe that point wasn't rape. Maybe that point was two murders.

Connors told them that with the tape and Iris's testimony, they had Jason on the rape. They also had him on Aggie's murder. They had found her blood in the Mercedes, as well as on the shirt Randy had kept for insurance. Jason's blood had been on that, too.

The attorney, whom you've probably seen on *Larry King Live*, asked Connors what kind of deal he could give them. If he tells us about Aggie and gives us the weapon, if he cops to Randy,

Connors said, maybe the D.A. will take the death penalty off the table, but I can't promise.

I didn't kill Randy, Jason said, sitting up straight as though he had just woken up with a start from a nightmare. The words *death penalty* will do that. Let's hear what they have to offer, son, Horton told him. I didn't kill him, Jason repeated. I can tell you about Aggie, I didn't mean for that to happen, I was stoned, but no way am I going to take the rap for Randy.

Come on, Jason, Connors said. We know you killed Aggie, we know you killed Randy. You tell me what happened and I'll go to the D.A. right now and talk to her about dropping the death penalty. Maybe they'll give you concurrent terms, Horton said. Is that on the table? he asked Connors. That would be a good deal, Jason, I think you should take it if they offer it.

"That's when it got interesting," Connors told me.

Jason glared at his father. You want me to cut my losses, Dad, is that what you're saying? Or maybe you'd like to cut *your* losses? Shut up, Jason. Maybe we'll diversify, Dad. I told you to shut up, Jason, you're making things worse for yourself. I'm going to cut *my* losses, Dad. I'll cop to Aggie, and you do the same for Randy. Ask him about Jim, Jason said to Connors. Ask him whose idea it was to trash Trina's apartment. Ask Trina how it is that Jim phoned when I was with her? Ask my dad why he told me to say I was with him the night Randy died. Ask him how much he paid Doreen to spy on Randy, how much he paid her to move out of town.

I talked to Connors this morning. He's having a hard time proving what is spite and what is truth, though we both believe that Horton killed Randy. Jason says he told his father Randy was to blame for his drug addiction, and maybe that's what drove Horton that night, though he won't admit to anything. He has his own high-profile attorney, one whose face you've also seen on *Larry King*. But Connors is smart. He has a lead on Doreen, and

Jason does have an alibi for the night Randy was killed, although he wasn't keen on his wife's finding out her name.

Jason says he never intended to kill Aggie. He followed her to reason with her after she turned down an offer from Horton, much like the one he made me. *I'll pay these women, I'll write a check to any institution you want.* Jason was stoned that night, and when Aggie wouldn't talk to him, he became enraged and before he knew it, she was in his car, the knife was in his hands, and she was dead.

Horton's Mercedes, by the way, is a black SUV. Horton claims he was working late in his office the night I was on Arroyo Seco, and that Jason had borrowed his car all day.

Bubbie G says no one has a monopoly on regret.

I haven't talked to Bramer and probably won't. My guess is that he has had many sleepless nights over the past six years about Iris and Aggie and the things he didn't want to think about when Aggie was killed.

I imagine that Sue Ann, despite what she told me, wonders how much she is to blame for the way Randy turned out. And Alice may have a twinge or two about the advice she gave, though I suspect she wishes there were thousands of miles, not fifteen, between San Marino and Culver City. I don't plan to tell Roland Creeley about his ex-wife, and Connors doesn't see why it would come up. I doubt that Sue Ann will suddenly develop an interest in meeting her grown-up daughter, or that Trina will decide that she'd like to meet her mother, though you never know. Trina's back in her apartment, with a new lock on her door.

I wish everything could be fixed that easily.

Jason's arraignment is tomorrow morning. Connors asked if I was going to be there, but I told him I'd pass.

I'm getting married.

CHAPTER FORTY-EIGHT

Wednesday, March 3. 7:15 P.M. 100 block of South La Peer Drive. A woman reported that unknown suspects threw several glasses over her bushes, nearly hitting her. (Wilshire)

I HAD TO SEND MY DAD BACK TO MY APARTMENT TO PICK up the gold cuff links I would give Zack after the ceremony, in the private room where we would break our fast and share our first kiss, not necessarily in that order. Mindy thinks Zack is giving me pearl earrings because he asked her if I had a pair.

And the plate my mother had picked up at the 99 Cents Store wouldn't break. My mother and Sandy, Zack's mother, had slammed it repeatedly, with growing frustration, against the corner of a table in the room where our fathers and two witnesses had just signed the betrothal agreement.

"Raul brought a hammer, tied with a bow," my mother said when she resumed her seat next to me on the elevated platform in the reception hall.

The breaking of the plate, like the breaking of the glass under the chuppa, is a reminder of our grief over the destruction of both Holy Temples, a reminder that even the happiest occasions have echoes of sadness. Early Tuesday morning, my parents and I visited the graves of Zeidie Irving and my father's parents and invited their souls to the wedding. I placed a pebble on Aggie's headstone, just a few rows away from Zeidie's, and invited her soul, too. And inside the white leather-bound book of psalms I now held on my lap was a small sheet of paper with the hand-written names of individuals who needed prayers. People who were ill, others who yearned for children or mates. A bride's prayers, I have been told, have a unique potency.

I was surrounded by family. My mother, my sisters and sister-in-law, Bubbie G. My mother-in-law, Zack's aunts and mine. My nieces sat cross-legged at our feet, their tulle gowns mushrooming around them. The room was crowded with guests, most of whom had come up to wish us mazel tov before helping themselves to hors d'oeuvres. Ron was there, too, with a statuesque blonde. I saw Isaac, proud in his new suede yarmulke. And the Lashers.

I have come to accept that I will never know why Aggie didn't confide in me. Maybe, as Connors said, I had put her on a pedestal. Maybe six years ago she didn't want to complicate my fragile return to Orthodox observance. Maybe she knew I would have tried to talk her out of doing what she felt was right.

The photographer and videographer were busy capturing memories that Zack and I would enjoy long after the evening was

over. I was compiling my own. The swelling of my heart as I saw
Zack, escorted by our fathers and a jubilant entourage of men
and boys. His whispered "I love you" and the tender look in his
eyes before he lowered my veil. My father's tears, and mine, as he
placed his hands on my head and blessed me. The sweet strains of
"Adon Olam" as Zack's parents walked him down the aisle to the
outdoor chuppa and helped him slip on his white *kittel.*

It was a day of joy and solemnity, a day of atonement for both
of us. New beginnings. Earlier today I had recited the Yom Kippur confession. Last night I submerged myself in the rain waters
of the *mikvah,* the ritual bath. Now I was under the chuppa, a
symbol of the home Zack and I would build. His family's heir-
loom white satin *tallit,* luminous against the darkening sky, bil-
lowed above us. Guided by my mother and Sandy, I walked
around Zack seven times, forming the walls that would complete
our home, the same number of circuits, I realized, that I had
made as I wound my red thread around Rachel's Tomb.

We stood side by side, suddenly shy, sobered by the import of
the moment as the rabbi, Zack's mentor who had flown in from
Israel, recited two blessings over a silver goblet filled with wine.
Zack took a sip of the wine, and my mother lifted my veil so that
I could take a sip, too. Then Zack placed a simple gold ring on
the index finger of my right hand and recited the blessing in
Hebrew.

We were married.

We gazed at each other while the rabbi of my parents' shul
read the *ketubah* in its original Aramaic and handed it to me. Seven
more blessings, more wine. Now my mother-in-law raised my
veil. Then Noah and Judah sang, "If I Forget Thee, Jerusalem."
Zack stomped on the glass someone had placed under his foot,
and everyone yelled, "Mazel tov!" as the band burst into song.

Zack took my hand. He held it tight as we walked down from

the chuppa and made our way through a throng of family and friends who showered us with kisses and beamed their joy.

I wished Aggie were here.

Edie asked me yesterday if I feel better knowing why. I told her I do. I will never get over Aggie's death, but I take some comfort knowing she wasn't mugged for a locket and the contents of her wallet.

But if I could, I would rewind the video of her life and make some edits. I would cut the scenes where she meets Randy and Horton, and probably the scenes with Iris, too. I would stop her from walking up the stairs to Jason's room.

The truth is, I'm not sure Aggie would want those edits. The rabbi at her funeral said she was like Rachel, and maybe he was right. Rachel, who stole Laban's idols to wean him from his idolatry, and hid them in her tent before moving them to her camel's saddlebags when he came searching. Rachel, who didn't tell her husband what she'd done, and died in childbirth because Jacob had sworn to a furious Laban that whoever had stolen his idols would die.

If Rachel hadn't stolen the idols, if she had told Jacob. If Aggie hadn't urged Iris to go to the police, if she hadn't stolen the tapes . . .

If Jason Horton hadn't been the man he was . . .

Not *God's* plan, my father had said. *Man's* plan.

I think now that God watched Aggie as she walked from her car on that July night.

I think He turned His head away, because He couldn't bear to see what He knew would happen.

I think He cried.

Glossary of Hebrew and Yiddish Words and Phrases

Adar (noun, a´-dar, or a-dar´). The Jewish month in which Purim falls, known for celebration.

"Adon Olam" (noun, a-don´ o-lam´). A daily prayer, often sung. Literally, "Master of the Universe."

Amidah (noun, a-mi´-dah). A daily prayer composed of eighteen blessings.

aufruf (noun, auf´-ruf). The calling up of the groom to the Torah, usually on the Sabbath before the wedding.

ayin harah (noun, a´-yin ha´-rah). Evil eye.

Az me laigt arein kadoches, nemt men arois a krenk (Yiddish proverb, az me laigt a´-rein ka-do´-ches, nemt men a-rois´ a krenk). If you invest in a fever, you'll realize a disease.

Bedeken (noun, ba-deck´-en). Ritual before the wedding ceremony during which the groom lowers the bride's veil.

Baruch Dayan ha´emet (ba-ruch´ da-yan´ ha-e-met´). Blessed be God, the Righteous Judge. Recited when one hears that a person has died.

bashert (noun or adjective, ba-shert´). Destiny, or destined.

bentch gomel (bentsch go´-mel). To recite a prayer of gratitude in synagogue after surviving a dangerous journey, illness, or accident.

bima (noun, bi´-ma). Elevated platform on which the Torah scroll is placed for the reading.

bli ayin hara (bli a´-yin ha´-ra). A phrase to ward off the evil eye.

bubbie (noun, bub´-bee). Grandmother. Also, *bubbeh, babi, babbi.*

challa (noun, chal´-la or chal-la´). Braided loaf of bread. Plural is *challot* (chal-lot´) or *challas* (chal´-las).

chesed (noun, che´-sed). [Acts of] loving-kindness.

Chevra Kadisha (chev´-ra ka-di´-sha). A community organization that prepares a body for burial.

chossen (noun, chos´-sen). Groom. Also, *chattan* (chat-tan´).

chuppa (noun, chup´-pa). Wedding canopy.

davened (verb, past tense, da´-vened). Prayed.

gleyzele (noun, diminutive, gle´-ze-le). A small glass.

greeneh (noun, green´-eh). Newcomer, immigrant. (Colloquial).

Halevai (ha-le-vai´). I wish that it were so.

hamantaschen (noun, ha´-man-ta´-schen). Traditional Purim three-corned cookies filled with poppy seeds, prune butter, or apricots. Literally, Haman's pockets.

Hashem (noun, Ha-shem´). God.

Hashem feirt der velt (Yiddish saying). God rules the world.

kenehoreh (ke-ne-hor´-eh). A frequently used phrase that is an elision of *keyn ayin horeh* (kān a´-yin ho´-reh). Let there be no evil eye. Also, *kenayn-e-horeh* (ke-nain´-e-hor´-eh).

kiddush (noun, kid´-dush or kid-dush´). A prayer recited over wine at the beginning of a Sabbath or holiday meal. Also used to refer to refreshments served after synagogue services on the Sabbath or other Jewish holidays.

kittel (noun, kit´-tel). A white ceremonial robe worn by married males on Yom Kippur and Passover. Males are also buried in it. Yivo spelling is *kitl*. Plural: *kitlen,* or colloquially, *kittels.*

kugel (noun, ku´-gel). A puddinglike dish, usually made of vegetables (like potatoes or onions) or noodles.

loshon horah (noun, lo´-shen ho´reh). Slander, gossip. Also, *lashon harah* (la-shon´ ha-rah´).

maksim (adjective, mak-sim´). Enchanting.

mazel (noun, ma´-zel). Luck; often used in a phrase, *mazel tov,* wishing one good luck or congratulations at a celebration or happy occasion. Alternate spelling: *mazal* (ma-zal´) *tov.*

mechitza (noun, me-chi´-tza). Partition used in a synagogue or hall to separate men and women.

Mishpatim (mish-pat´-im; mish-pat-im´). Literally, laws. A portion of the Torah.

mitzvah (noun, mitz´-vah or mitz-vah´). Positive commandment. Plural, *mitzvot* (mitz-vot´); colloquial plural, *mitzvos* (mitz´-vos).

naches (noun, na´-ches). Proud pleasure, special joy, as in one's child's accomplishments.

nachon (adjective, na-chon´). Correct.

nehedar (adjective, ne-he-dar´). Gorgeous, marvelous, superb.

onen (noun, o´-nen). Term used to describe someone who has just learned of a close relative's death. He or she retains this status until the funeral, and during this period does not perform any religious commandments, e.g., praying, reciting blessings.

Pesach (noun, pe´-sach). Passover.

Rachel mevaka al baneha (ra-chel´ me-va-ka´ al ba-ne´-ha). Rachel is weeping over her children. From Jeremiah 3:15.

seder (noun, se´-der). Feast held on the eve of the first day of Passover commemorating the Exodus from Egypt. Plural, *sedorim,* or colloquially, *seders.* Orthodox Jews living outside of Israel observe a second seder on the eve of the second day of Passover.

Shabbat (noun, Shab-bat´). Sabbath.

Shabbat Kallah (shab-bat´ kal-lah´). The last Sabbath before a bride's wedding; a festive day on which the bride's friends and family come to her house to celebrate with her. Variation, *Shabbos Kalleh* (shab´-bes kal´-leh).

Shabbos (noun, shab´-bes). Sabbath; also, *Shabbat.*

sheitel (noun, shei´-tel). Wig.

sheitel macher (noun, shei´-tel ma´-cher). Wig maker, or stylist.

shidduch (noun, shid´-duch). Arranged match between a man and a woman.

shiva (noun, shiv´-a or shiv-a´). Literally, seven. The seven days of mourning for a deceased relative.

shul (noun). Synagogue.

siddur (noun, sid-dur´ or sid´-dur). Prayerbook.

simcha (noun, sim´-cha, sim-cha´). Joy, or happy occasion, e.g., a birth, bar mitzvah, wedding. Also, *simcheh* (sim´-cheh).

tallit (noun, tal-lit´). Prayer shawl. Variation is *tallis* (tal´-lis).

teffilin (noun, te-fil´-lin; te-fil-lin´). Phylacteries; black boxes containing verses from the Scriptures that males use in daily prayer.

teshuvah (noun, te-shu´-vah or te-shu-vah´). Repentance.

Torah (noun, to´-rah or to-rah´). The Bible; also, the parchment scroll itself.

yarmulke (noun, yar´-mul-ke). Skullcap. The Hebrew is *kippah* (kee´-pah or kee-pah´).

yeshiva (noun, ye-shi´va or ye-shi-va´). A school of Jewish study.

Yom Kippur (yom kip´-pur or yom ki-pur´). Jewish Day of Atonement.

Za nisht kayn k´nacker (phrase, za nisht kayn k´nock´-er). Don't be a big shot (show off, know-it-all).

zeidie (noun, zā´-die). grandfather; also, *zeidi, zeide, zeideh, zaydie.*

zemirot (noun, ze-mi-rot´; plural of *ze´-mer*). Songs usually sung during Sabbath or holiday meals.

About the Author

ROCHELLE KRICH is the author of many acclaimed novels of suspense, including *Blues in the Night* (which introduced Molly Blume), *Shadows of Sin, Dead Air, Blood Money,* and *Fertile Ground.* An Anthony Award winner for her debut novel, *Where's Mommy Now?* (which was adapted as the TV movie *Perfect Alibi*), Krich lives in Los Angeles with her husband and their children.

Visit Rochelle Krich's website at www.rochellekrich.com.